GATES OF HOPE

AULIREAN GATES I

J E HANNAFORD

For Asa
Your belief made this possible.
Thank you for supporting my dreams.

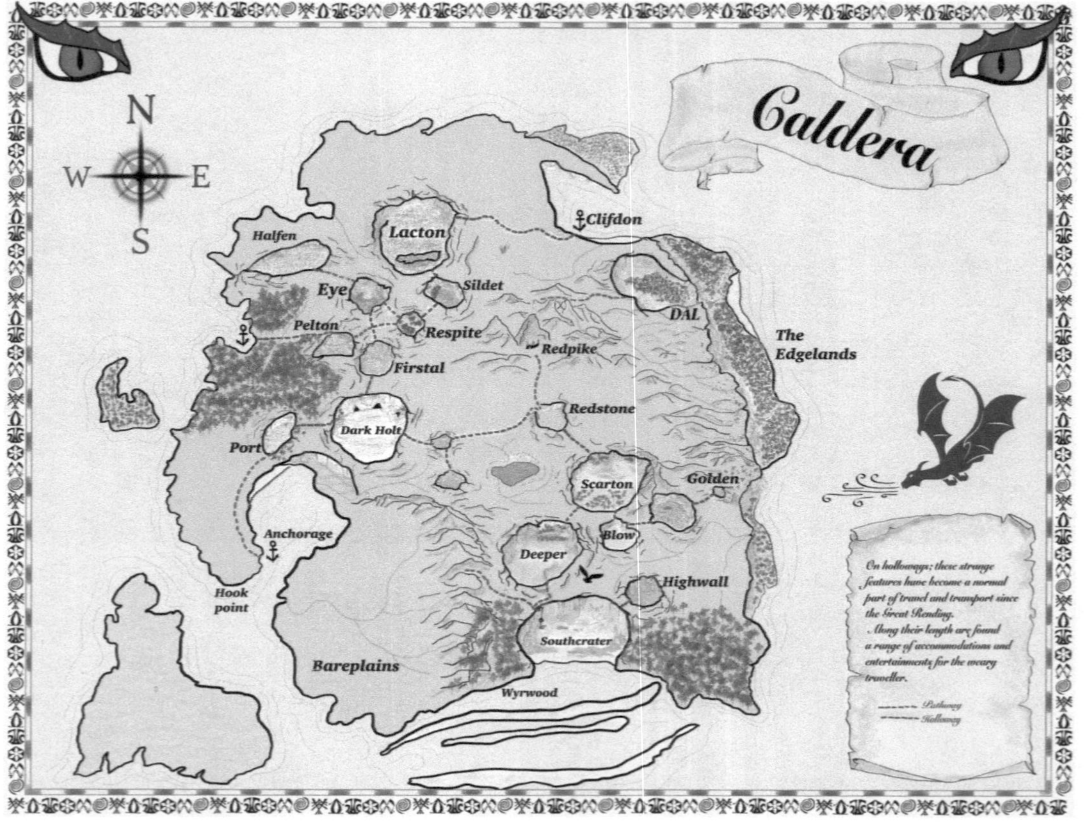

Caldera
N
W
E
S
Halfen
Lacton
Clifdon
Eye
Sildet
DAL
Pelton
Respite
The
Edgelands
Firstal
Redpike
Redstone
Dark Holt
Port
Scarton
Golden
Anchorage
Blow
Deeper
Highwall
Hook
point
Southcrater
Bareplains
Wyrwood
On holloways; these strange
features have become a normal
part of travel and transport since
the Great Rending.
Along their length are found
a range of accommodations and
entertainments for the weary
traveller.
Pathway
Holloway

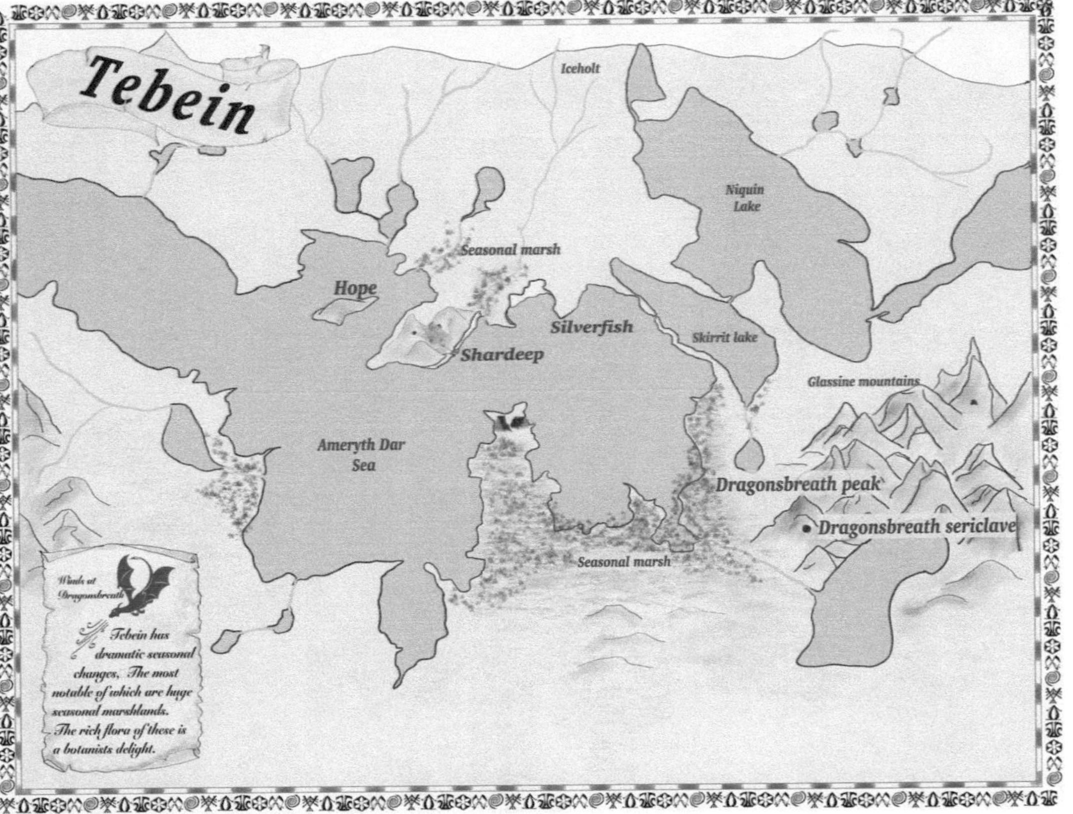

Tebein
Iceholt
Niquin Lake
Seasonal marsh
Hope
Silverfish
Skirrit lake
Shardeep
Glassine mountains
Ameryth Dar Sea
Dragonsbreath peak
Dragonsbreath sericlave
Seasonal marsh
Winds at Dragonsbreath
Tebein has dramatic seasonal changes. The most notable of which are huge seasonal marshlands. The rich flora of these is a botanists delight.

The Closing

Committing a once immortal race to slow, unstoppable death was never an aspiration of mine, but sometimes we must do what is right, not what is comfortable. Today, we choose the lives of many over the longevity of a few.

Exhaustion fills my muscles and thickening air pours into my lungs like syrup as I descend toward the surface of my home moon of Mythos. Enjoying the taste of home on my tongue, I turn back for one last glance at the planet we orbit before diving below the clouds. I have always loved the sight of Lieus shining like a green and blue gemstone in our sky. Now, the continent of Caldera, once green and lush with vegetation, is blackened and pockmarked. Even across the great distance, I see new shadows of giant craters sunken into its surface.

I draw my wings close to my sides, plunging toward home. The screech of my talons on the courtyard tiles echoes off the surrounding wall, and all aerial grace departs me as I careen across the grounds of the Gate Hall. My size and age are ever-increasing, and landings are getting tough.

I shake my black scales out and give my wings one last

stretch before folding them back. Shifting my weight back on my haunches with neck stretched upward, I scan the skies as I await my accomplices in this unpleasant business; Sorrow, Hope, and Regret.

I have barely regained my breath when I hear Sorrow roar out their impending arrival. Slow, tired wing beats reflect their fatigue – all three gasping for lungfuls of clean air. They alight in the courtyard of my hall with rather more elegance than myself, but then they hatched long after the Gates were built. Age is a long way in their future. After the last tide's events, I hope it will be a future without war.

Their arrival confirms the completion of our task. A heavy weight drops into my stomach, and I know its presence will never leave me. The tiny outer moon of Tebein is now isolated, the awldrin's immortality checked. The inevitable sacrifices of those trapped on the wrong sides of the shattered gates were a small price to pay compared to the devastation these two races had wrought over the last 100 cycles.

Sorrow speaks first.

'The Gates have been smashed and the site melted into the mountain. Watcher, the crystals are shattered and spread throughout the seas and lakes of Tebein. Have the humans on Lieus kept their end?'

I give a single nod in reply, feeling the ache of cold from both my return and my age as the scales grind past each other. 'I oversaw the shattering myself. It is done. The Anchor has put in place our agreed-upon strategies so that no So'Dal ever wields such power again.'

'Will they keep to it?' hisses Regret.

'They must,' Hope says, dark eyes meeting mine.

'I put safeguards in place. Not even the Anchor knows the full details.' I look at each as I speak. 'Human lives are short. They forget quickly, but their books hold memories. Those tomes which could teach them to break the accord have been hidden. We can trust those who care for them.'

As one, they bow their long sinuous necks toward me, then soar off into the Everdark side of Mythos. Once again, I am alone.

Towering wooden doors behind me beckon. For centuries I have been the Watcher, enabling the passage of both humans and awldrin through the Aulirean System, between Lieus, Mythos, and distant Tebein, but today, the Aulirean Gates closed for the last time. No one will ever use them again.

I lean onto the heavy doors, swinging them open, and step in. The dark, void-like space of this room always makes me feel small, distorting all sense of my size. Dominant in the centre of this edgeless space are the Aulirean Gates. Golden filigree designs surround the spherical crystals integrated with and woven throughout glimmering spirals. I sense a kinship with these beautiful and powerful creations. Their patterns are as familiar to me as the scales on my feet. I was present at their construction, and now I am responsible for their closing. These crystals showed me who, or what, awaited a crossing for hundreds of cycles.

I walk closer and reach out to touch a shattered crystal on the Lieus gate, fracture lines visible even from the doorway. Its surface is crazed, no longer unblemished and clear. As my claw touches it, I see movement; inside the crystal is no longer a single view, but many. I see different scenes and landscapes across each fractured section. Checking the other crystals, I find the same effect repeated – my window into Lieus is no longer limited, but multiplied by thousands.

I swing my head toward the Tebein gate. The crystals show fractures from being smashed, but the remains show little – no movement bar that of water and creatures living in it. Relief washes over me; not an awldrin in sight. This changes things.

Rather than leave the hall for the last time, I settle down in its centre. My eyes readjust to the dark, and I do what I have always done. I watch.

⊤ ✳ ⩔ ⫝ ✦

The last entry in the Watcher's log. Day of the Closing, Cycle 5697.

XOTRYL

CHAPTER 1

DARIN

SUMMER, 504 POST CLOSING. CALDERA, PLANET
LIEUS.

Evening sun reflected from the scarlet veins of staramine crystals streaking the black stone, causing the Black Palace of the So'Dal to shimmer with flashes of red. Its tall towers nestled against the mountainside, surrounded by imposing walls. It was Hal's home, and his, too, if he passed the test today.

'Are you sure we don't have time for one?' Darin asked. The market stalls creaked under the weight of fresh food and his mouth watered from the scent of hot, spiced ale drifting through the market. A woman peered out from behind the flower-laden canopy framing the ale stall, her scarf-wrapped hair hidden. She held out a jug in his direction, and Darin glanced hopefully at Hal.

'Not long enough to earn a meal.'

'I still have some coin ...' Darin reached into his pocket.

'It's no good to you here. Anyway, there will be food and spiced ale enough after your test.'

'Watcher's breath, how long will that be?' Darin muttered.

The look of frustration Hal shot in his direction did little to settle the nerves rising in his gut. He hoped the ale inside the palace tasted even half as good as this one smelt. Casting one last longing glance at the jug, he trudged after Hal.

⭐ ✻ ☿ ⚜ ✦

Flags of scarlet and black flew from towers peeking above the walls of the Black Palace. The symbol of the So'Dal emblazoned on the closest, which descended as they approached.

'Perfect timing.' Hal glanced at him and tipped his head toward the palace gates. 'Stop dragging your feet or you'll miss the start. You'll have to wait tides for the next trial, and that's not going to help your family. Mind you, I reckon we could find some work for you until then. There are always animal pens to clean out.'

Darin quickened his step, and they made it through the gates before they closed.

'You cut it fine this time, Hal,' one of the guards said, laughing.

'I timed it perfectly. It's been a long trek from Eye,' he replied. 'You're on your own now, Darin. Remember everything I've taught you, and may the Watcher be with you.' Hal glided toward a group of other black-robed So'Dal who stood near the gatehouse, although Darin still felt his watchful eyes on his back.

He studied the other occupants of the courtyard. Those two with the loud voices were barely into manhood, wearing fancy clothes they didn't fill out, with ornate, empty sword belts. Like Darin's staff, their swords would have been left at the town gate. He missed his staff.

A man similar to his age stood on the far side, alone. He appeared fit, relaxed, and confident – everything Darin wanted to be. A new flag rose, unfurling as it caught the breeze, and Darin recognised the new symbol dancing atop the pole from one of Hal's drawings. The trial had begun. He took a deep breath and felt for calm, as Hal had taught him over the last few tides, then closed his eyes and focused on breathing. He needed to be prepared for anything. *Shut out the noise, be ready to fight.*

'Welcome to the Black Palace. May I offer you a drink?'

'Oh yes, I'd love one.' Darin reached for the jug, but withdrew his hand quickly. *Everything I've taught you.* 'What can I offer in return?' *I almost made a mistake with my manners before I even started.*

Purple-stained lips parted in a broad smile of greeting as she studied him. Her skin was golden and freckled, her hair wrapped in an intricately knotted maroon scarf.

'We've a barrel of ale that needs putting on a rack for the celebrations after your trial. Could you help with it?'

Darin scanned the courtyard again. The two young men had taken their drinks without a glance at the woman offering them, and the man on the far side was looking back at him. The man shrugged and spoke to the woman stood nearby who led him toward an archway. Darin guessed that he'd remembered his manners too. The ale smelt good, and if he was going to have to fight soon, he could do with a drink first. It was how he'd usually fought at home, although admittedly, that was usually against drunk patrons as he threw them out.

'Of course, I'll help. Let's get this barrel moved.'

It was huge. The man from the courtyard was staring at it as he arrived.

'Hi, I'm Darin. Are you helping them move this too?' Darin gestured to the barrel standing between him and his drink, then offered a hand in friendship. The man took it in a firm grip and grinned.

'Conor, yes. Let's get this done so we can get back out before our trial begins.'

They each took an end and pushed. Slowly, the beast began to roll up its ramp.

'One, two ... push.' The barrel reached the top and dropped into place with a bang. The rack shuddered, then stood steady. They grinned at each other.

'Can I have that drink now?' Darin asked.

'Of course.' The woman he had followed in handed him a jug. It was delicious, cool, and sweet. Darin swirled it round his mouth, delighting in the taste.

'I needed that. Have you travelled far?' he asked Conor.

'From South Crater. I've wanted to visit Redpike for cycles so I couldn't turn down this opportunity. You?'

'Eye – it's near Pelton, much smaller than your home. Does South Crater really open on to the ocean?'

'It does.' Conor smiled. 'I miss the sound of it already.'

They drank companionably for a few minutes, then Conor took a final mouthful before placing his jug on a nearby table. 'We should head back out.' He gestured toward the archway just as the door closed with a thud. Darin took a last swig of drink, reaching for the door handle as he swallowed. It turned, but the door didn't open.

'You will not be going back out.'

He snapped his head around toward the women.

'But we came for the testing,' he said, his heart racing. He needed that wage, his family was relying on him. Watcher, he couldn't return home having failed at the first step. 'Please, I need to take the trial.'

'You passed the first step,' the freckled woman said. 'My name is Lea, this is Fresna. Showing you understood the most basic of our society's rules *was* the first trial.'

A loud shriek came from the other side of the door, and voices raised in challenge.

'Then what's going on out there?' Conor asked, staring at the door.

'They failed, so now they fight for the chance to join the guards,' Fresna replied.

'But that's what I came here for!' Darin's pulse raced. He focused on finding his calm – imagining his mother's voice always helped. *Breathe in, feel the breath out, in ...* 'You said we'd be finished in time.' His nails dug into his palms. *Stay calm, be calm.* 'There must be another way out. Surely if they've only just begun, we can rejoin them. I need to join the guard.'

Conor watched in silence, although Darin could see the muscles in his jaw working. 'Let's try one more shove together? Could be it's just stiff.'

They put their shoulders to the door and pushed. Darin's calm was slipping, along with his feet. He hadn't walked for all those tides across Caldera to be beaten by a door. The need to shout at the door – or the woman who had dragged him in there – rose.

'There's no point in shoving. It isn't going to open until

they're done,' Fresna said. 'You still have more stages of the trial left.'

'What position are you testing us for now, if failing the first was a position in the guard?' Darin asked in frustration.

'To become a So'Dal, of course.' Lea shrugged.

'I don't want to be a healer. I'm not interested in recording births and deaths. I've trained for years to be a fighter.'

'You may yet be one.' Lea smiled. 'Meanwhile, your trial continues. We have some time before the next stage. Would you like to walk in the palace gardens?'

'Hmm, if we can't get back out there, there's not a lot else to do,' Conor replied. *How was he so calm?*

'I didn't think there were gardens in the Black Palace?' Darin frowned. He'd talked a lot about the palace with Hal, and read about it so much before deciding to journey there, that he thought he could draw it from memory, but nothing and no one had ever mentioned a garden.

'There are many hidden features to the Black Palace. The gardens are just one that we keep private,' Fresna replied. 'Lea and I can show you, if you want?'

'Is there any food?' Darin asked. 'I'll do some gardening for food. If there are more tests later, I need to eat first.'

Conor chuckled. 'I'll help him. Watcher's wings, I could eat a whole faat, I'm so hungry.'

Lea laughed. 'We'll take you to the hall for a meal later. It won't be ready for a while though. Fresna and I will show you around the gardens.'

'Lead on.' Darin's mind whirled as he followed the others. A walk might help him work out his next move – it usually did.

A So'Dal? By the moons of Lieus, what skills did he have in healing? He should fail the next tests deliberately, then go back and do the combat trial. He was good at hitting things, and there would be pay sent home. Or maybe he could find some

other work. There must be jobs either here or in the town –
taverns that needed security like his family inn.

Maybe So'Dal got their pay sent home too, and it would
still help his family. He should have just taken the drink.
Sighing deeply, he looked up just in time to avoid walking into a
black-robed So'Dal. He dodged to the side as the So'Dal passed
without a break in his stride.

Black brickwork gave way to sleek blackness. Veins of red
crystal running through the polished surface glinted in a warm,
steady glow from globe-shaped lights mounted on the walls.
The corridor widened as they entered a large chamber. Brick-
less walls rose, carved and smooth. A shaft of light shone from
far above, illuminating a platform at the centre of the chamber.
Fresna led them toward it. A wooden handrail ran around the
platform's perimeter. As they approached, the sound of
running water grew louder, and Darin searched the cave walls
for the source so intently that he walked fully into the back of
Conor.

'Is that what I think it is?'

Darin stared at the platform and could only shrug. 'Is what,
what you think it is?'

'That platform … it's a steam lift, isn't it?' exclaimed Conor.
Frustration and tension dropped from his posture and he
grinned widely, gesticulating as he spoke. 'I thought the only
remaining one in Caldera was in South Crater? It's so high!
What's up there?' He gestured to the hole far above them, and
Darin's heart rate quickened as Conor continued. 'How's it
heated? Are we going on it?'

Fresna laughed at his excitement. 'Lea, can you answer him?
You know more about it than me.'

Lea led Conor to the edge of the platform. 'A stream flows
out into the chamber.' She pointed to water gushing from a
hole into a small pool. 'When we want power to push the lift,

we funnel the stream down that other tube to its right instead. They named Redpike red for more than one reason – the red rock *and* the fact that it was an active volcano once. The mountain has been dormant for thousands of cycles, but deep down in its heart, there are still pockets of intense heat. That's where our steam forms. We then channel it back to the lift mechanism and *whoosh*.' She gestured upward. 'Shall we take a ride?'

They climbed aboard the platform and Lea waved at a tall, robed figure stood near a long lever. They pulled it down and the running water stopped. Darin attempted nonchalance as he gripped the rail and tried to focus far away from the platform. His palms were sweating – he was going to lose his grip. It was a long way up.

Around the edge of the chamber were other entrances, differing in both size and decor to the one they had arrived through. Most were open, but there were balconies in front of closed doors farther up the walls. He studied them – anything to distract himself from what he stood on.

As the whistle of approaching steam rose in his ears, a glint caught his eye. Inlaid in one door was the same So'Dal symbol that flew on the scarlet flag. Darin turned to ask Lea about it as the platform shot up toward the hole in the cavern's roof. Disorientated, he gripped the rail as his stomach was abandoned on the floor and his unfaithful legs wobbled. Watcher knew, heights were not his thing.

The lift burst into bright sunlight, illuminating a rainbow of colours. All around him were plants and trees – a garden in the palace after all.

⊤ ※ ⚹ ⚸ ✦

Craters made up the fabric of the habitable landscape in Caldera, although he hadn't passed through any for at least a tide's travel from Redpike. Yet, here they were, in an enormous crater with sides so tall and steep that there was clearly no way out over the rim. It must fill the top third of the mountain.

Darin stepped off the lift, trying not to contemplate the height of the cavern beneath his feet. He followed Conor, Lea and Fresna between winding flowerbeds and paths. Darin recognised flowers that grew on the crater rim of his home, and to the side of the path were vegetables he'd tasted in homes on the way to Redpike.

There were a variety of medicinal herbs arrayed around the edges of a flower bed. Their subtle colours and petals contrasted with the gaudiness of the Agriums behind them. Lea led everyone toward the far outer wall of the crater. As they got closer to it, he realised that somewhere during the last few twists and turns, Fresna and Conor had peeled away and headed down another path. Conor was deep in conversation with Fresna, pointing out flowers. They appeared to be heading to a pavilion.

'Did you notice they went that way?' he asked Lea. She gave him a thin smile, and he saw a slight shake in her hands as she pointed ahead.

'Oh, that's fine. We'll catch up with them again soon. There is a really interesting set of plants in this direction.' She winked. 'Tasty ones too.'

Darin laughed and the heat of an embarrassed blush rose in his cheeks. 'You heard that rumble earlier. Okay then, let's visit the tasty plants.'

They wandered between columns of flowers and processional rows of fruit trees. Everything growing to one side of the path originated from the same area of Caldera; plants he had seen on his journey there – near Dark Holt, maybe? Darin was staring at the star-shaped fruits, trying to recall where he'd eaten them, when a small child ran toward them, stopped in front of

Lea, and tugged at her hand. Panic was written across her face and her little voice quivered as she begged for help.

'My friend ... she ate something. I told her not to eat the fruit, but she did. Help her, please. Please come ... she is very cold – very, very cold. Please help!'

They ran as fast as the child could lead them. Sat in a small grassed lawn was an even smaller girl with lilac hair in disarray around her shoulders. Darin tried not to stare, he'd never seen hair that colour before. He took one look at her face, and her hair was forgotten. She was pale and her lips – stained purple like Lea's – were turning blue underneath. Lea rushed to her, her own skin becoming ashen as she embraced the girl.

'Cousin! Lucia, I'm here,' she said, cradling the girl in her arms with tears streaming down her cheeks.

She got out of the girls that Lucia had eaten a berry from the bush next to her. It seemed familiar; Darin had only seen it dried, but he was certain it was frostbant. The blue berries appeared suitably tasty on the branches, and he could understand why Lucia had eaten it. Frostbant was not normally found in craters, but on the Surface. They wouldn't have long to help her before she would be lost to them.

ᛉ ⚑ ⚜ ⚕ ✦

On the way, Darin and Hal had stayed at a farm where the daughter had eaten a poisonous berry. Hal treated her, explaining that the cure came from the same location as the poison for most plants. He'd explained that they were usually paired, poison and cure. They spent a lot of time searching for paired plants after that.

'It's frostbant.' He tried to keep his voice calm, not to give away how serious it was. 'Lea, is there any ridgeweed in this crater?'

She looked up at him, tears rolling down her cheeks. 'I don't know. We plant everything from one region near to each other. The Gardeners insist it is the only way to help them survive.'

His hands started to shake; she didn't know. *Breathe, stay calm ...* Darin hunted around quickly. Tucked behind the frostbant he found the tiny, triangular-leaved plant. Delicate flowers adorned its stems. He'd seen it as a bunch before, never realising just how many plants that one bunch must contain.

Darin picked a handful and passed it to Lea. 'She needs to chew slowly. Only swallow the juices, not the plant. If she does that, we have time to get help.'

Lea pushed ridgeweed into the girl's mouth. 'You heard him, Lucia – chew it, don't swallow. Just keep chewing.'

Darin watched closely, a knot of fear tightening in the pit of his stomach as a drip of green juice trickled out the corner of Lucia's mouth, but she kept staring up at Lea and chewing.

'Where can I get help?' he asked. 'I could get Fresna. I think I can find my way back to them.'

Lea smiled softly and pointed behind him. 'Thank you, but it seems help is already here.'

A tall figure strode into the clearing. He wore dark robes like the other So'Dal Darin had seen, but these were green-trimmed.

The man glanced at the ridgeweed stems in Darin's hand, his gaze darting between them and Lucia. He nodded slowly in acknowledgement and met Darin's eyes as he spoke. 'She'll be fine, thanks to your quick action. Lea, I'll take her now. You may visit later.' He scooped the small child up in his arms and glided out as quietly as he'd arrived, the grass springing back after his steps as though he had never been there.

Lea began to follow the So'Dal, took a few paces, then stopped. Her serene composure had abandoned her, and she fidgeted with her scarf as she waited for Darin. She must be desperate to return to her cousin.

'Let's head back to the courtyard? You can guide me back to the second trial and then visit your cousin?' he offered.

'I hope you pass it,' she murmured. 'Thank you for your help. If you don't mind, I'll take you back. I promise I'll show you the rest of the garden another day.' They wound their way back through the plants to the lift. As they approached it, she stared up at the wall of the crater and an almost imperceptible smile crossed her lips.

'Darin, you've had a long journey. I'll take you to your room and arrange for a meal to be brought to you. You can rest and be refreshed and ready for tomorrow's trial.'

Gratefully, he nodded and let her lead him to the lift. He sighed as he gripped the rail tightly, waiting for the drop to the cavern floor. It had not been the mind-clearing walk he hoped for. Some time alone would be good – Darin needed a plan.

Chapter 2

Suriin

Sparkle like the most glorious night
Glow like a fire sprite
Smile with the warmth of Suns
Your new day has just begun
Children's rhyme

Summer, 504 Post closing. Caldera, Planet Lieus

'I wish I could get out of this crater and meet new people. I wish for new experiences,' Suriin called upward, sending her wish chasing after the shooting star, which crested the only circle of sky she'd seen in her entire life, over the top of Golden. A shadow cooled her back and blocked the heat of the fire.

'Really, Sis? You aren't wishing for love or something, I don't know – exciting? You're wishing for something you know will definitely happen. What a waste of a good star.' Gwynn laughed. 'Shuffle over.' He flopped down next to her and they stared out into the night. Suriin let her thoughts drift as she leant against her brother. She'd miss him.

There had been occasions when Suriin wished her parents had not been So'Dal; that she'd not been born with lilac hair, marked as talented herself. Days when she'd craved a normal life – to have friends who didn't stay for fleeting visits.

That night was one of those when everything felt on the edge of balance, so she'd chosen her favourite spot on the kitchen step to relax after supper. The night sky never failed to calm her.

Gwynn was right. She'd be leaving soon. Only ten more tides remained before she left for Redpike to start her own studies. How long would it be before she returned home again? Maybe years. That was a long time to meet new people and see new things. She felt a smile grow and embraced the joy; she couldn't wait for a life outside Golden's walls. Like all the craters, it was created by So'Dal magic in the war against the awldrin that the Watcher had ended. She couldn't imagine anyone having that much power. Somehow, the So'Dal must have been so much stronger then.

Suriin had been sheltered within her own So'Dal family for her whole life, stuck on their farm in that tiny legacy of the most powerful magic ever unleashed on Lieus. Soon, she'd get to learn it for herself. What would she be able to do – how much power was inside her? Suriin shivered and wrapped her arms tighter around her knees. It was both exciting and terrifying.

She'd begged her mother to teach her, but all she'd received was a stern look and a promise that she'd be taught properly at the Black Palace. Suriin could hardly wait. She'd always known her mother protected them – they lived in the closest crater to the Edgelands, after all. When she returned from her studies, maybe she'd understand how her mother did it.

Gwynn fidgeted next to her. He'd suggested a million and one different and equally crazy things to do each day for the last tide. She was sure it was his way of trying to make up for what he saw as a dreary future filled with compulsory education. Suriin really hoped he'd show talent as he got older – then he could join her in Redpike. He'd soon see it was so much more, and having him with her would be even more fun. She waited to see what he'd suggest next.

Her mother talked about Redpike with fondness. She described the hidden caverns, the tunnels, and the sparkling red of staramine crystal veins that ran through the walls, as though they were the blood of the mountain.

Suriin would walk in the libraries and explore the crater garden. She would probably get her own moonhound – that was her true aspiration. It would show that she'd made it, completed her training, and was a Soul Anchor like her mother.

'Shall we check the skaa-rak or go hunting farbrox cubs?' her brother asked.

'I can't imagine the skaa-rak have left their barn. It's dark.' Suriin chuckled.

Despite her brother's fears for her boredom and jokes about love, she was actually a bit tingly about meeting all the young men at Redpike. Maybe a handsome stranger would sweep her off her feet, and they would ride off on the adventure of a lifetime. It was Gwynn she really felt for. He might be alone with their mother until either he was old enough to take a trade and travel for himself, or showed magical talent. No wonder he wanted to do fun things while she was still there. It might be dark, but maybe they should do something.

'What would you like to do, Gwynn? You choose.'

'I was thinking, as Mother has gone to bed ... maybe we

could go up to the Surface?' He leant forward eagerly, and it was clear that he really wanted to do it, but the Surface at night was forbidden. The plants were toxic that close to the Edgelands, and there was always a chance of bumping into Surfacedwelling creatures. But he looked so keen, so eager. He reached for her hand. 'Please?'

'Okay, I'll come – but we stay near the top of the steps, and we tell Fluffy.' Moonhounds chose their own names, but she really hoped hers would be called something more noble and less like a small fuzzy farbrox.

She took the steps to their mother's room two at a time. Once outside the door, she sent an image through it. [*Her and Gwynn climbing the crater steps for a look at the Surface, stopped at the top step.*] In return she felt a wag – there was no other way to explain it. Her mother had taught her how to send to Fluffy, but not being the one bonded to her, she couldn't receive any real messages back.

When she returned to the kitchen, Gwynn had already put on extra layers and wore an old leather plant pouch. Suriin threw a cloak over her clothes and pulled fur-lined boots on. 'Come on then, little brother, before I change my mind. Let's see if the Surface really does glow at night!'

ⵝ ❋ ⚘ ⚶ ✦

The higher up the crater path they ascended, the narrower the steps became, and the wider the expanse of visible sky. Green light from the moon, Mythos, illuminated enough to see their way safely.

'Why a plant pouch, Gwynn? You don't know how to use any of them. You can't pick plants without gloves either.'

He lifted his hands so she could see from behind that he was fully gloved up. Suriin bit back a laugh – of course, he had gloves. She didn't bother asking where he'd found them. Their farm had been a Witness home for generations, and Gwynn had a knack for finding legacy items from the previous family in the oddest of places.

'I do know what I'm looking for, actually,' Gwynn said. 'I was reading one of Father's books. It mentions a plant that glows at night with a golden light. It has flowers like an open-bottomed teardrop and heart-shaped leaves.'

'You want to collect love-lies-weeping? What are you going to do with that?'

His muffled reply was lost to the wind the moment they crested the first ledge. Golden was a small crater, with just enough room for their farm and some wildlife to live side by side. At the top of the steps a path to the right descended into the deep holloway leading to the next crater. To the left, a narrow mud track marked the route to the Surface. They followed the path and as it sloped steeply upward, Suriin became uncomfortably aware of the deep, black drop into the crater below.

A gentle glow lit the rim of the crater as they ascended, bringing to mind cautionary tales of those who went to the Surface and never returned; of near misses with sudden sink holes and people returning with rashes and strange ailments. Suriin paused in her stride and glanced back. Had they come far enough? She'd promised Fluffy they'd stop at the step. She opened her mouth to suggest they turn around, but Gwynn forged ahead. Watcher's breath, she couldn't leave him, and they wouldn't be long anyway. She'd always wanted to see the Surface glow if she was honest with herself. Suriin grinned, she'd wished for adventure, so she could hardly deny her star-granted wish. At a wider point, a few paces from the crater's edge, their view opened up. Tiny points of light darted from glowing flower to flower.

'Fire sprites,' she gasped. 'They're beautiful. I've never seen them so bright before.' They danced and spun as if the stars themselves cavorted amongst the plants.

Most plants glowed faintly, a hint around the edge of a leaf here or a gentle spotty pattern there. Some were as bright as a glow lamp. As they stood drinking in the beauty of their surroundings, a dark shadow passed silent and low overhead, blocking the moonlight.

'What was that?' Suriin whispered.

She didn't need the encouragement of Gwynn's finger on his lips to remain quiet. As the creature moved on, she followed its flight with her eyes until it was out of sight.

Suriin spotted a golden glow to the side of the pathway and pointed it out to Gwynn. He tried to reach over the other plants with his long gloves to capture the tears, but as he reached out, he lost his balance. Suriin made a grab for his other arm. And as she pulled him upright, they exchanged a grin that turned into relieved chuckles. Having to wake Mother because he'd fallen in a bush of rakbane would not have been a pleasant end to the adventure, let alone the discomfort he'd suffer.

'Let's mark this bit of the path and come back in daylight if you want it so badly?' suggested Suriin, conscious that the creature might still be out there. 'Why do you want it, anyway? Come on, own up!'

'That's a good plan actually. Now I know where to find it, I may be able to grab it later when I can see what else is here. I'll show you what I've made when it's done.' Gwynn winked at her. That particular conversation was over for the moment. Suriin shrugged. It wasn't like he could do anything with it like their father did. As her eyes adjusted to the glow, she saw the expanse of beauty opening up. Glints of colour wafted in the surface winds. She wanted to see more – one visit would never be enough.

'It's beautiful up here, Gwynn. Thank you for suggesting it. Should we walk a little farther before we go back down?' She glanced up at the sky, searching for shadows against the stars, and found none.

'Yes. Oh, look at that tree!' Arm in arm, the siblings wandered deeper amongst the plants and away from the holloway.

Clouds of fire sprites parted as they moved through them, and the glowing vegetation brought out a beauty not found anywhere else on Caldera – aside from the Edgelands.

They saw a shadow fly overhead again and froze. Nothing happened, and after repeated passes, they relaxed, growing complacent. Gwynn pointed out more plants as they walked.

'That one is fuzber rudis – see the fluffy flowers? In daylight they're red, and the narrow hairy leaves are all furry and white. It's used in food to make it taste sweet. Over there is one of the poison pairs that grow here. See that one with the big wide leaves? They have a slight white glow. Its flowers give you blisters. Next to it is Gloria's salve. It helps to ease them.'

'Gwynn, where have you learnt all this?' Suriin asked. 'You shouldn't know the poison pairs, let alone be able to recognise them. You have gloves and a bag. This is the kind of information that you only find in Gardening books.' As she tried to work out the best way to drag out of him exactly where he'd got the information from, she heard steps behind her from more than one set of feet ... and really close.

'I'd rather like to know the same thing. What in the moons of Lieus are you pair doing up here? At night no less! You are making enough noise to attract a legion of creatures. Gwynn, where did you get that bag and gloves? Suriin, you should set an example for your brother, not go haring off on his crazy schemes at this time of night!'

'Father!' Suriin spun around and engulfed her father in a

hug. Over his shoulder, a second hooded figure watched silently. The So'Dal's face was impossible to read, so deep inside the hood that the plants couldn't illuminate it. Oh, Watcher, she was being told off in front of another So'Dal. She was thankful for the dim light hiding her furious blushes.

Gwynn walked up to their father. 'I—'

They all heard a crack. Her father tensed, and she released him. The same noise broke their breath-held silence, this time from behind Gwynn. A huge section of glowing leaves shook as the creature moved closer – it was something large. Her father took immediate charge, pushing her behind him, all else temporarily forgotten.

'Get behind me, *now*. Ronin, escort my wayward offspring back to the holloway. I will be with you shortly.'

The hooded So'Dal gestured for them to pass him and walked behind, herding Gwynn and Suriin away from their father.

'What is that thing, and what is he going to do? Why doesn't he come too?' Gwynn asked, as he tried to return to his father. Ronin held his arm firmly and steered him away.

Suriin risked a glance back. Her father stood directly between them and the source of the noise. A long, pointed snout protruded over the bushes alongside the path, its toothy mouth lit by the swirling globe of light balancing in her father's hand. The creature was at least twice his height, and light reflected off its hairless hide.

Her father stood facing it, alone, because of her. Because she didn't say no to the crazy idea. 'Can't you help him?' she pleaded with Ronin.

'He won't let me. I'm still training and could be dangerous to the beast.'

'The beast? What about the danger to him?' Suriin turned to take a step back and felt a firm, gentle hand on her shoulder move her along. A low roar rumbled behind them, followed by a single sung note, clear and unwavering. A flash of light split the sky. The roar turned to a yelp and a loud crash reached their ears. Then the sky went dark, and there was silence.

'That's why you don't come to the Surface without me or your mother.' Out of the darkness her father limped, carrying a small glow lamp. He was sporting a few scratches to his right arm and blisters swelled on his hands. Worry turned to guilt as Suriin saw the damage. 'Let's get home. We'll talk more about this in the morning when we are rested. Your mother is worried about you.'

The descent was considerably less exciting than the climb up the crater wall. Suriin let her brother and Ronin go ahead as they snaked their way down to the grassy paddock at the base. A quiet, repeating melody of three notes carried down to her ears, and she glanced around to see her father at work, pouring a glowing mix across the top of the crater steps while he sang.

She completed the descent in the muffled silence of the crater's protection. Her mother's outline in the doorway was sharply visible against the fire glow behind her. Fluffy bounded across the paddock toward them.

Suriin sighed. It didn't matter that she was almost old enough to go to Redpike; she was definitely still about to be told off. Soon, she'd be master of her own decisions, and maybe someday she'd have the kind of connection her parents had with someone. They always knew what the other was thinking. Would she learn and understand more of the skills her father used – how he'd made that flash of light? Despite the mistakes of the evening, a little buzz of excitement reappeared in her gut. Her adventure was not even partially begun. First, she had to endure the oncoming storm. Suriin stepped into the kitchen and braced herself for the 'I am so disappointed in you' speech.

CHAPTER 3

ELISSA

History becomes legends; become stories.
Stories not told are soon forgotten.
In the darkness, keep our legends alive. We must
*   remember.*
Found on a scrap of hide in the Shardeep
**   caves**

WINDS, 504 POST CLOSING. OUTER MOON OF
TEBEIN

Desperation and hunger drove her to fish farther downstream than she'd ever been. Thin sunlight sparkled off hundreds of tiny ripples, and waterside plants' reflections wavered over an eddy as Elissa studied it. It appeared a promising pool to catch sprill. The memory of how delicious the oily fish was spurred her into motion.

Shimmering scales deep in the pool caught her eye, and she smiled. Elissa plunged her arm in to grab at the fish but came up empty. She tried again and again, hunger and frustration making her careless, but there was no chance she'd catch one by surprise now. Elissa sat back on her heels and sighed.

Rains was late by at least a tide, and she was starving. The sooner the wind calmed and the edible plant life could recover, the better – for the whole sericlave. The wind had blown as hard as anyone alive could remember and scoured the remaining plants away.

Elissa had visited the secret places where root vegetables grew to supplement their meagre diet of grains. There were none left. If she started searching for new locations someone else might notice, and that was a risk she couldn't take. So, today she fished.

Reed beds flourished along the stream, their roots nourished by all the silt dropped in by the winds. Juicy green stems gave no hint of the unpleasant stomach cramps they'd confer on anyone unwitting enough to eat them, but she was hungry enough that even the reeds looked tasty. Windweed made a good basket, or maybe even a net woven correctly, but it was useless as food – a shame as it was the only plant life that benefited from the wind.

Elissa gathered a few handfuls of the reeds, resigned to the fact that extra food was not on the day's menu. She dried the roots and secreted them inside her ill-fitting, dusty clothes. When she next returned, she'd be better prepared and those sprill wouldn't evade her.

⊤ ✳ ⚶ ⚴ ✦

The advantage of being who she was meant that, as long as she was back before her duties began, no one would miss her. Elissa scanned the mountain-side in search of the lookmen. Makin stood on the southern scree slope, so her preferred route wasn't an option. She had no bribes, and so getting past her brother was the only way in.

Inhabitants were officially forbidden to leave but many of them did. Their rations were so poor during Winds that the lookmen turned a blind eye if they received something for their trouble.

The scree slope on Dragonsbreath Peak was a jaggedly sharp, melted mass of glass. There were a number of other melted patches around the peak, but this was the biggest. Makin had told her that on the top of the south slope, sunlight reflected off one with such focused intensity that it hurt and the awldrin gathered there every time the eclipses aligned. Officially, no human had been allowed to see what they did on those nights. Elissa thought it more likely that no human had survived to tell of it.

Her filthy clothes stood out against the glossy rocks, so she skirted the scree slope behind loose boulders and jagged shards, using as much cover as she could. A small black shard ahead reflected light into her face. She picked it up and aimed a reflection toward her brother's eyes. From her position behind a large, upright stone, she saw him wince as light hit his face, then peer down, searching for her.

He called to the lookman closest to him and pointed away from Elissa's direction. They both turned to stare at some imagining of his as Elissa took a deep inhalation of free air and ran. The sticky soles of her tattered boots gave her purchase, and she reached the top swiftly and with no mishaps. They'd performed their little routine often enough over the years that they were in synch. By the time the lookman turned back to Makin, Elissa was through the entrance.

Once safely inside the cave, she began the circuitous route back to her nook where she could stow the reeds. No one came near her nook – not even her brother. She was Untouched. The lilac curls she'd been born with had marked her. From birth, her parents had covered her hair with a sticky mass of cha leaves and calfa, and once Laytha had taken her in after her first bleed, she'd been taught to do it herself in a routine they followed together.

Elissa's mother had instilled in her an understanding that should any awldrin see her natural hair, the whole community would die. That weight of responsibility lay heavy on a child's shoulders, becoming a burden that weighed yet more as she'd aged. Her mother had also told stories of how once, a survivor from another sericlave had reached them. A solitary survivor of a massacre. The awldrin had found a single lilac-haired woman and gone crazy, killing the entire sericlave. Elissa was aware with every hair on her head that one wrong step or missed dye could doom them all.

The trouble was that no one could predict when a lilac-haired child would be born – or who to – and although occasional mutterings about killing newborns reared their head, she was sure that many elders had Untouched in their own families. Instead of infant death, through the cold of Winds, those like her did the most dangerous jobs, the filthiest ones that caused the most accidental deaths.

No Untouched would ever bear children – it was the solution Dragonsbreath sericlave had adopted, so they were never allowed to be alone with a member of the community. Elissa hid her loneliness, like her hair, under a layer of grime as all others born like her did. Her brother had also chosen not to risk having a lilac-haired daughter and lived alone in their old family hut. Their family would end with them.

Untouched only saw their families when they worked, so the chance to mix was valued – a treat in their mundane existence of darkness. To hide in plain sight effectively, they could never appear to be shunned, especially in front of the awldrin.

Dragonsbreath portrayed themselves as a seamless community, a unified team heating the high reaches of Dragonsbreath Peak for the awldrin. They knew their place, and their place was to survive.

Elissa reached the hut hiding her nook's entrance, passed the heavy, hide door, walked past the fire pit, then slipped around the false curtain wall at the back.

Once, there must have been more Untouched, but most of the dark nooks hidden behind carefully positioned huts at the back of the cave now stood empty. No lilac-haired women had been found by awldrin in Dragonsbreath for hundreds of cycles. *Keep unnoticed, stay Untouched.*

Unquestioned rules decreed that they had to sleep alone, surrounded by rock. She'd often wondered why, but the elders either couldn't or wouldn't tell her; they simply insisted it was for her own safety. Each Untouched had their own nook cut into the walls of the cave. It was just how things were, how they survived.

Elissa knew her way through the dark tunnel by touch, the space as familiar to her as the shape of her own hands. She ran her fingertips along the wall, past two nooks, and followed the carved groove until it ended at the entrance to her own space. She didn't feel safe sleeping right next to the hut, so her nook had always felt the right distance under the mountain.

Two paces to the bed. Turn right. Five paces to the far wall. Elissa reached forward and put a hand into the storage shafts, feeling for the empty one. Once she'd found it, she removed the sheaf of windweed from inside her clothes and pushed it in, then reached into an adjacent shaft and pulled out a roll of dry clothes equally as dusty as the ones she wore. She changed into them then returned to the main sericlave, strolling past the huts lining the edge of the cave. As she walked between two smaller buildings, she smiled at a group of young children playing in the entrance. They waved enthusiastically. At that age, they usually did.

The golden glow of the rota crystal filled the cave, pulsing as it changed from orange to yellow. Elissa climbed into the cage, and the liftmen lowered her and two others to the pit below. She would work until the crystal changed again, and when it did, night would have fallen.

At the bellows station, her neighbour, dressed in orange clothes, looked up in relief. An unspoken question in her eyes was met with a downward twitch of the lips from Elissa. They shared everything they had. All Untouched were women, and a sister-ship had grown between many of them. Laytha had been there for her since she was ten cycles old, and after sharing the nooks for over twenty-five cycles, their communication barely needed words.

Laytha was as desperate for food as she was, so Elissa couldn't meet her eyes. She'd failed. Her gaze dropped to her hands.

The cleanness of one arm struck her; it was unusually pink. Resolute, she fixed the sparkling fish and clean stream in her mind. Focusing on that image would help her through the dry heat of the bellows shift. She dragged her hands through her hair once more and surreptitiously rubbed dirt back onto the clean arm.

She shovelled ash. Her sole job was to keep the bellow's outlet clear. Maintaining airflow in the stagnant environment was the least demanding of Untouched roles, but hot ash burnt and – as with all jobs there – people died regularly. Staying alert after her stolen time at the river would be a bigger challenge than usual without the reward of extra food.

As Laytha left, Elissa took her seat by the bellows. The rhythmic whoosh of air from the pullers marked time. Firestone was added in at the top of the system and its ashes floated down to her floor. The bellows forced air through to keep the fire-stone glowing and heat moving upward toward the caves at the top of the peak. Throughout Winds, the awldrin required a constant temperature. As the three seasons cycled, needs of both the inhabitants of the sericlave and the residences at the peak changed. The awldrin left them to their work, mostly. As long as there was heat in their quarters at the top of the peak, they were satisfied.

Awldrin were obsessed with order – every part of the sericlave had to work properly. As long as everything they needed was in the right place, the sericlave was left alone under the gaze of the glowing crystal. What kind of creatures could create something like the rota crystal? It changed twice in each night and twice each day, a constantly glowing reminder of the power the awldrin could bring to life should the sericlave fail them. She often wondered how they could have made something so amazing, but not found a way to stay warm without forcing her sericlave to work.

Rains couldn't come soon enough. Newly fertile soil would sprout to life with a carpet of green and the crops would need care and tending. Food became less scarce, and they could restock their stores for the hot weather of Canicule that followed after. She stood smiling whilst she imagined the green fields stretched out below the peak.

A puff of ash in her face broke her reverie.

'Elissa! Clear it. Now.' She grabbed the shovel before the pullers were forced to stop and settled into her rhythm for the next few hours. *Keep unnoticed, stay Untouched.*

At the end of her shift, Elissa climbed into the lift, her feet dragging with exhaustion, desperate for her bed and rest. Her room may not be the comfiest, and she had no way to light it, but the complete peace at the end of a long shift made up for it all.

A bowl of food and some water had been left out for her inside the hut. Gratefully, she swallowed it down and then moved through to her nook. She tugged off her dirty, yellow clothes and placed them neatly back in the storage shaft, swapping them for loose woven trousers to sleep in. Her eyes were closing as her head hit the pillow, and within moments, she was asleep.

Morning dawned somewhere above the peak, although Elissa was unaware of it. In her world of mountain caves and ash, the changing of the great crystal in the centre of the cave governed time. Days stretched into a tide, and she continued her routine of sleep, work, collect rations, cook. At the end of each crystal rotation she would shuffle the windweed in her storage to help it dry. At the end of each tide, the rotation would change and she would have a day free. She needed the net finished by then; her brother worked an alternate shift to her and would be back on lookman duty that day. Elissa counted eight crystal rotations, then began weaving her net.

With no light in her nook, she wove it in the hut as she cooked. Ground meal tasted awful, but it gave her enough energy to keep going. She'd always noticed that, until Rains, awldrin weren't keen on the sericlave stores having any variety, or quantity. Were they feasting on rich food up in the peak while the humans starved? Or was it more practical, and it suited them more to keep humans tired and lethargic during Winds – they were less likely to rebel. It certainly made her more inclined to work hard when the rain arrived, bringing with it the promise of more food and more variety. The harder they worked, the sooner they could see rewards. It made a sad sort of sense.

Two rotations later Elissa finished her net. Makin had left his shoes outside his hut door, a coded sign that he was on watch. She headed to her nook straight after her shift, changed into her outside clothes and, ensuring the sticky-soled boots were still tacky, tucked the net into her tunic and waited. As the crystal turned from orange to red, reversing the rotation, she moved, first with the general flow of people, then toward the cave perimeter before scuttling through the exit to hide behind the closest jagged boulders.

From the corner of her eye, she saw someone else slipping out. Elissa paused behind a spotted rock and watched to see which way they went – toward the fields. She sent a silent wish of luck to them. Where they headed was too far round for her liking; she'd found a body there once with claw marks through it. Elissa had always suspected that humans who didn't work as part of the sericlave were seen as unnecessary. When she was a child, she'd seen an awldrin hunt a man down and kill him for being too far away from the fields in Rains. There wasn't much to be had in the fields at the moment, certainly not enough to risk being seen. While sprill fishing was riskier as she was further away, she was both careful and desperate – the food would be worth it.

Once at the stream, Elissa searched for patches of windweed and back-eddy pools. She followed the water as it meandered from the Black Lake toward the Ameryth Dar Sea. It had dropped much lower than last time; the lake must be starting to run dry. Flames, she hoped Rains would come soon.

The pool where she'd found the sprill sparkled with life. Elissa stretched her woven funnel across the stream by hooking one edge over some reeds. The other side she weighed down with a stone, then removed her foot wraps and rolled the fabric of her tattered trousers above her knees before entering the water.

Free in the knowledge she was alone, she splashed happily to chase darting flashes of silver into the net. Small flaps of tails and flashes of fins signalled a good number of small fish fighting through the windweed to avoid the net. Several minutes of wading and chasing resulted in a reasonable catch; they would eat well.

Elissa gathered the edges of the net together before searching for the easiest way out of the water. She pushed off the stream bed to climb out on a lower section of bank just as something sharp sliced into her foot and ribbons of red swirled downstream. With no one to watch, she allowed herself a sigh, a moment of frustration. She finally had food, and she might lose the entire catch hobbling up the scree slope injured in front of the lookmen. The moment passed, Elissa pushed her shoulders back and gritted her teeth. That wasn't going to happen – Laytha needed those fish as much as she did. She reached down to pull the offending object out, but her hand closed around the edges of a much bigger shard than she'd expected. Flames, she'd have to be careful. Elissa twisted carefully and shuffled further back on the bank, so as not to put more weight on the offending bit of rock, then lifted her foot out.

She crossed her leg onto her left thigh and saw that, contrary to her expectation, it was not dragon glass. A crystal shard was embedded in her foot, its opalescent surface shimmering like oil on water. Elissa wriggled it gently, easing it from the arch of her foot, but just as she thought it was almost out, the shard snapped. The larger section came loose in her hand and, despite the searing pain, she couldn't help but notice it was beautiful. She put it on the bank and returned her focus to the remaining fragment, but it was too small, too far in her foot to reach. Trying to remove it now would be messy and probably cause more blood loss – still, probably better than trying in the darkness of her nook. She washed around the wound for a closer look. The last remnant was in deep. Although the crystal had snapped cleanly, she could see no way to safely remove it.

Elissa gathered a handful of moss from the water's edge and padded her foot up. She'd simply have to poultice it and hope that the shard would work its way out. In the arch of her foot, at least she wouldn't have to bear her full weight on it. With the moss held still, she replaced her foot wraps, tying them slightly looser around the injured foot.

Splashes in her net reminded her to haul out her catch before they all escaped. Six small sprill remained in the funnel, more meat than they had eaten for almost the whole of Winds. Elissa killed each with a quick blow to the head before wrapping them in a cloth bag and hiding it under her tunic. She needed to hurry – the walk back would take longer with the injury, and she still needed to both sleep and cook the fish before the crystal turned yellow.

As Elissa turned to leave, the iridescence of the crystal she'd pulled from her foot caught her attention. She dipped it in the water, then tucked it into her tunic. It had sharp edges and it was dazzling, she could make use of it. Pretty and useful things were always good to have, either for trade or her own use.

She tested her weight on the injured foot. Flames, but it hurt. The scree slope would be almost impossible to run up, and speed was the only way to defeat its slippery texture – speed and her special foot wraps. Hopefully, her brother was still in the same lookman spot. If he wasn't, she'd happily sacrifice a fish to get back in without word getting to the elders.

Cursing her luck with each step, Elissa turned upstream and headed back to the sericlave.

CHAPTER 4

DARIN

To trust a dream, you must first be awake.
Engraved on a table in the Windwhistle,
    Redpike

Darin enjoyed rising with the sun and watching the world wake. Years of helping his parents with the inn had built an appreciation for early starts. Until the fire. Until their home and business burnt down, and they all moved into his grandfather's cramped cottage. Darin was going to give them the chance to rebuild. As sure as the Watcher had wings, he was going to find a way to support them, and the trial was his best chance.

He warmed himself in the morning sun filtering through his window, while marching boots rang out in the courtyard below as a group of guards crossed toward the hall. At the back of the group, bruised and battered, were the two young men he'd seen in the trial yesterday. If that pair of over-dressed ignorants had passed the guard test, he could too.

Darin stifled a yawn and turned back to his room. His dreams had been even more vivid than usual, but then they often were when he slept in a strange place. Last night, he'd walked in the tunnels under the mountain with a giant hound; the events of the garden had plagued his dreams too. Darin hoped Lucia was okay. He would go down for breakfast and try to find Lea. Maybe he could get an update on her to settle his mind before his testing.

Darin pulled his clothes on and was tying his boots when there was a knock at the door. He opened it to find a teenage boy carrying a tray.

'Chef says you'll need all this today! I wish I could have more. These flatcakes are amazing, especially with the brose.' He thrust the tray toward Darin.

It was laden with a toppling heap of golden-brown flat-cakes. Darin's mouth watered as fragrant brose drifted toward him. The words left his mouth before he realised it – Hal really had trained him well. 'Thank you for bringing it. Do you want to share?'

'Whoop!' The boy was through the door like a flash. He placed the tray on the table by the window and, from inside his robe, he produced a second plate. 'Not everyone in the guest quarters or guard-house remembers their manners. Thank you …'

'Darin.'

The boy reminded him of his younger brother, but with black hair like his own. Laughing, dark eyes peered back at him from between the tight curls, and he wore a long robe which lacked the coloured trim of the So'Dal he'd met.

The boy chatted cheerily through mouthfuls of food, brose dripping from his spoon as he gesticulated. 'I'm glad it's you. I wanted to meet you. My father said you came from Eye, you can use two weapons, and that you're not afraid of the Surface as much as he expected. He also told me to bring my second plate this morning when I delivered breakfasts.'

Darin chuckled; the boy must be Hal's son. 'He told me a little about you too. I can see you share your father's love of brose!' Darin glanced out the window and noticed a change in the tower flags. Scarlet stars danced in the breeze on a sky of silver. As he savoured his breakfast, he realised he'd seen that flag in his dream.

'What does that flag mean? You So'Dal use a lot of flags.'

'I'm not a So'Dal yet. I'm not old enough to be one, but when my powers become active, I will be. That flag is because it's a choosing day.'

'Is that part of the trials?'

'No, it's for the Soul Anchors – the female So'Dal – to bond with their moonhounds. It's not normally at the same time as the trials, but the Hound Master insisted the yearlings were ready.' A howl broke the quiet as a pack of enormous, shaggy hounds loped into the courtyard. 'Darin, you look like you've seen a ghost. What's wrong?'

'Those hounds are huge. What are they? Where do they come from?' A bundle of puppies came running behind the main pack, all wagging tails and big paws.

'Those are moonhounds.' The boy rushed to the window and gazed down at them. 'They're magnificent, aren't they? They decide for themselves who they want to bond with. One day I hope one chooses me. But I'm too young, and they haven't chosen a male since forever.' He rolled his eyes dramatically.

'They choose? How does a dog choose?' asked Darin.

'Oh, that's easy ... They dream of you and you dream of them.'

Darin almost choked on his mouthful. Most of the hounds milled around the courtyard, but some sat on their haunches, staring up at the building Darin was in.

'Why are they staring like that?' he wondered aloud.

'Probably waiting to meet their Soul Anchors. Would you like to go down and meet them? My mother has one, and she'll be there.'

They certainly looked like the hounds in his dream, but the boy said they didn't choose men. He must have seen one without noticing. After all, a lot had happened since he'd arrived.

'What did you say your name was? I'm sorry, I'm sure Hal must have told me.'

'I didn't. I'm Jaer.'

Swallowing his last mouthful, Darin stood. 'Well then, Jaer, lead on. I'd like to see those hounds up close.' The whole idea of dreaming hounds bemused him, but the sequence of events was too odd to ignore.

The worst that could happen would be meeting those majestic moonhounds. He'd stroll out nonchalantly, pet them, and put his mind at ease. Once he had met them, he'd find a training area to prepare for the day's testing. Maybe Conor would warm up with him.

ᛉ ⚒ ❀ ⚔ ✦

Up close, the moonhounds were even bigger than they'd appeared from his room. Their shaggy hair was wiry, and their long, slim heads were level with his chest. Wide-set, triangular ears flapped like miniature wings as they ran about. Their coats were predominantly grey, but the tips of all their tails were brilliant white. Some had four white feet, some only one, and each had a varied pattern of spots and patches in black or white. A few robed So'Dal walked amongst them, and two women with scarves wrapped elaborately around their hair stood with the mother and puppies.

'Jaer,' called a woman, 'you're out early this morning. Have you completed all your tasks already?'

'No, but Darin' – grinning broadly, Jaer gestured at him – 'wanted to meet the hounds. Is that okay?'

'Did he? I am sure we can accommodate that.' She turned toward a tall, slim hound with a black patch around its right eye, and it loped over. 'Greetings, Darin,' the woman said. 'I believe you arrived yesterday for testing?' Darin nodded, and she continued. 'I am the Anchor. Please be welcome in our palace. This is my moonhound, Sulki. You can say hello to her.'

Jaer's mother was *the* Anchor? The person in charge of the whole Black Palace. What did that make Hal? *My mentor. The same person he's been for tides. Breathe and focus. One thing at a time.*

Tentatively, Darin reached for Sulki's shoulder. Before he touched her, he spotted Conor walking out to see the huge dogs. When he turned back to Sulki, he found he could no longer quite reach her.

Sat between himself and the adult hound stood a tall, young hound. Lean and lanky, it had yet to grow into its legs. It was fuzzy grey all over, with no markings other than jet black ears and its tail tip. Tilting its head to one side, quizzical wrinkles appeared across its forehead. Darin felt under inspection.

They stared at each other for a moment. The hound was fuzzy, fluffy, and yes, he fancied a stroke, but no more than any other hound. Exhaling softly, he realised he had been holding his breath. Dreaming hounds! He could dismiss that idea and focus on the day ahead. Not wanting to appear rude to the Anchor, he returned to Sulki to stroke her. As he reached out, the young hound let out a bark, and a strong sensation of upset washed over him.

'You want a stroke instead, do you?' As Darin bent to the youngster and stroked the fluffy, dark ears, happiness and contentment flowed through him. 'Do you have a name?' He half directed this toward the Anchor, but she was frowning, her lips tightly pursed.

'Ask him,' she replied, 'not me.'

'What is your name, pup?' Darin asked, to smothered laughter from Jaer.

'You don't understand moonhounds, do you?' he asked. 'Darin, first picture yourself and picture your name. Then try to ask, feel the question. If he wants to tell you, he will.'

Slightly offended by the laughter, Darin concentrated on the suggested task. *What does Darin look like? Can hounds spell? No, that's just stupid.* He closed his eyes and formed a picture of himself in his mind whilst saying *Darin* in his head as clearly as he could. He kept the image in his mind and opened his eyes. Who would know other than him? He could make up a name, right? Would they really know any different? Darin fixed the question in his head and pictured the hound.

As he held the image, it was replaced with one from his dream the night before. The moonhound in front of him was fully grown, big, and powerful. They walked under the mountain and the hound stopped to nudge a rock with his nose. It sparkled and glittered red, illuminated by the light in his hand. Again, he nudged the stone; a staramine crystal.

'Staramine.' Darin tried it out. 'It's a bit long. Can I call you Star?' A paw on his leg made him open his eyes again. He'd spoken out loud to a hound. The heat rose in his cheeks as he noticed numerous watching faces amongst the So'Dal. 'He says his name is Staramine.'

His hand shook, and his heart was ready to burst from his chest, it was beating so fast. *Keep breathing. Look calm,* he thought, trying to project the So'Dal composure he had seen on Hal so many times.

Every face in the courtyard turned his way. The only noise aside from birds was Staramine's wagging tail thudding against the cobbles. Even the moonhounds stared at them. An old man with hunched shoulders limped into the archway. A hood covered most of his face, but Darin was sure he could see a smile grow in the shadow.

'Send word to ready an extra kennel bedroom, please,' the Anchor called to the old man. She waved over to someone behind Darin. 'Please have this man's bags taken over. He will be in for the best night's sleep he's had for a long while.'

She looked at Darin next, her blue eyes still, calm, and almost unreadable.

'Well, that was ... unexpected. I withdraw you from the remaining parts of the trial. If a moonhound has chosen you, you clearly dream walk. He will now shield you from any further dream testing. You may continue to train at arms, but for now, you need urgent training in moonhound care.' She waved her arm toward the pack of hounds. 'Continue your preparations. The Soul Anchors will be out shortly.' And, just like that, the courtyard returned to life.

Darin felt the burn of glancing eyes and was relieved when Conor came over to him. He'd overheard the conversation and patted him on the shoulder.

'Sorry, looks like you'll miss the fighting again, Darin.'

The Anchor studied them both, fixing them with her gaze. 'Neither of you need to fight. You passed the first trial already. The minute you offered to help the Soul Anchors, you showed you understood our ways. Everything you have done since you entered this palace has been a test. So far, you've passed them all.'

Darin felt nauseous, surely something at least was an accident? 'The poisoned girl in the garden?' he asked.

She nodded.

'A child I met in the garden was poisoned too,' said Conor.

'You both knew what to do and how to heal them,' the Anchor replied.

'Watcher's great claws! What if I hadn't known what to do?' Darin was stunned.

'Someone else would have stepped in. Darin, your trial is over, and your acceptance here is now certain. The hound has chosen you, therefore you have innate magical talent. You will begin training soon. The Master will send word.'

'Conor, you still have trials to face to determine your final role in this palace. I will meet you again in time, when your talents have been revealed.' She turned to Jaer, and a smile broke through the veneer for a moment. 'Go, get some breakfast. I'll see you later.'

'Yes, Anchor.' Jaer bowed, then winked at Darin before he sped off through the archway to the kitchen.

Darin cleared his throat nervously. 'Umm, Anchor? I came to test as a guard. My family lost everything, and I'd hoped that working here would help them have a chance to rebuild.' Was he actually asking the Anchor about money? Yes, he had to.

'Your family will be taken care of,' she said. 'You have other things to worry about now.'

He felt his shoulders drop as the tension released, and he swallowed hard to hold back the tears of relief threatening to rise. He'd done it. His family would be secure. A hound and a life as a So'Dal were never the plan, but the Watcher must have had other ideas, and his main goal was achieved.

Wait, had she said magic? He was about to ask, but she gazed past him toward the buildings, a smile playing on her lips.

'This is always one of my favourite days,' she murmured.

⁂

The guest quarter doors opened, and a group of the women Darin knew as Soul Anchors came running out, lilac hair flying behind them and faces adorned with broad smiles. A few more, who looked only vaguely hopeful, followed hesitantly. Lea was one of the first through the doors, and Darin stood with his hand on Staramine's head, ruffling his warm, soft ears as she ran toward the hounds, her eyes searching the pack. A hound similar in size to Staramine, calmly padded toward her. She was as tall as Lea's waist already. They stopped and stared at each other for a moment before sheer joy exploded in a wagging, woofing bundle of grey fur as the moonhound put her paws on Lea's shoulders and nuzzled her face.

Around the courtyard, other greetings took place. Some were as effusive as that of Lea and her new moonhound, whilst others were more restrained. Barks echoed from the high walls, it was one of the most joyful things he had ever seen.

⁂

New partners moved away from the pack and sat in quiet spaces, getting to know each other as calmness descended. With the greetings over, Darin noticed that many So'Dal and Soul Anchors in the courtyard still took sideways glances at him and whispered. He grew increasingly uncomfortable with the scrutiny and focused on Star instead, desperate to get away from their stares. He crouched down, eye to eye with the pup. Staramine responded by licking his face with enthusiasm.

Conor tapped him on the shoulder as Darin wiped ribbons of slobber from his face. The old man had returned to the archway and gestured him over. Darin strode across the courtyard toward him, away from the stares and into a new life with Staramine trotting at his side.

CHAPTER 5

SURIIN

*On holloways; these strange features have become
a normal part of travel and transport since
the Great Rending. Along their length are
found a range of accommodations and entertainments for the weary traveller.*
A Traveller's Guide to Caldera

Branches formed a living, vaulted roof high above her head. Mottled light dappled the muddy path, and roots protruded like grasping fingers from the walls of the high, moss-covered sides of the holloway. The journey from Golden crater had taken several hours, and they'd left almost as soon as Ronin and her father had resupplied.

⁂

The holroom door was halfway up the living green wall. It would have been level with the path once, but hundreds of cycles and thousands of footsteps had worn the base of the holloway increasingly deeper. Suriin idly wondered how many times her own father had passed along its length, his footsteps contributing to the deepening hollow.

She climbed the steps cut into the wall and reached for the handle, caught her toe on the door frame, and fell into the room as the door swung open. The tiled floor surprised her. Rather than the dark, damp cave she'd expected, shafts of light lanced down from above, illuminating groups of seats arranged around small tables. Several open doors led to small chambers off the main room. The whole place was homely and welcoming. She picked herself up and hobbled to a seat at the nearest table. Her feet were so sore she desperately needed to rest. Her new shoes had not been as well-softened as she'd thought. Maybe the older boots her mother had suggested would have been a better idea after all – not that she'd ever admit it.

Ronin entered the holroom behind her, crossing to a cupboard marked with the So'Dal symbol. He arranged vials from his bag onto the shelf, matching them to patterns painted inside the door.

'All stocked up,' he called. 'Anyone for a drink?'

'Please,' her father replied from the doorway. 'Suriin can have one too.' She was about to reply that she could make her own decisions when Ronin fetched tankards from under the counter and pulled three ales from a pump. Maybe she'd just stay quiet. Her mother wouldn't have offered her ale; sometimes it felt as though they thought she was still a child.

Outside the door, her father sung the three note melody she'd first heard a few days ago – after the incident with the beast.

It had been a difficult few days with her parents arguing throughout. Her father wanted to keep her there until her nineteenth birthday, follow the old tradition. Her mother was concerned about her recklessness and curiosity. As usual, her mother had won. Suriin was on her way to Redpike to begin her training early.

Golden was several craters away from Redstone crater, and after that, there was the final surface path to Redpike town and the Black Palace. It would be a long journey. She'd studied a map with Gwynn one evening as the arguments continued and Ronin had been out gathering plants. They worked out that it might take about three tides to reach Redpike on foot – if there were no delays. Tomorrow they'd continue down the holloway to Nameless crater. After that, it would be onward to Blow and the first town.

It would be the first night she could remember being away from home. Maybe wishing on the star had sped the adventure up? No, that was silly. Only children believed things like that – it was coincidence.

The door closed with a heavy thud, interrupting her thoughts as her father joined them. He didn't slide the bolts across and smiled as he noticed her watching him.

'It isn't dark yet and, unlikely though it may be, this far from any towns, travellers could still be out,' he said. 'I'll bolt them later.'

'Stores are refilled and the other vials checked,' Ronin said, strolling round the counter to join them. 'No one has been through since our stop on the way here – as expected – but at least next time you visit, you won't have to continue on through the night.'

'Thank you, Ronin. It's a good thing we did though.' A sideways glance at Suriin reminded her it would take a long time to live that down. He took their drinks and sat at a well-lit table.

'Come and join us, Suriin. We need to get a few rules on the table before we meet anyone else.'

She picked up her bag and joined the two So'Dal.

'You will not speak of what you saw me do to any who aren't So'Dal, and you will mention nothing about my sung wards either. I know you've noticed – you're my daughter, and it would disappoint me if you hadn't. We have brought you up as if we lived in Redpike around normal So'Dal behaviour.' Suriin self-consciously touched her lilac hair, and her father nodded.

'A lot is about to change for you, my heart. The population of Caldera knows the So'Dal as caretakers, administrators, builders, and herbalists, trusting us to provide potions and treatments for their health, and to record moments of great importance in society. They put our skills with healing down to the care with which we grow herbs, and our songs are in demand as entertainment. They've forgotten that magic is real. To those outside our society, it is a myth, a legend, and no more – something for children's rhymes. Our charmed potions are created in secret and your power, like your mother's, will never knowingly be seen outside our society. Much of what we were is lost, and it's better that way for everyone. We were once the defences of Lieus against things long-forgotten and happily left that way. Watcher knows, I hope we never have to be again.'

'The people of Caldera are right to have faith in us, and we must live up to it. We're caretakers and record keepers, paid in kind for our services, seen as humble servants of the people. That's why women in our society wear head covers in public to hide the sign of their gift. It's easy for society to forget you're anything more, if you don't show it.'

Suriin nodded as her father reached into a pocket of his robe and handed her a plain blue scarf. It was as light as an enna bird's feather and incredibly soft. The plainness of the fabric hid the fact that it was very special material. Some of what he explained, she knew, but a reminder of the responsibility that came with the power was inevitable given the last few days.

'People will see you wearing it and think nothing of it. Your hair colour will attract no attention, and you may cover your hair in any way you see fit. Many women you meet will take great pride in their choice of styles and colours, matching them to every outfit.' A wry smile crossed his face. 'Your mother has more scarves than I thought could possibly exist stashed away in her rooms!'

Suriin tried to remember her mother wearing the scarf in her hands. 'She's never worn this one? I don't recognise it.'

'No, I bought this one for you. You should have had time to learn how to tie it before we travelled after your birthday. You'll have to work it out yourself, I'm afraid.' He shrugged and took a drink.

Ronin leant forward and smiled at her. 'Don't worry too much, Suriin. The closer we get to Redpike, the more women you will meet with a variety of head covers. Most of them aren't gifted.'

'But we could pass other travellers from tomorrow?' she asked.

'Yes, Nameless crater is neither abandoned nor empty – it merely has no big settlements in it. We will no doubt meet someone.'

Suriin tried to remember how her mother tied her scarf and grimaced at the complex knotting she did.

'Is there a mirror in this place? I think this may take some practise.'

Ronin pointed to a door alongside the bar. 'That one has a mirror. It's old and clouded, but it should be sufficient.'

As Suriin walked off to attempt coaxing her long, unruly hair into a tidy, hidden arrangement, the men quietly continued in conversation. She left the door slightly ajar while she braided her hair.

'While we travel with Suriin, I'm limited in what I can teach you. I know you understand this,' her father said in a low voice.

'It is how it needs to be, Yorynn. One of the most important parts of your teaching has been to accept that we only learn what we should learn at the time we need to learn it. That to learn the work of the other is to hold more power than is safe. No one wants another incident of ground-shearing!'

'I'm glad you understand. We'll focus on herb-lore until we reach Blow. From there, we will work on your singing. Maybe we can earn our bed or some faster transport with a performance or three.'

'How do you think she'll cope with the difference, you know, being out in the normal population?'

'We'll stay in crater-edge lodgings where possible. Suriin has never slept near anyone other than our family. I don't know how she'll cope, untrained and unexposed as she is. Usually, two full So'Dal accompany a bond-less Soul Anchor, so I am aware of the extra pressure on you. I am sorry, but her mother and I still feel it is for the best.'

'Reporting for babysitting duty then, Yorynn. Shall I take the first shift tonight?'

Suriin could hear the laughter in Ronin's voice, but the comment stung. Great. So first, she showed herself to be irresponsible by joining her brother on a whim, and apparently they thought she needed babysitting. She had no plans to go wandering anywhere at night, so they'd both be sorely disappointed. She wanted to learn magic with every fibre of her being and resolved to note down as much of what Ronin was taught as she could. Maybe it would help her in the future – give her extra talents. Suriin checked in the mirror one last time. She looked older. Not a hair showed, and the blue scarf was tight to her scalp. It wasn't particularly pretty knotting, but it would do.

Both men glanced up from their ale as she walked back in. Her father with affection while Ronin held a neutral, cool expression.

Suriin hadn't seen his face properly until that moment. The whole time they were at Golden, he'd been in her father's study, reading and researching or out gathering. He'd even kept his hood up all day as they travelled. Long, dark, wavy hair reached to his chest, and dark eyes looked out at her from a golden tanned face spangled with freckles. Suriin recognised his features as being from the west of Caldera. Which also explained the soft accent. Pretending to ignore what she'd overheard, she collected her drink and joined them.

'Do we have any food?' she asked her father.

'Yes, but it's all dried. I never know how long things will be stored here. Ronin, could you rustle us up some supper before the light fades?'

Ronin nodded and rose, disappearing through the door opposite the main entrance. Quiet singing drifted back to them as he worked, and a smile twitched at the corner of her father's mouth.

'Suriin, if you check under the counter, you'll find a stones board. It's been a long time since we played. Do you fancy a game?'

She did. Time with her father was rare, and she planned to make the most of the journey in that respect. She found the board and all the coloured stone pebbles.

They were mid game, Yorynn about to outmanoeuvre

Suriin into a defensive position, when Ronin reappeared, bearing plates of steaming supper.

He'd used ale to rehydrate the food, and the end result was delicious. They ate in companionable silence as the shaft of light finished its journey across the floor, fading into patches of diffuse brightness.

Yorynn rose, stretching as he crossed the room. He opened the door and had one last look down the holloway before dropping the heavy bolts in place.

'It's time we bed down for the night. Suriin, use the room you were in earlier. Ronin and I will share the bunk room next to you. I'd like to arrive in Nameless tomorrow with enough daylight to find a place to stay, so we need to leave early.'

Suriin rose to hug her father. Three tides with him would be a treat. After her recent behaviour, she was keen to show she could follow orders, even if it did smart that he felt she needed watching.

⊢ ※ ∰ ∰ ✦

Her room was sparsely furnished, but the bed was soft, and as she rolled out her blanket, she felt the ache of the long walk setting into her calves. Suriin stretched them out as she relaxed.

The solid walls reminded her of home; as first nights went, it wasn't too strange. Her father and Ronin talked quietly as she flexed her ankles.

'She's always slept under stone and with Fluffy nearby. These rooms only have wooden doors.'

'I've dream-shielded plenty of times. I can protect myself from her visiting accidentally,' Ronin replied quietly. 'She's unbonded, though – surely she can't?'

'You would think. I remember,' said Yorynn, 'as a babe she used to wander into my dreams and demand more food! Hopefully, those innate skills are buried deep, or one or both of us could be in for some interesting nights.'

'What do you want me to do if she does visit me?'

'Walk her back out again. Make sure you almost walk into hers with her. As soon as she's safe, let me know and I'll wake her. We may have to teach her to shield, but I hope we can do without that lesson just yet. Especially as she needs to do it differently from us once she's crystal-bonded.'

Suriin heard one set of feet walking and a door shut. She could still hear her father in the main room, muttering about weddings as he cleared what sounded like the stones board away. None of it made sense to her and, as the noises quietened, she lost track of his movement and dropped off to sleep.

CHAPTER 6

ELISSA

*Human survival on Tebein requires that we as
humans exploit the short good times to
survive the remains of each year.*
The Black Moon

Four plump sprill simmered in the pan along with some dried roots Elissa found deep in a storage shaft. They would feast, and her mouth watered with anticipation. Laytha pulled the entrance hide to one side, peered in, and inhaled deeply as she closed it behind her.

'What are you cooking? It smells incredible.'

'If I told you ...'

Laytha laughed. 'Okay, okay, don't tell me. I'll just eat it!' She sank to the ground alongside Elissa and hugged her. 'Thank you.'

Elissa served the fish into a pair of dragon-glass bowls, their sides thick enough that the heat didn't reach her hands, and steam rose to the ceiling, lifting their spirits with it as the pair savoured their meal in quiet companionship. Elissa released her smile as she saw obvious enjoyment on Laytha's face. It was always a pleasure to be able to make her life a little more comfortable.

'Did you hear the elders have called a meeting tomorrow?' Laytha asked as she placed her bowl on the floor. 'That was delicious.'

'No, but it's usually only good news at this time of year. Maybe they feel Rains is finally close.'

Her friend nodded and ran her finger round the inside of the bowl. Elissa followed her example – every drop was precious. 'I really hope so. The stores are even lower than normal, and the river is drying up. If Rains is much longer, we will lose more people than usual. Have you seen how starved some of the children are? All bones and elbows.'

Laytha closed her eyes for far longer than a blink should take and sighed. Neither woman needed to elaborate; both were old enough to remember the last famine caused by late Rains when the toll on the population of Dragonsbreath sericlave had been severe. The Untouched were first to have their rations reduced. With no dependent families, they were the most expendable, and their numbers, already low, were cut in half. That was the year Elissa first sneaked out. She knew her brother had hated seeing her so emaciated, so he turned a blind eye to her forays.

Laytha was older than Elissa, more like a mother than a friend in those early days, and her kind words and company were one of the few things that kept Elissa fighting for survival – for both their survival – all those cycles ago. They needed to know what was in store for them, to have a chance to prepare and lend help to others if needed. She hated that she'd miss the meeting.

'I'm on bellows tonight,' Elissa said. 'Will you go?'

'Yes. I'll let you know what they say.' Laytha looked appraisingly at Elissa's cropped hair and frowned. 'You need more dye. I'll fix you some later, but you'll need to do something to dull the colour until then.'

Elissa grabbed a handful of the dirt surrounding the rug. 'I needed to sort my legs and arms out anyway.' She closed her eyes tight as she rubbed it all over her face and worked it into her hair. Despite her best effort, it still went up her nose. 'Every time,' she spluttered, then studied her arms, covering each clean patch thoroughly. Once finished, she was filthy. She hoped that any suggestion of lilac in her hair was entirely hidden under the mud.

'There are less filthy ways to cover the evidence, Elissa,' Laytha choked out between bursts of laughter.

'This suits me just fine! Who do I need to be clean for?' Elissa rose and walked tentatively toward the back wall. She was well-fed, but exhausted. 'I need to sleep before my shift. Can you wake me when it gets close?'

The older woman nodded and, although she said nothing, Elissa felt her eyes on her back as she hobbled toward her nook. She trod gently, trying to conceal the twinge of pain shooting through her with each step. There was no need to worry Laytha. The shard would work its own way out soon enough.

The end of the shift came, signalled as ever by the descent of the lift carrying the next crew. Elissa cleared her area ready for the next worker, but instead of the green-clad people due to replace her, an immaculate pair of booted legs descended into view. Boots made from the shining hide of creatures from north of the Ameryth Dar Sea. The legs were followed by an incredibly tall, slender body. The lift's occupant wore iridescent, scaled gloves which stretched up the arms to the top of their shoulders.

Before they could see her, Elissa stirred up a cloud of ash and, momentarily hidden, she grabbed a handful, scrubbing ash through her hair, then angled herself so that she could watch the visitor without it being obvious she was staring. They didn't usually come so close, or even come down there at all. Flames, she needed some more ash to shovel!

An awldrin was on that lift, and the narrow, crystalline, lidless eyes would miss nothing. Though she didn't look directly, she knew that any moment, the lift would reveal the hairless head covered in translucent green or grey skin, so thin it flaked off like tiny scales where it hung in thin folds. Every feature in the face – other than those wrinkles – would be unnervingly symmetrical. She could picture the row of pointed, black teeth exposed in the lipless mouth, even without seeing it for herself. More than anything else in that moment, Elissa knew she really didn't want to be noticed.

She tried to be as inconspicuous as possible. Barely daring to breathe, she focused on her task, staring intently into the bellows and hoping there would be a need to shovel soon. At least if she worked up the dust, the mess might be enough to keep the awldrin away.

From the corner of her eye, she watched the tall creature step off the lift and move toward her. There was finally sufficient ash to be busy, so she began to shovel it clear. Clouds of grey rose around her feet in an ever-thickening cloud and shrouded her in tiny fragments of burnt-out firestone. She stirred as she shovelled, trying to make the cloud as dense as possible.

The awldrin kept well away from her soot-covered self and the ash storm. Dimly, from within her personal cloud, she saw the lift return to collect the next shift.

There would be another Untouched on the lift – flames, Elissa hoped they knew what awaited them. She kept up her technique of shovel and stir, shovel and stir, so that the cloud remained in place, ready for her replacement.

The awldrin headed directly toward the team leader at the end of the pit, but her ash cloud was so thick that Elissa could only just make out the tall, shadowy form. The strange protrusions that ran down either side of the awldrin's back were no longer visible through the ash. Maybe it was nothing sinister, and the awldrin also believed Winds was ending. Maybe the plans for the new rota were being discussed, and the freedom of the outdoors would be theirs soon. The awldrin needed fewer people there as the top caves warmed.

Rains. She dared to hope. Although Rains was wet, there were spells of warmth between the showers, and the hot sun on her skin always felt amazing after the cold of Winds. Elissa was good with plants; she had an eye for tending them, and the elders quietly appreciated her skill with herbs. It was as close to feeling a real part of the sericlave as it would ever get for her.

⋎ ⁂ ⚇ ⚌ ✦

A group of green-clad people descended as the awldrin strode back toward the lift. It turned its head toward her, and Elissa found herself looking directly into the crystal eyes, her ash cloud having thinned. She quickly averted her gaze and focused on shovelling. The awldrin made as if to move in her direction, but as the cloud re-thickened, it tilted its head to one side and stopped. She felt it staring, but didn't dare look up. It stood for what felt like an eternity before it spotted the waiting lift and strode to board it.

The green shift exited the lift and shuffled toward their positions, apparently studying the floor ahead of each step with great focus. Elissa searched for the Untouched she knew would be there; she was in the centre of the group and appeared a lot more relaxed than she herself felt. The group of workers moved as one, a herd of prey animals under the gaze of a sharp-eyed predator. They bunched nearer, and Elissa's shift prepared for a swap. As the choreographed changeover took place in the narrow confines of the pit, the awldrin boarded the lift and was borne back up to the sericlave.

Much as the green shift had done, her shift enveloped her into its centre without a word. It usually took two lift loads for the full shift exchange to take place, and as the lift arrived with the remainder of green shift, it was clear they were unsettled.

'Something feels very wrong. There's five of them up there, searching for something,' whispered one in passing. 'Be careful.'

Elissa toyed with the idea of staying down in the pit, but they'd made eye contact. Could it be called that with those strange eyes? She forced herself to board – it would be more suspicious if she wasn't on the lift. She gritted her teeth and, trying to appear outwardly relaxed, joined the others. As the lift rose, so did the worry in the pit of her stomach; she always felt like that around *Them*. Makin said that never changed – he still felt *wrong* around them. The lift reached the top, and Elissa strolled casually off, trying to act relaxed. She wouldn't head straight for her hut. Laytha might still be there, and she had no intention of leading suspicious awldrin to their home. Instead, she nodded her thanks to the liftmen and moved with the flow of the group toward the main circle of houses.

An awldrin left the elders' meeting hut as they passed, and another stood near the top sericlave entrance. Elissa couldn't help but think that she'd have been fine, if only she had dyed her hair more recently. The worry of exposing herself overrode her usual rational thought. What she needed to dye it should be in her brother's hut; he drank loads of cha and calfa. Watcher knew entering his hut might break the rules, but he was her brother and she needed to protect everyone – especially herself – by covering up.

Inside Makin's hut, the fish she'd left him was still on the table. Elissa quickly hid it and hunted around for some knocked-out drink powder. She found a pile in the corner of the hut and added water from his stores to make the paste – she'd have to replace that later. Elissa applied the dye as well as she could on her own. A proper covering wasn't possible without help, but maybe she could do just enough to get home unnoticed.

After covering her head in the sticky, leafy mess, Elissa realised that she had nothing to brush it out with. In her panic, she really hadn't thought it through. The door covering twitched, and she heard heavy breathing from outside before Makin slipped in.

'What in the Dragon's name are you doing in my hut?'

'It seemed like a good idea at the time!'

'Where's my fish?'

Elissa grinned. 'Would you believe me if I said it swam away?'

'Not a chance, but knowing you, I'm guessing it's somewhere obscure.'

'Just remember to check under your pillow before you go to sleep.'

Makin reached out to touch her hair and frowned. 'There are awldrin all over the sericlave, and you stopped by to put that on? Why didn't you do that in your own space?'

'It made sense at the time, but now I can't get it off. Do you have a brush?'

Makin lifted the lid of his heavy chest, and after a quick

rummage, came up with one. Elissa removed the leaves from her hair quickly and ran her fingers through to check. It felt sticky, but sticky was good. If she could feel it, then it must be covering that much of her hair. 'Better?' she asked.

'Elissa, you walked past me twice today, and on neither occasion did I spot anything wasn't ok. I know you're careful, but you worry more than you should.' Makin leant close. 'The limp you are trying to hide ... now that is new. What on Tebein have you done? It's not like you to get injured out there.'

Elissa thought about telling him the full truth, but something stopped her. 'I stood on a rock and cut my foot catching your fish. It'll heal – Oh, do you have any of that salve left? The one I made you last year.'

Makin returned to the big chest, had another dig around, and came up with a small, wrapped parcel. 'There's not much left. Elissa, the elders said that we would set the fields ready next tide. If you want to be considered fit for field work, you need to be steady on your feet.' He passed her the pot and moved to the door.

'I can't see any of *Them* around,' he said, as he retrieved his shoes. 'Slip around the back, and you should be able to work back to your section of the cave. Take care. I'll watch you from here. I've a few minutes to sit for a cup of calfa.'

⊤ ⋇ ⋇ ⋇ ✦

Elissa slunk around the edge of the cavern, watching out for awldrin. She reached her hut and paused at the door to check on Makin. Across the cave, she saw him stand and enter his home. As she watched, an awldrin passed his hut, its head turning side to side. She watched until it was past, then wasted no more time.

Once inside her own home, she rushed to her nook and

gathered a bag of essential belongings. A brush, some clothes, and her sticky-soled boots. She crossed the tunnel and tapped on Laytha's door. She'd probably be asleep, unaware of the danger.

A simple four beat sequence, twice. One they'd practised many times. Tap, tap-tap, tap. *I'm moving deeper – we have visitors.*

After a short pause, Laytha replied. Tap, tap-tap tap-tap. *I will follow and shut the wall.*

Elissa followed the trail of grooves along the wall, deeper into the mountain. They'd hidden in the far caves for days in the past, and no one in the sericlave would expect to see them again for a few days. Removing herself made life safer for her brother, and she'd do it every time to protect him. Elissa continued along the passage until her fingers hit the flat edge at the end of the groove. She felt around the wall until she found the protruding stone, then pressed it hard. Footsteps behind grew louder and faster as Laytha caught up.

They passed through the small gap that opened up and dragged their few belongings with them. Once inside, they pushed the wall back into place. All nooks in the sericlave had tunnels leading back there, and they'd soon be joined by the others. The women dropped their bags in the middle of the large cave and sat to catch their breath.

The caves contained odd things – things they never discussed with the elders or any of those who Elissa considered normal. There were smooth balls embedded around the walls, and small sleeping chambers cut into the walls between them. Old, dusty books filled shelves along one side of the space – the sealed state of the caves kept them well preserved. There was no need to read in Dragonsbreath, so few people ever learnt, aside from the elders.

Elissa liked to run her hand along their sleepy spines as they languished unread on their shelves, imagining what they contained. The lack of light in the huge cave meant that she'd never tried to open one. Laytha had taken one out to the hut once; it was filled with pictures of caves full of light and people reading. There had been pictures of awldrin amongst humans, working and living together. They looked very different to the awldrin they were used to around Dragonsbreath, but it was clearly them.

Every time they retreated there, Elissa was reminded of that book. If the pictures in it were true, if the two species had a joint history, how had they ended up where they were? Hiding from awldrin in fear of their lives.

She desperately wanted to see the caves lit up herself, but she had no firestone. One day, she planned to return and explore them properly, but she made that plan every time they hid there, then cycles came and went, and she still hadn't done it.

As first in, it fell to Elissa and Laytha to find the food stores and evaluate them. They needed to know how much mash was left before trying to feed lots of mouths. As they walked toward the alcove where the bags were stored, more Untouched arrived. The tapped-out greeting rang through the space as each small group entered.

Tap-tap tap tap tap – *entrance hut three here.*

Tap-tap tap – *entrance hut one here.*

Each hut signed in at the hollow tap pad positioned by the end of their tunnel. Soon, all five huts were safely in, and Elissa's tension drained slowly away. Aside from the one woman still in the pit, they'd removed themselves from discovery. The woman on green shift would join them soon, and once she arrived, they would remain there for the next few days.

Fourteen Untouched. That's all they were. Just fourteen women in a dark cave. Waiting.

CHAPTER 7

DARIN

*A fascinating property of Calderan Surface
plants is their ability to glow at night. When
the plant extracts become exposed to So'Dal
magic, the same effect can be created. This
was once in great demand as entertainment.*
Botanicals, an Encyclopaedia

Prior to arriving in Redpike, Darin had thought himself well read. He usually had a book on hand while working in the inn and had read anything and everything he could get his hands on. He read histories, stories about battle strategies, and tales of fantastical imagination filled with magic.

Only a couple of days after arriving in Redpike, he realised that he knew almost nothing. He'd only ever been given a partial truth. The magical fantasies filled with strange creatures, magical plants, and powerful women were the true reality of Caldera, buried from common eyes in plain sight.

Darin picked up the open book on his table. Moonhound

History and Care was beautiful; the illustrations delicately coloured, and the moonhounds drawn around the margins appeared ready to leap off the pages and play. It was full of new ideas. That single book contained more information about the continent of Caldera than the entirety of his previous knowledge. He sighed and turned the page.

⁜

Many have wondered, do animals dream? In the case of moonhounds, dreaming has proven to be very much a defining feature. Their ability to walk in the dreams of their choice has taught and inspired generations of So'Dal. The reason for the development of this trait is unknown. It was first recorded after the events of the first great ground-rending and the magic storms that brought it about. Many creatures and plants were changed by the events of those years, and it is possible moonhounds are one of these altered creatures.

⁜

Star could certainly dream – and invade his waking thoughts too. His new training mostly comprised of hound care and learning to communicate with Star. Add to the melting pot of new knowledge Star's badly timed visions, and he shouldn't be surprised concentration was hard. He rubbed his eyes and turned the page.

Darin persisted with reading in his spare time, desperately needing to know his place in an unfamiliar world. He felt adrift on a sea of ideas, far from the sanctuary of his parents' inn. Seeking a quiet space, he adopted a carrel in the deep library and collected together the books that he thought would help.

He placed Moonhound History and Care back on the pile and looked at the rest of his stash. Darin ran a finger down the ornate spines as he read them. Even saying their titles aloud didn't make his new life real.

'Animalis of Lieus. The Animalis Non Localis. Botanicals, an Encyclopaedia. New Maps of the Craterlands and Their Flora. History of Caldera, Post Rending. The Bond of Three. A Traveller's Guide to Caldera. Basic Musicianship. It's going to take me tides to read this pile and cycles to learn it.' The last book on the list was going to be the most challenging. Music, he had been told, was inseparable from magic. And, judging by his first singing lesson the previous night, it was going to be a long journey before he had mastery of either.

He reached instead for the pair of red, leather embossed books on top of the pile. Intricate gilded animals, hounds, faat, and farbrox cavorted around the cover alongside beautiful birds and rarely seen animals of the Bare Plains. His mother would love it.

The second was illustrated with the beasts his grandparents described, whilst explaining why people didn't go to the Surface at night. Darin suppressed a shudder and pushed it away. Definitely not a book for reading so late at night. He'd leave it there for the following evening.

A tug for attention and a strong sensation of hunger filled him as Star asked for food. Darin tried to picture getting food for himself and Star. He couldn't send images like the pup did to him if they were far apart, but he'd discovered that if he thought it, then Star reacted to it. At the moment, all their conversations were to do with food or grooming. It was slow progress and each image he sent gave him a headache, but it was slowly getting less painful the more he practised.

A So'Dal Gardener strolled around, activating the glow lamps with a quietly sung note as he left the library, bound for the hall and food. At the gentle sound, the globes lit with the same steady glow Darin had noticed on the first day. The man made it look so simple.

He walked past more Gardeners lighting lamps on his way to the hall. It shouldn't have surprised Darin that everyone in Redpike helped with a variety of jobs, especially after Hal's lessons, but he'd not expected the So'Dal or Soul Anchors to take turns helping in the kitchens. He'd seen Fresna there most days, and the chefs were welcome in lessons on herb combining for healing. Children ran errands to help out. Whatever your particular skills, once you arrived at Redpike, that was what they expected in contribution.

Fresna was there again and waved cheerily at him. The queue was fast-moving, so he was served quickly and took a seat on one of the long benches. Darin scanned the hall for familiar faces and spotted Conor on his way in. He waved him over.

Conor couldn't dream walk, so his testing had ended. That had delighted him, and he was accepted as an apprentice to the builders. After his excitement about the steam lift on their first day, the choice didn't surprise Darin.

'Hi! You've put that mountain of books aside then, have you?' asked Conor as he plonked his plate down next to Darin.

'For today. I have singing practise again this evening.'

Conor grimaced. 'Thanks for warning me. I'll stay well clear of the training rooms then, after last night's disaster.'

'That's a good plan. The Master says I have raw power, but I can't control it. I broke two empty Gardener's globes last night – it's going to be ages before I'm allowed near any filled ones.'

Singing was not a natural talent, and he was sure it would

take him longer to learn true control of a single note than it would to read his entire pile of books.

They finished their meal in companionable quiet. After returning his plate, Darin grabbed Star's meal from the hound table and made his excuses to Conor as he passed.

ɤ ⚔ ⚔ ⚔ ✦

He strolled across the courtyard, enjoying the fresh air and fading light. Sounds of chatter and laughter followed him from the dining hall, and he smiled. Darin was slowly starting to settle into the routine of his new life. Evening sun warmed his shoulders until he passed under the arch into the grassed dog paddocks. A fuzzy bundle bounded over. Star cleared the small fence with ease and knocked his feet out from under him, enveloping Darin in a happy, wagging sensation. He quickly handed the food over before he was doused in drool.

With Star preoccupied, he created a mental image, then sent it [*Darin standing in front of his teacher, singing*]. Star stopped eating, and a returned image [*Darin singing with Star howling alongside*] overwhelmed him. He rocked back on his heels in surprise. If he concentrated, he could see the paddocks through it. After a few moments, it faded away, and Star returned to eating.

It was an improvement; they'd almost had a conversation! A wide grin split his face. As good as it was, if that happened when he was walking, he'd probably trip over. He sent one more copy of his first image, but clearly with Star not present, and gave the moonhound a scratch before heading off to meet the Master in a new practise room. After the Master's discovery that Darin couldn't sing and the subsequent damage he'd caused by trying, they'd moved to a more secluded location.

It took Darin a while to find the new room, despite having a map. Was he really so awful at singing that he needed to be so far under the mountain? He cracked the door open. The So'Dal singing Master waited alone in a small chamber. Two stools sat in the centre. He gestured for Darin to close the door behind him, then took a seat.

'Good evening, Darin. Hopefully, today we can make more ... useful progress,' he said. 'You've clearly got magical strength, but it is wild. As discussed yesterday, So'Dal magic requires *precise* control of your power. Without control, you cannot channel power into potions. You will fail at simple daily tasks, such as illuminating glow globes or adding extra potency to a gardening recipe.' He leant forward as he spoke, gesturing expansively to emphasise each point. 'To control our power, we channel it through sound. The volume and pitch of your music, along with the complexity of the weft, will help you imbue potions with extra healing, create your own light globes, and eventually, complete more complex and powerful spells.'

Darin shuffled in his seat. He was still unsure if he was excited or terrified by magic, but he liked being in control, and music was one aspect of his life he had none over.

'I understand. I'll work hard, I promise,' he said.

The Master nodded. 'I know you will. Now, sing a single note. Whichever you choose, try to hold it steady.'

Darin nodded and stood. He breathed deeply, imagining air filling him up as the Master had taught him the day before. Then he tried to sing.

'Aaaaaaaaaaaaaahhhhhhhhhhhhh.' Darin looked around. Everything was the same, and he felt no different. He sounded awful though – even he could hear the note waver.

The Master winced, though Darin saw him try to hide it. 'Do that again, but focus more on the note you're singing instead of the volume.'

'Aaaaaaaaaaaaaahhhhhhhhhhhh, oh!' A burst of *something* left him. Darin sat abruptly, slightly shocked.

'You felt it?'

'I felt something, like something flowed from my chest.'

'I'd like to try something else. This is a good start – better than I expected after yesterday.' The Master pulled an unlit glow globe from his robe and placed it on the floor. 'This is a training globe. It will glow brighter the more you direct your sound. Remember, hold the note steady and focus. This time, when the flow leaves you, try to steer it toward the globe.'

'How? What if I break it?' After the last time, he was worried about damaging another.

'This is special. It's thicker, tougher, and far less fragile, even though it's outwardly similar. Give it a try.'

Darin sang the same note, trying to focus, and tentatively aimed it at the globe. He was running out of both breath and hope when a tiny flicker of light appeared.

'Was that me? I did that?'

'Yes. It's a small light but big progress. You need practise. With one note, you should be able to adjust your flow. As we add more notes, we call it a weft, a weaving of sounds. Brighter and dimmer light reflects the amount of flow you are letting out with the song. Once you can do that consistently, we will move into more complex techniques.'

The Master began to sing quietly; no words, just notes. He sang scales, and the globe changed colour. He sang louder, and the glow became brighter.

Darin watched the display in awe as the colours changed; faster, slower, lighter, and dimmer. It was beautiful. He needed to try again with more confidence. He stood, prepared for what he felt sure would be a long evening.

Hours after beginning, Darin could hold a steady glow in the training globe for about five counts. He hadn't broken anything, and the Master offered him a smile.

'That was good. At this rate, you might be able to try a light globe tomorrow, but this won't be easy, and you will need to continue to work hard.'

'Um ... I don't want to moan, really I don't, but my throat hurts from all the singing. How will I be able to practise this much every day?'

'You will learn faster, or you will hurt longer.'

The rawness in Darin's throat grew even more painful as he swallowed that idea. Maybe talking would be out during the day.

As he wound his way back through the passageways to his temporary rooms, he had to pass the kitchens.

'Darin, hey, I've got something for you.'

'Jaer?'

'I remember Master's singing lessons. He used to make me sing for hours. My magic hasn't even come in yet, but I can sing like a chorus bird.' Jaer rolled his eyes. 'My guess is you could use something for your throat right now.'

Darin took the strange-smelling concoction offered to him and sniffed. It had a sweet and sickly aroma. Trusting Jaer, he gulped it down. The mixture coated his throat and seemed to make it less painful.

'Thank you! What's in it?'

'No idea, Dad sent it. He also said if you wanted, you can

meet him for sparring practise tomorrow to take a break from reading.'

Some fresh air and physical exercise were just what he needed, so Darin accepted the offer. Giving his thanks again to Jaer, he dragged his exhausted self to his room.

With his arm around Star, he fell into a deep, dreamless sleep.

Chapter 8

Suriin

Many creatures roam the Surface lands, which an unwary traveller may encounter in a holloway. The strangest of these creatures come from the Edgelands and can, on occasion, be found roaming closer to the craters.
The Animalis Non Locales

The scent of hot fruit drifted through the door, enticing Suriin out from her warm bed. She stretched and eased movement into her aching legs, flung her covers off, and followed her nose into the main room.

Ronin had created something delicious with berries he'd collected the previous day from the holloway walls. He'd mixed them with some dried grains, and three bowls of it steamed on the table. Warmed, and drizzled with syrup her father offered her with a conspiratorial wink behind Ronin's back, it was delicious.

Her father's and Ronin's packs were already by the door, so she returned to her room as soon as she finished, gathered her belongings, and quickly retied her headscarf. It was a little easier than the first time, and she was sure that seeing how others did it would help. When she got to Redpike, she'd be able to copy the fashionable styles the women there would no doubt wear.

Suriin's feet and calves still ached, so she stretched them out some more before she rejoined her father. After the last few days, there was no chance she was going to mention it. She doubted there would be any sympathy offered.

⟡ ✳ ✴ ✴ ✦

Morning light filtered through the holloway's canopy. It must have rained overnight, and the soft mud along the base of the path was covered by the trails of nocturnal creatures. Most prints were shorter than a finger's length and, to her relief, there was nothing remotely big enough to indicate the passage of the huge beast they'd seen near Golden.

She knelt down and examined the tracks. They had three toes and a small indentation from a claw at the tip of each. Hundreds of prints ran in and out of the holloway, scaling the sides in numerous places.

Her father traced the outline of one footprint with his finger. 'A herd of graaken. We don't have them in Golden. They're small and not a particular problem, but in these numbers, best avoided.'

'Why?' Suriin asked.

Her father chuckled as Ronin answered instead.

'Believe it or not, the smell! They eat the glowing plants that make us ill, but the end result is lots of gas. They also emit a foul stench when upset.' The two men smirked at each other as Suriin grimaced. *Did men never grow out of finding that sort of thing funny?*

The morning's journey was long but uneventful. Occasionally, they'd spot a different plant hanging down from the lip of the holloway or growing from the walls. If it was useful, her father would scramble up the steep sides to collect some – or more often send Ronin up. Once, he asked Suriin to collect a small-leafed plant growing in cracks of the holloway wall. It had a fresh and fragrant scent as she broke the stems.

'What's this used for?' she asked. 'It smells lovely.'

'It's a herb,' her father called back.

Suriin was slightly disappointed that it didn't have a more exciting use, but she collected a small sprig for herself as well. It was delicate, with small pointed leaves and blue feathery flowers.

'Can I eat it raw?' she asked.

'I don't see why not, but it might taste a bit intense raw. Some people use it crushed as a drink.'

Suriin tentatively tasted a leaf. It was strong and astringent, but not unpleasant; strangely, the taste didn't quite match the smell. In a cook-pot, it would lend its flavour well to meats.

'Are there many other wild plants we can flavour things with?' she asked quietly, as she examined it. Suriin had a sketch-book in her bag and resolved to fill it with as many notes as she could over the journey. Maybe once she reached Redpike, she could fill the gaps in her knowledge.

'What's this plant called?' she asked, running to catch up. While she stared at the delicate flowers, they'd moved ahead and not heard her.

'Nolethm,' replied Ronin.

When they sat down for lunch, Suriin searched in her bag for the sketchbook. She sat in the brightest patch of light she could find and carefully copied the shapes of the leaves and the way they were arranged around the stem. At the top of the stalk, she drew the small, feathery flowers. Once complete, Suriin added a description of the plant and its location, then a clear annotation as to its use as a flavouring.

When she finished drawing the plant, she flipped the book over and, on the back page, tried to sketch the tracks they'd seen that morning.

'There are often spur marks behind the heel pad too. May I?' Ronin reached for her drawing. 'This is really good, especially from memory.' He gestured for the pencil. Suriin handed it over, and Ronin added two small marks behind the back pad. 'There, that's it now.'

'It looked a little odd before. Now it looks bizarre.' Suriin frowned.

Her father glanced over and nodded. 'They are odd creatures. We may see some later, but it's unlikely – the farther we get from Golden, the lower the chances. We should catch a glimpse of the large birds, though.'

'Bigger than skaa-rak?' The riding birds stood well above her shoulder. Birds taller than that seemed almost impossible.

He shook his head. 'Only garants are bigger than that, there's one in South Crater we might see. There'll still be plenty more creatures for you to draw.'

Suriin was delighted there was the possibility of more than just plants to break up their journey, and the thought perked her up considerably through the trudge of the afternoon walk.

They rounded a corner, and the holloway appeared to end in open sky. They'd reached the top of Nameless. With the sun behind them, afternoon light shone brightly, illuminating the full extent of the vast crater spread out below.

'It'll take us at least three days to cross.' Ronin stared across it. 'I love the views from the top of craters, but it really brings home how reliant we are on their sanctuary,' he said with a sigh.

As Suriin followed his gaze, she saw herds of grazing animals and a few houses scattered sparsely around. The descent to the base was almost vertical, and she peered over the edge, curious as to how they would get down.

'Unlike us, they can't guarantee that their routes in and out are warded,' her father said. 'There are no permanent So'Dal residents in Nameless. This side, closest to the Edgelands, is dangerous, and the livestock in the crater supplies a lot of towns in Blow and beyond. It suits the residents to make it hard to enter from this side. We'll hook our bags on the pulley and drop them down first. You'll need both hands for the descent.'

It made sense, she supposed. Suriin looked over again – it was a long way down, but there did appear to be plenty of handholds and thin ledges to use. She passed her bag to her father, and he hung it onto a weighted hoop he hauled up from part way down the wall. They added the other two packs and carefully lowered the bags all the way down to the crater floor.

'Ronin, please go after my daughter. Suriin, keep an eye on where I go and follow my route.' With that, he strode to the edge and with grace and agility his robes should hinder, he clambered down the narrow route.

⊤ ※ ⅏ ⅏ ✦

It was a long, tiring descent. Sometimes vertical, but at other points she could walk comfortably. Suriin was grateful for the daylight, even if the evening sun cast the cliff into deep shadow. Many handholds were small and some footholds so smooth that her foot slipped. They were, however, regular and well placed, so although it was slow, it was not difficult as long as she concentrated.

Finally, they reached the base, her legs slightly trembling with exertion. She sat on the ground and glanced up to see how much farther Ronin had to go. Suriin blushed as she realised that the robes her father wore were the same as Ronin's, loose and split into wide trousers. How had she never noticed that before? She thought about the skirt she wore, understanding why her father wanted her to climb below Ronin. They'd likely have to do that more than once; maybe other craters needed climbing into. Suriin needed to get some trousers in the next town. If her mother hadn't been rushing her so much, maybe they'd have realised she needed some – although Suriin couldn't remember when her mother had last left the crater. How did Fluffy get down?

Ronin landed next to her with assured ease as he sprung from the wall, and as he landed, he caught her staring and winked.

'Ready when you are,' he called to her father. 'Are we stopping at the same landhold as last time? They made excellent food.'

'Yes, we'll sleep in their barn again if it suits them. Suriin, do you have the nolethm?'

Suriin nodded, but checked the bunch was in her bag anyway, just in case.

'It only grows in holloways, so it's a valuable trading commodity, along with some of the potion vials we made at Golden – you have those safe, Ronin?'

He grinned. 'I do, plus a special one for the particular landholder here.'

Yorynn nodded approvingly. 'He'll be pleased. That was good thinking.'

They followed the narrow, overgrown trail through grazing land. It was cool in the shade, and the crater felt similar to Golden – there was just much more of it. A herd of dusty brown faat grazed, their young fal gathered toward the centre of the herd. Occasionally, a bearded animal raised its horned head to observe them.

A wooden house appeared as they crested a gentle hill, and alongside it stood a small stone barn. As they neared, a figure ran toward them.

'So'Dal Yorynn, can you help? Please!' the woman shouted. She stopped, panting for breath. 'We had a night attack when you left. The xotryl tried to take a fal. My husband tried to fight it off. It caught him with a wing tip, and now he has an open wound and it won't heal. Please, do you have anything to help?'

Yorynn placed a hand upon the woman's shoulder and nodded. 'We can help, Trudie.'

'Xotryl?' Suriin asked Ronin quietly.

'The flying beast you were so careless about back at Golden. They're native to the Edgelands but sometimes travel farther to hunt. Golden, whilst closer, is warded, so they don't notice it. Here, they try to fly in and grab faat without landing. It's rare for one to attack a person.'

'What my father faced a few nights ago?'

'Now's not a good time for a zoology lesson on the Edgelands. We need to go help this man.' Ronin's curt reply ended the questions.

Her father nodded. 'Suriin, take our bags to the barn. If you could help Trudie prepare food, Ronin and I will go and see the landholder. It's incredibly lucky that it was the wingtip and not the claw that cut him.'

'Thank you, oh thank you, So'Dal Yorynn. Come child,' the woman said.

Suriin balked at being referred to as a child, but biting her tongue, did as her father asked. She took the bags to the barn under Trudie's guidance.

'If So'Dal Yorynn is with my husband, he has the best care.' She paused. 'I've never seen him travel with a woman before?' The question was implicit in her voice, and Suriin forced a smile as she found a spot to leave the bags. Once she knew how to use her power, she wouldn't be the one relegated to chatting, but the one helping people, just like her father.

'He's my father. I have a gift for you.' Remembering it was valuable, she carefully chose a few sprigs of nothelm and offered them to Trudie. 'Can you show me how best to use it? Ronin tells me you're very skilled.' Suriin had been told nothing of the sort, but her father's instructions were effectively, 'Keep the woman away while we work.' Having seen him do things she'd not known he could over the past few days, she understood that her apparently trivial task could be significant in its own way, even if it wasn't what she wanted to be doing.

Trudie took the nolethm and crushed a leaf before inhaling its scent. 'Oh, thank you. Yes, of course, I can show you. It's a real treat to have this! Should I go and check they have all they need?'

'I'm sure they'll ask if they need something,' Suriin said. 'Please, show me around?'

They continued chatting about the farm, but Trudie's cheery tone no longer hid the wrinkles of worry on her brow. She allowed Suriin to steer the conversation to care of the faat as they crossed the open yard to the main house.

It was a solid building with several spacious rooms. The kitchen had an open hearth at one end, and as they passed the stairs, Suriin heard her father talking in a low voice while an unfamiliar male voice groaned in pain. She glanced up and spotted Ronin rummaging through a bag at the top of the stairs. He found a vial and stood up. Seeing Suriin staring up at him, he gestured with his head for her to move away, and she quickly recovered her senses to follow Trudie.

As they chopped and prepared the meal, Suriin asked questions about other flavourings the woman added. The distraction worked for them both, and it was a considerable while later that two So'Dal descended from the room, her father was clearly exhausted.

'He'll be fine. There will be scarring, as you would no doubt expect. Had we been a few hours later, I'm not sure that any poultice would have been able to help him. I've given him herbal tea to help him sleep, and you need to let him rest until morning.' He took a seat and gestured to the pot. 'That smells incredible, Trudie. Could we please have a small portion? We'll rest in the barn to save you preparing guest quarters.'

'It would be no trouble, none at all. If you've saved his arm, then you've saved our landhold. As soon as he's up again in the next few days, we can make the small barn secure overnight and gather the animals in.'

'Do you have a skaa-rak?' Suriin asked. 'I can gather them in for the night now.'

'Between us, we can do that.' Suriin found Ronin standing alongside her. The smile he flashed at her came from his eyes. He looked tired, but not as much as her father.

They slurped their meal, then Trudie led them to the barn. 'We have this pair if you can saddle them. They're a bit cantankerous.'

'What skaa-rak aren't?' Ronin chuckled.

The huge birds curled their necks down toward Suriin. One massive red beak opened, and the tongue flickered as it squawked in her ear.

'Skaaaaaa.'

'Looks like this one's mine,' she said, reaching up to stroke it.

'Raaaaaaak.' Its head plumage rose erect, the long feathers fanning out widely as it waggled them at her.

'You're going out for a ride,' she muttered as she took in how huge the male bird was. His thighs weighed more than her and Ronin combined, and his stubby wings, whilst useless for flight, showed bald patches from fighting.

She strapped the neck collar on first, its beaded handle giving her a small degree of control, then hoisted the saddle onto the flat part of the bird's back. 'Down.'

It responded immediately and allowed her to fasten the straps above and below the wings to anchor the saddle.

'Oww.' She swatted its beak away as it went in for a second bite. 'You might be a pretty boy, but your manners are awful.'

'Aren't you ready yet?' Ronin's bird had tail feathers bouncing with every stride of its clawed feet.

Suriin swung up onto the saddle. 'U-up.'

Her skaa-rak lurched upward, tail puffed up in absurd competition with its flock-mate. She rode alongside Ronin, trying to ignore it scratching at the ground.

'I wouldn't have had you down as a herder,' she laughed as they rode out.

Ronin ignored the comment and pushed his bird into a run. 'It was a kind offer you made. You'll make your parents proud one day. Now, let's go and get these faat in.'

CHAPTER 9

ELISSA

*Dragonsbreath Peak is the pinnacle of awldrin
and human co-operation. For hundreds of
cycles, they worked in seamless co-operation to
develop a method of cultivating the inhos-
pitable moon of Tebein. The rock-working
skills of the awldrin and the magic of the
humans together created many of the most
beautiful artworks of the pre-closing. It is
unknown how many of these treasures
remain.*
Preface to a map of the Blasted Mountains

Elissa and Laytha stared at the paltry pile of dried, ground meal.

'Either someone has been back here for extra, or we've used a lot more this Winds than we realised.' Elissa sighed. There were only two and a half bags.

'If we're careful, it might last half a rotation,' Laytha replied. 'It's still dry, at least.'

Dim light transmitted through the veins of crystalline lumina from far above the mountain. The caves were threaded through with them, so patches of dappled light broke the monotonous darkness. The crystal veins, which illuminated their sorry store, gently increased in brightness as they stood silent for a moment longer.

'Let's not share how low the stores actually are,' whispered Laytha. 'It'll only panic the younger ones.'

Elissa could make out huddles of women around the room as they returned. She stretched out her cramped legs from the cold of the cave and winced. Her foot was growing more painful by the hour. She hobbled to a puddle of light and sat down.

'What've you done? Shall I take a look?' Laytha asked.

'I stood on a sharp crystal catching supper. It's stuck in my foot, and I can't get it out. Don't worry – it's deep in the arch, so I can walk on it. The dressing needs changing though, as I did it at the river. Makin gave me his jar of ointment.'

Laytha rummaged in her bag, then pulled out a small bandage and a vial. 'Or, we could use this?'

Elissa grinned at the small vial. 'You are amazing, as ever. Where did you find that?'

'While you slept off supper, I took a walk. I noticed your limp, and I know what you're like – you always cover things up and pretend nothing happened. It's my way of saying thank you for the fish.'

Elissa accepted it gratefully. Laytha was right. She had numerous scars under her clothes from close calls with various parts of the mountain. The big scar on her shin had needed a lot of help to heal, and Laytha had been the one who assisted her then too. Elissa often wondered if she'd have survived as long without her.

As the light brightened enough to see the chambers around

the edge of the room, Laytha and Elissa dragged their belongings to the closest one and made it comfortable and ready for the night. Once the sun passed to the other side of the peak, the crystals would go dim, and they wanted to be prepared.

'Let's see that foot then,' Laytha said.

They found the brightest spot they could, and Elissa removed both her wrap and the makeshift moss dressing she'd applied at the river. It seemed a long time ago.

'It's not as bad as I expected. There's a clean cut in the arch, and I know this light isn't good, but I can't see any discharge. It doesn't smell bad either. You're lucky.' Laytha gently ran her finger along the cut.

The combination of pain and tickling was too much, and Elissa pulled her foot back quickly to avoid kicking Laytha.

'Only I could be lucky enough to have a bit of crystal stuck in my foot!' she said, taking a deep breath and returning her foot to the light.

Laytha poured some fluid from the vial gently across the wound. Elissa gritted her teeth. It stung at first, but then started to numb the ache.

'Tell me again why you didn't remove this at the stream where you had clean water and light?' sighed Laytha. 'Actually, no don't,' she said, as some women headed their way.

'Ouch, that's a big cut!' said one. 'You need to be more careful in your nook! Maybe you should clear it out so you don't catch your foot next time.'

Elissa nodded. 'Trust me, I've already moved the stone, and won't be putting my foot where I did this anytime soon.'

Laytha shot her a bemused glance, and Elissa struggled not to laugh. She masked the chuckle with a groan of pain as Laytha bandaged her foot back up.

'We'll try again later, Elissa when we have better light.'

'Why were there so many of them today?' a younger girl

asked. Her long, dyed hair made Elissa smile. So much effort. She didn't begrudge the girl that small vanity, but Elissa, like many of the others, had cut her hair short years ago. It was easier to dye.

'Rumours are they were searching for something specific, but no one knows what it is. Apparently, they turned up this afternoon while yellow shift was on,' said another woman.

'I saw one,' Elissa said. 'With the half scale. That's a highly ranked awldrin to be scouting around the bellows chamber.'

⁂

Rumours and discussion circulated for much of the morning. With Rains so overdue, the dribble of water that ran through one of the far rooms hardly flowed. Their communal meal was cold and barely wet as a result. The food adhered to the roof of her mouth as she chewed, and anywhere else a drop of moisture could be found.

Elissa was restless. They were all used to waiting in there and she'd borne it many times before, but something was different – maybe it was having been so close to them. She struggled with an irrational itch at the back of her mind and needed a distraction.

'I need to walk,' she whispered to Laytha.

'On that foot?'

'It doesn't hurt as much now,' she lied.

'It will if you walk on it! Where are you going? We're stuck in a cave – it's not like there's any scenery.'

Elissa pointed at a tunnel next to their temporary bedroom. 'That one has a vein in it, so there should be some light. I just need some space to think. I promise I'll be back before the veins fade.' She pushed herself to her feet and quietly hobbled toward the passage.

The dark walls were smooth and flat, the ceiling high enough for an awldrin to walk without having to stoop. The floor was smooth and level – as easy as it could get for her injury. As Elissa followed the dimly lit passage, she felt calm descend and let her mind wander.

Their refuge must have been special once. Who'd lived there and when? What did they do? Every time they retreated, she wondered why her people had forgotten about them.

Out in the main sericlave, they lived a simple existence in small huts inside a cave. That's all they really did; the people of Dragonsbreath sericlave existed. Admittedly, some of them loved and lived more than others – they had children, and she saw with envy, families with a purpose. Without those bonds of family, she stood detached and saw them for what they were. More mouths who, in turn, would slave away to provide heat to those living above. And yet, to their parents, they represented hope.

What had the humans and awldrin been through to separate them so distinctly, to create such an imbalance?

She wound her way down the passage, lost in thought, contemplating those who had walked the path before. If she reached up, she could feel spheres embedded in the walls. What were they for? Were they everywhere in the caves, even in the side chambers? She wandered down the passage much farther than she ever had, her thoughts running away with her feet. As she ran her hands along the wall, more from habit than for guidance, she noticed a change in texture.

A very dim light emitted from the lumina crystals, barely enough to see her own hand. She peered close and ran her fingertips across the wall; some kind of picture or symbol was stippled into it. Elissa could make out most of a door shape around the picture. At least, if she could reach the top of the seam, she thought that's what it would be. There was no obvious handle and no push rocks like the ones they used to enter the main chamber. She tried to shoulder it open, to no avail. Another thing to add to her *to do one day* list.

Elissa continued down the passageway, keeping her fingers alert for more texture changes. She was so focused on the walls that it took a few moments before she realised the air had changed. A breeze moved past her face, cool and fresh.

Cautiously, she moved forward, reached a fork, and followed the fresh air down the right-hand passage. At the end, it doubled back and bright daylight flooded the last curve.

Torn between the desire for self-preservation and the need to know how at risk they were, her heart raced as she closed on the exit. If there was another entrance to the tunnels and chamber, were they actually safe? Had they ever been?

Elissa rested for a while, leaning against the wall to ease her foot. Curiosity and concern for her friends won over, and she edged closer to the entrance cautiously. It took a sharp turn just before the end. From outside, it would look like a recess in the rock, not an entrance.

Clouds drifted over the plains and marshes, then beyond to the purple-grey waves that rolled gently across the Ameryth Dar Sea. Clouds of dust swirled along the land, and a dried lake basin was visible to her right. At first, she didn't recognise where she was, until she spotted the small crop buildings scattered around the ground between the mountain and the marshes. The opening was directly over the fields.

Several terrace-like plateaus dominated that side of the peak. The top of which was the dragon-blasted face the awldrin were so secretive about, which meant there would be no lookmen above her. She cautiously peered upward to find a capstone obstructing her view. The entrance would not be visible from above either. Braving a step farther, she scanned her immediate surroundings. Large boulders stood to attention on either side and several more guarded the approach from below – like rock sentinels permanently on duty. If you were looking from the fields, you would not see it.

Elissa took a step back so she'd be fully out of sight and sank to the floor. She desperately needed to rest her foot, and bravado could be dispensed with in private. The afternoon was wearing on and the lights in the passage would soon fade, but she had time to relax for a few minutes. She closed her eyes and rested, feeling cool stone against her back, and enjoyed the fresh, sea-scented breeze.

⊹ ⚝ ⚜ ⚶ ✦

'Where are you? Stay relaxed – just tell me where you are. You need me, and we need you. Quick, before *They* find you.' The male voice was calm and reassuring. Elissa tried to locate the speaker, but her limbs felt heavy and slow. 'You're asleep. Don't panic. Please, tell me where you are and keep the crystal safe,' the voice calmly continued.

'Asleep?' Elisa mumbled.

The male voice grew more insistent. 'You're in danger, and I can help.'

'Dragonsbreath. I am at Dragonsbreath,' she replied. There could be no harm in replying to her own dream, after all.

'I will see you soon. Don't sleep outside again. They are hunting for you.'

Elissa found herself pushed forcibly awake. The odd daydream had done nothing for the itch in her head – if anything, it felt stronger. She took one last glance outside and sighed. Fresh air always did give her odd dreams. It was a shame; she loved the idea of sleeping under the stars. Elissa placed her left hand on the wall for stability and limped back to the central chamber and Laytha.

CHAPTER 10

DARIN

The huge, accumulative surge of power being
*   discharged had a backlash; the ground shook*
and the very land beneath their feet sank.
In that moment, the So'Dal changed the land-
*   scape forever.*
In that moment, the So'Dal changed forever.
History of the Craterlands, Post-Rending

Red, orange, yellow, blue, yellow. Darin slammed his hand on his bed in frustration and the training globe's light faded. Why was it so hard to sing a scale? Even Conor had tried to teach him. But every time he tried, he got it wrong. What use was a So'Dal who couldn't use magic?

Star licked his hand and sent *[Walking in the garden]*. A companion who could sense his mood took getting used to. Whenever he struggled or felt frustrated, Star tried to make him feel better, even though his suggestions didn't always make sense – like the time he had suggested sniffing other moon-hounds' rear ends to make Darin feel happy – but he could see how they'd improve Star's mood. He had a gardening lesson shortly, so they could head up to the crater early before they met Tralkion, it was a good idea.

Darin stuffed a blanket into his bag and carefully placed the training globe on top as Star picked up a tooth-scarred bone and tilted his head hopefully. Darin grinned, but sent *[Bone left on Star's bed]*. Star dropped it without fuss. Darin blew out the candle and they left. He felt a little brighter already.

His lesson times had been swapped because later, he'd put his new knowledge of Edgeland plants to the test. He'd been engrossed in books about their bestiary and flora for days. Darin's gardening tutor, Tralkion, took him to the fenced-off area the day before to show him where they'd be meeting. Glowing plants! It was going to be exciting. He knew some were found on the Surface all over Caldera, but as they'd only travelled in the holloways at night on the journey there, he'd never seen them. Having recently read about the nocturnal animals which roamed the Surface, Darin was glad they'd stayed in the depths of the holloways.

But the Edgelands ... The descriptions of Edgelands beasts caused a shiver to run down his spine. It was as though someone drew the darkness out of a story and spilt it over the land – equally fascinating and terrifying.

⸕ ⁂ ⚔ ⚜ ✦

Dim, green moonlight illuminated the lift platform from far above. Despite having used it several times, the steam lift hadn't lost its novelty, nor Darin his fear. He grinned nervously as he climbed on. Star pressed close against him, so Darin placed his hand on the hound's back. He tried to swallow his fear. *Breathe* ...

The hooded figure waited until Darin had both hands back

on the rail before releasing the steam. They rode up into the dusk, and both walked off the lift with trembling legs. Darin tried to walk confidently to the nearest bench and sat for a few minutes, staring up at the circle of stars way above his head. Once they'd recovered, they wound through the paths to the small gated area where Tralkion awaited them.

'Star needs to stay outside,' he said.

[Star sitting outside the gate]

[Star not sitting, Star chasing a bird, or a smell]

'Fine,' said Darin. 'Don't go far, and don't get lost.'

Tralkion laughed. 'Lea does that too. A whole conversation between them, and I pick up the tail end.'

'Has her hound moved in to your rooms yet?' Darin asked. He knew that Lea's hound was only just older than Star, so once they were out of the kennels, he wouldn't be far behind.

'In the morning, I believe. It's my last night alone for a long time!'

Darin grinned. 'And you're spending it with me!'

Tralkion opened the gate. 'I wouldn't have it any other way. You were so quick with responding to Lucia that she suffered no adverse effects at all. Lea insisted I asked to be your Gardener. She also said you're using a candle in your room?'

They walked in and closed the gate, ensuring Star couldn't push it open.

'Yes, I still can't light any of the globes.' Darin was glad the darkness hid his embarrassment.

'Then tonight's lesson is even more important. Instead of plant recognition, we'll make your own glow globe.'

Something else for him to shatter, but being amongst the Edgeland plants made more sense. All around him, Darin saw what he assumed were fire sprites flickering green and blue amongst shifting leaves. He reached toward one, then realised that he was looking at the leaves and flowers themselves. He'd expected them to glow, but hadn't anticipated them being quite so bright, nor in so many colours.

'Can you find our plants?' Tralkion asked.

Darin scanned the surrounding vegetation and pointed out the open, golden flowers to his right, like small, luminous teardrops. He searched carefully, ensuring he didn't make contact with any foliage, and found the plant with small spotted leaves tucked behind a group of other plants. The spots pulsed with gentle light.

'I can't see the third one?'

'You shouldn't be able to. It also grows in the west of Caldera, and it's used in other potions, so it will be across the garden. We'll get it after we finish here.'

Tralkion gave him the Gardener gloves and a leather bag. The thick gloves were surprisingly flexible and protected his entire forearm from toxic plants. Carefully, he gathered the flowers and spotted leaves he needed and slipped them into separate compartments in the bag. Then they left the enclosed area and called Star.

Ten days before, Darin had seen the unflickering globes in the passageways for the first time. He'd never have thought he'd be wandering around a garden at night with a So'Dal and a hound, collecting plants and learning how to make one himself.

After collecting the last plant, they took a winding route toward a large door in the crater wall. Inside, a spiral staircase wound tighter and tighter as they climbed and – just as Darin thought the next spiral would be too narrow for his shoulders – it widened into a chamber with one side open to the crater.

'Welcome to my workshop.' Tralkion gestured broadly around as he sung the glow lamps alight.

'It's, um, pretty high,' replied Darin, realising that the open balcony had no railing, and they were quite some way up the side of the crater. Other lights shone from around the walls.

'Are those other workrooms?' he asked, trying not to think about the drop.

'Some of them are, yes. Some are private rooms. Nissa – the Anchor – has one that opens out to the crater. It lets her watch the poison test section of the trials, and several Senior So'Dal watch from there too.' He gestured to the workbench in the middle of the workroom. 'Shall we?'

'Let me just settle Star.' Darin gently placed his training globe on a workbench and laid his blanket far from the edge of the crater. Star slunk onto it and rested his head on his paws, watching Darin's every move.

⊤ ✵ ✻ ⟁ ✦

Under Tralkion's supervision, he ground the glowing flowers into a gently fluorescing paste, then added the third plant. Its astringent scent overwhelmed the perfume of the Edgelands flowers. Tralkion leant over the bowl to inspect the mixture.

'It needs to be a bit finer, then we'll be ready to add a weft. Once all the big lumps are out, I'll do that part for you.'

Darin ground up the paste in the marble bowl for a few more minutes, and when he had checked it again, Tralkion began to sing. To Darin's ears, the tune sounded impossibly complex; delicate melodies woven around each other. The paste glowed brighter, and Tralkion gestured for Darin to continue mixing. As the last notes of the melody echoed back from the walls of their workroom, Darin sighed.

'That was amazing. I have so much to learn.'

'You have, but you have plenty of time. We are all always learning. Now, paint that around the inside of this globe, evenly and thickly.'

Darin took the globe and coated the interior carefully.

Tralkion watched over his shoulder. 'Before you put the lid

on, I'll sing one more weft, then it needs you to add your trigger note. The one that will light it.'

Darin's breath quickened. A real, useful bit of magic. 'Which note?' he asked.

'Whichever you are most confident you can hit and use.'

'Green. I can normally hit green,' he said, after some thought. 'Can I use the training globe to pitch myself right first?'

Tralkion grimaced. 'It would be better if you don't. Trust yourself.'

'Okay, then I'm done.'

Darin stepped aside to let Tralkion get closer. He took a few deep breaths so he was ready to sing when Tralkion signalled. As soon as Tralkion nodded to him, he poured himself through the note. The globe shuddered slightly, then lit up. He'd done it! His hands shook as he screwed the lid on.

'You did it.' Tralkion's grin was almost as wide as his own. 'I knew you could.'

Pride swelled Darin's chest. *It was one note, just one step, but my first real step.*

'Thank you for your help. I think it will be a while before I can sing that first weft – it was really complex. Will we make something next lesson too?' Darin picked up his glow lamp, cradling it in his hands.

'We'll make a healing draft. It's a less complicated weft. I'll let you try it yourself, if you can show me the correct sequence on the globe.'

'I'll try. I'll practise even harder. Your weft tonight showed me how much more practise I need.'

'That's a basic one, Darin – only four notes. The only ones simpler are wards and the general healing draught.'

'That's not reassuring, you know.' Darin sank to the bench, his excitement quenched by the reality of the task ahead.

Tralkion smiled. 'You didn't even know who the So'Dal really were until a tide ago. Don't worry. Can you imagine how our recruitment dreams would go otherwise, sword swinging and singing?' He laughed as he tidied the table. 'They might raise more than curiosity!'

'Recruitment dreams?'

'Of course. How do you think you had the idea to join us? The Soul Anchors work together to send out powerful dreams. They amplify them out to the population with emotional resonance added. Those with potential to become So'Dal receive them and come here as you did, to become part of our guard. We do still get applicants who just want the prestige of being guards, so we can't always assume you dreamt your invite. The trouble with hiding ourselves from the general population is that no one really wants to be an administrator.' He shrugged. 'I can't blame them. It sounds boring, but it means there are far less new So'Dal discovered in the last hundred or so cycles.'

'What about you? How did you arrive here?' The question tumbled out, and Darin worried for a moment that he had overstepped a mark.

Tralkion looked thoughtful. 'My parents lived here in the Black Palace, so I grew up here. My sister has lilac hair, so we knew she was talented. But no one tells you about the trials as a boy, just in case you aren't. Then, if you don't pass them all, you can choose to leave here and live a normal life.'

Darin glanced down at the long, split black robe he was wearing. 'Normal's not so bad.' He shrugged. 'It's what I've always been. If I walked up to my parents' home wearing these black robes and accompanied by a giant hound, I don't think they'd consider me normal anymore.'

Tralkion picked up their tools, turned the tap on a vat of water, and rinsed them under the flow. 'You won't be doing that soon, Darin. Not until you learn more control and a lot more wefts. You need to be able to earn your way before you travel, unless you're on an apprentice journey. Your money is no good as a So'Dal.' He put the tools back on the shelves and gestured for Darin to pass him the rest of the items. Then he froze, his eyes becoming unfocused. 'Can you find your way back out?'

'Yes, I think so.' Darin replied.

'We'll meet up here tomorrow, first thing. You may leave.'

Darin shuffled Star off the blanket, wrapped it around his training globe, then slung his bag across his back *[Their bedroom, lit by a glow globe]*.

Star stretched his front legs out, touching his nose to the floor and yawned *[Star asleep on the bed]*.

Darin scratched his hound's ears, and they wound their way down the stairs and across the garden. His globe gave out a steady light as they strolled back through the palace, and his smile was just as bright.

⌐ ※ ※ ※ ✦

Star peeled off to the hound paddocks as they passed under the archway. Back in their kennel bedroom, Darin placed the globe on its flat lid and admired it. His painting wasn't as smooth as the ones in the walls, and small flecks of flower and stem were still visible, but it was his.

As he gazed at the glowing ball, a familiar canine presence intruded in his mind. Pride seemed to be order of the day – Star was proud of something too. The moonhound trotted up the stairs with a small, furry animal in his mouth, then curled up in the corner to eat it. The cracking of bones wasn't an ideal sleeping accompaniment, so Darin tried to send *[Himself asleep]* to Star, who obliged him by eating faster. If Star was hunting, maybe he was ready to leave the pack. A proper room with a real bed wouldn't go amiss, in his opinion.

As he waited for Star to finish, Darin took the training globe out and practised his exercises. He worked quietly, and after several repeats, managed to get a clear, consistent colour change between a few colours. Maybe the confidence of achieving something truly magical had helped. Star finished crunching, and Darin put the training globe away. He sang the single note to turn his lamp off, smiled broadly as it dimmed, and allowed sleep to claim him.

⊤ ※ ⚓ ⚓ ✦

Light speared through Darin's window, piercing his eyelids and bringing him abruptly into wakefulness. He sang the glow globe into life. Fierce energy filled him – he was going to work so hard. His new path wound into a musical distance in his mind, filled with glowing plants and magical happenings. He could do it! He'd proved it to himself. Darin stretched out and looked for Star, but he wasn't in their room. That was hopeful – maybe he'd gone to hunt his own breakfast. Small rodents wouldn't fill him up, even if he was trying to be independent; he wasn't going to find enough food there, so Darin would get them both something.

He pulled his boots on and ran for breakfast. Jaer passed him in the courtyard, bearing plates of food and a wide grin. Darin smiled and waved; he felt lighter. The whole atmosphere of the palace was happy, and everyone wore a smile. Lea passed him on her way back to the hounds with an armful of hound meals.

'Lea, if you see Star, can you feed him too? He's out hunting.'

She stopped. 'Again? That's wonderful news. Of course, I

can. Tralkion left already because he was keen to get started early today – apparently, he has a promise to keep.' She grinned. 'I hear you made a glow globe last night? That's great.' She was dressed in loose, feminine clothes, very unlike her usual tunic around the hounds. Her scarf was loosely draped around her shoulders.

'You look nice,' he said without thinking, then felt his cheeks burning. 'Sorry, I didn't mean—' She was Tralkion's bonded anchor. He hoped she didn't think he was flirting.

'And I don't normally?' Lea laughed, interrupting his thoughts as he blushed. 'It's okay. I know what you mean. There's no mud or hound fuzz stuck to me. Go on, get going!'

Darin ran to the hall and grabbed a plate of food. He sat at a bench, savoured the fruity brose, and took in the buzz around the room. Conor plonked down next to him with his breakfast, also dressed in smart clothes; Darin glanced down at his own hound-hair covered robes. What had he missed?

Through a mouthful of flatcake, he mumbled, 'So ... what are you up to today, then?'

'We're going into Redpike. It's the full moon market today. I thought I'd go and explore since we've all got the day off.' He stared at Darin. 'Are you going out dressed like that?'

Darin sighed. 'I haven't got the day off. I'm due up in the garden first thing.' He loaded his fork with another heap of food and grinned. 'I made a lamp yesterday!'

'On your own?' Conor's eyebrows shot up. 'No offence meant, but is your singing actually good enough to make it work yet?'

'That's a fair comment. No, Tralkion helped me. He sang, I harvested and prepared the plants. It was still exciting, though. I can show you later?'

'Sure, why not?' Conor rose to his feet and stabbed the last portion on his plate. 'Have a great day. I'll catch you later.' He almost inhaled the last mouthful of flatcake and, patting Darin on the shoulder, left him to finish his food.

A full moon market. He'd no idea what that entailed, but memories of the market stalls laden with food and ale flooded back. He'd have liked to go. Maybe if he asked Tralkion, they could finish early – he'd still have to be back for the Master that afternoon, but a chance to get some real free time would be too good to miss. As he scanned the room, he realised that every woman in the hall wore a hair cover, not just those Darin knew had lilac hair.

It was a style of dress he'd noticed more often as they got closer to Redpike. He'd never met a lilac-haired woman outside of the palace, but over his lifetime, he'd known many who always wore scarves, hats, wraps, and other hair ornamentation – his mother included. Had he met Soul Anchors and never realised? Was it a deliberately cultivated fashion?

Darin washed his plate and put it on the stack before spotting Tralkion standing in the doorway, chatting with Lea. She smiled as Tralkion reached out and squeezed her hand. After Lea left, Tralkion caught his eye and gestured him over.

'Let's get started. If we get through your lessons quickly today, you can go to the market.'

'Really? Thank you. Although,' – he grimaced – 'I have singing practise with the Master later.'

'I may have made a deal with him.' Tralkion winked.

Darin's hopes rose as he strode through the corridors ahead of Tralkion toward the steam lift. That spiced ale was calling. He'd do whatever it took to get to the market.

⊤ ※ ✵ ⚏ ✦

They climbed the spiral staircase from the garden up to the workroom, where Tralkion gestured toward the open side.

Darin shuffled as close as he dared and looked across the gardens in amazement. What had felt like a random layout with plants vaguely grouped to their region was, in fact, a rough map of Caldera.

Some flower beds were planted in shapes that represented the craters and others grew in between, just like the Surface. The paths were arranged like the main holloways between them. It was beautiful.

Tralkion stood at his shoulder. 'It's impressive when you see it properly, isn't it?' He pointed across the garden. 'The pavilion represents the mountains and Redpike. Today, we'll visit that area.' He pointed across to some flower beds arranged around a cross in the path. 'Your home region of Eye, Pelton, Respite, and Firstal. As we walk, I want you to show me what you know about your local plants.'

ᛉ ⚜ ⚕ ⚚ ✦

Darin had enjoyed evenings with Hal on the way to Redpike. Once they were settled in a holroom, Hal would lay out the plants they'd gathered that day and explain their uses. As he walked through the garden, he tried to remember what he'd learnt.

He pointed out which plants were used for healing aches and fever and those that were good for burns and stings. Darin was pleased to remember one that was best if a fire sprite scorched you. He wandered along the paths, stopping and telling Tralkion about as many as he could recall.

Tralkion followed quietly, asking little and letting Darin talk. Occasionally, he asked for more details or about a particular plant that Darin hadn't mentioned.

Eventually, they reached the part that represented Eye crater. Darin reached for a flower with relaxed familiarity. His mother had those in a vase on her window; his father used to give him that one for stomach aches. A pang of homesickness hit him. When would he see his family again? *Would* he see them again? They had no idea what had happened to him. He looked up, away from Tralkion, blinking away a treacherous tear, and as he did, he saw movement high on the crater wall. The outlines of two figures on a ledge who appeared to be facing in their direction.

Darin narrowed his eyes, to squint up at them 'Tralkion, are we being watched?'

Tralkion nodded. 'I would imagine so. Lea is desperate for me to accompany her into town, and the Anchor will be up there with her. I'm not sure if it's because Hal brought you here or it's the moonhound, but she's very interested in you.'

Darin wasn't sure he liked being noticed that much. 'Is that a good thing? How can they see much from up there?'

'They aren't, really. I am talking to Lea, and she's relaying it on.'

'How?' Darin frowned. He wasn't sure he enjoyed being listened in on either.

'The easiest way I can explain it is that Lea says it's similar to how you talk to the hounds.'

'I make a picture in my head and send it to him,' Darin said. 'You can talk in pictures?'

Tralkion shrugged. 'Well, it's a bit like that. I don't aim the thought at her, though – I aim at her crystal. I can't explain it better than that. You've read about the wars?'

Darin sat on the grass and nodded. He ran his fingers through the soft blades and breathed in the scent of home as Tralkion talked.

'So, you know we were considered much too powerful. After the Watcher closed the gates and smashed the echoglass, our predecessors split the responsibility for the talents between the genders. So'Dal always learn one set of skills, one set of magic, the gardening, and singing-related crafts and uses of our wefts.'

'What do the Soul Anchors learn, then?' Darin asked, squinting up at the ledge.

Tralkion collected as he talked, filling his satchel with the plants they had come down for. 'The women use the crystals and work with emotions and dreams. I don't know the details, but I understand they don't need to use song to weft their magic. Women are always stronger. They can even amplify out our magic somehow.'

He closed the satchel. 'Without their level of power, we can create portable gardening potions and enhance their properties, make globes, and activate some special potions – like flashballs and some small wards. But the days of one lone So'Dal or Soul Anchor having the ability to tear the ground asunder is gone. No one alive now knows how to do it all.'

Darin could see a sense in it. What he'd researched had been terrifying, and the knowledge that he could potentially be in control of that much power had frightened him, though he daren't admit it to Tralkion.

'Is that why there are separate women's and men's libraries?' he asked.

Tralkion nodded. 'There are duplicates of relevant texts, but much has been separated. Some older texts – the most powerful – were lost. It's generally thought the Watcher took them back to Mythos. Come on, let's get back to work.'

They walked back through the twisting paths, and Darin tried to process everything. 'So, can you work with any Soul Anchor?' he asked.

'No. Usually, the person you work with is the one you feel closest to, most bonded to. In many cases, they will be both your partner in life and the wefts. It's easier that way. I have known siblings to work as a team and have non So'Dal partners, but it's far less common. Soul Anchor Aslin works with her brother, for example. Her partner in life is another Soul Anchor, so he's the Gardener or Collective member that she's most closely bonded to.'

Darin wasn't sure who Tralkion referred to, but it made sense to him. If you had to work with someone of the opposite skill set, then a sibling could work well. He considered the women he had seen since arriving and wondered who he might be paired with. None of them had paid him much attention; everyone just wanted to meet Star. As they reached the archway to the spiral stairs, he asked, 'Do you get to choose?'

Tralkion nodded. 'We don't force partnerships on you – it has to be mutual. Many women have been here from a very young age, especially if they were born to non-So'Dal families. That lilac hair marks them from birth, so they are brought in early by So'Dal Witness families in busy craters. They may have grown up alongside their future partners.'

'The next group of women the Witnesses are bringing for training should arrive over the next few tides. Don't be too hopeful, though. Many have already met their match – especially if they're from Witness families who see many visiting apprentices.'

Darin rubbed Star's fur from his hound-hair covered robes as they climbed the stairs.

'Well then, it's probably a good thing that I'm not after a woman. I wasn't ready when I left home, that's for sure. My mother was pressing me to consider it, to give her grandchildren.' He laughed, remembering the awkward meals in his family home. His mother had invited different women each tide, all appearing as trapped as he'd felt. 'Aside from helping my parents to rebuild, part of the reason I came to Redpike was to escape!' He rolled his eyes as he continued. 'Her friends' daughters were always being invited over for dinner. Now, between singing, hound training, and learning from you, I'm exhausted, so I'd have no time to give anyone. I rarely get to practise sparring, and sleep is a luxury. I'm simply too busy for a woman.'

Tralkion paused at the entrance to the room. 'You have an extra complication with Star. Unless he likes someone, a connection between you won't be possible because Staramine can block it. Then there's her hound too – if your future Soul Anchor bonds.'

It all sounded way too much to deal with; a partner was definitely something to worry about much later. Tralkion dumped the bag on the workbench and looked expectantly at him.

'I'm ready.' Darin walked up to the table.

Tralkion placed a slip of paper by three bowls. 'These are the symptoms and requirements of three people in Redpike who have asked for our help. Here are the plants I gathered, but I've picked more types than you need. For each case, choose the best plant or combination for their symptoms. If you choose correctly, we'll make the potions and deliver them. Then, you can go to the market.' He handed Darin the bag and stepped back. 'Go ahead. You have the glove. I've already spoken to the Master, and if you can do this, he'll excuse you from singing today to accompany me.'

Exploring the market was a great incentive, but a day off from singing? Watcher, he needed that badly. Darin read the symptoms of the first person on the list, then turned toward the bag of fresh plants and additional dried plants Tralkion had laid out. He could definitely do it.

CHAPTER 11

SURIIN

*There are many theories of how Nameless crater
ended up with its title. In reality, it is probably not due to nameless terrors hunting the
faat and haunting the skies. It is more likely
that it was simply one of the only craters
formed during the Rending without a town
already present from which to take a name.*
A Traveller's Guide to Caldera

Suriin shut the barn door, dropping the heavy bars into place once all faat were safe inside – as safe as faat in a barn with a hole in the roof could be. It might have been kinder to leave them in the open with at least a chance of escape, rather than gathered up, ready for a living banquet if the xotryl returned. The one they'd seen near Golden was certainly big enough to take a fal.

The dividing wall between the faat's section of the barn and the part they would sleep in felt very flimsy in light of the danger, but the hay bales would make comfortable beds, and she could snuggle into it for warmth. Maybe bury herself a little – and they had a roof, unlike the faat.

A distant shadow in the sky didn't reassure her that the xotryl had left Nameless. The wide-winged silhouette over the top of the crater was huge, even from a distance. It flapped slowly as it circled over the edge of the crater for lift. If she squinted, it could be a garant. They lived on the opposite side of Caldera, but if she believed hard enough ... she pulled her attention away from it

⌐ ✳ ✳ ✳ ✦

Suriin's father glanced up between mouthfuls of stew as she walked in. He had dark rings under his eyes and appeared exhausted. Whatever he'd done took a lot out of him. She gave him a quick hug, then crossed to the hearth to warm some feeling into her fingers.

Once he'd finished and Ronin had eaten his fill, they bid Trudie good night and returned to the barn. They pulled the solid door shut behind them, and her father bolted it shut. Suriin laid her bedding across some bales, built a pillow from hay, and tried to get comfortable. She wriggled into the hay, watching Ronin and her father prepare their beds.

They planned to take turns sleeping again. Although frustrated by their over-caution, Suriin decided to ignore them and rest while she had the chance. They would traverse the huge crater the next day, and after that, it would take at least two more before they'd be in the next holloway and headed to Blow for her first real experience of a town.

Would it be full of noise and people? Would it smell of spices and other goods? What would it be like to hear the laughter of so many children and the conversations of people from all over Caldera? Would there be people from farther away? From other parts of Lieus?

She drifted off to sleep. Her dream wandering took her along imaginary wisps of streets and paths with twists and turns. People bustled around as children played in fountains. She noticed someone walking nearby. Her location changed; the streets became wider and the houses different, more solid. As she walked after the shadow companion, featureless people developed faces. The houses were no longer in a crater, and the person alongside was her father.

He touched her shoulder, and she was surprised at how real the dream felt.

'Suriin, this is something you must be careful of. You're dream-jumping, and you have crossed into my dream,' he said. 'Don't panic. It's better that it happened now and in my dream.'

'I'm in your dream?' Suriin asked.

'Yes, and now you need to learn how to get out safely. The next few nights will be hard for all of us. You must first learn to walk out, and then how to stop others walking in.'

'Am I dreaming that I am dreaming your dream?'

Her dream father wrinkled his forehead. 'Not if I understand your question properly. You're asleep, but instead of being in your dream, you walked into mine. When you're safely out of my dream, Ronin will wake you.'

Suriin tried to hold back panic. She had somehow walked into his dream? Why now? Surely, she could have done that any time he was around.

'I'm eighteen cycles old. Why have I never done this before?'

'You did as a child, but as you got older, we kept you secure from this possibility. As we get closer and closer to others, we won't always have the ability to enclose ourselves in rock overnight. Rock helps stop unintentional dream walking.

Fluffy kept your mother's dreams wrapped from you and Gwynn doesn't yet show any talent, so this is the first real opportunity.'

She looked around at the town her father was dreaming of. Market stalls grew either side of the road, plants wild over their canopies, and cobbled streets ran off in various directions.

'So how do I get out? Where is this place?'

'This is Redpike. You see that group of towers on the mountainside? That's the Black Palace. I usually meet your mother here in the market, if she is able to join me.' He smiled. 'It's where we first met.'

'Will she be here soon? Can I see her too?'

Her father shook his head. 'We're a little early, and I'm not due to meet her tonight. I was just hoping. We didn't have long together this visit.'

That was her fault, and they'd argued most of the time too. Her father didn't come home often, and she felt a little guilty. At least they could still talk, still see each other in their dreams. She hadn't known that; maybe she could talk to both her parents once she'd learned the skills. A scarf fluttered in the breeze on the nearest stall and she reached for it, but her hands went through it.

'Why can't I touch it, but you can touch me?'

'It takes practise. Let's worry about getting you safely out of here first.'

Suriin focused on her dream father. 'I'm listening.'

'To get out of someone else's dream, walk to a place where you'd expect to be alone. Try to create it in your mind, then walk there. I'll follow you from a distance to check you are safe. Once you vanish from my dream, you should be alone again.'

Suriin tried to picture somewhere she'd be alone. She considered home in Golden, but Gwynn might still be awake. The only place she could think of, where she expected no one to be and could picture clearly, was the holrooms they'd been in the night before.

She walked away from her father and pictured the door as clearly as she could. As she approached it, something felt wrong, but she wasn't sure what. She turned to run back toward her father's dream, but he wasn't there. His town had gone.

Suriin didn't feel alone in her own head; something else was there. Something ominous and dark. Panicking, she tried to picture somewhere different. Golden, the farmer's hut at the end of the paddock ...

She gained on the door, pursued by heavy footfalls of something huge. Suriin reached the door, threw herself in, and slammed it behind her. She could still hear footfalls growing louder. It was her dream. Hers! She needed to go somewhere else – and fast. Suriin tried to picture the door of the hut as the one to her home, opened it, leapt through, and slammed it behind her.

The sensation of being chased vanished.

She opened her eyes; Ronin stood over her, gently trying to coax her awake. She flung her arms around him and hung on. He didn't push her away, but let her hold on to him until she calmed down.

'Tough one, huh?' he asked, eventually.

'Something was chasing me, something big.'

'Where did you picture being alone?'

'The holloway. I tried to go into the holrooms.'

'From the holloway? That was dangerous. Suriin, we're not the only creatures that dream walk. Try not to choose an area where you risk wandering through some unpleasant creature's dreams next time.' Ronin shook his head as he spoke.

'Lesson learnt, I promise. If I can barely escape a single creature in one dream, how will I avoid hundreds of people in a town?'

'We'll take crater-edge accommodations. Your father knows where we can stay and have solid rooms. If it's any consolation, during my first time sleeping in a room with others, I sat in on a dream all night because I was too scared to move. The most important advice I can give is to always wake from your own dream. If you don't, you leave a trace in the other dream. They can find you easily then – anywhere you sleep.' Ronin met her eyes, and she saw the depth of his own, deep and dark and lost in his own memories. She also realised she was still holding onto him like a small, desperate child.

Suriin untangled herself from his neck, brushed herself down, and sat opposite him. 'So how do I sleep now? There are tides of travel ahead.'

'Find your safe place and stay there. Keep a clear mind when you fall asleep and try to focus on your safe place. Never places where you could be stalked.'

'That's easier said than done!'

He shrugged. 'I know. Sorry. A few creatures stalk the night – moonhounds are one. Fluffy protected you in Golden. Creatures from the Edgelands make up the rest.' Ronin rubbed his beard with his hand as he spoke. 'They seem to have abilities we don't. Over the next few nights, you must practise leaving our dreams if you end up there. Go to Golden if you feel you crossed over. Now, try to get some rest. Yorynn will have his guard up now. You should be able to drift back off while he is in deep sleep.' He smiled at her and returned to his bedding.

Suriin laid down and tried to relax. He was right – she needed sleep. She tried to remember to use the relaxation techniques her mother had taught her as a child. Maybe that had been why! In the morning, she would ask her father about them. For the moment, she'd think of home, her mother's room, Fluffy, and all the happy moments there before she closed her eyes.

Ronin watched her from a distance, glancing over occasionally. She took comfort in his quiet presence, although she tried not to blush at the way she had thrown her arms around him in panic. Once again, Suriin had shown her immaturity. Every time she thought she gained some credit in his eyes, she followed it with something that showed how incapable and inexperienced she was.

Suriin wanted her father to see she was ready to train at Redpike. She would learn fast and make him proud.

When morning dawned, Yorynn paid a quick visit to the landholder to check on his progress while she and Ronin readied their belongings to leave.

Suriin checked in on the faat before they left and went to scratch her grumpy skaa-rak mount on the beak.

There had been no disturbance overnight, and she was faced with contented chewing from the herd. She hoped they would be okay for another night. There wasn't a huge amount of hay left, so she dragged a new bale through to them before closing the doors.

The walls of the crater shrunk behind them as they set out toward Blow. They would recede into the distance over the day, and she hoped that the xotryl would too. There was no sign of it at the moment, so she relaxed a little, enjoying the new sights and wildlife.

Whilst a lot of rarer plants were on the Surface, many that

the So'Dal discussed were new to her. Yorynn explained the uses of various herbs and their healing or flavouring properties to Ronin as they walked, then Suriin made copious notes and sketches of the dried flowers and leaves when they stopped. She tested their flavouring over lunch. It was dry food, chewy and tasteless, so she added some herbs. A few mouthfuls later, she struggled not to spit the food back out. The herbs were much too strong on their own. Maybe she should have spent more time helping with cooking. From her mother's tales of growing up around the Black Palace, she knew she probably wouldn't have to cook a lot once they arrived, though. Food was made for everyone there.

⊢ ✳ ⚜ ⚜ ✦

As the day drew on, no houses or buildings squatted in her sight. Nameless was mostly flat grassland with occasional mounds. Fence posts formed wooden crowns on a few of the larger ones. The faat there had no shelter, but their long, thick coats meant they had little need for it. They clustered in herds, rounding their fal up to the centre for the night.

The Aulirean sun dropped below the horizon slowly, warming the cool greens of the crater, and Suriin was admiring the glowing skyline as a silhouette rose above the northern crater edge. Wide wings and a heavy body gave it a mismatched appearance as evening sunlight glinted off the creature's hide and leathery wings.

Mesmerised, she recognised the shape of the snout and teeth. It was the same type of creature that been at the top of Golden. Maybe even the same one. Her heart raced; they were in the open! They were dinner.

She shouted to her father, but he'd already seen it. He stepped forward and pulled her hand.

'Follow me. Now.'

Suriin wasted no time. She dropped his hand and stayed close as he ran. Then he stopped, turned toward her as she gained ground, and pointed to a small hill ahead.

'Run for that hill and don't stop. At its base is a cave. I want you in there as quickly as possible. Ronin, follow her in and make sure she's safe. I'll come last.'

The xotryl flew ever closer to the herd of faat, swinging its monstrous head from side to side. Long, shiny, sharp talons hung from claw-like feet. It was more than twice the size of a skaa-rak, and it had seen them.

Its head swung to the side, and the large eye stared right at Suriin before it straightened its neck, changed course away from the herd of faat, and headed in their direction. She held back a scream and ran.

The dark patch at the base of the hill gave her a target; it must be the opening. The xotryl's wing beats were audible as the gap between them narrowed.

Oh, Watcher's breath, she was running directly at a hungry xotryl that flew toward her. Suriin kept running, her breath ragged gasps as she struggled to get enough air into her lungs. Her legs burnt with every step.

She was so focused on the cave that she lost her footing and tripped. The entrance was only twenty steps away, and the xotryl rose over the crest of the hill.

As she hit the ground, Ronin grabbed her and pulled her to her feet. He practically dragged her the last few steps to the entrance. Suriin tucked into the gap in the rock and collapsed, searching her for her father.

He'd made it to where she'd fallen watching the creature as he ran. It couldn't fly straight at him, as he was too close to the hill, so it had banked around and was headed at him from the side. Yorynn held a globe in his hand and sung quietly as he ran.

He reached the base of the hill as the creature pulled its wings in tight and dived, catching his shoulder with a long, curved talon.

Suriin screamed.

He ducked free of its grasp and, in the process, dropped the globe, which rolled across the grass toward them. Her father dropped to his knees, his face twisted in pain, and crawled toward the cave entrance. Suriin couldn't watch him struggle any longer and broke free of Ronin's restraint. The xotryl had flown around to line up for another attempt. They wouldn't have long. Suriin dragged her father toward the cave, but he crawled excruciatingly slowly. They weren't going to make it.

'Come on! Not far now,' she encouraged him.

'The globe, Ronin,' he whispered.

'Ronin, the globe? Can you do it?' she shouted, still gasping for air after her own dash for safety and pulling her father with the last of her strength.

Ronin grabbed the globe that had rolled to his feet and held it ready to throw. His hand shook as he sang. At first unsteady, then gaining power, his song weft rose.

Suriin concentrated on getting her weakened father into the cave and didn't look back at the xotryl. She would trust Ronin. Her only focus was the cave entrance.

'Eight steps more. Come on ... you can do it. Seven steps, six ...' She cajoled him forward. Time seemed to stretch, and her focus narrowed to the world around the two of them.

She barely heard her father's voice over the song.

'Eyes down, now!'

Suriin obeyed. Ronin's voice hit a final clear high note, and the globe burst with a brilliant, blinding light. She felt wind on her skin as wings flapped and the creature turned away from the light, screeching in blind panic.

'Three steps ... Two ...'

They fell into the cave. The entrance was too narrow for

anything bigger than a human to get through, and the shrieks of frustration from outside, whilst deafening, were no longer a threat. Ronin helped carry her father to a flat area, and her eyes slowly adjusted to the dark as the flash wore off. Inside, the cave was big enough for all three of them to lie flat with space between them. There would be no need to go back out until morning.

Ronin pulled a small glow lamp from his pack and lit it. In the gentle light, her father's skin was pale, and his eyes more tired than the previous day. He gestured them both over.

'Suriin, get my pouch. There are a few vials in there. Bring them all over. Ronin, come here. How bad is it?'

Ronin sat next to him and pulled the robe off his shoulder. A fresh gash ran across the very top of Yorynn's arm, oozing a mixture of blood and a black substance.

'It's not as big as the injury we dealt with yesterday, but it got you with a talon, and the wound is turning black.'

'You will have to do it, Ronin. It's draining me already.'

Suriin brought over the vials, each a different colour. Some swirled when she looked at them closely, just like the globe had before it flashed.

'Use a bottle of draw. Once the poison's out, I can start to heal naturally. It'll be slow, but we can't afford the risk of using the others – not until we know we can restock. You know the weft, Ronin. I know you can do it.'

Ronin nodded once. 'I can. Suriin, get the fabric wedge from the same bag and some moss from the walls if you can find any, but don't leave the cave.'

Suriin handed Ronin the cloth and stepped back, watching in silence. He poured the contents of a vial onto the cloth, applied it to the gash, and then placed both hands over it. As she headed to the entrance – more light might mean some moss – Ronin began to sing with a deep, mellow voice. The tune started out wavering but, as he sang, she heard his confidence grow. He repeated the same refrain over and over; it was complicated, and the melody would have been soothing and calm under other circumstances.

There was moss near the cave mouth and no sign of the xotryl outside. Hopefully, it had taken one of the faat and would leave them alone. She returned to the men as Ronin began a fourth repeat. He stared intently at the bandage, reached for the moss without dropping a note, lifted his other hand, and placed it underneath the cloth, keeping the melody unbroken.

The air seemed thicker in the cave, and Suriin felt useless. Ronin appeared exhausted, and the strain showed. Without asking permission, or even thinking, she sang alongside him, the melody fixed in her head from Ronin's repeats. She hoped that if she helped him sing his song, it might help them both.

Her father's eyes flicked open. He stared at her in surprise and opened his mouth to speak. Gently, she shook her head and placed her hand reassuringly on his other arm.

'I love you. Rest.'

As she continued to hold the melody — staying in tune with Ronin – she felt odd, as though something was leaving her. Instinctively, she placed her hand on Ronin's hand whilst continuing to sing. He'd been singing with his eyes closed for the last few repetitions, and at the gesture, he started. His eyes met hers and he frowned, but didn't break his song.

They sang until they could continue no more. She had no idea why she'd done what she had, or whether it had helped, but she certainly felt empty and drained.

'Stop,' Ronin said, and leant over her father, holding the glow globe closer.

He was asleep, his breathing shallow, even, and regular, and he'd regained a more normal colour. Ronin removed the dressing. It was completely black underneath, and her father's shoulder was almost pink again. Ronin stepped away and beckoned Suriin over to the other side of the cave.

'Xotryl talons are dangerous. I honestly don't know if we did enough. But for now, rest.'

CHAPTER 12

ELISSA

*We needed them, and they needed us. What we
could not know at this point, was how much
more they needed us. More than we could
have ever imagined. As we shrouded our
Hope, we hid from them. They were forced to
hide in plain sight.
One day, I fear we will meet Regret over our
behaviour.*
**_Diary of the Shardeep Elders. Entry dated
504, Post-Closing_**

With little else to mark time, the gently glowing lumina governed their days. Days dominated by the sole task of preparing and eating food. The rest of their time was spent sitting or pacing in the gloom.

Once Elissa was aware of the passage to the mountainside, she couldn't shake the feeling of insecurity. Usually, their cave felt like a safe haven, their undiscovered retreat. The itching disquiet in the back of her mind wouldn't leave her alone either.

Its constant presence generated an increasing desperation to get back to the sericlave and normality.

Elissa considered telling Laytha about the strange daydream, but decided it was just that – a dream. They had enough real concerns to worry about. Only the last two meals remained. Someone would have to find more food, or else they needed to rejoin the main sericlave. Laytha hadn't been able to hide the food situation any longer and decisions needed to be made. Elissa did not look forward to the making of them as the silhouettes of the group closed in on their pool of light.

⋎ ⁂ ⚶ ♏ ✦

'We should go back out. Maybe *They* have gone and we can leave.'

Elissa wasn't surprised at the voice. The long-haired girl had not yet developed the patience that came with age and waiting out the awldrin many times.

'We can't all return at once. A few of us should check things out to begin with,' Laytha said. 'Hut five, how many of you live there? It's closest to the other huts and easiest to blend in from.'

From the other side of the group, a quiet voice answered. 'There are four of us. Two can return easily enough.'

Elissa heard the low murmur of voices, then two shadows separated from the group and left the chamber. She sighed quietly with relief. Lack of food was bad and the itching in her head was annoying, but being the first out when your daydreams were telling you that it was you personally *They* were after, was very unnerving.

She could deal with accidents, and arguments didn't faze her either. Even hunger was an opponent she had beaten many times in the past, but taking on an awldrin was beyond her; they were the one thing that frightened her.

The temptation to leave through the tunnel with Laytha had come more than once. They could see if the sericlave had started on the soil and whether Rains had arrived yet – they could slip out and blend in.

Two things held her back. It was a long way down to the fields, and hiding from both above and below whilst hobbling and less than agile would be hard. She desperately needed her mobility back. Vulnerability was not within her usual range of feelings, and Elissa hated it. She cradled the sticky coated shoes in her hands, glad she'd brought them. They gave her a goal. As frustrating as it was, waiting for others to take action first, it was the right choice. Getting fit to work had to be her main objective.

Elissa continued her new habit of walking circuits of the cavern. She ran her fingers over the spines of the books, along the walls, and across the small chambers. It would probably only take a few more circuits before she could work out where in the chamber she was, just by feeling a short section of wall. But she would walk, and the shard would come out – it wasn't much of a plan, but better than nothing.

The women from hut five had been gone for a while, and tension in the chamber was rising to a palpable level. Hut five's two remaining women sat at the other side of the room, waiting on the signal indicating it was safe to return.

Elissa began yet another circuit. The part that went past the books was her favourite section. There must be so many answers in those books, vast amounts of lost history. Where had they come from? Why could they only eat the crops they grew or planted from their stores and nothing wild grown? Everyone who ate wild vegetation had fallen very, very ill. Wild-caught meat was no good either. Only occasional creatures like the sprill seemed tolerable to them.

Tap-tap tap tap tap tap tap.

Elissa rejoined the others and sat alongside Laytha once more as the woman began her report.

'They stopped searching two days ago, and the last awldrin left today, so it should be safe to return. The work parties headed out to the fields this morning to begin breaking ground. Rains has not arrived, but immense clouds are finally building on the horizon.' She paused, peering at them all in the dim light. 'If we want to get into those parties, we need to be out there as soon as we can.'

'So should we go back tonight?' another woman asked.

Silence fell, and she realised they were waiting for an answer. Elissa glanced up to see who they were looking at, momentarily thinking they were waiting for a response from her, but it was Laytha they all faced. As the most senior of them, she was the most respected. In the dim light, Elissa saw her rub the back of her neck, which usually indicated Laytha was deep in thought.

'Yes,' she said eventually. 'We won't come back for another day or two. Elissa's injury makes her too conspicuous and will hinder her getting selected for crop teams. She needs rest. The sericlave is used to a phased return, so we'll be last out and seal up either tomorrow or the morning after. Take care of each other. Let us hope not to return here any time soon.'

Elissa bit down the urge to argue and scream that she needed to go back, that she could prove that she was fit. But Laytha was right. The idea of the whole Rains season working on the bellows, trapped in the cavern, made her feel sick. She needed to recover, fast.

The others slowly gathered their belongings and melted away toward their sleeping chambers. They would pack up, ready to move home to their normal nooks and to their repetitive, recurring existences. Still, she envied them the chance of true daylight.

In the crystal dawn of the next morning, there were only a few of them left, and soon afterward, Elissa and Laytha were alone. Finally, confident in not being overheard, Elissa shared her experiences of the first day.

Laytha jumped to her feet as soon as Elissa finished talking. 'Show me.' She paused before running to the wall of books. 'Shall we take a book?'

'What? Why?'

'Because if we take one, we could look at the pictures when we reach the end. You'll need a break when we get there, Elissa. You're tough, but there's no point in pushing yourself. You need to get fit.'

'Then I want to take one particular book,' Elissa said. The anticipation of feeling something other than fear or pain for the first time in days caused her to break out in a big grin. 'Every time I walk past it, I can feel the cracked leather shapes on its spine. I want to see what's in it.'

'Then let's find it!' Laytha said. 'Show me.'

Elissa got to her feet carefully and walked along the book wall; she moved quickly, pushing her weight to the outside of her foot as she walked and ran her fingertips across their spines until they found the book she was after.

'I've got it.' Elissa pulled the book out, and Laytha took it from her.

'You concentrate on walking. Lead on.'

Elissa followed the wall back to the passageway. She aligned her hand on the smooth right wall, and they walked quietly as she felt for the carved doorway. It was a lot farther from the main cavern than she realised before her fingers found the stippled texture that had caught her attention previously. 'Feel this,' she said.

Laytha ran her hands over it. 'Oh, I wish I could see it! It feels as though it's a picture.'

'I thought that too. There are small carvings.' Elissa moved Laytha's hand. 'This one has wings, I think.'

They felt around the door, trying to make sense of the patterns, finding other animals and what they thought might be plants. But neither of them could work out how it opened.

From far down the passage, toward the outside of the mountain, a singing voice broke their focus. The hairs on Elissa's skin stood on end.

'Laytha,' she whispered. 'The walls … the balls!'

They stood in silence, frozen against the stone as the balls began to glow weakly. A shadow moved toward them, tall and indistinct. The singing stopped abruptly as it neared them.

'Why are you in the dark?' the voice called.

Elissa's knees almost buckled, but she stood tall, leaning on the wall for support. It was him. The voice from her dream who told her he was coming to help her; the one who'd told her she was being hunted. If he was real, then what did that mean about the other things he'd said?

As he closed in on them, they could see he was human. His fitted clothes were of a quality matching those of the awldrin. No tattered rags in sight. His broad shoulders and build spoke of athleticism.

He pulled his cloak hood back and stared directly at Elissa. The man appeared well-nourished and healthy – more so than anyone she'd ever met.

'We meet again. But seriously, why the darkness? Where's the rest of the sericlave?'

He peered at the symbol on the door, clearer in the dim light, and his eyebrows rose. 'You want to go up there? Are you mad? That's the route to the awldrin accommodations, according to my map.' He unfurled a small map showing what

Elissa presumed was the layout of their passage and others connected to it. It showed the nooks with a big empty cavern beyond them, but no huts or houses. The exit from the sericlave cavern was also missing from the map. She pointed at it.

'That's where everyone else is. Everyone except us.'

'Why are they all hiding?' He studied Elissa with one eyebrow raised. 'Your hair? It's not ...'

'It's just messy,' she blurted. 'Nothing special.'

The stranger frowned. 'Nothing special? I spoke to you. What are you doing? Why are you hiding your gift?'

'Gift!' choked Laytha. 'We are Untouched. You must know that, and you are being unacceptably cruel to make light of it. Speaking of which, why are you in *our* caves with a map and acting as if you know Elissa?'

He stood in the fully lit passageway and looked at them one at a time, studying them, really taking them in.

'You're serious, aren't you? You have no idea.' To Elissa, he said, 'Please tell me you've at least kept the crystal safe.'

Elissa laughed, breaking the tension. 'The one in my foot or the one around my neck?'

'There are two?'

So, she knew at least one thing he didn't. 'Strictly speaking, there was one, but I stood on it.'

'That explains both the red tint and the fact that I could find you easily. You must have blood-bonded to the crystal accidentally.' He spoke so casually of things that meant nothing to her: blood bonding and gifts, speaking to him in her dream ...

'Red tint?' Elissa crossed her arms and glanced over at Laytha, who nodded and continued to watch the man intently.

'Our crystal got a faint red tint along the edge where presumably it matched with yours once. We were worried in case you caused a tint on any awldrin sections too,' he said. 'It's why we reached out as soon as we found you.'

'We?'

'The elders of Shardeep.'

Laytha crossed her arms and strode closer to him, staring up at the man. 'Shardeep? I thought we were the only humans. How are you so well-dressed? Are you in league with your awldrin in Shardeep?'

The man chuckled. 'In league? There are no awldrin anywhere near Shardeep. The only ones we know of live here. We are just a normal human sericlave. We may be small, but we stick to the old ways – something Dragonsbreath has clearly forgotten about.' He rolled his shoulders and grimaced as he adjusted the weight of a bag. 'Can we find somewhere to sit or eat? I've been travelling for days.'

'If we go deeper, it gets darker. The light will fade soon,' Laytha said. 'We should head back closer to the way you came in.'

'Darkness isn't a problem. Now I know we're alone, I can do something about that.' The stranger reached upward. As his fingers touched one of the glass spheres, he sang a single note. The ball under his hand sprung to life, vibrant and bright. The strange symbol on the door and the entwined animals illuminated clearly for the first time in hundreds of cycles.

Both women gaped. Then Elissa laughed. What started as a small chuckle soon became a full belly laugh, and she gasped for breath as she spoke.

'You mean we've sat in almost total darkness for our retreats all these years, and all we had to do was sing?' It was such a crazy idea that once she started laughing, she couldn't stop. Laytha looked at her as though she was mad, then slowly her own mouth twitched, and she joined in.

The stranger could do nothing but stand and wait. Elissa wondered what he must think of them. Two tired, scruffy women who, rather than being upset at discovering things were not as they had assumed, laughed uncontrollably.

He stood quietly while they tried to regain their composure. Elissa watched him out of the corner of her eye. The man appeared kind. He'd told her he was coming, and then had been true to his word; he knew things they had forgotten as a sericlave. Elissa regained a modicum of control and nodded. He had a map. There was little point in refusing the man.

'Let's take him back,' she said to Laytha. 'I want to see that chamber lit up.'

Laytha held Elissa's gaze and smiled. 'So do I, but,' she turned to speak to the stranger, 'you should know that here, we are forbidden to be alone with men. That we are classed as cursed or Untouched by our community. Most of our elders would not take you seriously should we take you to them. With respect, I would request that you keep yourself hidden until we know more of both you and your singing.'

The man nodded. 'I understand. I will not endanger you.'

⊤ ※ 类 ⅏ ✦

As reality sank in, Elissa wavered between worry and excitement. The idea of seeing all the books and their pictures, to see what secrets they hid, was enough temptation to let him in. They walked back to the cavern in silence, bar the occasional lighting of a new ball, and each time he sang, it drew her back to his strangeness – his warning. Others were hunting her, and the itch at the back of her mind inflamed further.

The stranger stopped after one lighting and consulted his map. He pointed to a door to his right. 'There used to be two work areas down there. Do they still exist?'

'I don't know. I stuck to following this tunnel. This is only the second time we've used it.' Elissa ran her hand across the door. Its silent, stone presence a reminder of the hidden secrets in the tunnels. 'I didn't even realise there *was* a door in the dark.'

He nodded. 'I'll check them out later, then.'

'Not without us,' Laytha retorted. 'How do we know what you're after? What you might find? Today, we discover we're not the only sericlave left. For all we know, you might want to exploit us for resources. This season has been hard and long. No, I think you return with us first and explain what you want from Elissa and why she interests you so very much.' She planted her hands on her hips, daring him to argue.

He didn't say a word.

'Once we hear what you have to say,' Laytha continued, 'then we will decide what to do next.'

Elissa studied his face, but he didn't react at all to the tirade. No signs of stress or guilt crossed his features. He merely inclined his head to Laytha respectfully and gestured for her to lead the way.

They approached the main chamber, walking by the dim light of the lumina alone. Elissa gestured for him to stay round the corner, hidden from sight at first. But as she adjusted to the darkness, she saw it was clearly empty. One of the others must have returned while they were walking and had kindly left them a small pile of rations in the centre of the room. On tapping the pad, they heard no reply.

'You can light a couple of the balls at this end of the chamber,' Elissa said.

'We call them glow globes,' he replied. As he lit up the room, Elissa winced from the brightness before she noticed, for the first time, the deep red of the walls.

A faded rainbow of books in all sizes and colours sat arrayed on the shelves. Two upright bars she'd encountered in her wanderings appeared to have been a ladder once. The small alcoves they'd slept in were painted with flaking and faded green and black decor. Elissa raised her eyes to the ceiling; the marbled smoothness and its white crystal pattern were gorgeous. Light reflected off the tiny crystals, casting splashes of light against the walls. It was beautiful.

'You set up in the main chamber of records? Where have you been sleeping?' The man was walking along the shelves, touching books gently. He pulled one out and opened it, then studied it for a moment. 'How can you not know your own history when all these books are so well-preserved? Our records are nothing compared to this!'

'No,' said Elissa, reluctantly bringing her gaze down from the ceiling. 'Let's start with you. Your name and why you were so desperate to find me.' She sat on the floor to ease her foot and gestured for him to join her. 'I'd also really like to know how you got inside my head.'

⊤ ⁕ ⚙ ⚙ ✦

He folded himself into a seated position and smiled. 'My name is the easy bit,' he said, placing his hand on his heart. 'I am Rossi. We need you, Elissa Shard-Bonded, to get home.' He paused, and when they said nothing, he continued. 'Several hundred cycles ago, we were part of an established trade and travel agreement with two other realms, Lieus and Mythos. Strictly speaking, we did little trade with Mythos, but to reach Lieus, we had to pass through it. Lieus is where our people are from. You can see it on a clear night – the green and blue planet in the sky.'

'Our people?' asked Elissa. They were from that green planet? She leant forward, trying to hide her eagerness to hear more.

'On Lieus, with powers and knowledge, we ruled and prospered. It was a green and fertile land. Those with your gift and mine have power deep inside and were trained to use it and channel our energies through song. We could walk in dreams, plant ideas and suggestions in minds. We had everything.'

'Then the awldrin arrived with their own unique abilities. They communicate with certain animals and many had incredible strength. They don't age as long as they can access a rock called staramine. Over time, they had mined all the stores here, so they traded for it with Lieus. It was a successful partnership for a long time, until in Lieus, the occupants noticed that some plants and animals seemed to be drifting through the gates and growing there, too, affecting the local wildlife.'

'The influx of awldrin into Lieus was not sudden. They moved gradually and built a home in the mountains. A sprawling mine well away from the main cities where they extracted staramine and sent it back here. Everything started going wrong when they decided to use humans to do the work. Despite the wonders they'd begun to create alongside magic users here, they regarded the normal humans of Lieus as beneath them.'

'In response, the most powerful members of our community banded together and called themselves the Souls of Dal. They worked in secret and honed their talent, practiced making weapons with plants and animals they hoped would be toxic to awldrin. Over time, they developed a range of effective battle tactics. One of which used whole gems of echoglass from their Gateway to pour magic into, creating a deep, powerful sound which could be amplified enormously. Filled with emotion, it could elicit fear and terror in all nearby – or so the histories say.'

Elissa hung on every word Rossi said while Laytha paced around them. She stopped in front of him. 'So if these Souls of Dal were so powerful, what are we doing here now and why aren't the awldrin working for us?'

'The Mythese acted.' Rossi shrugged. 'So, no one won. The war raged for years. Small skirmishes mostly, but it was ever-present. Those who live on Mythos were getting fed up of living on a war staging post and watching the two realms tear each other apart. They came here and melted the Aulirean Gates into the mountainside. They shattered and spread the echoglass that powered them all over Tebein, and as a result, they trapped us.'

'Were the Mythese not trapped too?' asked Elissa.

'No. Dragons do not need the gates to pass between Realms. In fact, it is likely that they made them in the first place as they are the only beings who can travel freely.'

Elissa's head was reeling. 'So this shard I found is one of these ancient relics, these bits of echoglass?'

'Yes, and you have inborn power yourself through your blood. All those with lilac hair have it. By stepping on the shard and blood-bonding to it, you have also made yourself visible to anyone searching for you or it. May I see it?'

Elissa reached inside her tunic and pulled out the large crystal. It was as long as her finger and as wide as two fingers together. In the illuminated chamber, its contents appeared to swirl, yet it didn't reflect any of their surroundings.

Laytha looked at it, her eyes wide. 'It's beautiful!'

'You've seen it now,' Elissa said to Rossi, tucking it back inside her clothes. He wasn't getting to hold it. Not yet. 'You've given us a lot to think about. Thank you, but I think I need to sleep on it. Tomorrow, I want to study those books. If what you said is true, there will be evidence to back it up.'

Rossi nodded. 'I'll sleep in one of the other rooms off this chamber. The glow globes will go out on their own without being reactivated. It's been a long ride to find you. I can't guarantee you're safe now I am here, but I can promise I'll help.' He left them alone and wandered across the cave into a small chamber.

'Elissa, we have light. We should try to remove the shard from your foot.'

Laytha was right. Elissa unwrapped her foot and crossed it over her lap. 'Have you got anything left in the vial?' she asked. Laytha wandered over to their bags as Elissa twisted herself to investigate the sole of her foot. 'And something sharp,' she called as she gently poked the wound. 'Maybe we can persuade it out.'

The edges of the wound were clean, and it had stopped bleeding. The finger-length wound ran along the length of her arch, and she tried to pull the sides apart gently to see if there was a glint of the shard inside.

'I can't see it,' she muttered. 'It has to be in there somewhere. I can feel it.'

Laytha's shadow blocked the light as she crouched next to her. 'Let me see.' After poking and prodding at Elissa's wound, she glanced back up, her brow deeply furrowed. 'Are you sure it hasn't come out? There's nothing there. I can see all the way to the top of the wound – there's no shard.'

'I can feel it! When you poked it, it pushed into my foot.'

'That doesn't make sense – it's healed below it already. I don't know what to say, Elissa. If I dig around more, I might damage other parts of your foot. Maybe these other women can magic it out when you get there.'

'Fine. I'll have to just manage until then,' Elissa replied. Rossi had claimed it took days to get here. She'd already walked on the foot for days by that point, so what were a few more?

Laytha enveloped her into a hug. 'You always do.'

CHAPTER 13

DARIN

*Gaudy ornamentation is not the way of those who
live in Redpike. Yet they live life in a riot of
colours, as if in deliberate counterpoint to the
sternness of the mountain and the black castle
on top. The colours come from the plants and
paints, as well as the silks and cloths worn by
its occupants.*
A Traveller's Guide to Caldera

The sibling moons graced the sky in a rare show of togetherness. Darin looked up at them with fresh eyes; there really were dragons on Mythos, he knew that now. The smaller, more distant black disk of Tebein shimmered occasionally. Humans lived there, too, once. It was almost impossible to comprehend – Gates that let people travel between the moons and dragons that could fly there if they chose. Had they ever been back? Since the Gates closed, had dragons visited other continents of Lieus?

He imagined what his little brother would say if he knew dragons were real or that he could do magic.

'Come on. You'll fall over your feet if you keep staring skyward like a moon-struck fool.' Tralkion nudged Darin. Once they'd delivered the potions, there would be time to daydream with a spiced ale in his hand. Darin checked the potions in his bag one last time and followed Tralkion out through the main gates.

The swollen market bulged from alleyways, and temporary stalls filled every gap between the permanent traders of Redpike. Darin took it all in, noting which stalls he wanted to revisit. The older the stall, the more of its canopy was covered in plants. Some had such well-established floral canopies that they were more plant than man-made. The scent of flowers intermingled in the air. One old stall was covered in climbing plants of so many varieties that Darin decided he needed to return to it. If it had traded for long enough to grow such a thick canopy, then the food must be worth earning. Maybe he'd go there for supper later.

An array of coloured scarves floated on the breeze, dancing for Darin's attention; one in particular lifted higher than the rest. Embroidered birds spiralled upward as the scarf rose on the warm breeze. It would make a wonderful gift for his mother.

'Tralkion, is there a way for me to send something home?' he asked, eying the scarf.

'Of course. Leave it with the gatekeeper to sort out. It will be on the next rider to Eye.'

Darin hurried to catch up. He'd get that scarf once their jobs were done. 'How much can I tell them? I know I can't tell them everything. Not now I know what I am.'

'You're a long way from a So'Dal yet. Traders here have an understanding of the coloured bands on our robes, but they won't take your money.'

Darin had expected that. 'What should I call myself? When I introduce myself to earn a scarf or food.'

Tralkion paused in his stride. 'Or spiced ale ...' He winked. 'You're an apprentice. In herb lore, if you wanted to expand.'

'Are there many apprentices?'

Tralkion shook his head. 'No, and we only took one other this cycle who wasn't born to So'Dal parents.'

Darin, the apprentice So'Dal, walked proudly through the market with one of his masters, his head held a little higher. He hadn't realised how rare the opportunity was.

⟋ ⚝ ⚹ ⚶ ✦

They left the noise of the market behind as they walked through narrow alleyways to the first patient's house. Their first delivery was a potion for easing aching joints. Would it work as he watched? It had been the only one Tralkion had added a weft of magic to. The others were simple potions relying on the plant potency alone.

A young child answered the door of the small yellow house. She studied them for a moment, then smiled.

'Hello, Sho'Dal Tralkion,' she lisped through gaps in her front teeth. 'Da ish over there.'

The man warming himself by the hearth was still in his prime; tall and muscled, but his hands were gnarled, stiff, and blistered. Darin watched from a respectful few steps back as Tralkion knelt by the man's feet, then Darin pulled the vial from his bag and passed it to him.

'Master carpenter, the So'Dal regard your craftsmanship as the finest in Redpike. We heard of your returned affliction and bring a small token of our gratitude for your beautiful work. This will numb the pain for several tides, and my apprentice' –

Tralkion gestured at Darin, who once again felt a small glow of pride – 'will return with more in the future.'

'My thanks, So'Dal Tralkion, but please stop the formal address. Wilf does just fine – especially when you give my hands a few more tides of work to complete.' Wilf smiled as he took the vial in his gnarled hand and unscrewed the cap. He looked up at Darin. 'I'll see you again soon, young man. Do you have a sweetheart? I can make you a small token for them as thanks for your errands?'

Darin grinned. 'Thank you, but I only have a pet hound.'

The image of Star as an obedient pet elicited an emotional response from the hound, who was somewhere in the palace. The surprise must have shown on his face, as Tralkion smiled wryly at him.

'We should go. We have others to visit,' he said.

Wilf drank the potion and handed them back the bottle. 'I'll look forward to seeing you again.'

They closed the door behind them, leaving the carpenter and his child sat in the warmth.

'That potion makes you sleepy as it works,' said Tralkion. 'In a few hours, he will wake to improved hands, his swelling reduced, and hopefully, he can get back to doing what he loves.'

ᚣ � ✷

Tralkion handed over a vial of orange fluid to the next patient with a smile, and she took it gratefully. They walked a little farther to the last patient, who took their vial and gave Tralkion a small purse of coin.

As they began their walk back to the market, Darin itched to ask about the coin.

'Tralkion, I thought we didn't deal with money as So'Dal?'

'Where do you think the money for your parents and all the guards and other families comes from?'

'I assumed it was from the fees we pay to each crater's Witness house for registrations, and all the other small things they do for us, I suppose.' Darin realised he hadn't really thought about the details at all.

'Mostly, yes.' Tralkion patted the pouch. 'But we also provide extra services, those beyond the essential. Things like anti-aging or potions to help with more ... personal problems. Those, we charge for.'

Darin was desperate to ask for permission to explore and to get back to the stalls he'd seen earlier, but he held out – just. Outwardly, he showed calm patience, but in his pocket, he fiddled with a pebble to keep himself distracted.

'Thank you for your help, Darin. Enjoy your afternoon off,' Tralkion said as they turned into the market. Darin was released.

He didn't need telling twice and flashed a grin at Tralkion before he headed for the scarf stall. It was easy to find again, and to his delight, the birds still sailed on the breeze.

After asking for a price and admitting he couldn't yet make any potions to trade, Darin found himself weeding market stall footings and running errands. Much to his amusement, he saw Conor out the back, washing up in a bar, earning his own treats. Conor shot him a wink and called for him to return once he'd finished.

An hour or so later, and happily carrying the scarf, Darin returned to the Wandering Star. Conor sat outside at a street table with two tankards of warm ale. It didn't smell quite as amazing as the one at the market stall, but Darin accepted it gracefully and pulled up a stool.

'I saw you at that scarf stall and figured you might be a

while. Are you preparing for the new group of Soul Anchors arriving this tide?'

Darin chuckled. 'Everyone's a matchmaker! No, it's for my mother. I thought I'd let them know how I was doing and send her a gift. Being a So'Dal may not be what they had envisaged for me, but I'm beginning to like it. Well, all except the singing – and if me singing is rebuilding their inn, it's worth a sore throat. How's your training going?'

They spent the rest of their jugs discussing buildings and machines, some of which sounded almost magical in their own right. Conor was a great speaker, and Darin found himself engrossed in the visions his friend conjured with words.

As they mulled over their first few tides at Redpike, a huge shadow fell across the square. A giant bird-like creature flew overhead, heading straight for the palace.

Conor squinted at it. 'What's the garant doing here?'

'What's a garant, and … is it carrying people?' Darin squinted as the giant creature passed the sun. 'Should we go?'

'The garant is from South Crater,' replied Conor. 'The So'Dal Witness family there keeps one for emergencies. I've seen them send it out, but never knew where it went. Wild ones nest around Caldera, mostly in the Bare Plains.' He grimaced. 'Those garant are definitely not tame. I can't imagine anyone trying to harness one. In answer to your other question, yes, let's go and see.'

As they rose from their stools, *[A giant bird with three people on board]* superimposed itself on Darin's view. Star must be watching. He sent *[Himself walking through the palace gates]*.

He stumbled as his vision blurred repeatedly. Star sent image after image. After the third stumble, Conor took notice and grabbed Darin by the arm, guiding him.

'Are you always this poor at holding your ale?' he asked.

'Watcher's scales, no. I grew up in an inn. Drink isn't the problem – it's Star. He's too strong to block out, and he keeps sending me pictures.' Darin stopped walking and shook his head. It was ridiculous. He clearly needed to practise walking and sending more often. 'It's got three people on its back. One woman and two men – one man is injured.'

⁂

They struggled through the crowd drawn by both the old market stalls and the garant and waited by the palace's portal gate. The guard captain waved them through.

'Darin, you'd better get in fast. That hound of yours has been roaming the courtyard, unsettling the bird.'

Darin and Conor ran to the hound paddock while Darin concentrated as hard as he could on persuading Star to come to him. Thankfully, he eventually did, with his tongue lolling daftly from one side of his muzzle.

The So'Dal surrounding the garant were able to calm it down and allow the passengers to dismount. Had Star been that much of a nuisance? The Anchor glanced toward him, and rather than draw any more attention from her, they retreated behind the arch to watch from a distance.

Two passengers wore So'Dal robes. One was hooded, the other not; he was older, maybe Hal's age. His face was pallid and his robe ripped across the shoulder. As he moved, he favoured that side.

The third passenger was a young woman with her hair tied in a blue wrap. She surveyed the courtyard wide-eyed as she fiddled with her straps. When her eyes rested on Star, then him, he smiled. It seemed the right thing to do if Star had stopped them dismounting. She frowned at him, then her eyes slid past.

The Anchor glided over to the group.

'We should move away from it,' Conor said. 'How about you show me that glow globe you made last night?'

'I'd love to!' Darin replied, sending *[Star in their room]*.

Star ran ahead as they walked through to the hound paddocks, the garant already forgotten.

Darin took a quick glance back. He couldn't see the visitors any more – just the garant, its head dropping with exhaustion while So'Dal fussed around it. What was that all about?

Chapter 14

Suriin

Copper-brown feathers grace the sky,
Clouds and mountain peaks we pass by.
Rare to see, ride with me.

To send our message by Golden's grace,
Her beating wings send her at pace.
Rare to see, ride with me.
Children's rhyme from South Crater

Suriin sat astride the garant, her legs locked into the leather harness straps, unable to move. Her father sat in front, his hands rested either side of the garant's neck as he communicated with the bird. Fatigue overcame him again. He wilted – softness crept into his core, his shoulders stooped, and his head dropped unsteadily.

'How long?' she whispered over her shoulder.

'Long enough to be a problem,' replied Ronin quietly. 'You see the mountain range? It's the dark one in the middle.'

The blackened peak rose from the bristle of mountains

ahead. Thank the Watcher – she'd hoped that was Redpike. It was still a long way off, but at least their destination was finally in sight.

'The palace is built into the mountain. I am sure your mother will have sent word ahead, and someone will be waiting for us.'

Suriin was certain she would have. The garant flew unsteadily over the top of a sprawling crater town, its sloping floor rising to meet the rim of the Surface. Faat pulled carts, and skaa-rak ran beneath their shadow along the black stone path to Redpike Mountain and its town. Fortified inns provided refuge from the Surface, and the undergrowth was cut back a long way from both sides of the path.

Suriin glanced back up at her father. His head was lolling. He was using his own dwindling reserves to keep the bird in the air, to will it on.

They'd be forced to land soon, or Yorynn would fall asleep and the garant would land anyway, too far from the help he desperately required.

'He needs it,' Ronin whispered. 'You're going to have to help me again.'

The exhausted garant eased its tired wings into a glide. It descended as Yorynn's head did, his hold on it sliding away.

Suriin felt a hand on her neck as Ronin reached up under her scarf. For the second time since they left Nameless, he sang, quietly and insistently.

She reached for her father. A fingertip touch. Gently, carefully, she allowed the music to pass through her, adding a quiet echo of the melody. She hoped and willed her father back to health and consciousness as she passed the weft forward. His head rose again; the garant rose with it, and they were back on the ascent toward Redpike. The relief that they had kept him awake just a little longer, despite his obvious need to rest, was bittersweet.

The mountain range grew from a bristle on the horizon to towering peaks, and the Black Palace peeked out from the top of the town, its towers nestled snugly against the mountainside. They passed low over the town walls. Bright market stalls flashed past as the crowded streets rose to meet them. The garant skimmed over rooftops, wing beats slowing to a glide. They barely cleared the walls of the Black Palace and passed so close to the So'Dal flag, Suriin could have grabbed it.

ᛉ ※ ※ ※ ✦

With a careful back-beating of wings, they landed gently in a courtyard. Suriin fought to release her harness so she could help her father with his. A tall moonhound barked nervously at them while it evaded capture, and the garant hopped agitatedly until the moonhound was restrained. Ronin beat Suriin to the ground and was assisting Yorynn by the time she'd fumbled the buckles off.

Her father looked as pale as he had two days prior, just after the xotryl attack. He favoured his shoulder and stood unsteadily. A tall So'Dal strode across the courtyard and tucked an arm under his, while a tall woman glided behind him, accompanied by a moonhound. She appeared younger than Suriin's mother, with a distinct aura of authority.

Suriin watched her approach and found her gaze coolly returned. She must be the Anchor herself; they had indeed been expected. The Anchor gestured, and the courtyard sprang to life. People ran forward, carrying water for the garant, and the loose moonhound was taken through an archway by two men who ran into the courtyard and caught it. She watched them go. The one in robes stared back at her for a moment.

'Nissa, thank you for your assistance. I'm sorry to bear such dire news and be in an ill state,' her father whispered, leaning heavily on Ronin and the other So'Dal.

The Anchor placed a hand reassuringly on his shoulder. 'Don't be sorry. You're here now. You made good time from Nameless, despite having an extra passenger.'

Suriin flinched at the look shot her way as Nissa continued. 'Your Soul Anchor didn't mention a third in her dream walk? I anticipated the garant would be bringing just yourself and your apprentice.'

Nissa waited for a response as Suriin saw her father struggling. He twisted his body, unable to turn his head. He met Suriin's eyes and looked pointedly at her, gesturing with his right eyebrow that she should step forward.

Subtle as ever, she thought.

'This is my daughter, Suriin. Events,' – he paused, looking at Suriin directly – 'led to me bringing her several tides earlier than she was due. It would appear, however, not too soon for her gifts.' A wry twist at the corner of his mouth indicated a conversation for later. She wasn't sure if the comment was aimed at herself or the Anchor.

Suriin bowed her head in greeting. Embarrassed by the introduction, she felt her cheeks heating. The Anchor's eyes bored holes in her scarf, and Suriin wanted to be anywhere else other than the centre of the courtyard. It felt as though there were people hiding behind windows and in shadowed corners, staring at her.

Suriin stood tall. She was above average in height, but the woman made her feel tiny. She moved closer to her father, and he leant heavily on her, freeing the two So'Dal for a moment to discuss something in low, murmured tones.

'Can we get my father indoors? He needs rest and food.

He's flown this garant without a break and is still weak from the attack,' Suriin said.

Nissa nodded. 'It's fortunate, Yorynn, that you had previously met the garant, and she was willing to carry you. Otherwise, you might not have made it. Now, an apprentice healing – even one from your apprentice – will need checking to ensure it is clean and complete.' The Anchor turned toward the tall tower with its star flag flapping merrily in the breeze. 'I have both food and a bed prepared. Come with me.'

Suriin took her father's weight on her shoulder, and they followed. He managed a few staggering steps before his knees gave way and he crumpled to the floor, despite her best effort to hold him up.

'Help!' she called, and Ronin dived forward to take the other side. Suriin was gently moved aside to make way for the big So'Dal. Together, the two men made a chair with their arms and lifted her father from the ground, carrying him through the tower door ahead of the Anchor at a jog.

ㅜ ※ ㉆ ㉓ ✦

They allowed her to stay with her father as he slept. Pink curtains across an open window reached for him with gossamer fingers on each breath of the mountain breeze, and the green moon hung low on the horizon. Her father's icy-grey complexion contrasted sharply with the warmth of the room's colour palette. Ronin sat in the opposite corner of the room. He'd not left them aside from a quick chat with the So'Dal, Hal, who'd helped them on arrival. They hadn't talked to each other, and as yet, neither of them had slept.

Before they left the cave in Nameless, he'd told her she should never mention helping him weft. That she could only do it because she was unbonded, and it would cause serious trouble for both of them if someone found out that she'd used her power, untrained. Having to help him twice afterward was even worse, given what she then knew, but the garant wouldn't let Ronin fly it and totally ignored Suriin, so it had given them little choice.

⚜

A group of Gardeners had been in to see her father too. They'd huddled around the bed and poked and prodded the wound while he slept. She shuddered at the memory of his shoulder when they checked it. If she were to open his shirt, the black poisoned spider of veins would be back, leaching his life force with its toxins.

The weight of her eyelids eventually won the war against her will, and Suriin fell asleep on her chair, only to wake moments later on the floor. The thud of her face on the rug had drawn Ronin's attention, and he chuckled.

'Go and sleep!'

Indignantly brushing her clothes smooth and trying to appear as dignified as an exhausted teenager who just fell off her chair could, she knew her response was petulant, but the words slipped out.

'Where exactly am I supposed to sleep? You told me to sleep alone. I've nowhere to go aside from here, and I don't want to leave my father.' Suriin watched realisation dawn on Ronin. He stood smoothly, to her irritation. How could he do that after the journey and all that wefting? He must be tired, too, surely.

Ronin strode to the carved, painted wall next to her. It was decorated with deep, rich colours and highlights of gold. He pushed a gilded disk at the central point, and the panel slid sideways, vanishing into a channel between the neighbouring walls.

'When you get in, push the gold disk on the other side to

close it. I am sure they'll give you quarters with the other apprentices over in the main peak soon. You won't stay in here,' he said, before returning to his seat.

Suriin tried to stalk into the neighbouring room but almost tripped over the sill with exhaustion. Two falls in as many minutes would be ridiculous. Not that she cared what Ronin thought, except that he would tell her father. But he'd also saved her father, with her help. Even though she couldn't tell anyone she had helped, which was disappointing. It would have made a good conversation opener.

⛋ ※ ✖ ⚒ ✦

It turned out that Ronin was right, and before her father woke up, Suriin was reluctantly taken to her new room.

Her small bag of belongings was on the bed awaiting her. She sat next to it and took in her surroundings. The bed was comfortable, and unlike the room in the Star Tower, there was a solid wooden door that swung on heavy hinges – far more normal. When Suriin looked at it from the edge, she spotted a thin band of stone sandwiched between the wooden panels. There was her dream protection.

Suriin unpacked her washing items and took her scarf off, draping it over a hook by the door. When her mother arrived, she could help her choose more scarves and would heal her father. Suriin hoped she was coming soon. She missed her steady presence and, after the last few days, she'd give anything for a hug from either of her parents.

A big mirror hung next to a nightstand with a glow lamp on it. She tapped the lamp, but nothing happened. She sang the note that her lamps at home worked with – still nothing. Then saw the note scribbled on a scrap of paper. Relieved and thankful for the singing lessons her mother had insisted on, she lit it and closed the door.

Finally alone, Suriin collapsed on the bed and shed tears born of exhaustion and fear. Her father was still not awake; maybe her help had caused his condition to be worse than it should be. The birth of a gnawing guilt chewed at her. If she'd not caused them to leave early, then the xotryl might not have been there. Had her dream walk called the creature to them?

She was filled with the realisation that she'd endangered him with another of those animals only days before. How close might it have been for her and Gwynn if her father hadn't saved her, not just once, but twice in the same tide? Looming over everything, rode the frustration that she had no idea how he was, and she was sequestered far from the tower, surrounded by strangers. It wasn't the entry to Redpike that she'd dreamed of for most of her life.

A thump on the door intruded on her misery. She pulled the pillow over her head and ignored it. The thumping repeated. Suriin turned her back on the door.

When it happened for a third time, she shouted, 'Leave me alone!'

Suriin listened to the muffled voices, unable to make out the conversation, then silence. She was alone with just her thoughts for company while her stomach churned itself into nausea. Suriin had no way of knowing how he was – could she even find her way back up to that room through the maze of tunnels?

'What would he want me to do?' she wondered aloud. She sat up and sighed. 'He wouldn't want me sitting here like a moonstruck farbrox, that's for certain. I'm here to learn, and I will make him proud.' As she approached the mirror, Suriin could see how red-rimmed and swollen her eyes were.

She poured a little water out of a jug on the nightstand. It smelt fresh, so she splashed her face, then retrieved the sketchbook from her bag before tucking it into the long pocket of her dress.

Suriin puffed out a small breath to focus herself and tried to retie the scarf. She didn't think she needed to wear it inside the palace, but her father had given it to her, so it felt like having a bit of him with her. Several botched attempts later, Suriin decided to drape it over her head and threw the ends round her neck and over her shoulders.

⋎ ✳ ⚳ ⚸ ✦

Her room was not the only one in the corridor, and each had a unique pattern engraved on the door. Suriin traced her design with her fingertips, committing the plant engraved on it to memory.

She had a notepad – why was she trying to learn one of a hundred patterns? Shaking her head at her own folly, she took it out to copy the picture. The flower wasn't one she recognised, with its long petals and feathery leaves.

'It's pretty, isn't it?'

Suriin turned. The speaker was tall, elegantly clothed, and maybe a year or two older than herself.

'There's a much easier way to get a likeness. Pass me your notepad.'

Suriin passed over her sketchbook, anticipating some magical trick. The woman took the pad and placed it carefully over the pattern, reached inside her own flowing dress, and pulled out a pencil. She rubbed it gently over the picture, and a likeness came through on the page.

Suriin's mouth twisted into a smile. She chuckled, and the woman smiled back at her. For the first time since arriving in the palace, Suriin relaxed a little. Shyly, she offered her hand.

'Hi, my name is Suriin.'

'Fresna.' The woman clasped it in both of hers. 'Have you eaten? I'm on my way to get food.'

'Thank you, I haven't eaten since ...' Suriin realised just how long it had been. 'Since yesterday. Yes, please, can we get food?' As if on cue, her stomach rumbled, and both of them laughed again. 'I guess I must be hungry!'

⋎ ※ ⚒ ⚎ ✦

Suriin ran her hand along the wall as they walked, feeling the textures of the staramine veins running through the smooth black walls. Most people were going in the opposite direction.

'Where are they all going?' she asked Fresna.

'The full moon market. They'll be getting ready for the evening's festivities.'

'But you are still ... Are you not ...?' Suriin stopped herself.

'I've already been this morning. My duties in the palace are this evening.'

They continued in companionable silence for a while. Suriin noticed a change in the wall. Smooth, carved rock gave way to black brickwork, and her footsteps tapped out on the tiled floor. Only in the presence of such a contrast was the silence of her steps in the tunnels so obvious. Suriin wondered how it was possible and mentally added it to her list of things to research.

⋎ ※ ⚒ ⚎ ✦

The smell of food assaulted her nostrils. Rich and fragrant, it was enough to make her mouth water. Long tables ran from end to end of the large hall, and small groups sat on benches along their length. Most people were dressed simply. A number of robed So'Dal gathered at the table furthest from their entrance, leaning in close and deep in conversation. Suriin saw the green robe-edging of Gardeners, mixed with the red of visiting Witnesses.

Sat amongst them were men with shaven heads, their gilt-edged hoods pushed back and the black So'Dal tattoos on their cheeks fully visible. She'd heard of the Collective from her father. Maybe one day, one would go to Golden for Gwynn; the thought brought a small smile with it. She'd love it if he showed talent! Then they could be together.

⚹ ✻ ✖ ✦ ✦

Suriin collected a plate of steaming meat and vegetables, then followed Fresna to a table along the centre of the hall. Surrounded by the buzz of quiet voices, Suriin engaged with her food like a starving hound. Gobbling it down with minimal decorum, she spared little energy to chat. Fresna was pointing out people and telling her what they did, but Suriin couldn't concentrate.

'I am so sorry! You'll have to repeat most of these names later,' she mumbled through a mouthful of vegetable.

A familiar face walked behind Fresna. Suriin opened her mouth to talk, but Ronin caught her eye and shook his head before he returned to a conversation with his companions – a group of men, all similar in age and with no noticeable banding on their robes. She watched him walk off, confused.

A short, soft-faced woman strode toward them. Her floor-length trousers flowed liquid blue as she moved, and her simply-cut tunic was tied in an ornate knot at the waist. She wore no scarf, and her short, dark lilac curls bounced as she approached them.

Fresna noticed her approach and straightened up, sitting a little taller – if that was even possible. Following Fresna's example, Suriin sat straighter as the woman approached. It seemed like a good moment to remember all the manners her mother had insisted on.

⁂

'Suriin, I presume,' the woman said. 'I'm Soul Anchor Aslin, and I'll be in charge of your training once the next cohort arrives. As you are rather' – she paused, resting a hand on her hip – 'unexpectedly early, you cannot begin training yet. I've therefore attached you to the kitchens for now. In your free time, you are welcome to explore the Women's Library. Fresna, once you return to your duties, please take Suriin with you if she's back. Chef will be expecting you both.'

'Of course, Soul Anchor Aslin.' Fresna inclined her head in acknowledgement, and they watched Aslin continue her almost unbroken passage past them.

'By the way, Suriin, you may visit your father now. He's awake,' she called back.

The forkful of food midway into Suriin's mouth retreated to her plate at speed.

'Which way is the Star Tower from here? Please, will you show me?'

Fresna nodded in assent as she chewed the last mouthful of her own meal. Suriin grabbed both plates and took them quickly to the washing pile.

As Fresna started toward the exit at the far end of the hall, Suriin took off at a jog across the dining hall to catch up, weaving through So'Dal and Soul Anchors alike. She muttered her thanks as they parted for her. The hall had a short passageway exit that ended in a gated arch into the yard, where she could see the Star Tower.

'Thank you,' she called back to Fresna whilst running toward the tower. 'I'll be back to help.'

'Don't worry. I'll let Chef know and find you later,' Fresna replied. 'I hope he's feeling better.'

So did Suriin.

CHAPTER 15

DARIN

*Deeper and deeper you walk. Deeper into the
library, and deeper into the knowledge of the
ages. The spiral stairs surround the central
pillar of knowledge, holding up the So'Dal
above all others.*
The Bond of Three

The glow globes dimmed, and Darin was plunged into the
musty darkness of night in the deep library.

'Every moonstruck night,' he muttered.

From the next carrel along, he heard a snort of laughter.
'You and me both, lad.'

The steady glow of a lamp illuminated the area, growing
brighter as the speaker approached Darin's carrel. The light
illuminated a haggard face, pale and drawn with age. He had a
So'Dal facial tattoo, but even faded and folded like a crumpled
drawing on the wrinkled face, Darin could see it was neither
the symbol of the Collective or the Gardeners. Age and knowledge were etched in the lines of his face, and humour danced a

jig on the speaker's lips, while his glow lamp illuminated pale eyes.

'When I was your age, I did the same thing. Course, I already had a pack. Knew my place.' He gestured toward the stairs. 'Need a guide out?' the old So'Dal asked. 'I've been losing myself in books since before you were born, so now I come prepared. This way, you won't be shouting for the librarians again.'

Darin cringed. He'd certainly done that a few times, but thought he was the only one down there when it happened. The old man had already turned and illuminated the spiral stairs that climbed the edge of the deep library.

'Books and hounds ... get one and the other becomes a companion for life,' the old man mumbled. 'As long as the life together lasts. Never got a Soul Anchor, I didn't. My hound was all I needed. Eyes, ears, and a stomach that's never happy with the amount of food you give them.' He half turned and called back, 'Am I right or am I right?'

Darin grabbed a book and hurried after the old So'Dal. Did he just say he'd had a hound? He said he had a pack too.

'I didn't think any other moonhound-bonded So'Dal lived in the palace,' he said, hoping to encourage more out of the man.

'The So'Dal, we still does, but our hounds, they run no more. Our pack has departed on its final hunt.'

They continued up the spiral, and Darin's legs ached from the pace. Despite his younger age, Darin struggled to keep up, and further chat was out of the question while they climbed. He snatched a breath as they reached the last turn, and just as he opened his mouth to ask that they slow a little, the So'Dal stopped.

The arch of the doorway loomed from the darkness ahead, with glow lamps embedded either side, quiet and dark.

'Go on then, lad. Let's have some light for the last bit.'

Darin gathered his calm and breath, feeling for the power in his core. He inhaled deeply then creaked out a note that just about flickered the globes to dim life.

'So ... you truly are one of us.' The old So'Dal sounded excited. 'Not a one amongst us hound-bonded So'Dal ever could sing well. Earned us our nickname – Howlers. Nothing to do with our hounds, all to do with our singing!' He chuckled quietly and continued up the rough steps.

Howlers? Darin had never heard of them. To be fair, he hadn't heard much about the So'Dal at all before he arrived, so another group within their ranks wasn't really a huge surprise.

The old So'Dal balanced a pile of books on one arm as he walked, like a child testing their limits. The man was odd, yet Darin felt drawn to him – there was something familiar about the man that he couldn't place.

The top floor of the library was still illuminated, and library keepers sat in a corner, deep in conversation with a group of Gardeners. The gestures of escalating frustration from both parties were easy to understand.

'They're still searching for a cure for that So'Dal who arrived by garant yesterday,' his companion said. 'Xotryl claws, I hear.' The old man shook his head sadly. 'Personally, I think they'll search until the Gates reopen. You'll work out how to find me when you have questions, and you'll have more than these books can answer.' He gestured around them. 'Let us as have already done the reading, help you.' With those parting words, he slipped away on silent feet into the staramine-veined corridor.

'That was all a bit strange,' Darin said, watching the old man vanish. It was good to know that other hound-bonded So'Dal were still in the palace. Maybe they could tell him how bonding might work with a Soul Anchor and her hound – or help him with the communication side of things. It didn't seem to work exactly the same for him as Lea, so some hints would be great.

Darin took one last glance after the man, then shuffled his way back at a relaxed pace toward the courtyard, stifling a yawn. He opened his eyes in time to dodge some So'Dal, who were deep in conversation as they walked. They were older – did they used to have hounds? He span around. No, they had green and red-trimmed robes. He racked his brain to remember if the Howler So'Dal had a trim. Why hadn't he thought to check?

He fought back another yawn. Darin had fewer dreams since Star had adopted him, that was for sure, but the bed in their room was really uncomfortable. It was his last night on that itchy, straw-filled mattress. He was so glad that Star was ready to leave the pack; sleeping in a private, quiet room without six large puppies making a heap of noise through an open door would be peaceful, although a little odd. It was surprising how quickly he had adjusted to their energetic, if loud, presence in his life.

Darin stepped over and around young pups as Star bent his head down to exchange greetings with younger pack members. While he waited for Star, he lit his glow lamp. It was so much easier than the library one, but he'd still managed it, and in front of the old So'Dal. The Master would be pleased.

He reflected on the old man's words as he fussed over Star and packed their few belongings. Just because he'd bonded to Star, why wouldn't he be able to sing? Surely, they were entirely different things? After all, he'd made the glow lamp, and Tralkion hadn't given up on him, nor the Master. It just took him longer to learn, that's all.

As he paddled and swam through the river of his thoughts, one jumped out at him. *How did the old So'Dal light his own glow lamp?* Darin hadn't heard him sing. The light had gone on after the library lights went out with neither word nor note. With that puzzling thought running through his mind and his moonhound's steady warmth by his side, Darin was claimed by sleep.

⁘ ⁘ ⁘

Curiosity continued to gnaw at Darin the next morning as Tralkion taught him a new poultice recipe. Despite the plants being perfectly blended into floral works of art, he found the simple weft to increase its potency nigh on impossible.

After several botched attempts, Darin flopped onto the bench more forcefully than intended. Wincing as he rubbed his tender behind, he finally broached the subject.

'Have you ever heard of the Howlers?'

Tralkion glanced sideways at him, pausing in his own preparations. 'The Howlers? I vaguely remember something to do with an old Edgelands patrol, if I recall correctly. I haven't heard of any active patrols out there in my time at the Black Palace, so it must be a long while ago – well over twenty cycles.'

Something to start with. 'How many So'Dal like me are there in the palace? Moonhound-bonded ones?'

'None I know of. I think you're the only one. I remember there used to be one who'd visit.' Tralkion touched his own tattoo of winding vines, which climbed up his cheek, as he talked. 'He had a howling hound tattoo and no outer robe trim ... oh.' He laughed. 'A Howler.'

'Howling hound?' Darin tried to picture the old So'Dal's face, but the marking had been too worn. 'How long since you last saw them?'

'Ten cycles, maybe more.' Tralkion rubbed a hand around the back of his neck. 'He must have been at least that much older than me. I had just started my Gardener training, much like yourself. He'd visit the old Anchor – the one before Nissa – then vanish into the palace. We'd never see him leave either, only ever arrive.' He paused, staring out into the garden. 'Which is really odd, now I think about it. He had a gigantic moon-hound, the biggest one I ever saw.'

Tralkion looked over at one of Darin's half-completed poultices. 'That's nicely built, well-layered. You'll make a great Gardener if you can master the wefts. I'll activate this one so it doesn't go to waste. Ask the Master to help you learn the weft, and then you can practise the colour sequence on your globe.'

Darin was proud of the poultices, so was glad they'd use at least one, but the continued problem with his wefting gnawed at him. Would he ever be a Gardener? He helped Tralkion clear up the rest of the mess and resolved to find the old man. He'd try the library again that evening once they'd moved rooms.

ⵔ ✳ ◈ ⵣ ✦

'How do I know this Howler is even still here?' he mumbled through a mouthful of stew a few days later. A berry popped as he spoke, leaving a trail of red spray across the table.

Conor raised an eyebrow. 'This, again? You tried the library, you've sat in the dark like a farbrox for the last three nights, and you haven't seen the man. Maybe he's left, or maybe you're missing something obvious.'

He wiped the spray up quickly before Soul Anchor Aslin swished past, then took another mouthful and chewed on the thought.

I've only met him once. How on the moons of Lieus am I supposed to find one person in a palace of hundreds.

'He knew who I was and said I'd know where to find him. But I don't. I'm treasure hunting with no clues.'

Conor shook his head, one side of his mouth curling in a

repressed smile. 'I think you've missed something. Who have you asked?'

'We've been through this. Just Tralkion and you. I don't want to go around asking about people who are apparently not here!'

'So you've still not asked the most important one?'

Darin felt blood drain from his face. 'The Anchor? No chance, Conor. She's not going to tell me where some old So'Dal lives, if she even knows. Anyway, she's always rushed and busy.'

He saw Conor check left and right, but wasn't prepared for the roll that hit him square between the eyes.

'You're such a moonstruck fool sometimes! Darin, you are searching for a Howler. A man bonded to a hound. Have you asked Staramine?'

'He's just a youngster,' Darin said, rubbing the spot where the roll had hit. 'You threw that way harder than you needed to.'

'A waist-height young hound who can smell things or, I don't know, talk to the other hounds. Can he do that?'

Darin thought about the conversations he had with Star – if they could be called conversations. They were still more like pictures, shared images or moments. Maybe Conor had hit on something, though, and it wasn't such a crazy idea.

'It's worth a try,' he conceded. 'It's got to be better than sitting in the library when Star sends that he is on my comfy new bed again while my backside is freezing on the carrel benches. I'll ask him.'

Conor fiddled with a small gadget as they walked, the clicking noise of its mechanisms punctuating their footsteps until they reached their corridor.

'He'll be on my bed, I guarantee it,' Darin muttered as they arrived at his door. They were greeted with a reclined moonhound, his legs flopped apart like a dog-shaped starfish. Star snored fitfully on his back, right down the middle of the bed.

Seeing his hound's big paws flopped at the ends of his ridiculously over-long legs always made Darin happy. He still had so much growing to do! Almost before he knew what he was doing, he buried his hands in the fluffy belly-hair to stroke his hound.

'Star.' Scratch, scratch on the hound's lean, lightly muscled stomach. 'Star …' A shove with his hands. 'Star!' Darin hung his sleeve next to the soft muzzle, its hem soaked in the dribbles of stew from lunch. A large weight of small moonhound rolled over at speed, tail wagging and … eww, was that drool on his sleeve? 'Star, I need your help,' Darin said, more for Conor, who was sat on the chair by the door.

'Go on. Betcha he knows.'

Darin concentrated hard, then sent *[The old So'Dal in a long robe]*. He tried to add all the details he could recall. On opening his eyes, he saw Star's tail wagging excitedly.

As usual, the response was as clumsy as his own, and Star sent Darin *[The same So'Dal, in the courtyard, playing with all the puppies]*. Another image replaced it almost immediately. It was very fuzzy, like a copy of a copied picture, the original details lost in time. But it was clearly him. *[The So'Dal was a lot younger and stood taller. By his side was an aged hound, almost shoulder height and proud.]*

'He knows him. Conor, you were right – he knows! Can you take me, Star?' He sent *[Himself and Star meeting the old man]*. It was a rough image, crude, but he hoped it would get the idea across. Star's tail whipped his face as he leapt off the bed and barked. 'We'll see you later,' Darin called to Conor as he chased Star out of his room. 'Don't wait up!'

Star led him down passageways, through the courtyard, and up along the palace walls. They rushed past bemused guards as Darin ducked under spears, shouting apologies as he went, then followed the wall around the top of the hound paddocks and away from the main buildings.

At the rear of the palace, where the wall merged into the mountain, was a small tower. Star ran through the wall as Darin slid to a halt in front of it. Confused, he reached forward, and his hand continued on through the wall. He felt a wet lick – at least, he hoped that was what he felt.

Staramine's head popped back out at chest height and sent *[An open archway with stairs. Staramine was standing on the first one while Darin stood outside the arch].*

'This wall isn't real,' Darin tried to convince himself. Maybe if he closed his eyes, he could pretend he wasn't trying to walk through a wall. He put one hand on Star's collar and let himself be guided through; a prickling sensation passed over him, then he stubbed his toe on something hard. He yelped in pain and opened his eyes to see he was at the base of the steps. Behind him was a perfectly clear archway. Darin stared out in amazement. Every time he thought he had a grasp of what the So'Dal could do, he discovered something new. He stuck his hand back out. It looked normal. But, under the middle of the arch, the prickling sensation cut across it.

Star started whining at him and running up a few steps, then coming back for him, so Darin followed.

The old So'Dal gave a wide grin as Darin and Staramine entered the room at the top of the stairs.

'Well, that took you longer than I expected, but you worked

it out in the end. You have questions. I see them burning in your eyes. Where do you want to start?'

'I'd like to know how you lit that lamp without singing, about the Howlers – are there any left? What did you do in the Howlers? Were you a separate class of So'Dal?' Questions tumbled out like a small avalanche.

'Well, best I show you rather than talk at you,' he said. 'Come with me, and we'll get started.'

He opened a small door into a mountain tunnel. 'You know, it's only because this Anchor forgot we still exist that she sent you for Gardener training. You should learn as much as you can before someone, somewhere, realises they have classed you wrong. It happens. We Howlers are rare these days.'

The passageway sloped slightly downward with a rough untiled floor. Once the door closed behind them, a whistle rang through the tunnel.

'It will get quite loud,' the old man said. 'And my hearing isn't what it was. We'll talk when we get there.'

He was right. The noise became almost unbearable as it echoed up the tunnel, and Darin struggled to resist covering his ears. Star sent *[pain]* to him, further amplifying his own discomfort, so he was grateful when the passage widened into a small chamber. As they entered, the noise died down to a bearable volume. Levers and pipes protruded through the wall.

'The back of the steam lift. Well, a part of it,' the man said, bringing his head close to Darin so they could talk.

He pulled open a door and poked his head through it. When the lift chamber was clear, he gestured Darin through. The prickle ran across his skin again, and when he turned around, he couldn't see a door, despite knowing it was there. How many of those things were there? More importantly, why hide them?

The hooded figure, ever-present on the lever, nodded in

greeting as he returned the lever to its upright position, clearly unfazed by people walking out of a wall. Darin started to walk toward the lift before realising his companion had stopped by another door. He had been there for tides, but he'd never noticed that door either. The day was getting crazier by the moment. The So'Dal dropped a clenched hand from his mouth and beckoned Darin over.

He pushed a button, and the door slid into the wall – just like the ones in the main castle. It must be an original tunnel. Water sprayed the floor from a small waterfall flowing down the wall to form a pool on the chamber side. Was that the source of the steam lift's water? The scent of brown earth and green moss permeated their surroundings like expensive perfume. Under the waterfall, light suddenly illuminated the running streams dropping to the chute near his feet. He glanced behind, and again, caught the lowering of a hand.

The path curved ahead, its pick-carved walls and rough stone underfoot didn't feel part of the castle; they were too rough, unpolished. They emerged into a large chamber where a musty scent replaced the fragrance of the waterfall.

Hide-curtained alcoves surrounded the room, a few of them pulled open. Inside the closest two, glow lamps sat on small tables, and inviting warm ochre walls offered a relaxing feel. Heat globes dominated a sort of fireplace in each room, and deep fluffy pelts on the ground added to the cosy feel.

His damp feet sunk into deep rugs on the floor of the main chamber, and he felt guilty for his wet boots. Dust particles danced in light lancing from channels – bored out, presumably, through the crater walls above. Star ran around the room, wagging excitedly and sniffing at chairs and tables gathered in small groups. A stones board sat between two stools, with a game underway. Darin moved closer to see what positions the pieces were in. He chuckled – red was going to win easily. He reached forward and slid a piece to the next role.

'Welcome home, Darin,' the So'Dal said, gesturing at the furthest room with its door open. 'It's all yours – and your hound's of course.'

'Mine? But I have a room in the palace,' Darin replied.

'And you'll want to keep it too. Better to be visible if you're being trained as a Gardener, and we're all too old to spar with you.' He chuckled. 'It's hard to attend lessons if you aren't there. We'll teach you to be unnoticed in time, but until Chase gets back, come and go as you wish.'

Darin looked around the room more carefully. There was a galley at the far end, and a couple more passageways led from the main room.

'You keep saying *we*, but there's no one else here. How many people live here? And what *is* here?'

His companion winked. 'Meet your new pack,' he said as three figures resolved themselves on the seats. Friendly faces greeted him as he stared in amazement. Star lolloped around the room, greeting the Howlers with puppy-like enthusiasm, and received many pats and scratches as a welcome. His happiness was infectious, and Darin began to relax.

'My name is Bones. This is Boulder.' His companion gestured to a small dark-skinned man who'd resumed his game of stones with concentration. 'His gaming partner is Waterfall – we usually call him Fall.'

Fall waved cheerily. 'Thanks for the move. That role will take him a while to respond to.'

'And this is—' Bones was interrupted as a firm hand gripped Darin's own. He met the hard eyes of a tall, broad So'Dal. He matched Darin in height, but unbent and younger, the man would have towered over him.

'My name is Aggi. Welcome to the Howlers, Darin. Our

names are given to us by our hounds. One day, Star will probably give you one. The name he uses to refer to you when he communicates with other hounds.'

'How do you know my name?' Darin asked, more bothered by that than their strange names.

'There aren't many new Howlers these days. Word gets about. The Watcher did a good job – hiding the magic of the So'Dal worked rather too well,' Bones replied. 'Not enough people come to trial any more. Less people, even less chance of a Howler. Look at how old we all are! It's been a long time. Of course, we noticed you.'

Aggi nodded slowly in agreement and returned to his seat. 'We've got old and can't keep up anymore. The responsibility's all been on Chase for too long. One Howler and his moonhound simply aren't enough to keep the Edgelands at bay. When Chase is back, he'll find out from his moonhound, Sandy, what your Howler name is – if Star has chosen one yet. It will be the one you'll eventually become known by outside these walls.'

'Thank you. I'm used to being Darin for now, though, if that's alright? You said, "Keep the Edgelands at bay?" But they haven't caused a problem for hundreds of cycles.' Darin tried to steer the conversation back to his questions.

Bones patted him on the back. 'Until Chase gets back and Sandy tells him anything different, Darin it is. You're right, of course. Everything has been quiet as far as anyone is concerned. That's our job, and it will be yours. We'll teach you the skills you need – ones they won't teach you out there. You won't find the tricks that make you a Howler in the library, either.'

'Why not? Surely if you're low on numbers, you could ask the Collective? They're fighters.' He sank to the floor, sitting on the rug with Star's head resting on his lap. Star was relaxed and happy. Darin scritched at his fur and was rewarded with a belly to rub.

'He's a lovely hound,' Boulder said. He moved his piece and sat with a triumphant smirk as Fall studied the board with a frown. 'The books we have here aren't in the main library. We guard the oldest books – the most dangerous ones. In return, we use a few of their tricks to allow us to do our jobs. The guards and Collective may guard the So'Dal against discovery, but we are the guardians of Lieus from the far bigger risk of the So'Dal themselves. Oh, and the occasional xotryl.'

Darin struggled to understand Boulder. 'So you don't count yourselves as So'Dal?' he asked finally.

'Yes and no. We're Howlers first. We can't use song as they can – if we could, we'd have far more power. Our magic is accessed differently.'

They let him sit quietly. There was no pushing, no questions; just an air of expectation. He studied the four old men, their faces turned toward him with hope writ across each, and then he saw it – the tattooed hound. Different bits of it remained in each of their cheeks, and like a jigsaw, they fitted together.

'How has no one noticed you're all still here? Isn't it easier just to destroy the books?'

'Because we like to be forgotten, and because about a hundred cycles ago, an Anchor died suddenly. Her successor was not fully informed of everything in the palace. Howlers back then decided that it was an extra layer of protection if the new Anchor forgot we existed – she was selected by strength, in a rush, far from the calm leader an Anchor should be. In fact, I suspect she would have been unable to resist using the knowledge we have,' replied Bones, pointedly ignoring the question about destroying books.

Fall rose to his feet. 'I'll beat you next time, Boulder,' he muttered and wandered off to the galley.

'Has Chase been away for ten cycles?' Darin asked. 'Tralkion said that was the last time he saw any other moon-hound-bonded So'Dal.'

'Chase spends a lot of his time in Dal, but he's only been away for a few tides. He needed to do a quick trip to Dal to check on some rumours. I'm sure he'll have news on his return and not of a sort we hoped we'd live to hear. Your appearance is more than lucky – it's Watcher sent. But for now, check out your room, then sit with us and play stones. I'll take you back out when my turn on the lift lever begins.'

From out in the galley, Darin heard a shout from Fall. 'Want some ale while you play?'

A third kind of magic to learn ... in secret? The weight of the Howlers' expectations was heavy. They appeared kind and friendly, but the old men had been fighting xotryl and strange creatures in secret his entire life, and some of them, most of his parents' lives too. Watcher's flames, if he couldn't talk about his day-to-day training with his parents, how would he ever explain everything else? Would he ever be able to? Darin tried to put a smile on his face.

'Yes please, Fall,' he replied. It was going to take far more than one ale to come to terms with everything.

Chapter 16

Elissa

Love-lies-weeping: origin unknown, but thought
to be from the dusk zone of Mythos.
Uses: glow lamps and flash globes
Stability: very stable, especially once sealed.
Availability: limited to import only. Cultivation
being attempted near Shardeep.
Herblore Volume 1. Tebein Edition

Elissa found herself wishing desperately that she could read. Since Rossi's arrival, she'd spent hours engrossed in the ancient, leather-bound books, staring at the pictures she could find and trying to make any sense of the words. It turned out that most books were openable with care, their secrets finally exposed by Rossi's lights. The words remained far from her grasp, but the faded pictures in the ancient books showed wonders she could never have dreamt of.

They all explored together at first, eventually leaving Rossi to search through the bookshelves alone. As they left the chamber of records, a small pile of books grew at his feet. Elissa found herself grateful for the space as she wandered through the complex with Laytha, investigating relics of time long gone. Rossi's map had proven accurate, and the majority of chambers on it were intact. They found abandoned workrooms with equipment stacked on ancient shelves – most of it crumbling and fragile – but the larger of the two workrooms was well-supplied with undamaged glass containers.

It was as though the people who lived there had simply closed the doors and walked away from everything they owned and knew. She couldn't help but wonder why the past inhabitants of their specific sericlave had stopped educating themselves and sharing their history. Had they known how steep the cost would be for those left behind?

'If any Untouched return, it's better that they find the chamber empty,' Laytha said as she looked around the workroom.

'We could set up in here? If they come back for us, they'll just assume we left.' Elissa tested the door, and it swung closed easily enough.

Laytha nodded and gestured for her to lead back to the hall of records. 'We'll need to be out of there with the lights off by nightfall.'

Rossi glanced over as they picked up their belongings. Elissa couldn't help but notice how light the food bag was, even topped up. 'Have you found somewhere better?' he asked.

'Yes, and if the others reappear, we need to be gone – it has to look as though we've rejoined the sericlave.' Laytha gestured at the lights. 'These need to be off too.'

He put a book back on the shelf. 'Agreed. I'll start bringing the books I want to study down to one of the other chambers.'

With so few possessions, it took little effort to clear the room. Once they were settled into their new hideaway, Laytha was clearly on edge. She paced the room several times before saying, 'I'm going to return to the sericlave, put our names on the soil and tilling preparation lists so we won't be missed on the bellows.'

'Can you stop by Makin's hut – if it's safe to – and leave a fish bone under his pillow?' Elissa was confident that Makin would understand the message; that she was safe, regardless of whether or not he saw her.

Laytha smiled. 'You two have some weird ways of communicating, you know? That's going to stink.'

'I'm counting on it.' Elissa grinned as she laid out a blanket on a nice flat area to sleep on. 'If it stinks, he might notice it.'

While Laytha was away, Elissa joined Rossi in checking through books he'd brought into the workroom. She stared in awe at the illustrations while Rossi scanned the pages, flicking through at speed, his eyes flickering as he read. A pile slowly built near his feet before he moved them back down the passage to the other workroom and swapped them for more.

Elissa fought the urge to ask what he wanted, a part of her dreaded the answer. After all, he'd come bearing warnings and concern for her safety. Sometimes not knowing was better. Occasionally, Rossi would glance up at her, open his mouth to speak, then glance at the door before shaking his head and returning to his book. The globe had begun to dim, and Elissa had taken to squinting at the pictures, rather than asking Rossi to re-light it, when Laytha reappeared.

'All done,' she said, sitting next to Elissa and peering at the book. 'It's a little dark in here. Can you relight that globe?' She looked over at Rossi.

He put the book down and crossed his right leg so that his ankle rested on his left. He leaned forward and rested his right elbow on his knee, draping his left arm over the raised ankle. 'No. You can relight them,' he said. 'If you can relight them, you can always have light.'

Elissa sighed as quietly as she dared. He really, truly believed they could use his song technique to light the lamps. He'd insisted that morning that they needed to learn to sing, and explained it was the easiest and fastest way to access their talent, but she still hadn't expected him to actually try to make her use it. It didn't matter that she'd seen him light the globes a few times already. It still felt too strange, too dangerous. If she was honest with herself, Elissa didn't want talent and power. It would be another thing that marked her as different – something else to hide.

She glanced at Laytha, who smiled and gestured up at the globe. 'You should try it.'

Elissa knew she was merely putting off a choice. Rossi had said he wanted her to go with him to some place where she could help his people and, by extension, her own. He was being very patient – probably aided by all the books he was searching through, but they really needed to make some decisions about the new information they had, and whether to share it. Lighting a lamp was both a step toward accessing that lost knowledge and accepting that Rossi's words held substance and truth.

What she had not known hadn't been missed. Knowing that her sericlave was neither alone nor living as others were unsettled her. Centuries of subjugation had left an indelible mark in Dragonsbreath. Knowledge without the tools to bring about change would only lead to malcontent, putting their people at even greater risk. It was on her and Laytha to give them what knowledge they could glean from Rossi.

She needed Laytha to help her decide what to do. The older woman was respected, and her opinions held weight with the others, as well as power in Elissa's own heart. Without the ability to read the books or use them, it left Laytha with nothing more than piles of paper with drawings on them and the knowledge that they could have helped once.

'You should go,' said Laytha suddenly. 'What you learn will help us, if these pictures are anything to go by.'

Reluctantly, Elissa nodded. 'Is there something you could do here in the meantime? Something to help all our people? Rossi, is there anything she can do without a crystal?'

He leaned back in his chair and smiled. 'She doesn't need a crystal. No one does. What Laytha can do depends on her natural ability to learn. We usually teach song wefting to much younger people.' He winced as he said it. 'Sorry, Laytha, I don't mean to be rude. If you can pick it up, there are some skills you could work on.' He paused. 'You mentioned lists and names. Whoever puts them together must be able to read. You need to gain their trust and learn yourself.'

Laytha smiled. 'That might be less difficult than it appears.'

'Only the elders can read or write.' Elissa narrowed her eyes at Laytha.

'We all have families, even if we don't talk about them. In my case, to protect them. You know my brother's an elder. He has a good heart and – much like you and Makin – we meet in secret when we can. I'll ask him to teach me. He's always refused before, but now he'll see why it's important. I know he will.'

Rossi nodded. 'A good plan. I'll find the most helpful books and bring them here. First, we need to teach you to light the lamps so you can read, away from crystalline eyes, once I leave.'

⊤ ※ ※ ※ ✦

Over the next few hours, Rossi went through some skills with Laytha. Elissa watched them while she pretended to look through books; realisation of what they could have slowly dawning as dim light bloomed in a bulb in front of Laytha. Flames, if Laytha could learn how, then thirteen more women could potentially use what Rossi called *wefting*. If Elissa left with Rossi, maybe she could find somewhere safe, away from awldrin, for them to live. Maybe even find a way to improve the quality of life for all the sericlave.

ⵜ ※ ﮊ ﮊ ✦

Thirteen. Women. Rossi was no woman, nor did he have lilac hair. She'd been so focused and fixated on the sericlave and the possibility of leaving her home that the obvious hadn't occurred to her.

'Rossi, this is probably a stupid question,' she interrupted them, 'but your hair – is it secretly lilac?'

'Not stupid at all. No, talented males don't have lilac hair. They are born with black hair. Most of us have other clues to our talent, though.'

'Such as?' Elissa asked.

There might be a significant number of people who could do the things in those books – encouraging crop growth, producing light ... producing warmth! The implications shook the foundations of her world. Some of the pictures appeared to show people tending to wounded and sick; the potential for what they could reclaim was staggering. Elissa's mouth was dry as he continued talking.

'Probably half of the talented males will have a lilac-haired sister. They will be likely to have vivid dreams – ones they can't control. Maybe they are very good with potions, or their singing has an unusually emotive effect on people.'

Elissa saw sudden motion to her left.

Laytha sat bolt upright, staring at Rossi. 'My father, my brother ... we always thought bad dreams just ran in the family. They could be like you?'

'And like you, Laytha. Yes, it's possible – probable.'

Elissa ran her hands over her filthy hair. Did Makin have talents or dreams? She'd moved to Laytha's care so young that many of her childhood memories were faded. She was sure she could trust him, though. 'This changes everything. What's your plan?'

'We need to get you and the crystal away from the awldrin. Maybe with the size of it, we can somehow communicate with Lieus and figure out a way home,' Rossi replied.

Elissa closed her book with a bang. 'I'm not going without our people from here, and especially not now I know this.'

'You have to, Elissa. We'll come back for them, I promise. In the meantime, Laytha can begin to recover the knowledge here. You have twice as many books and tools as any sericlave I've ever seen – somehow, we need to get everything away from here and get your people trained. This won't happen overnight, and needs to be carefully done. Awldrin are long lived. Many of them will remember the war on Lieus, have experienced the power of our magic in person. North of the Ameryth Dar Sea, there are no awldrin, and we live in peace. If we'd known you still lived ... were under their control ...' He hung his head. 'I'm sorry.'

'If I accept that we need to leave, how will we know what's happening here? How can I know they're safe?'

Rossi pointed to the exit. 'We need a willing volunteer open to dreams who can be our contact. Someone you trust. From what you have said about the way the awldrin view your sericlave, it can't be Laytha. We need to find a talented male. Someone who could sleep outside without arousing suspicion.'

'I trust my brother, Makin, but I don't know if he can help us. He also can't enter here through the nooks. No man could. We'd need to bring him in the other way.'

Laytha interrupted them, taking control of the situation. 'I'll go and speak to my brother – get him to take a tour of the crop preparations. Makin will be his lookman. Rossi, collect them from outside and bring them in. You've done it undetected once, so you can do it again.' She pointed at the map, authority pouring from every pore as she spoke. 'Some books showed more than five passageways with nooks. While I'm gone, you need to locate one of the others so the men can use it as access from the sericlave once we identify who is talented.'

She stood up, and Elissa watched the leader who could have been step from the shadow of the woman who'd lived her life in fear. She believed that if Laytha was in charge, it would be okay.

'Elissa, you need to be on your way in the next couple of days. From what Rossi said, you need to go through the marshlands to reach his home. You need to hurry before they become impassable with Rains. Once you are through the marsh, you'll be hard to follow.'

Elissa nodded. She was no leader, and Laytha's plan made sense, but she had one last bit of preparation to complete before they could leave. She rose and embraced Laytha. 'Be safe. We'll search for the other entrances.'

Laytha nodded and left the room. Elissa reached for the map, then saw Rossi sat staring at the empty doorway, a small smile playing across his face.

'Did you feel it?' he asked.

'Feel what?' Elissa frowned, confused.

'She was pushing emotional wefts at us. How did you feel when she spoke?'

Elissa frowned. 'She always makes me feel positive – she's good with words. In tough situations, she always helped me find a way through. Laytha's a good leader – even if it has only been of fourteen women. Coming from a family of leaders, she must have had good examples as a child.'

'Yes, you would feel positive. She is wefting hope and determination. She doesn't even realise she does it. With early training, she would have been incredibly strong. It really is no wonder there are elders in her family.'

'Do we tell her?' Elissa asked.

Rossi's eyes roved the room as he replied. 'Would it help her to know? If she thought she was manipulating people, would she be different?' He returned his gaze to Elissa.

She thought for a few moments. 'No,' she said finally. 'We don't tell her. The sericlave needs all the hope and determination we can get. If the Rains are much later, they will all starve.'

They studied the unrolled map on the table where Laytha had sat. Alcoves were drawn all around the chamber of records' walls. One or two alcoves had identical symbols on them, one had a series of radial lines drawn in, and another had a unique symbol on it that was different to the one on the awldrin door, yet still felt familiar. Elissa stared for a few moments, running her fingers over it until she recognised its form. It was a symbol found on many of the books in the selection they had with them. She wondered if Rossi had spotted it, but decided to keep the finding to herself – for the moment.

'Let's go and explore,' she said. 'We'll need your singing to light up what we can as we go.' Elissa pointed at the radial drawing. 'Could this be stairs?'

Rossi grabbed his bag. 'Let's go see.'

They headed back to the main room. The alcove with the radial sign in it was on the wall next to hut one's entrance. As Elissa had hoped, a globe was embedded in the wall.

'Sing us some light, then,' she said.

Rossi sung it to a low glow, enough to illuminate a doorway at the back. Elissa tried a gentle nudge to either side, but it didn't swing. She spotted a groove in the door and tried to grip her fingers into it and pull. Nothing happened.

Rossi felt around the edge of the door, stopping his hand halfway down the left edge. 'I think it might slide. Try using that groove along the door, not against it.'

Elissa tried to slide the door using the groove. At first, nothing happened. She pulled harder, and a small click she felt rather than heard preceded the door's movement. It slid easily into a slot in the wall, allowing them passage.

⊤ ✳ ✸ ✵ ✦

The stairs curled downward; the air was dark, dusty, and mouth-shrivellingly dry. Elissa found the descent hard on her foot, but was determined not to show it. If they left within the next few days, she would walk on far rougher terrain than a few carved steps. As they descended, warmth built through the walls and air.

'I think we're headed toward the bellows and the firestone heating chimney,' she said. 'It would make for good cover, but on the other hand, if an elder vanished down the fire pit too often, someone would notice.'

The stairs ended abruptly in a blank wall. They checked for grooves or handles, and Elissa checked for push stones, but to no avail. If it was a door, it wasn't opening by any physical methods from this side.

'Back to the books and maps then.' Elissa sighed. Maybe the extra tunnel had been blocked up – it had been hundreds of cycles after all. They'd be leaving another mystery to Laytha and the brothers. 'Maybe we have time to check the other one.'

'It's worth a try. This hasn't taken us too long.' Rossi gave the door a last shove before turning back to the stairs.

They carefully closed the sliding door behind them before

turning their attention to the other marked alcove. It wasn't in the main group, but off to one side at the opposite end of the chamber, and much smaller than the others. Maybe, at one time, it had contained a single table rather than the two or three that occupied the other alcoves. They searched the walls and floor, but the symbol on the map wasn't anywhere.

A frustrated pair returned to the workroom. Rossi's map held no more detail than the ones in the books. Laytha had clearly seen something else that they had missed. They divided the ones on the table between them and pored through, page by page, checking all the pictures they came across for a clue.

The light had faded again by the time Laytha returned, and they still hadn't found the extra tunnel she'd mentioned. As Laytha touched the glow globe and sang to relight it, the page Elissa was gazing at changed to show an extra passageway on the map – from the same alcove the stairs were in.

'Sing again, Laytha,' she said. 'Look at this.' She showed the others, pointing at the side wall just inside the entrance. 'It's there. It must be well hidden. There's another symbol on it. Laytha, can you sing again? Rossi, does this mean anything to you?' How had they missed a second door?

'I recognise it, but I don't know it. The answer will be here somewhere. Laytha, I'm afraid we are leaving you with more mysteries than help. When do I need to collect your brothers? We need as much time with them as we can get before Elissa and I leave, which needs to be as soon as possible.'

'But—' Elissa started.

'No, you have a crystal – that the awldrin want – embedded in you. I don't understand why they want it so badly, but it cannot be good news. The Gate was melted, though perhaps they've rebuilt some section, or hope to use it in some way. If you leave, you'll gain knowledge and skills that you never knew you could use, and draw them away, keep them from hunting the sericlave for you. You will keep Dragonsbreath safer by leaving.' Rossi indicated Laytha as he spoke.

'With all these books, surely that applies here, too, now. Why can't I be taught here?' asked Elissa.

'You could, but self-learning would be slow, and you're a danger to your sericlave. The awldrin hunted for you once, and they'll be back, unless they no longer feel that the crystal is close. There is one skill I need to teach you before we can leave. You must learn to shield your dreams and be able to keep others out. Tonight, sleep in a room with me, with no walls between our beds, and I will teach you some very basic dream safety. Elissa, what you've found could change the lives of all humans on Tebein, if we can just get you to the right place, the right teachers. I didn't want to say too much, put too much on you, but you may carry the key to free us all. There's a chance that the shard you carry could open a gate back to Lieus.'

Elissa stared at him. 'I stood on a shard. It was an accident.'

'They should be there soon, Rossi.' Laytha interrupted, breaking the building tension in the room. 'Elissa, he's right. If you go, you can learn – can help us all. If you are really able to change things, to get us all away from here … A day ago I'd have said he talked nonsense, dreams, and madness, but these books! Look at the things they could do. The awldrin didn't make the rota crystal – we did. We are the ones with the power. No wonder they oppress us. They are afraid of us.'

She clasped her hands together. 'Imagine the life we could lead! Do you really care whether it was an accident or not? If anyone can do the impossible, it's you. We'll be safe here – I'll make sure of that. Go in the morning. The sooner you go, the sooner you can come back and help. Now, you don't want to be carrying much with that foot, so let's sort out a light bag to carry. Take essentials only. I'll take care of anything else until you return.'

Elissa nodded in grudging agreement. As much as it felt that Laytha was pushing her away – and she could feel the push once she knew it happened – she knew it was the right thing to do.

The women rose and left the room to pack as Rossi said nothing, and walked down the other passageway to collect the two waiting men.

CHAPTER 17

DARIN

*That evening, we took residence in a holroom. It
was richly furnished and the owner offered
us a hearty meal. We were lucky to arrive on
the same night as a pair of travelling So'Dal
Witnesses. The power of the songs they
performed that night and the complexity of
the harmonies still haunts me to this day.*
A Journey to the Barren Plains

After the initial surprise, the most challenging thing about discovering he was a Howler was keeping their existence secret, even from Conor. Aggi had impressed the importance on him in no uncertain terms.

'He may not be So'Dal, but your friend is still a builder. So he need not know we're here.'

Bones had joined in. 'Only the Master Builder knows about the passage behind the waterfall. If the lift gets stuck or too much steam evaporates, then the waterfall gets topped up from back here. Otherwise, we stay invisible in plain sight. Just old men working the lever.'

Old men who could battle monsters. Darin had been wanting more than study; maybe he'd finally get to learn some new fighting techniques too. On the way back out, Darin briefly met the last Howler, Claw, who swapped places with Bones, then headed into their home behind the waterfall. Darin watched the door vanish with awe. He wasn't sure when the next opportunity to visit them would occur, but he hoped it would be soon.

As he sat with Conor the next morning, he tried to weave untruths with a calm, steady voice.

'So, it turns out that the old So'Dal is just a librarian. That's how he knew where he was going and that I always shouted for help,' Darin lied, a knot of guilt tightening in his gut.

'What about the glow lamp?' asked Conor.

'Um, that was simple. It turns out it was already lit and hidden up his robe sleeve. I felt pretty foolish when he showed me that.' Once he'd started the trail of lies, they just seemed to keep coming. The knot of guilt tightened, and his palms grew clammy.

Conor shrugged. 'So, you got all worked up about a librarian. What about these Howlers?'

'A couple of old men who used to have moonhounds. Nothing special.' Darin held his breath, hoping that Conor would accept the answers and leave it there. His hand rested on the treasure the Howlers had given him, and which he'd hidden under his bedcover.

Conor rose, but didn't meet Darin's eyes. His casual shrug

was at odds with the tightness in his shoulders. 'Let's go get some sparring in before breakfast.'

Darin had never been a good liar, and it was not going well. He hated it. Star nudged his wet muzzle at Darin's hand and sent reassurance through their bond. Taking comfort from the moment, he pushed himself off the bed and followed Conor out of the room with Star close at his heels. Conor's set shoulders and lack of conversation continued until they reached the courtyard.

'Spears or swords?' Conor asked, monotone.

'Spears.'

It was going to hurt.

⊢ ※ ✲ ✦

Darin's muscles burnt with exhaustion, and Conor still rained furious blows on him. Blocking Conor with the shaft of his spear, Darin pushed back to try to twist his body away from the incoming spear-tip. They might only be practise spears, but they gave a nasty bruise, and he already had plenty of cuts to show for Conor's efforts. The butt of the spear connected with his leg instead as Conor swung it around, and Darin's knee buckled. He flipped his own spear as he struggled to stand and felt Conor's spear point pressing deeply into his neck.

Conor grinned, some tension dropped after their exertions.

He leant in close and whispered, 'I know you're lying. I don't know why, but for the sake of our friendship, you'd better have a bloody good reason.' He pulled away, threw down his spear, and offered a hand to Darin.

He was forgiven – for the moment. Darin grinned back at Conor.

'Do you know what's for breakfast?' he asked.

'Flatcakes and brose.' Conor grabbed his spear and jogged

to the weapons rack. 'If we sneak in through the kitchen, maybe we'll be able to get hot ones from Fresna before they go out to the main hall.'

Darin grabbed his own spear from the dusty ground and chased him down. They dived through the archway side by side, almost knocking a bemused Jaer down. He grappled with his tray, saving a pile of flatcakes from falling as Conor caught the brose.

'Sorry, we didn't see you.'

Jaer arched an eyebrow. 'I hadn't guessed.'

'So where are you taking those?'

'They're headed to my stomach,' Conor said as he winked at Jaer.

The boy pulled himself up tall. 'No, they're for one of the new Soul Anchors. She arrived late last night and is over in the guest quarters.' He brandished a spoon. 'Bring back any memories, Darin? Wish me luck.' He walked past, then turned and called back, 'Fresna just put the next batch of flatcakes on the grill. If you don't take Star in with you, you might have a chance of getting some.'

⋎ ⁂ ✹ ✺ ✦

A full stomach is a happy stomach, Darin thought as he collected his moonhound after eating. Puppies wove around their feet, the smallest running under and between Star's legs. Star was already a hand's width taller than the next largest youngster and seemed to grow by the minute. Darin reached out and scratched the little ear of the closest puppy, then sent Star their plans. They needed to go to Tralkion's workroom soon for more plants and more failed singing, then he had singing practise with the Master in the afternoon. Star followed at his heels through to the steam lift.

Darin climbed aboard and studied the hooded figure on the lever. Which of them was it? Should he be saying hello? The Howlers had suggested he try to pretend he didn't know them or recognise them, so he resisted the urge to wave. A tall So'Dal joined him on the lift, with long, curly hair cascading from under his hood. A Witness apprentice, Darin decided as he took in the thin red robe trim but lack of tattoo. The So'Dal nodded a greeting as they rose to the garden. Darin gripped the rail, feeling the usual nausea begin to brew when the lever was pulled.

Sighing deeply, he looked at the clear blue sky they shot toward, wishing he could enjoy some real time outside with Star. Not just in the crater or the paddocks, but a walk outside the walls. The palace grounds were massive, but he wanted – needed – to feel free.

⊢ ※ ※ ※ ✦

After another day of failed gardening wefts and being told it would all be okay if he just practised enough, or harder, or for longer, Darin was drained. Frustration built up, and he thumped down on his bed.

He was trying his hardest. That had always been enough – until he got to the Black Palace. What more could he do? Darin reached under the covers and pulled out the Howlers' gift. He turned the set of whistles over in his hand thoughtfully as the seed of an idea grew. Darin uncovered the training globe and raised the smallest whistle to his lips, pushing his magic through it. As he blew, the globe flickered. He couldn't hear anything, but Star sat up and pricked his ears. When he tried again, the globe glowed bright white. Star shuffled along the bed to sniff the whistle, his ears flicking back and forth as he tried to lick it.

Darin scratched Star's head gently, then tried the second

whistle. The globe changed again to white with a hint of blue in the centre. The third whistle was similar, but the mid-point was lilac. He couldn't hear any of them, but Star's response – along with the glow – showed that they worked.

Could they be the answer? If he would truly be alone with Star one day, and there was no longer a full Howler pack – if he really did have a Watcher-given responsibility – then he needed every advantage he could get. He needed to be able to weft. More than that, if the Howlers' hunch was real, and things were getting out of control, then surely giving more of them the ability to weft would help. They might be too old to wield a sword or staff in battle, but maybe their hidden books contained magic they could use in defence of the craterlands.

Darin turned the idea over as he turned the whistles around. It would mean trusting someone to make him some new ones, small enough to carry and use at speed in a tight situation. He studied them carefully, deciding that they were all made of the same type of wood.

He could get a whole set of whistles made and claim it was for training Star. Even better, he could get a sliding whistle! It would allow a range of audible notes as well, and he could try wefts. If he didn't have to sing, he could do everything the Gardeners could with a whistle. The whole pack could! Darin smiled; he had a plan, but he needed someone to make it happen – and he might know just the person. He just had to keep his head down for a few days and take the chance.

⟡ ✳ ✤ ✦ ✦

Tralkion loaded Darin up with vials ready to take to their patients. 'Are you sure you can find them yourself?' he asked for the second time.

Darin sighed with impatience and recited the directions

Tralkion had given him. 'The general heal to Wilf, the fever-down to the third stall down from the scarf one. The last to the baker three doors up from the Windrush Tavern.'

'I'll see you in a few hours, then. Thank you, Darin. I'm sorry I can't come with you today. This meeting I have with the other Gardeners cannot wait.'

'Don't worry. I can do this,' Darin replied, eager to be off.

He delivered the feverdown and the potion for the baker first, then headed toward Wilf's home.

'Hello, apprentice,' Wilf said, shaking Darin's hand firmly. 'It's good to see you again, although a little sooner than I anticipated.'

'So'Dal Tralkion didn't want you running out and having to call us,' said Darin. 'This way, you can let us know how long the first potion lasted without having to wait for a new one. We can work out the right timing for your next deliveries, then.'

Wilf looked thoughtful. 'I can only presume that they anticipate a need for my services soon. Be sure to inform Tralkion that I'll be ready for the order. I'm sure he'll pass that on to the right people.'

Darin put his hand in his pocket and drew out the whistle.

'Would you be able to make a gift for my mother? I'd love to send her a whistle. One that slides and you can play a tune on. She's always wanted one.' He was shocked how smoothly the lie came out. His palms sweated as he held one of his whistles out. 'Something like this, but with a slider?'

Wilf took the whistle and turned it over over appraisingly. 'I can do that. Would you like it engraved as it is a gift?'

Darin hadn't thought about that and nodded quickly. It would sound more plausible, he thought. 'That would be lovely. What can I do to help you as repayment?'

Wilf furrowed his brow. 'You already do it by bringing Tralkion's potions to me. I offered you a gift before, and I meant it. I'll send it up to the palace for you. It shouldn't take long.'

Darin inclined his head in what he hoped would be seen as respect. 'Thank you. My mother will be so pleased.'

He left Wilf's home with an extra spring in his step and a flicker of excitement growing in his stomach as he walked. Darin didn't like having to lie to good people, but it wouldn't hurt anyone. In fact, it would help everyone if the Howlers did their job a little longer and he could keep training Star.

CHAPTER 18

SURIIN

*The Anchor must be a hold-fast in the strongest of
storms. Rippling waves on the surface and
movements of those on the ship are of little
consequence to her. A good Anchor allows her
ship to bob and drift around her position.
But always, she keeps the ship where it needs
to remain for both the safety of the crew and
the integrity of her ship.*
**So'Dal Brand, The Anchors of the Black
Palace**

Suriin's heart sank with every groan that struggled from
between her father's lips. His sweat-drenched covers were
heaped on the floor – thrown off in another fit of tossing and
turning – and dim glow lamps illuminated his wasting form.
His ribs showed clearly through ever more translucent skin,
where new threads of the toxic web appeared daily. He needed
more help. Why hadn't they stopped the spread? Suriin
watched him struggle and wondered for the thousandth time if

her father would be fit and well had she not helped Ronin, or maybe if Ronin had been more experienced.

Xotryl poison had passed deep into his body. The Gardeners tried new draws and remedies throughout the last tide. At first, the symptoms had disappeared, and they'd even walked in the gardens one sunny day. Then something changed, and the dark patches had reappeared, crawling outward from the wound site.

Suriin picked up the damp cloth on the washstand and wiped a light sheen of water across his back; it evaporated away, much as wisps of hope departed from her daily. The heat pouring from his body made it hard to keep him comfortable. Rarely in the last few years had she wanted her mother to be with her as much as she did right then. She hoped that they'd come soon, but her mother would never leave Golden unguarded; until someone else arrived, she'd not leave.

Footsteps rang on the tiles outside, so she gave him a farewell kiss on the cheek and prepared to leave. It must be Fresna to ensure she wasn't late to the kitchens. Through the cracked-open door, she heard an unexpected voice.

'More of them?'

An unknown voice replied to Nissa. 'Yes, we have reports from the Witness family in Dal that another has been seen overhead. One of our Collective members has also seen graaken tracks close to Lacton Crater. It's only a matter of time before the populations of Sildet and Lacton run into them. The Edgelands are spreading.'

'Then we desperately need to know how this poison is acting, what it's doing, and how to treat it. Without knowing which organs it's affecting, it limits our treatment options. How does he fare?'

Suriin considered interjecting. Her impetus found her within reach of the door, and she opened her mouth to speak when the unknown speaker's reply shut her voice off like a steam valve. Stunned, she held her tongue and her breath and listened.

'If he lives, we will have found something that works. If I'm honest, though, it's unlikely. I suspect it's more likely we will have a chance to see how his organs have failed.'

Nissa replied, 'So be it. I hope his Soul Anchor arrives in time. I sent a replacement to Golden, but it's a long journey.'

The valve inside re-opened, and Suriin burst through the door, her words pouring out in a torrent.

'My father will not die. My mother will not need to be in time. He healed a xotryl wound in Nameless, so maybe you should start there for your cure – ask Ronin. He helped. My father will not die. He mustn't!'

Suriin ran down the corridor with tears streaming from her face, decorum forgotten and all control lost. Her pounding feet and tear-blind eyes found their way to the kitchens. Chef took one look at her and his face fell.

'Oh, Suriin, I am so sorry. Yorynn was so respected, such a good man.'

'He's not dead – not yet! Why does everyone think he'll die?' she shrieked.

'Suriin, I know it hurts, but you'll be a Soul Anchor one day. You need to focus on facts and learn to control your emotions. I'm relieved he is still fighting – but remember, it is a long-forgotten poison. Even So'Dal cannot cure everything, though I'm sure they are trying their best. I know that doesn't help, but maybe some time out from the kitchen would? I need these tonight. Go and collect them.' Chef handed a list of plants to her.

Suriin unfolded her arms and took the list. He was right; she had to focus. Taking her frustrations out on others was not behaviour either of her parents would accept.

The plants were mostly from the Hook Point area of Caldera. She liked that section of the garden. There were few poisonous plants and many beautiful flowers.

'The linj seeds ... will they need drying?' she asked hopefully.

'They will. If you go to the hot-room, there should be some ready. Replace those with fresh ones?'

'Thank you, I will. Sorry for shouting.' Suriin took a proffered cake, managed a weak smile, and left the kitchen to head down the silent black corridor toward the steam lift.

⋇ ⚹ ※ ⚌ ✦

Sunlight rippled through the thin cloud layer, and shadows drifted like small wavelets across the crater garden. Alone in the Hook Point section, Suriin drank in the sunlight greedily. The flowers stood proud and tall, soldiers of the soil. Rank upon rank of red and silver goblets faced her with unblemished green spears held proud and straight in salute.

Passing between their lines, Suriin reached the smaller, more fragrant linj plants. There was no organised planting, they grew rambling and low, tripwires across the path for the unwary. She stood on one, and the crushed seeds released their fragrance. For the first time in a tide, Suriin took out her sketchbook to draw.

She let her mind focus on tiny details as she filled in the leaf veins. Suriin took careful note of the way the oval leaves were arranged at cross angles all the way up the square, hair-covered stem. The flowers had long gone, and the full seed pods were ready to burst. Suriin recovered the bag Chef had given her from another pocket and gently pulled it over the pod, trying not to catch it. Once the pod was fully inserted, she tapped it. There was a satisfying pop as the pod burst open, spraying its seeds into the bag.

When she removed it, the curled pod showed a new beauty with its five arms rolled back on themselves. Suriin began to draw again. The curl of the pod casing as it spiralled tightly reminded her of the woven rug in her parents' kitchen. Her pencil made its familiar scratch across the page, fast strokes and slow strokes, creating its own soothing music and easing her soul.

With notes made in the margin and pods drawn, she collected more seeds, feeling the pop against the bag each time, then little seeds hitting the sides like rain. Once the bag was full, Suriin uncurled from the floor. She'd better sort them out first; herbs in the hot room would wilt.

Suriin wandered around the edge of the steam lift to a door alongside it. She ran her hand along the wall, feeling for patches of heat. Warm steam ran behind the walls on its return to the pool below, making the little room dry and hot as a result. Shelves lined it from floor to ceiling, with rows of paper packets arranged and labelled on each. Trays of brown bags with their tops gaped open allowed their contents to dry.

They were mostly plants used by Gardeners, leaves here, seeds there. Suriin peeked inside a packet of vibrant red flowers. Someone had knocked over a packet, and its precious contents had spilt on the shelf. She picked it up, checked inside, and replaced the matching seeds carefully. The air was warm and comfortable in there, and the wealth of potential plant life from all over Caldera in this one small place made her feel warm inside, but maybe that was just the room. There was another space somewhere deep inside the mountain where rarer dried seeds were stored; from all over Lieus and beyond. She imagined a much bigger room like the one she was in, where she could spend hours wandering.

In the back corner of the room was the section that the

kitchen used. A dedicated area to reduce the risk of contamination.

The doorway shadowed as Fresna appeared.

'Chef said you'd be up here. He also said you might need company.'

'Thanks.' Suriin forced a smile. 'I overheard Nissa discussing how she planned to cut my father open when he dies to see the poison's effects. I'm probably not the greatest company right now. I don't want him to die.' She spun and faced Fresna, knowing she sounded desperate. 'There must be something that can help him. If xotryl were part of the great battles of the closing, surely accidents happened, and we know something about their poisons? Although, if the Gardeners are trying all they know, I'm not sure where else I could search for help.'

'Gardeners don't have all the answers. We can try the Soul Anchor library. It's not as big as theirs, but it covers the magic of our crystals. I'm not sure how emotional amplification can help here, but maybe we'll find a clue.'

'We? You want to help?'

Fresna grinned. 'Of course, I'll help. That's what friends do, right?'

Suriin felt the taller woman's arms wrap around her and gratefully leant into the hug, returning it with a squeeze. She sniffled a little and swallowed the rising lump in her throat.

Fresna continued cheerfully, 'Let's get these seeds in and the rest of Chef's list picked and dug up. Oh, I nearly forgot – your first classmate is here. Not long now, and you'll be able to start your first lessons.'

'That's not good, Fresna. When that happens, I'll have less time to spend with him.'

'You'll have classes each morning with Aslin. We should make the most of the next tides to see what we can find out.'

She leant past Suriin and pulled open the small room divider. The drying tray was full of linj seeds. Suriin emptied them into a bag left alongside them, then poured all the seeds from her own pouch, covering the tray in a thin layer of gold. Their tangy fragrance filled the room, and she could almost taste the brose it would be used to make. They closed the door behind them, careful not to create any breeze to dislodge packets, and left the hot room to gather the rest of their list.

Splattered with mud and laden with a feast of root vegetables and edible leaves, they descended the steam lift. The hooded figure on the lever nodded as politely as ever when they dismounted the platform.

'That must be such a boring job,' Suriin remarked to Fresna.

'I think they're old builders who can't use their tools properly anymore,' Fresna whispered. 'There's a few of them, I think. They've always got those big hoods on – maybe steam leaks through the lever, so they need protection. One is much taller than the others, and at least two of the shorter ones have different accents.'

'I still think it must be quite boring!'

Fresna laughed. 'I suppose they can at least still feel useful. Come on. Let's get these into the kitchen, then we can go hunting for something to help your father.'

Suriin glanced back at the old So'Dal, who inclined his head in her direction as they walked past. *He must get really bored,* and as quickly as the thought came, it disappeared. The corridor toward the kitchens beckoned, as did a warm breakfast and a plan to help cure her father.

Jaer was dancing around the kitchen as they returned,

waving a spoon and chattering about the new arrival. 'She was really nice. She shared her food with me. So tall and strong – like a Collective, not like a Soul Anchor. Suriin, I met your new classmate. She is nice.'

Fresna rolled her eyes at Suriin. 'He does this every time! You should have seen him the day that Darin arrived.'

'Darin?'

'The apprentice with the bonded hound. The only man bonded to one I've ever heard of. He was nice to Jaer, then they went out and Staramine chose him. Jaer couldn't stop talking about it for days! Seems to think he'll bond his own hound one day, now he's seen it happen.'

'I will!' he shouted across the kitchen. 'I'll have a hound, too, and be a Gardener, just like him.'

Suriin mentally filed away the information for later. She had seen the man, but hadn't registered that he was special in any way. In fact, he appeared anything but special. One could ignore him altogether if it wasn't for the large moonhound accompanying him everywhere. She'd just assumed it was his Soul Anchor's hound.

⚜

The Soul Anchor library was decorated with ornate and beautiful paintings around the walls. Women and hounds ran side by side, and rainbows cast by the painted crystals hanging from their necks appeared to light up the room. It was open and well lit. Wooden roof beams carved into many animals cavorted over their heads, and coloured windows cast warm light across the floor.

Older frieze panels were set between the shelves, out of direct light. They looked as though they'd been removed from other walls at some point in the palace's history. The librarians projected a serene quality. It was a calm and pleasant place.

The teetering pile of books between Fresna and Suriin grew as they read, each rejected as irrelevant or unhelpful. The guest quarters were below the library and, it was easy to get distracted by the comings and goings. She wondered which of the women leaving them was her new classmate.

'My father will. Not. Die,' she muttered, turning away from the window and returning a book to the shelf. She picked up another, *The Bestiary of the Edgelands*.

The Edgelands are a newly created habitat, rife with strange flora and fauna. It is thought that there was a leakage, or carry-through, of the species from Tebein and Mythos at some point in the past. The glowing plants we are now familiar with are presumed to come from the dusk zone of Mythos, and several of the creatures colonising the Edgelands have been brought through inadvertently from Tebein.

'Fresna, this could be more hopeful,' she called. They shuffled closer together and turned the page.

Many of the new plants have been found to have medicinal effects, further details of which are now passed on through training in the arts of the Gardener. There have been no positive effects found from any of the animal species. Graaken are the biggest in number, xotryl the most dangerous. Xotryl are known to have toxic poison, which responds to no recorded Lieusian treatments or magics.

ᚱ ※ ⚜ ☩ ✦

'It doesn't say it's incurable,' said Fresna hesitantly.

'It doesn't say it isn't!' Suriin retorted. 'What it says is that we have no known way to treat this on Lieus.' She dropped the book back down on the table in frustration. As it hit the table, a small sheet of paper slipped from between the pages. In handwritten script it said,

ᚱ ※ ⚜ ☩ ✦

Though it is now often forgotten, we knew awldrin to ride xotryl in battle. Whilst they are not human, and therefore, medical implications are unknown, we have seen individuals known to have been caught by xotryl claws, who are recovered at a later date. They were heavily scarred, but alive. I must therefore assume that there is an antidote they have access to, which will aid in the relief of the xotryl toxins – within their species, at least. This is an area which requires future research. Currently, xotryl numbers are exceptionally low and they are a rare sighting outside the Edgelands, so it is unlikely that this will be urgent research. Recommendation for it to be a low priority.

ᚱ ※ ⚜ ☩ ✦

Suriin held out the scrawled note with a shaking hand. Fresna read it in silence, her eyes skimming across the scrap of paper.

'So, there is a cure – for them, at least,' Suriin said.

Fresna nodded slowly. 'So, do we research more about awldrin? It feels like our search just got a whole lot wider, not narrower. If xotryl are not from Lieus at all, it explains why it's so hard to cure their poison.'

'What makes awldrin so different from us? I've heard of them as a kind of folklore, but what do they really look like? What made them different?'

Fresna stood smoothly – *I really need to learn that grace* – and beckoned her to follow. 'Let's check out the histories as bedtime reading!'

Laden with several books on the war that led to the Closing, the two women struggled back to their rooms that evening. As they crossed the courtyard, the gates burst open. A hooded rider leapt from their skaa-rak, flinging the reins to a stunned guard. The rider ran at full pelt into the Star Tower. Suriin caught a flash of red trimming the cloak as the figure vanished into the doorway.

'That can't be good.' She turned to Fresna, who stared into the open doorway.

'No,' she murmured, 'I don't think it can be.'

CHAPTER 19

DARIN

*The magical powers exhibited by some humans
were first seen in Dal. The long term effects of
living so close to the gates – those beacons of
draconic magic – were felt by many living
things in the region. Most notable though
were the births of lilac haired daughters in
villages near the Gates, who exhibited unusually strong influence over their parents.*
Dal, Our Secret History

'Hey, Darin, you've got a parcel.'

Darin ran toward the gatehouse and grabbed it
from the bemused guard. He didn't have long before his lesson
with Tralkion to try the whistle out, so he sprinted back to his
room with Star bounding alongside under the bemused gazes of
sparring So'Dal in the courtyard. Darin ran through the corridors and dived through his door, closing it behind them.

The practise lamp sat on a small table and, full of hope, he
raised the whistle to his lips and blew. As hard as he tried, the

globe would not light up. He tried to sing a note and, yes, it was definitely working – a muddy colour glowed. Darin blew the whistle again. It sang out beautifully, and he could play notes he had never even sung before. The slider was smooth as dralowfly silk, and its tone deep and rich. He tried pushing the note through as he did when he sang, but the globe stubbornly refused to even flicker.

It was a lovely but useless whistle. At least his mother would like it after all. He wrapped it back up in the soft cloth Wilf had sent it in. Clearly, he'd missed something. Maybe it was the whistles that were magical, not just the tune that they made.

He turned one of the Howler whistles over in his hand. There was no obvious coating, so the materials the whistles were made from must hold power. The barrel was dark wood, with a strange, almost scale-patterned grain; a white band of something else was delicately embedded around the open end of each whistle. He tucked them all inside his robe and shoved Star off his snoozing spot on the bed. It was time to go.

⊤ ※ ⚇ ⚌ ✦

Darin thought about the whistle problem again as he collected ingredients for another of Tralkion's recipes. 'Let those that have done the reading answer your questions,' he murmured. He should stop trying to do things himself – Bones was right. Darin needed to speak to them. After all, with all their combined knowledge and experience, he couldn't be the first to have had this idea.

'What did you say?' asked Tralkion from the other side of the clearing.

'Oh, nothing. Just mumbling to myself.' Darin glanced up. The sun barely reached the edge of the crater, and shadows shortened across the windless garden. The plants felt eerily static. He had a few hours between the end of the session with Tralkion and singing with the Master. If he finished on time, they could just squeeze in a visit.

Darin called Star to him with an image of the Howler rooms. A large, hairy arrow shot across the garden. He braced for the inevitable impact as Star leapt at him, tongue flopping out the side of his mouth and whip-like tail wagging in circles. They hit the ground together.

'You have to come at me slower! You're too big for this already,' Darin said, sending *[Star trotting toward him and stopping in front of him]*.

'If you've got everything we need, head up to the workshop and get it prepared,' Tralkion called. 'I only need a couple more plants.'

Darin and Star ran through the gardens. He took pleasure in the burn of his muscles, a quick sprint to clear his mind; all the reading was great, but he missed the time to stay as fit as he'd like. Star was so fast that Darin couldn't keep up, and he arrived at the steps panting, but exhilarated. He looked up at the balconies and laughed. Who cared what anyone else thought of him running everywhere? Not him, that was for sure.

⌐ ✳ ✵ ✾ ✦

Usually, Darin enjoyed crafting healing drafts, but he couldn't focus. The whistles in his pocket were a constant reminder of how tantalisingly close he'd come. His first attempt to sing the weft resulted in several flat notes, rather than the usual one or two; he felt his magic fizzle away as he hit them wrong. Darin's frustration rose, and he tried to squash it down – if he could just get that whistle working! His hand strayed to the pocket where they were hidden. He'd go see the Howlers. Tralkion's raised eyebrow jerked him back to the moment.

'Concentrate. You almost had it yesterday.'

Darin took a deep breath. *Focus. I can do this.* He tried again, pushing the weft into the bottle. He only hit one wrong note. To his amazement, the magic didn't fizzle, and a gentle glow wound through the jar as he held it.

Grinning with pride, he offered the jar to Tralkion – who stared at it with his brow furrowed and his lips thinned.

'You might want to put that down before it gets—'

'Ouch, it's hot!' Darin released the jar, and it smashed on the floor. Steaming herbal aromas filled the workshop before drifting across the crater.

⋎ ※ ✖ ⅏ ✦

Tralkion chuckled. 'Congratulations on your second successful weft, but sadly the wrong one! It's useful for warming a poultice or heating ingredients when preparing them. Not one I'd use on a finished draft, though, and definitely not that strongly!'

Star had retreated to the corner when the bottle smashed to the floor but was back to nose around the mess. Darin received *[Star licking the liquid up]* and quickly replied *[Fire on the liquid]*. Star backed away with his ears flattened and watched warily as Darin and Tralkion cleaned the scalding mess up. Rumbles from Tralkion's stomach punctuated their work.

'Food then!' he remarked as they finished. 'I think we should call it a day. Shall we go?' Down in the garden, Lea sat with her cousin, and Tralkion waved at her.

Darin raised his soggy sleeve. 'I think I'd better change first.'

Tralkion winced at the mess. 'They won't love you for that in the laundry! Some of those ingredients stain. I'll see you tomorrow!'

They wound their way down to the garden together, where

Tralkion went to meet Lea. He'd just about got time. Darin and Star ran for the lift. They needed to get down before the others to slip through the passage under the waterfall unseen.

He could eat with the Howlers – their new pack. Darin smiled with excitement. It would be nice to see them again. He hoped they had answers for him, and maybe he could give them something in return. His busy thoughts helped override his fear as the lift dropped smoothly to the chamber floor; several people wandered through the space as they stepped off.

The hooded So'Dal on the lever nodded in acknowledgement as Darin gestured to the invisible door – someone that size could only be Aggi.

Darin ambled toward him, absently stroking Star's head. He watched the last people move through the space.

The chamber cleared, and Darin sent *[Door opening]* to Star as they ran toward it.

'Go now,' Aggi called and gestured for him to hurry. Darin blew the small whistle, pressed the button, and stepped through. He heard the swoosh of the steam lift start as Aggi sent it up, hiding the hissing noise of the closing door.

⁜ ※ ⚜ ⚜ ✦

Star ran ahead, surefooted over the slippery, wet stones – probably anticipating the fuss and attention he'd get as soon as he poked his furry head around the door. Darin was unsurprised to find Star lying on the rugs with two Howlers fussing over him when he entered the room.

A second hound stood outside the closed curtain of Chase's room. He was darker than Star, with a greying muzzle, and easily the tallest moonhound Darin had ever seen. His long, powerful legs were leanly muscled. Unlike many pampered moonhounds in the palace, he looked as though he could run for days. At first glance, Darin thought he had stripes. Then realised, with a moment of fear for Star, that they were scars shining silver by the light of the globes.

Bones patted a seat adjacent to him with a smile. 'Great to see you. How's training going?'

Darin laughed as he recounted the incident with the over-heating draft. From around the room, he was rewarded with chuckles and beaming grins.

'I set fire to the table once,' Bones said.

Boulder shrugged. 'I made a poultice glow.'

'I froze a draft,' Fall said in agreement, getting up and walking into the galley.

'And I heard Aggi turned his first glow lamp into a flash bomb.' Claw mimed an explosion.

All the Howlers chimed in, giving examples of mixed-up wefts.

'And it's because of you lot doing that, that I never had the opportunity to learn gardening at all!' Chase opened the curtain. He was younger than the rest of the Howlers – Darin guessed at about fifty-five cycles. If he'd bonded with his moon-hound at a similar age to Darin, it would explain the greying. Hounds, he'd learned, usually lived to about forty-five cycles old.

Like Sandy, Chase was lean, muscled, and scarred. He was almost as tall as Darin.

'It has been so long since a new Howler bonded!' He reached out to clasp Darin's hand. 'It's good to meet you. Given that our Anchor doesn't know we exist and appears to forget about me until she needs a messenger to Dal, you must be getting a decent teacher.'

'Tralkion. He's really patient, and I have singing lessons with the Master. Tralkion remembers you,' Darin responded without thinking. 'He is a Gardener, but last recalls seeing you over twenty cycles ago.' Seeing an expression of concern cross a whole pack of human faces, he quickly followed it up. 'I asked if he knew any other So'Dal with moonhounds before I came here the first time – that's all.' Shoulders around him dropped and relaxed.

'I do need to ask you some questions, though. It's about these whistles,' Darin continued. 'Bones, you said to ask those who've done the reading, so before I redo everything past Howlers did, and for nothing, I thought I'd ask you.'

'Have you eaten?' shouted Fall from the galley.

'No, I came straight here between tutors,' Darin replied. He sent *[Plate of food]* to Star and received a happy wag in response. 'Star's hungry, too, if you have anything?'

Fall returned with a plate of cold meats and steamed roots for Darin. Sandy and Star followed his every move and were rewarded with two thigh bones with moist meat still clinging to them. The echo of cracking bones filled the room.

The Howlers occupied themselves while Darin ate, but he felt them watching. Occasionally, one would catch his eye and smile. As soon as he finished, Bones returned to sit with him. He leant forward eagerly.

'So ... How can we help?'

'It's about the whistles.' Darin pulled them from his pocket and laid them on the table. 'I had this sliding whistle made, thinking I could use it like your whistles and use it to push magic through. It didn't work. I'd hoped that because they helped the magic, that if I used a sliding whistle, maybe I could get a full range of notes and create wefts. Then you could all use your magic, too, and if there had been bad news from Dal,' – he nodded at Chase – 'then we could all work together to fight it. But it just makes lovely tunes.' Darin turned it over in his hands, admiring the craftsmanship again. It really was lovely. 'It doesn't affect my training globe at all. So, what's special about the other whistles?'

'You have your own training globe?' Bones asked.

'Yes, my singing is so bad the Master makes me practise away from lessons. It's the only way I can tell if I've hit the right note most of the time,' Darin replied with a grimace.

'That's a rare thing to be trusted with!' said Bones. 'No one knows how to make those anymore – not even us. But back to the whistles. They're made from hollow stems of fern-trees found in the Edgelands. We believe the vibrating part is a very thin sliver of echoglass from the old Gates. They also have a small rim of dragon bone, just ... there.' Bones pointed at the white circlet around the bottom edge.

'Where did the dragon bone come from?' Darin asked, stunned. 'There haven't been dragons on Lieus since the Watcher left.'

'The Watcher left us with a single bone. A token to remind us to whom we made our promise to protect Lieus.'

'Do you still have it? Can I see it?'

'We have a small part left. It has other properties that have kept us alive.' Bones gestured to Sandy.

Chase leant over the table. 'Watcher's wings, it's a brilliant idea. Why haven't I thought of it before?'

Bones shrugged. 'Why didn't any of us? Maybe someone did in the past, and the records might hold something, but most of the time, we've been too busy doing the rest of our job. You weren't taught the wefts, Chase, and there was an entire pack of us before you joined. Every whistle was needed. Anyway, we've always had other ways to access our power.'

'May I have a look?' Chase asked. Darin passed it up and watched the inspection hopefully. Finally, Chase gave it back to him with a nod and a smile. 'It's well made. It might just work if we take the bone and echoglass from one of the original whistles and put them into a new whistle. We'd still need new fern-tree wood, but I really think it might work.' He looked around at the others. 'You could be useful again, old men.' It was said with the affection of decades of friendship, and Darin watched sparks of hope illuminate their faces.

'Imagine if we weren't restricted by the limits of these three. Maybe we could push them back before people get hurt without risking the Collective.' Chase pushed a little more.

'I asked before, but why not just let the Collective fight?' Darin took the whistle back and tucked it in his pocket.

'They'd lose and they would die. One talon in a shoulder and …' Boulder mimed cutting his throat, then collapsed off his stool.

'Give them the magic they need?'

Boulder raised his head from the rug. 'And break our word? Risk the power falling into the wrong hands? The So'Dal have successfully hidden for so long that their true nature slipped into legend. What do you think the population would do if they realised? Would we be safe? There are other safeguards the Watcher put in place restricting the powers of the Soul Anchors – ones they do not even realise they are bound by. None of them have the same ability to defend themselves that they once had.'

'Okay, so we guard them against themselves. What's to stop a Howler going bad? Has that ever happened?'

Bones nodded. 'It did. But he had an unfortunate accident, according to our records. I like to think that we were chosen by the Watcher in part because our inability to weft limited the possibility of us ever accessing everything. The hound-bond gives us enough strength to aid, to work some things, but never enough to do what those So'Dal of old could do. No Howler will rend the land.'

'So, any suggestion of being able to weft or raising our

strength to equal that which we are trying to stop ... It wouldn't have been accepted in the past?' A general shaking of heads supported his conclusion. He closed his eyes for a moment to think. It wasn't those times anymore – there was only him and Chase. Their words reminded him of the dying So'Dal in the Star Tower. It was just the beginning of a change in the balance, and he couldn't do it alone. He had to convince them to try the whistles.

'I've only used the two you told me to so far – the lights and doors. What does the other do?'

'The other one triggers effects.'

Darin grinned. 'The invisibility?'

'Amongst others.' Bones nodded. 'We use a number of patterns to trigger each event. It takes a lot of skill to use it right. We tend to rely on a very limited number of magics not used by the other So'Dal for that reason.'

'Using the whistle costs less energy than singing a weft, and is far more reliable than our singing, so it's effective in battle,' Fall said as he joined them.

Darin blinked, his brain whirring. 'But there hasn't been a real battle for hundreds of cycles.'

'No big ones, no,' replied Bones, 'but we've fought the Edgelands creatures and kept their numbers low for all that time. Now, with only Chase and Sandy, it has become too hard. We cannot keep them away from the craterlands much longer. They encroach on human space. We nearly lost Chase twice last cycle. One Howler is not enough.'

Darin looked at the scars on Sandy's side. What type of creature could do that level of damage to a moonhound? How had Sandy survived? If they expected him to help, they needed every possible advantage.

'I think if we had a whistle like this, it would work.' He patted his pocket. 'If we can get the parts, could we make it? Or should I get the same instrument crafter who made this one to make it? I can hit things, but Star's just a pup. He's not ready to fight.'

'None of us could, that's for sure.' Bones raised his gnarled knuckles.

As soon as Darin could make a potion alone, he would bring Bones a draft like the one Wilf had. That and whistles would change so much. 'It would need someone with the right tools and an eye for copying, and it would have to be done in a single attempt. If the crystal shattered, we'd not have enough spares to try again. The dragon bone is even rarer.'

'Tian can do it,' said Chase through a mouthful of food. 'He still makes things in the old ways, and he knows how to repair one of these.' He held his own whistles out. One was a lighter colour than the rest. 'He put a new barrel on mine about ten cycles ago. He's never breathed a word to anyone else or mentioned it since. You all know how he feels about the So'Dal magic.'

'I'm sure Tian would if you asked, Chase. If it helped you in any way, you know he'd help,' Fall said. 'We should try it. We can't find more Howlers in time, and we can't risk sharing the knowledge widely.'

He stood and surveyed the rest of the pack. 'If we do this, it's a pack decision.'

Bones rose and joined him. 'I don't like the break in tradition, but desperate times call for more flexibility. We can destroy the whistle later if we feel it is a problem.'

One by one, the others stood and gave their agreement.

'Aggi would agree, I'm sure of it, but we'll get his final vote. Assuming it is positive, Darin and Star will join Chase when he next leaves for Dal and the Edgelands,' Bones said.

'Which will be as soon as we can,' Chase said. 'We need every edge we can get. It's getting difficult out there. Graaken roam freely, and it's only a matter of time before some of the other creatures reach the craterlands. Really, I need Darin trained up yesterday, but Star still has growing to do.'

A prickle of anticipation crawled over his skin, and a slight sweat of worry formed on Darin's palms. It seemed a great idea at first, but once they'd taken to it, he couldn't see how their extension of his plan would work. It was one thing getting a whistle made in Redpike, quite another going to Dal! Darin couldn't just disappear. *Keep calm – be like Hal,* he thought, suppressing the fluttering excitement rising in his gut.

'What about my studies?'

'Most apprentice So'Dal take a learning journey with a mentor at some point,' Bones said as he stood and paced the room. 'So, you leaving on one would not be a problem. It would be expected that you'd go with Tralkion eventually, but Star gives us a claim on you. However, exposing ourselves – and you getting withdrawn from your classes – would be a hindrance, especially if we lose access to the training globe. We'll need that to calibrate the whistle. By the moons, if we can get them working, imagine how much more use we could be.' He stood tall and looked around at the others, grinning. 'I could go out on patrol again!'

Chase snorted. 'Bones, you old fool. You are not fit enough to reach the holloway to Dal, let alone the Edgelands!'

Bones' shoulders dropped. 'Sadly true – but at least if you and Darin both had one ...' He trailed off. 'Fall, do you know how many whistle sets are still here?'

'Three sets from the original twenty,' Fall replied.

'So in total, we have nine sets?' Bones muttered.

Fall nodded agreement. 'They should take at least one set. Do you all agree?' He looked around at the rest of the Howlers. 'If they can get three or more sliding whistles, we'll have one ready for the next Howler as well.'

'If Darin can take classes as long as possible and learn as many wefts as he can while Star matures, he could really help Chase,' Bones mused.

'We don't have that long.' Chase sighed. 'If we don't get the Edgelands under control soon, we'll have to involve the Collective just to protect the people, and then we're risking inexperienced lives fighting xotryl. There will be no way to hide the power unleashed. Five hundred cycles of hiding, of change for the greater good of the population, would all be for nothing.'

'Who is the senior So'Dal on the council?' asked Fall.

A cough came from the corner. 'Last I heard, it was the Master,' said Claw before returning to his book.

Darin sighed. 'He won't let me miss lessons! Hal was my Collective. Can he help?'

Fall shook his head. 'No, we don't want anyone else involved for as long as we can avoid it.'

'Then we have one last choice,' interjected Boulder. 'The Master of Hounds clearly needs help with an essential trip in his old age and will need to take Darin along ... Bones, you'll have to appear to take him ranging.'

'But the Master of Hounds is an old man, he's—' Darin stopped in shock as he watched Bones pull his cloak far over his head and turn out the edge of the hood, exposing the brown trim. His face was hidden deep in its folds. He hunched over to hide even more of his face and walked with a limp. 'You? You were under my nose all that time? I knew you felt familiar.'

'Leave it with me,' Bones said in the Master of Hounds' South Crater accent. He pulled his hood back and, standing tall again, threw Darin a wink. 'I'll make a request to the Master for an essential trip and insist on your help. As you haven't left the castle with Star yet, it's urgent that you and your hound train without boundary walls soon. You are also young and strong, so you can help me with carrying the items I need to get.' He laughed. 'That should work.' He frowned at Darin. 'Talking of the Master, don't you have a lesson this afternoon?

'Yes, but I have plenty of time to play a game of stones before I need to change this wet robe.'

Darin was getting out of the palace and Redpike! His spirits soared, and even the thought of an evening singing couldn't dampen the rising joy he felt at getting outside the walls for a while.

Chapter 20

Elissa

Streams of stale calfa trickled into her mouth with each snatched breath. Rain dribbled down her neck and under her clothes as a cold stream ran between her breasts and down to her stomach. A break in the rain illuminated the grey sky for a moment, giving them respite from the downpour. Elissa stole a glance behind her, a last look at the place that had been home, where her closest friend remained. Laytha was as strong, as powerful as the mountain its self. Her presence was the one constant in Elissa's life, and she felt a yawning ache of loss as she fled with a stranger.

A flash of sunlight reflected off Dragonsbreath Peak, drawing her eyes skyward. Was a dark shape rising from it? Something blocked the dazzling reflection momentarily, then it was back. Adrenaline surged again, and Elissa turned away, increasing her uneven pace as they reached easier terrain.

The descent to the fields had been hard. Dodging from stone cover to cover had been tricky over the freshly slippery rocks, but she bit down the pain and continued onward, head down, following Rossi. His cloth cloak stuck to his legs as he walked, wrapping itself around his clean leathers. A stark contrast to her own ragged attire.

Upon reaching the fields, they walked along the fieldworker routes, stopping at the first hut. Makin had left them tools and food tucked in the corner. As she entered the familiar safety of the hut and found the small brush with a tiny fishbone tied to it, she drew a ragged breath and fought an urge to return to the familiarity of the sericlave. No. They needed her to go.

ɣ ※ ※ ﷼ ✦

They left the hut and followed the path Laytha's brother had said was the shortest route to the marshes. Despite the urgency of their escape, they walked casually, veiled tension in every step. Every few paces, they would both stop, bend as if tilling, and, carrying the tools left hidden for them, do some soil breaking.

There were enough people working through the intermittent downpours that they hoped their movements would appear natural, part of the pattern of people to any awldrin observing from the peak. New streams ran past their feet, running from the stones of the mountain over the parched earth toward the reed beds. Like sticks in the stream, they moved with the flow toward their shared destination.

Heavy rains greyed out the distant mountains; one of the next downpours might allow them enough cover to slip away from the sericlave's outer perimeter. As they reached the furthest field, Elissa felt a tickling sensation in her head and halted abruptly, turning to search the skies behind her. From high above the peak, a xotryl screech split the air.

Rossi turned to look with her, and his eyes widened as the shadow leaving the mountain grew more distinct. 'Do the awldrin usually send xotryl out while you work?'

'Occasionally, yes. They make me feel watched,' Elisa said, holding back a shudder, remembering the body she'd seen.

'You probably were. They have a strong bond with their riders.' Rossi grimaced. 'Let's hope it's just coincidence that they happen to be flying straight toward us as a break in the rain occurs.' He scanned the clouds scudding across the sky. 'There are more showers coming. That xotryl won't want to stay out long. We'd better hurry.'

The marshland filled quickly, and walking grew increasingly challenging. The tall tuffets of grass protruding through the soggy land were navigable and a way to stay dry a few moments longer, but one wrong footing would be unpleasant. Elissa's foot was throbbing with pain, and she was already finding it tough. Step by painful step, as the grasses pushed up into the arch of her foot, they continued onward.

'It's open and exposed out here. Our best chance might be the marsh itself,' Rossi said as he glanced back.

It wasn't Elissa's idea of great cover, but in their circumstances, anything would do. 'How deep is it?'

'Let's see, shall we?' Rossi hoisted his bag over his head and walked off the edge of the tuffets into a reed bed until he was deep enough that the water reached his waist. The reeds would be tall enough to hide him once they were in thicker vegetation.

Elissa sighed. So much for taking care of her foot, but it was already wet – maybe water would ease the pressure. She lifted her bag to preserve the few items she had brought and the books carefully wrapped in oiled cloth. Elissa hoped that would be enough. Her crystal shard was hidden under her clothes, hanging round her neck and bumping against her ribs as she lost balance. Cold water seeped through her clothes as she waded into the marsh; she'd be chest deep by the time she reached Rossi.

A screech split the air behind her. She dared a glance back, only to see the xotryl's shadowed form headed directly toward them. No routine patrol – they were being hunted. She gritted her teeth and waded onward. As the water reached her chest, the crystal submerged and bumped against her more gently, the xotryl shrieked again, its outline clear with the rider in stark silhouette against the grey sky.

It was being chased by a distant wall of rain but, for some reason, was no longer flying toward them. Instead, the huge head wove from side to side as it flew in an erratic pattern. Rossi and Elissa froze in place, trying to keep the reeds around them still. After more screeching, the xotryl stopped its erratic flight and began a broad pattern, weaving from one side of the fields to the other.

They waited until it flew away from them, then Elissa turned her back on the mountain for the last time and focused on following Rossi. They made steady progress through the reed bed. Tall, fluffy wind-weed flowers stood far above her head. She caught glimpses of the xotryl, still flying a sweeping pattern through an occasional thin patch. It screeched with a different timbre, as if frustrated or in pain.

'What did you do?' she whispered as she drew level with Rossi.

'Nothing! You saw me. I had no chance to do anything.'

'Then why's it lost us? It was heading right for us.' She couldn't see the xotryl as often, but they continued to hear it, shrieking from different places. Each screech sent a shudder down her spine. No one had ever got away. There was no way the awldrin would let them go.

Rossi glanced over his shoulder at her and shrugged. 'I've no idea, but I think we should stay in the reeds. My boat's that way.' He pointed to the seaward side of the marsh.

The xotryl's path was bringing them closer. It still flew a search pattern from side to side, but overall, it was headed in the direction of Elissa and Rossi.

How long did they have before the xotryl called for backup? Before they were caught?

Wading in such deep water was tricky. Tall reeds tangled around her legs, and Elissa's arms were exhausted from holding up the weight of her bag. They parted wind-weed stems slowly as they moved between them and returned them gently. She hoped that an observer from above would have seen slow ripples through dense flower heads, but nothing of the two cold, wet people beneath them.

As the day wore on, Elissa relaxed enough to notice other sounds – buzzing insects and the pattering of rain on leaves around her. The hissing of something deep in the reeds and the splashing of a large creature somewhere in front. The second increased in volume as it closed the distance between them. Rossi held up a hand to slow her, and they waited.

A head the size of Elissa's body appeared, plants protruding from both sides of its mouth as it chewed. Its leathery hide was decorated with narrow bands of light shining from between plant stems, and its thick, trunk-like legs waded through the reeds, breaking whatever they stood on.

Elissa had never seen a wildbeest so close. The creature was at least as tall as her shoulder and a solid mass of muscle; it swung its heavy head toward her, and tiny eyes glinted golden from high on its face. The hooked upper jaw was framed by a pair of short, downward-pointing tusks.

'It can't see very well,' Rossi whispered. 'Stay still.'

The coils of another creature wrapped around her legs and

then slipped away as she stood frozen to avoid startling the former. Finally, the short, thick tail of the wildbeest passed from view.

'Flames, what else is in the water? Something was on my legs.'

Rossi grinned, but it lacked the conviction of his earlier reassurance. 'I felt that too. Nothing like extra fear to get your heart pounding.'

They kept moving on, and the sky began to darken once again. If they could remain unnoticed just a little longer, the xotryl would have to turn back. The last rays of daylight faded away and rain fell heavily; greyness closed around them, providing a wet cloak of protection. The weather remained in their favour as they closed on the edge of the marsh.

Eventually, the stems thinned, and for the first time in hours, Elissa felt exposed. She found herself wishing they went a little farther.

Rossi pointed toward a slightly raised rocky area. 'That's where we are headed.'

Beyond it, wavelets on the Ameryth Dar glinted in the slices of dim moonlight slipping through gaps in the clouds. They reached a strange object hidden amongst the rocks, covered by a mottled cloth and filled with a pool of water. It was longer than Rossi was tall, and wider than she could stretch her arms. The boat looked smaller than she'd imagined it to be.

'I'll lift this edge to drain it, then we need to pull the cloth into the boat – it's our sail,' Rossi said. He untied the cloth to raise one edge and poured water back into the marsh.

Elissa scrambled in and helped haul the sail onboard. Rivulets of water ran from her clothes into the boat, filling it with a new, shallow puddle. As they squelched around, Rossi whispered instructions while Elissa threaded ropes through eyelets and held whatever he told her to. The rain continued, and she was sure they would fill up before they could go anywhere.

Finally, they were ready to leave. Rossi instructed her to sit low in the centre of the boat. He used a long pole to push them free them of the marsh, and once they were out on open water, he raised the sail. The boat rocked over waves, and Elissa found it difficult to adjust to the new sensation at first. Rossi watched her closely, but didn't ask her to help.

'We'll stick near the coastline to start with,' he said. 'Then we have to cross the open water to return to the village who lent me this. We'll sail as far as we can tonight, while it is too cold and wet for the xotryl to fly.'

The little boat slipped away from the edge of the marsh. As she stared into the darkness toward Dragonsbreath, Elissa saw occasional glints of light from the glassy peak. *I'll be back ... with help.*

Exhausted and unsettled by their trek, her eyelids flickered as she struggled to keep them open.

'Set your guard and rest,' Rossi said after she'd pulled herself upright from a nodding head for the third time.

Elissa lay gratefully in the bottom of the boat with her head resting on her pack and one arm in the small pool of water. As she dropped off, soothed by the gentle motion of the boat, she felt the cord rotate around her neck and heard the clink of her crystal as it, too, dropped into the water by her chin.

⊢ ※ ※ ※ ✦

Gentle, diffuse light woke Elissa. Rossi slept alongside her, and the boat rocked slightly. She moved and bright dots criss-crossed her body where the sun shone through laced-together eyelets of the sail overhead. Rossi had hung it over the bit he'd called a boom to create a tent-like structure.

As she moved to sit up, Rossi opened an eye halfway and motioned her down.

'You'll make us rock too much. Stay still. Were you safe in your dreams?'

'As far as I remember. I must have been pretty tired, but I remembered to sleep in the nook in my head.'

He nodded. 'Good. I couldn't find you, so you were well hidden. I spoke with the Shardeep elders before I went to sleep, to let them know them we're on our way, and ask about the strange way the xotryl stopped being able to track you. The elders were meeting to discuss the possible reasons, and I'm due to meet them again shortly. Stay still until I'm back.'

She watched him close his eye again. Elissa was never keen on being told what to do, a weakness she knew, but it had saved her and Laytha more than once. She was desperate to see what the sea looked like in daylight. She stared up at the eyelets, idly wondering if the fish in the sea were as easy to catch as the sprill back at Dragonsbreath. What she would give for a sprill! She was probably surrounded by them.

Fear was great motivation for a short time and overrode hunger, but she needed food to get her through the day. Elissa rummaged quietly through her pack and found a small, soggy bag of grain at the bottom. She scooped the top layer off hopefully, but farther down, she found nothing different – just more grains, all wet.

Wryly considering the meagre fare, Elissa decided it was a good thing that it had pre-soaked and had a quiet chuckle as she forced down the slightly salty, wet mush.

Once she'd eaten as much as she dared, leaving more for later and the next day, she levered herself up off the bottom of the boat, trying to keep her weight centralised, then reached out to gently raise the edge of the sail. Elissa glanced into the water and found herself looking into a pair of eyes. The deep green eyes looked *into* her. Elissa was certain that she was being read, as though the eyes dredged her soul. She reached toward them and, as her weight moved, the boat tipped.

⟡ ※ ⩖ ⁂ ✦

The huge, green eyes blinked. Then they were gone.

⟡ ※ ⩖ ⁂ ✦

The sparkling dark purple of the Ameryth Dar Sea was the only thing in sight, the rare sunlight between showers playing on the waves. Far away, to either side, all she could see was water.

She quietly laid back down. Rossi was still dreaming – or just sleeping. Should she tell him? Was it normal to see enormous creatures in the water? Surely it couldn't be good. Then again, did she actually see a creature? The eyes had grasped her, pulled her in, then vanished. She could no more describe what they had belonged to than she could her father's face, and she'd never really known him.

⟡ ※ ⩖ ⁂ ✦

Elissa gently ran her finger over her crystal as she thought.

'Put it back in the water – now.' Rossi stared at her. 'Water is like rock. It's all connected, so they can't pinpoint a crystal's location. That's why they never found it in the stream themselves. That's why they lost us yesterday. We need to keep it in water.'

'What about my foot?'

'Well, as long as part of you is in the water, it still connects you.'

Elissa laughed nervously. 'You want me to get in the water

with the giant creatures that live in this sea? All the way to the other shore?'

'The Ameryth Dar has nothing bigger than an occasionally oversized fish in it! And no. Trail a hand in the water as we sail. Keep the big crystal in the puddle at the bottom of the boat for now, and we will work out what to do with it once we are moving.'

Rossi frowned at her, shaking his head. Swallowing a retort, Elissa tied the cord from her neck securely around the mast base so that the wrapped crystal was submerged.

⋎ ※ ✖ ✖ ✦

Rossi shuffled gently to the front of the boat and opened a hatch she hadn't noticed. He reached inside and pulled out a bag of food. Dried meat, a bread-like substance, and dried fruit.

'Want some?'

Elissa held out the pack of wet grains. 'I ate already.'

'You didn't actually just eat that, did you?' Rossi looked at her food with disgust. 'I had all this food, and you ate *that*?' He reached for the bag.

'I didn't know about the food.'

Rossi took a mouthful of her food and gagged. 'Elissa, I know you are an independent, determined woman, but please let me sort out the food until we reach Shardeep. That's foul.' He swallowed it with effort and continued. 'Knowing what we do now, I'm tempted to keep moving during the day. If we rest for the least time possible, we might reach the village tomorrow. No sailing in daylight, even with the wefted fabric. It will blend us into the water, but in daylight, the boat itself is too visible.' He reached under the seats and offered her a long, flat section of wood. 'It's an oar. We'll use them to move along the water's edge.'

Elissa took the oar from Rossi. It was heavy and unwieldy. They rearranged themselves so that the grey sail hung across the boat from the boom, and they had a small window of visibility out the front.

Rossi helped her secure the oar. 'Put it in near the front of the boat – the bow – then pull it toward the back, under water,' he said.

Elissa took a while to master the technique, but after a few circles and spins, they were finally underway. By midday, a high bank rose ahead of them on the landward side.

'That's the land-passage between the Ameryth Dar and Skirrit Lake.' Rossi pointed at the land bridge. 'We'll be really exposed when we reach it. When we get close, we'll stay in the reeds along the edge until nightfall.'

They heard distant xotryl calls over the land throughout the day from multiple creatures. Occasionally, they saw one, and Elissa waited for them to catch up, to find them. She hoped that Laytha was safe, that the sericlave were being left alone while the xotryl hunted her instead.

Neither could relax until nightfall, despite the assurances from Rossi's elders that they were untrackable by crystal if it stayed wet.

The reeds thinned out as they approached the high bank. Pulling the oars back in and once more flattening the mottled grey sail over the whole boat, they took turns to rest and be on watch. A xotryl screech woke them part way through the day. It sounded closer than they had been at any point.

Rossi shook her awake. 'Elissa, I think you need to get in the water,' he whispered.

'All of me?'

He nodded. 'I'll try to sing the boat's camouflage into more strength, but you need to hide. Take the large crystal too. Be fast.'

He tied a rope around the mast and dropped it over the edge of the boat as Elissa slipped into the water alongside, wrapping it around her wrist tightly.

Rossi sang gently, and the sail draped over the boat appeared to shimmer like water.

Another screech split the air, and a pair of xotryl came into view, flying over the edge of the marsh toward the land bridge that connected the southern mountains from the far side of the sea. The area safe for humans.

'They're coming!' she called.

'Shhh, I'm getting ready to row. They won't follow me out across the water.'

Elissa couldn't see what Rossi did, but the xotryl were closing in on them. It didn't matter that they hadn't been spotted yet – they would be soon.

'Hold on.'

Rossi's oars dipped in by her head, and Elissa winced as one hit her. 'This won't work.'

'Trust me,' he hissed, then sang gently again. Elissa moved to be as close to the boat as possible.

Slowly, and with a lot of quiet grunting, Rossi moved them away from the protection of the bank. They would be visible, unless his magic worked, and surely the disturbance of the boat's passage would show on the water.

As the xotryl started to fly over the land bridge, she could see the creature beating its wings backward – could hear the shouts of the awldrin riding it – as the xotryl refused to fly. The narrow land bridge between the vast expanses of sea encircling the entire middle of Tebein was too thin to persuade it to cross, or at least she hoped it was. That xotryl's hatred of water was her ally in the direst of moments. They floated in silence as Elissa grew colder and colder, her teeth beginning to chatter, until the next rain shower passed through. It was the breaking point for both awldrin and xotryl, but before they turned, she was certain that something splashed into the water, part way between the xotryl and the boat.

Once they turned back, Elissa scrambled over the side of the boat, shaking and shivering. She replaced the crystal in the water and accepted Rossi's cloak gratefully.

By the time Mythos rose, they'd rigged the boat for the dash across the sea. Once they set sail and the land receded behind them, Elissa felt more and more exposed. They might have hidden so far, although she was sure that rider had spotted them. Surely, they could be seen from Dragonsbreath once exposed on the water? They were such obvious targets; a small moving object on an open sea.

Rossi radiated calm, so Elissa hid her own worries by throwing herself into whatever he asked her to do. The xotryl had turned back. They'd made it. After a few hours, she could make out stars low on the horizon.

'There.' Rossi gestured at the lights. 'That's where we're headed.'

They sailed onward, and as they drew closer, the stars grew bigger, gently bobbing with the movement of the water. A small group of boats sailed toward them.

'We've an escort back to Silverfish village as one of the fishing fleet. I hoped they'd be out. We'll stick close while they fish, then return ashore with them,' Rossi said. 'You'll have an opportunity to rest when we reach Silverfish. We'll stay the rest of the night in the inn before we continue to Shardeep tomorrow.'

Elissa felt a weight lift from her shoulders as they neared

the boats. There was still a long way to go, but safety in numbers was a far more familiar sensation to her than running alone.

⁘ ⁂ ⁑ ⁕ ✻

When the small fleet eventually docked in the fishing village on the northern shore of the Ameryth Dar just after midnight, Elissa was amazed by how healthy and happy the people were. She carried the crystal in a bag of water as they walked into the village, cradling it in her arms as they headed from the dock to the stone building dominating the seafront. Once indoors and surrounded by rock, she finally felt safe and able to relax. Someone had prepared beds, and they offered Elissa the chance to climb into a warm container of water as deep as her waist, that Rossi called a bath. A luxury she had never had the opportunity to enjoy – it was cold streams or nothing in Dragonsbreath.

'Wash that stink out of your hair,' Rossi commented as he left her to bathe in peace.

Elissa considered leaving the plants in, but rain had washed most of the herbs out, and the idea of being completely clean for the first time in her memory, won her over. She climbed into the carved tub and sank up to her shoulders. Warm water helped ease the aches in her muscles and the tension around her neck and jaw. It burned against her sore foot, swollen and discoloured after their escape.

She felt stings from bites and scratches gifted by inhabitants of the reed beds. Elissa took a deep breath, then sank down in the water until she was fully submerged, marvelling that she could hear her own heartbeats echoing through the water. Elissa counted them: ten ... twenty ... thirty. Breath bubbled out of her nose, breaking the stillness of the moment. She sat back up in the water, reached for the small bar of fragrant cleaner on the side of the bath, and washed.

⊤ ※ ✖ ☗ ✦

Elissa washed Makin's brush in the bath after she'd washed herself, and set about untangling years of knots in her hair. She wondered what he'd make of the village. Hopefully, one day, she'd find out. Dry and clean, Elissa felt like a normal person for the first time she could remember. It would be a few more days before her natural bright colour would show at the roots, and she felt a little safer knowing it wasn't obvious. For the moment, just a hint of lilac showed through her faded dye.

She gently tested her foot; it was incredibly sore despite the soak. Raising it across her thigh and resting it on her lap, she could see that the wound was clean and healing well, despite the strain she'd put it under.

The bath had washed years of accumulated muck off her, and Elissa's scars shone various shades of red through to silver – a map of her life, of the sharpness of living in Dragonsbreath. Scars from burns and scars from rocks, all making her who she was. Laytha would say it wasn't very ladylike. Thinking of Laytha spurred her into action. Elissa reached for the dress left for her and found herself glad it was a little too long. There was no need to show the scars off to the world; she didn't feel like talking about them all. Without leg coverings, she felt only half dressed – half dressed in better clothes than she had ever owned in her life.

Elissa slid her toes into the pocket of her foot coverings, feeling the familiar padded sole with appreciation. After wrapping the folds of leather, she tied them and readied herself to leave.

As she made her way out of her room and into the

communal area to meet Rossi before she went to sleep, it felt as though she walked into a new life. It was already abundantly clear that life away from awldrin was better for all humans. Despite Rains having barely started and the late hour, delicious smells emanated from the kitchens, and no one had the haggard, hungry appearance all too common at Winds-end in Dragonsbreath.

Elissa's hand rose to her neck before remembering the shard was still hidden in her bags. Rossi might want to get all their people back to Lieus, but she would settle for getting her seri-clave away from the awldrin first. They deserved a chance to live well too.

CHAPTER 21

SURIIN

*The Pagoda, that blissful symbol of youthful love.
Its many separate benches discreetly separated by
vine-covered trellises, make the perfect place
for early romantic trysts. This is a rite of
passage for most inhabitants of the Black
Palace.*
The Bond of Three

Suriin sat amongst glowing plants, accompanied by long-dead historians. No matter how many times she read the histories, something felt missing. Immense battles, and the subsequent collapse of a continent required enormous magical forces, which didn't appear possible with the level of So'Dal magic she'd experienced. Yes, people worked together. But, unless the histories weren't telling her something critical, So'Dal didn't have the power to do such damage.

That led to the conclusion that awldrin must have been incredibly powerful; they probably still were. She looked up at their dark moon. Up there, awldrin might still ride xotryl across Tebein.

Flickering fire sprites around nearby plants caught her attention and brought back memories of home. A smile crept across her face; her brother was so impetuous. She hoped he was all right – maybe he'd accompany their mother to Redpike, although he'd probably stay to help take care of the farm, ready for their parents' return. It was memories of that night and missing her brother which drove her to sit in that part of the garden. She was going crazy in her windowless room. She needed the stars. Suriin laid between flower beds, surrounded by the soft twilight of the plants, and continued to read.

'You're either incredibly foolish and lucky, or very wise and, therefore, after solitude.'

Suriin rolled over and sat up to face Ronin. 'If it was the second, why would you knowingly intrude?'

'I could claim it was to preserve your health in case it was the first option?' Ronin shrugged. 'As if your father getting hurt wasn't bad enough, here you sit, surrounded by the most toxic plants on Caldera, reading – what is that?' He reached for the book, and Suriin flipped the cover to show him.

'*Battle Strategies of the Awldrin*?' He raised an eyebrow.

'The plants remind me of the glowing crater rim at home. This book is research. I am not giving up on him, Ronin. No way.'

He gently rested a hand on her shoulder. 'We did the best we could. He'd already be dead if we hadn't.'

'Our best wasn't good enough!' Suriin cried. 'I *will* find a cure. It is my fault we were there that day. You shouldn't have left Golden so soon. If you hadn't both been protecting me, he would have easily reached the cave. Whichever way you look at it, it's because of me.'

'*If* doesn't change what has been. We can only affect our

futures – move forward, move onward. If all the Gardeners in this palace haven't found a cure, why do you think you will?'

Suriin crossed her arms. 'They're looking in the wrong place. I am sure of it.'

Ronin rubbed his hand along his jawline pensively. 'I would not see Yorynn die. I don't want to jeopardise my final assessment by doing something rash, but maybe I can help a little ... if I'm careful.'

Suriin nodded, understanding. 'You can help with getting books I can't. I don't know what's in your library that would add to what I already know.'

'Which is?'

'Awldrin heal from xotryl wounds. So, I want to know how and if it's something we can apply to my father.'

'Now that book makes more sense. I'll see what I can do. Your father's as stable as they can make him, so I don't think risking things by rushing round and attracting attention is a good idea. I'll meet you back up here in three nights' time. Not here, though – every Gardener working late can see you lying here. I'll meet you in the pagoda.' Ronin bowed his head in farewell and turned on his heel to walk away, straight-backed without a backward glance.

He may be arrogant, annoying, and think I'm a baby, but at least he's willing to help.

Ronin had a valid point, though. She was almost night blind from the glow, and had forgotten about the ledges and workrooms in the crater walls. Conscious of how odd she must appear to an observer, she finished the chapter, then avoiding the toxic blooms and clutching the book close to her chest, she negotiated her way back out.

Suriin rubbed her head. Her eyes pulsed with pain, and her forehead ached with the effort of continued reading. The pile of books dismissed as useless had grown. She stepped over them, knocking several botanical treatises and a full history of the events of the Rending off the pile. The latter was embossed with a beautifully detailed picture of the Watcher. Black scales covering a colossal body glistened on the cover; the dragon poised, and ready to fly off the page.

Over the past two days, she had learnt about magical techniques that were, as yet, far beyond her understanding. She'd found mentions of wondrous things she might one day be able to do, but as far as cures or xotryl went, her research remained barren. Suriin packed the scattered books into a bag, ready to return to the Soul Anchor's library before her meeting with Ronin.

She hoped he'd made better progress than her. A red book caught her eye – she hadn't meant to take that one back yet. Suriin picked *Moonhound History and Care* back out of her bag and, absently stroking the cover, replaced it on her table. Hoisting the heavy bag over her shoulder, she stepped out of her room to meet Fresna.

'Did you have any luck?' Fresna asked quietly on their way to the library.

Suriin shook her head despondently. 'No. Lots of general facts, but nothing of any real use. I feel like there are gaps in what I'm reading. Things unsaid. I can't put my finger on it, though – it's odd. You?'

'I found a list of the objects and substances that awldrin carried and the uses found for them. A few were marked as unknown or no use found. There were mentions of red, white, and black powders, as well as other unidentified substances in looted bags of captured awldrin. I do agree with you, though. It feels like something's not being said, but I can't work it out either.'

'I'd guess at the red one being staramine powder,' said Suriin. 'From what I've read, the historians still didn't really understand why they mined it, just that they did.'

'Yup – more missing information! So, all we need is a nice friendly awldrin, who can clarify their use then. That's easy. There must be hundreds around!' Fresna replied.

Suriin twisted her mouth into a half smile. 'I'm sure there's a few in the Collective So'Dal. They're all so tall – and you never see who is under some of those hoods. Or maybe the steam-lift men. They're always deeply hooded too. What do you reckon?'

Fresna laughed, and the resulting avalanche stopped all conversation as they recovered the books and checked them for damage.

⊢ ❋ ⚙ ⚛ ✦

They walked into the library, and the Soul Anchor in charge nodded acknowledgement of their presence, gesturing them through, barely lifting her eyes from the pages of her book.

'What next?' asked Fresna.

'Tomorrow, I have to meet Soul Anchor Aslin. Maybe I will start classes soon after.' Suriin liked Fresna, but letting her know about the meeting with Ronin didn't feel right.

'Tomorrow? But the class isn't all here.' Fresna's eyebrows creased in confusion.

Suriin shrugged. 'You and I know that. Presumably, Aslin knows that, but she still sent a messenger. As long as I'm still on kitchen duty, I can catch up with you. I'll just have to do my research at night. Come on. We'll be late, and Chef will not be pleased.'

'Have my list anyway. Maybe it will tie with some of what you've read when you look back at it.'

Suriin smiled her thanks, tucking it safely into her robe.

⊥ ※ ⅏ ⅏ ✦

It had been a long, hot shift, and she felt sticky and uncomfortable. But washing would have to wait. She tucked her hand into her robe, checking that the scrap of paper Fresna had given her earlier was still safe, and rushed off as soon as Chef released her.

The tall So'Dal working the steam lift lever that night seemed to watch her more than usual. She climbed aboard and concentrated on her feet as she waited for him to raise the lift. Thinking back to her earlier joking comment to Fresna about awldrin, she couldn't resist trying to see who was under the hood. Not expecting to see anything but an old and worn face, she was surprised by the clear, direct eyes that met her own.

Suriin forced a smile and attempted a casual, relaxed posture. He couldn't have heard her joking before. It was just paranoia. At some point, surely everyone walks in the crater garden at night? She was hot and bothered and everyone ate in the hall, so he'd be bound to know that she worked in the kitchens. The Gardeners did. Maybe she wouldn't look out-of-place cooling down to anyone on the observation balconies. She wasn't doing anything wrong by meeting a So'Dal in the garden. There was no reason to feel as edgy as she did. She glanced upward to the crater – she needed to get up there soon. Why hadn't he released the lever?

As she stared upward, the steam whistled, and she shot skyward.

⊥ ※ ⅏ ⅏ ✦

Shadowed forms sat around the pagoda. Most of them Gardeners, but a few So'Dal and their Soul Anchors were enjoying some time alone. *Great, so now it will look like a romantic tryst.* As she circled around, a So'Dal rose and walked toward her.

'Walk with me,' Ronin said. 'I am going to take your arm.'

'Why?' Suriin recoiled. 'You don't even like me!'

'Because it's less conspicuous if we are meeting for a romantic stroll, than if we stand here talking,' he said pointedly. 'I don't have to like you. I've already told you I'm helping you for your father's sake, not your own.' Without another word, he linked his arm through hers and steered her away from the other couples.

They wandered away from the pagoda before Suriin spoke again. 'As you didn't send me back to my room, I take it you found something?' It was dark, but even in the dim light of the crater, she could make out a nod before he spoke.

'Unlike us, they used their plants and other substances in a dried powder form. Several plants have been identified, as have their uses, and several other substances remain unidentified.'

Suriin sighed in disappointment. 'I've already found that out. A red, a white, and a black powder – am I right?'

'You are. Did you find out where the samples of the plants are kept, though?'

Suriin frowned. 'No. I sort of assumed that they'd have all been removed or lost years ago. After all, what is it? About five hundred and four years now since the last awldrin was on Lieus?'

'Yes, but we still have some artefacts. The treasury and armoury retained everything useful to us, but I also found a reference to the old storage vaults. Maybe if you can locate those, there could be something left of other awldrin artefacts? I'm grabbing at clouds here, and I can't help any more. My assessment date has been set for next tide. I did find you one other thing, though. I'll need to take it back in a few days, but I borrowed this.'

Suriin reached for the folded parchment he offered to her. 'What is it?'

'It's a steward's palace plan. I think they used them for defence – it was in the military histories section. I figured that as you were already researching that area, there might be something useful in it and came across this.' He shrugged. 'It might help. There's lots of doors and tunnels marked on it that I've never seen. Much of the palace has been rebuilt or built over since this was drawn, so it may be of little use. It shows the steam lift, so you can always work outward.'

'Thanks, Ronin. I may be a bit more occupied from tomorrow. What if I meet you back up here in a tide? I can copy it by then. You'll let me know if you hear anything new about my father, won't you?'

'I doubt I'll hear much more than you. Are you going to see him tonight?'

'Yes, although I think it might be a shorter visit than I'd like. The Gardeners tend to him fairly soon.' Suriin tried to keep her composure as she felt her lip wobble. 'I'd just like to be able to talk to him.' She wiped her eye and sniffed. 'Well, it looks like you've upset me now. That's a good reason to leave here alone, I suppose.'

'I'll accompany you back to the pagoda.'

The walk back was painfully slow. All she wanted to do was run off to examine the map after seeing her father. The faster she acted, the sooner she might help him.

CHAPTER 22

DARIN

Darin checked the list of plants was safely in his pocket for the third time. Everything on it grew in the crater garden, but Tralkion had asked Darin to find and preserve new seeds from any wild ones he came across to enhance their stock. That was the one part of the journey he was confident about. Tralkion had seen Darin's journey as a challenge and eagerly set about devising a list. The Master had not taken it quite so well.

'You need far more practise. I don't want you making mistakes where you could hurt people,' he'd said. 'I don't like this. You should be more ready first.'

Darin promised not to try wefting whilst away, but he'd secreted the small training globe inside his pack. They needed it for the whistles, and the Master hadn't asked him to leave it – even if, technically, he hadn't told him to take it either.

Neither Darin nor Bones carried much, as they were supposedly travelling to the Surface near Port, and could take advantage of hospitality along the way. A pack of wild moonhounds were known to live in the area, so it gave them a legitimate destination. That route also meant lots of towns to replenish stores at, and comfortable beds for Bones' old bones.

He doddered around slowly, hunched and leaning heavily on his staff. Bones took so long crossing to the Hound paddocks and back again that Darin thought they'd never be on their way.

Hal wandered over to Darin and patted Star on the head.

'It's good to see you. I bet you're desperate to get underway. Remember, when you pass through Eye, be careful what you say to your family.'

Darin had sent the scarf to his mother a while ago, so it should have arrived, and he couldn't help feeling sad that he'd not get to see her wearing it. But he hid that. Hal, as all the others did, needed to believe he was headed to the West.

'It will be good to see them and have an ale without having to earn it.' He grinned at Hal.

'This came for you.' Hal reached inside his pocket and pulled out an opened letter.

'It's open?'

'It has to be – I'm sorry. We have to check that all your communications appear to have been confidential.'

Darin would be aware of that in the future. He took the letter and read it quietly, keeping half an eye on Bones. 'They are well. The money is reaching them.' His mother wrote of starting to rebuild the inn and of how his wages had brought them hope and a fresh start – how one day, he could come home again. Darin couldn't see when that might be, but at least they were well. He folded the letter up and tucked it in his pocket.

'Thank you.'

Hal clapped him on the shoulder. 'Just be careful on the way back. Remember to restock your supplies.' He leant in close and whispered, 'Keep the Master of Hounds safe. He's a little frail these days.' Hal pressed a vial into Darin's hand. 'Tuck that into your supplies, just in case.' He nodded once more and walked back to the Star Tower.

Aggi and Chase waited somewhere outside the town walls for them with his real supplies. Fall, Claw, and Boulder were manning the lift on rotating shifts until Aggi and Bones returned. Everyone played their part, and Darin hoped he could repay them with whistles. He shifted his weight from foot to foot in nervous anticipation. Bones was so slow! Star nuzzled his hand, and Darin tried to relax. He was making Star nervous – he could feel it.

He tried to distract himself by watching Lea round up errant puppies in the courtyard. She was in charge of the palace pack while the Master of Hounds was away and beamed with pride. Her young moonhound worked proudly alongside her. She'd told Darin that she hoped to take on the responsibility permanently one day, so his journey was as important for her as it was for Darin.

Finally, Bones was ready. Darin sent *[Walking through the gates]* to Star, who wagged furiously with excitement.

His sight was suddenly flooded by *[Sandy and Chase with bags on, in a valley]*. He patted Star gently to try to calm him.

'Yes, boy, but keep it quiet,' he laughed as Bones turned his deeply hooded head toward Darin.

'He is just excited, Master So'Dal,' Darin explained. 'It will be his first adventure outside the palace.'

Gruffly, Bones replied, 'Let us hope you can keep that

excitement in check, apprentice. No upsetting the residents of Redpike as we pass through, please.'

'Of course, Master So'Dal,' Darin replied, loudly enough that anyone nearby could hear him.

They continued the charade of formality through the palace gates and out into the town. The main cobbled highway wove drunkenly between market stalls and the houses behind them, toward the town gates. A few children tried to stroke Star, but he continued walking with his head held high as he loped along-side Darin.

They passed through Redpike's walls, having had no real communication with anyone else. Once outside, they doubled back around the perimeter. A narrow trail cut around the town, and they followed it in a silence broken only by occasional twigs snapping underfoot. It was always Darin's foot.

Once out of sight from the town gates, Bones straightened up and pulled his hood back.

'Moons, it's good to be out of there! We'll be with Chase by midday. Keep Star on the path – there are unpleasant plants up here.'

'I see some,' Darin replied, pointing at a group of scarthorn bushes Star ran near. Their wicked points would do serious damage if they caught skin. Tralkion's list had them on it, but he didn't want the long thorns. Darin needed the leaves that spiralled around the stem like a tiny staircase for fire sprites; since they were so close to the town, he decided to get them on his way back. He sent *[Star and Darin walking along the path]*, and received a mental wag in return. Moments later, Star walked alongside them, his muzzle lifting intermittently and nostrils flaring as he took in the mountain air and its myriad of scents. To Darin's own less developed nostrils, the fresh smell of outdoors was a welcome sensation.

The path split into smaller trails as they reached the

ascending slopes marking the route toward the peaks. They grew narrower and less defined, a flattened gap between the vegetation the only clue that any creature had passed that way before. Bones pointed down-slope as they followed one of the small paths around the mountain.

'We need to be heading down now.' He sounded breathless, and Darin worried that they were setting too fast a pace.

'Don't look so concerned,' Bones wheezed. 'Age catches us all in the end, and it's downhill from here, in both senses of the meaning.'

Star slowed his pace and returned to walk with them after Darin sent *[Bones looking tired and breathing heavily]* to the moonhound. In return, Darin received *[Open area of grassland at the end of the trail. Two figures and a hound visible on the skyline]*.

'Not far now. Star can see them,' Darin encouraged Bones onward.

'It may have been twenty-five cycles since I came out here with my hound, but it hasn't changed so much that I don't know where I am,' was the retort. 'Clearing ahead, the other Howlers on the skyline?' He sighed. 'Twenty-five cycles, and I still miss that. My extra eyes and constant companion. I miss her.'

He glanced at Darin as they descended the last part of the path. 'Your Staramine ... he's my girl's descendant. All of the Howler hounds are from one line – they always have been. It's a strange thing.'

'So Sandy and Staramine are related too?' Darin asked.

'Yes. I've got all the records in the hound paddocks. I can't always track the fathers, but I record the mothers.'

A howl cut through the air, reverberating through Darin's core. His head snapped up as Star replied.

'Imagine how it used to sound with the whole pack,' Bones

said. His bright eyes lit up, focused ahead unseeing, and a grin split his face from ear to ear. 'It was worth coming this far with you just to hear that again.'

They reached the clearing as midday sun broke through the cloud layer. Both squinted in the sudden brightness as warmth took the damp chill from the air. Star bounded ahead, leaping on the incoming Sandy, and the two moonhounds rolled around in the damp grass like a pair of pups.

'You wouldn't think Sandy was almost thirty cycles old to see this, would you?' Chase smiled fondly at his hound, and the chiselled edges of his countenance softened with affection.

The four men stood in companionable silence, watching the pair of hounds rolling around and chasing each other for several minutes.

Aggi broke the moment with a gentle cough. 'Well, this takes me back. I wish I could join you on your trip.' He pulled out two spare sets of whistles from his pack. 'We decided you should take two sets. Then we can all have one if it works. We might not be fit enough to join you on patrols, but if things continue to get worse, at least we can use them closer to Redpike, or man a watchtower.' Aggi held out a closed hand. 'The third whistle in your set can be used to activate this dragon bone. With it, you will blend in, be effectively invisible.' He opened his fist to reveal a tiny fragment of white material strung on leather.

Darin took it carefully. 'Like the door?' he asked. 'And all of you when we first met?' He turned the tiny fragment over in his hands. The Howlers had trusted him with real dragon bone. It stunned him.

'Yes. Wear it under your tunic, then it will always be in contact with you. It's as hard as staramine, and only staramine will grind or break it, so don't worry about it breaking. Each shard is tuned differently, so it won't suddenly turn Chase invisible,' Aggi said and patted him on the shoulder.

'Do you remember when—' Bones broke in.

'Chase swapped Claw's and Boulder's whistles over,' Aggi said, a smile dancing over his face. The realisation that those men had faced so much of their lives together hit Darin hard. Yet, like Chase, he'd spend much of his time alone.

Chase laughed. 'Let's not give him ideas! I have a short time and a lot to teach him. Although, if we can get these whistles, and they work ...' He left the rest unsaid, but they all nodded at the unfinished sentence.

Darin's backpack gained more items from Bones, including two small vials of healing draft.

'These are all I could gather on short notice,' Bones said. 'Chase has been working hard out there, and we are extremely low on supplies. If we'd had more time ...'

Darin took the small vials and tucked them into his bag. 'Thank you. Two is still better than none and Hal gave me an extra one in the courtyard. When we have the whistles, we can make our own.' He offered a smile to Bones. Truthfully, he hadn't expected any. After all, the old Howlers probably needed their own doses just to keep going. From out of his own bag, Aggi pulled what appeared to be a skaa-rak saddle pack, but smaller.

'This is for Staramine. It was ours, and he's a similar size to my old hound, or will be. It doesn't carry a lot – but there will be times you need it. While he's still young, just get him used to wearing it.'

Chase reached down and picked up a similar pack. Sandy appeared at his side straight away. Darin copied Chase, putting the bags either side of Star and gently tightening the chest and stomach straps to stop it slipping backward.

Star wagged throughout and licked Darin's hand affection-ately as he tried to do the chest straps up.

Next, Darin rolled his shoulders and tested the weight of his own bag, his muscles straining at the weight. It would be a hard walk until he got used to it. Aggi helped lift it into place and passed him the walking staff he'd been holding.

'This is for you.' He reached into his robe and handed Darin a spearhead on a long screw.

'You can unscrew this' – he undid the top of the walking staff – 'and screw this tip on so you have a short spear. It's good to be less threatening in villages.'

The screw threaded a long way down inside the staff and felt secure. Darin nodded his thanks and secreted the cap inside his robes.

'Be safe, both of you,' Bones said.

'Bring us back some Edgeland delicacies for tea,' Aggi joked. 'We're going to have a short rest, then head back through the Howler tunnels. Bones will have me fetching him books, washing his clothes, and Watcher only knows what else that he can't do while you're gone, so please hurry back!'

'Ready?' Chase asked.

'Let's go.' Darin tried to cover up the nervous wobble in his voice.

'Sandy, to me,' Chase said. It was clearly for Darin's benefit, so Darin called Star close and followed Chase along the winding path that would lead them to the rising mountain pass, and the small, hidden holloway he had seen marked on the Howler maps, then on to Dal.

⊹ ※ ✗ ✗ ✦

They crested the ridge of the pass as the sun passed the mid-point of its descent; it bathed the open expanse in front of them in a blanket of shadow. At the shadow's extent, the twin peaks of the Fangs blocked the view of Dal crater. Smaller hills ahead rose and fell like the curves of a sleeping person under a blanket.

'We need to be on the lower slopes by dark. There's a small watchtower there we can stay in. It used to be manned, but without enough of us, all the Howler keeps stand empty.' Chase pointed down at a narrow gap in the foothills. 'It's there.'

Darin strained his eyes, but couldn't make out a tower – or any structure at all. *I bet it's invisible.* Excited for another secret reveal, he hurried after the already departing Chase.

⚹ ⚹ ⚹ ⚹ ⚹

The long descent hurt his knees, and the heavy pack dug into his shoulders. Darin's neck became sore, and tides of being stuck in the palace meant that unused muscles on his back and legs ached. Darin had tripped over his own feet on several occasions by the time they reached the base of the pass and was certain he had blisters. Although he'd travelled much farther with Hal, they'd carried very little, and he'd been used to an active life. This would be a very different journey.

The tower came into view as they rounded a foothill. Small and solid, it appeared to grow out of the hillside. Over time, moss had filled gaps in the stonework, and trees protruded from upstairs windows. It looked abandoned and unused. A relic of a bygone age when the So'Dal were the rulers of the land rather than keepers of secrets. Faded red symbols ringed the waist of the tower on a collection of feature stones. Central to them was the howling hound. To one side of it, the star, and on the other, the So'Dal symbol.

The door creaked open, hanging off its top hinge, whilst its base swung wildly. They were greeted by a room as overgrown and moss-covered as the outside of the tower. Echoes of their footsteps accompanied them upstairs, where the abandonment appeared complete.

'In here,' Chase said as he pushed open a small door. It had every bit as much moss on as the rest – light and rain streaming through the landing window were doing a good job of helping nature reclaim the place.

He followed Chase, who blew a whistle, and what Darin had expected to be another small damp room, lit up.

Clean walls, a dry floor, and soft beds met his eyes. Deep rugs like those in the Howler quarters were piled in the centre of the room, and soon, a heat globe filled the space with welcome warmth.

'There are blankets in that cupboard.' Chase pointed to the corner. 'I'll get some food for us. Nothing fancy – it doesn't last out here – but it will fill us up.' He rummaged in a different cupboard and quickly had a warm drink and some broth ready for them both.

Darin collected the blankets, made the beds, stretched his sore muscles out, and sat to eat with his new, small pack.

CHAPTER 23

SURIIN

Whilst it is common to have remorse after an action, encountering it prior to events is a rarer phenomenon. For, to be remorseful before you carry something out, is to carry it out knowing that what you do will be regretted forever.
The First Anchor appointed by the Watcher himself, had to make just such a decision.
So'Dal Brand, The Anchors of the Black Palace

'Take nothing that might distract you today – everything you do in her room is a test,' Fresna had told her before giving her a hug. 'Good luck.'

Suriin knocked on the door, her heart pounding. It was finally time. She'd waited so long!

'Enter.'

She opened the door and paused at the threshold. A circular

table dominated the room, and carved patterns radiated out from where Aslin stood in its centre. *Had she crawled under the desk to get into that space?* Suriin tried to find calm as her mother had taught her. Once her emotions had settled and nerves stopped seething, she stepped into the room.

'Welcome. Take a seat.' Aslin gestured widely around the table. A bench encircled it. Suriin moved closer to make out the symbols engraved in the wood. She walked around the table slowly and found that she recognised some symbols. There was joy; near it, she spotted love. Was that one anger? They were arranged in three rings with fewer symbols in the centre, closer to Aslin. As the symbols reached the edge of the table, they doubled in number.

Eventually, she decided to sit on the opposing side from love. After all, if Aslin had been observing her, she didn't want rumours about herself and Ronin flying around. She recognised none of the symbols on this side except anger. She deliberately avoided that one and chose one at random. This way, she could face the door in case of other surprises.

Suriin sat on the bench, then raised her eyes to meet Aslin's. She caught the woman staring at her, wide-eyed. The moment vanished as soon as it happened, and Aslin spoke, her voice melodious and smooth.

'That took you a while. Why that seat?'

Suriin considered her reply for a moment and decided not to reveal that she knew any of the symbols.

'It was facing the door.'

As she had walked around the table twice before she sat, she wasn't sure it would be accepted, but Aslin nodded.

'That is a reason. Why worry about having your back to the door?'

'I was thinking about being able to see who came in, rather

than worrying about not seeing who is behind me.' Suriin replied. *It would have been easier just to say it was random.* She ran her finger over the symbol on the desk in front of her, feeling its intersecting lines and points. As she did, she thought it lit for a moment, just a glimmer.

Aslin appeared to accept the reason and smiled. Her eyes flicked to Suriin's fingers.

'They're interesting, aren't they? This table is older than the palace. The earliest So'Dal used it. We are merely its current caretakers.'

'What does it do?'

'It is a tool to help you learn control of your powers. To channel through your crystal and focus them. Without crystals, we use our resources too fast. They help us to preserve them and allow us to apply them more often. Are you ready to take your first steps in becoming a Soul Anchor?'

'But the rest of my class?'

'Arrive daily. You were here first, so it's only fair that you are first to gain your crystal. The others will bond theirs over the next few days, and lessons begin before the tide is out.'

'Please, Aslin, I'm ready to begin. I'll work to be the best I can.'

Aslin smiled briefly, her serious eyes meeting Suriin's. 'Of that, I have no doubt. Your mother was the hardest working student in our class. It will be a pleasure to teach her daughter.'

'You know my mother?' Suriin asked, bursting with questions. Which seat had her mother chosen? Did Aslin know? She couldn't wait to show her mother she'd crystal bonded!

'A conversation for another day. Back to you and your own journey today,' Aslin said lightly, her tone not matching the slight tension of her jaw. *A conversation for another day, indeed! What's she hiding?*

Trying to keep her face smooth and quell her rising concern, Suriin re-centred herself. Aslin bent down to retrieve something from under the desk. As she straightened up, her curls bounced, and she smiled broadly at Suriin.

'Ready?'

'Of course. I was born for this,' Suriin said calmly. Aslin flinched again, her gaze flickering toward the symbol Suriin rested her hands on.

'Place your crystal on the closest symbol, cover it with your hand, and repeat the words after me,' Aslin said, handing her a crystal.

It was beautiful. Colours danced along the edges, reflecting light from the windows. Flashes of green shot from the fragmented sides as Suriin placed it in the middle of the symbol. She concentrated intently on copying Aslin; each phrase was short and hard to pronounce, in a language she didn't understand. As she repeated the words, light shone through cracks in her fingers, her crystal pulsing with light. When the last phrase left her lips, a flow of power ran from her core, through her hand, and into the crystal.

Then she could feel it. On the edge of her mind was a shiny, sharp feeling. If she turned away, she was certain she could find it. Suriin was aware of the table below the crystal through it, and the cradling warmth and softness of her own hand around it. She could feel the crystal with her hand, and her hand through the crystal. Suriin lifted her hand and gently dropped it. The two sensations separated.

'We usually wear them against our chests. It's easier to cope with, rather than dealing with all the sensations you'd feel were you to carry it exposed.' Aslin's voice cut through the moment. 'Here,' she offered Suriin a soft, leather pouch on a cord, pushing it across the desk to her. 'Put it on. You'll need to get used to the feeling before we start lessons.'

Suriin gently placed the crystal in the bag and hung it around her neck. The sensations it produced were muted enough that she could once again focus on what Aslin said.

'You should feel slightly different now? The seat you chose subconsciously represented a big store of the emotional reserve needed to bond. Can you feel how your mood has changed?'

Suriin reached inside herself, probing her thoughts for a gap. She still felt love for everyone. She knew it wasn't anger, but she couldn't work out what was different.

'I feel lighter,' she said finally. 'I want to do something outside palace gates. My parents wouldn't want me wallowing here.'

Aslin nodded. 'You used remorse – that is the symbol you chose.'

Suriin sat quietly, holding the pouch at her neck with one hand. 'I suppose that makes sense. It was my fault my father left Golden early. It was trying to save me that got him hurt, so I can see why that would be a strong emotion. When I use my power, do I use up feeling?'

'You do.'

'So I could effectively magic away my guilt over this, my role in it, and just accept he got hurt?'

Aslin nodded again. 'Yes. It's powerfully tempting to spend the emotions we don't like, but then we become less than human. The crystal helps us to keep that control. This is why we can't teach you to use your power until you have crystal bonded.'

'When do we start lessons?' Suriin asked. The logic made sense. Emotionally hollow magic users could cause chaos with no emotional checks, no guilt.

'In a few days. I'll send for you, and we'll meet here. Until then, go about your normal routine. Get used to the sensations and handle the crystal in solitude to learn how it feels.'

Suriin bowed her head. 'Thank you, Soul Anchor Aslin.'

She stood and bowed to Aslin, then circled the table to leave. Aslin's eyes were fixed on her, and Suriin was certain there was sadness in them.

Chapter 24

Elissa

Tebein has dramatic seasonal changes.
The most notable one is the development of huge
seasonal marshlands.
The rich flora of these is a botanist's delight.
The Black Moon

Lieus hung low in the sky, illuminated by their shared sun of the Aulirean system. Small and distant, yet beckoning her with new hope. Humans lived on that verdant world, green with edible plants, rich with food all year around; a place where she would have been at the opposite end of the social scale, born to power and influence.

Elissa gazed up, torn between anger they'd been abandoned and the tiniest flicker of hope that maybe Rossi was right – there might be a way back. She shook her head. Such thoughts wouldn't help. It was time to focus on survival, on learning and – as she put her discoloured and swollen foot on the floor – trying to walk.

Tentatively, she shifted her weight onto it and straightened her legs to stand. Elissa attempted a normal stride, digging her nails into her palms, trying to distract herself from the pain. It didn't work. Every flexion of her foot brought about eye-watering agony. If the awldrin continued their pursuit, she couldn't afford to be slow or immobile. She was both, but surely they'd got away ... maybe.

Elissa tried to walk on her toes, but the flexion of her foot made that worse. She gritted her teeth and shifted, walking with her weight through the heel and outside of the foot, the toes elevated. It was the most comfortable of the three.

She'd knew she'd look ridiculous, and no doubt hurt other parts of her body, but it would have to do. Rossi and Laytha had assured her that the actual wound was clean. Perhaps if she was careful, the shard might eventually work its way out, or at least into a less painful spot.

Elissa replaced her crystal in the small carved jar Rossi had given her before she went to sleep and tied it to her belt before heading down for breakfast.

The food was solid and nutritious – some dried fruits and grains, a cup of calfa, and a warm welcome. The owner offered a smile, and they chatted with some fishermen over their steaming mugs. Elissa felt truly relaxed until she recalled the reasons for running and the next stage of the trip.

On the journey to Shardeep they would ride wildbeest, to speed their journey and ease her foot; two tame ones were tied up in the back of the building. The thought of sitting on a moving animal made her stomach flip. She was certain she'd fall off. What if the animal didn't want to be sat on? Rossi had tried to ease her fears by discussing their broad backs and docile nature.

Rossi assured her that tame ones were docile. If it meant that she could travel at speed away from the xotryl and toward a future for her and the other Untouched, she'd do it with a smile.

Once breakfast was eaten, and before they prepared to leave, Rossi took her to the beach. Children played with pebbles, skimming them across the water to make them bounce; parents hunted in rock-pools and shared their finds with bright eyed toddlers. The whole place was suffused with joy.

That was what she wanted – the child who waved at her on the way to her shift on the bellows each day deserved a chance to be so free. The other Untouched deserved to eat and live. A few people glanced at her and smiled. Rossi soon gathered a cluster of children showing him their treasures and asking him to do magic. He looked at each shell and creature, making time for them all.

One young girl passed him a shell with a hole in it. 'I think this is my best shell. You can give this to your daughter? Will she come and visit again soon?'

Rossi took the shell and tucked it into his pocket.

'Thank you, Vinjii. I will pass it on. We'll visit later in Rains, I hope.' He stood and turned to Elissa. 'This is why we ride, why we hope – for our children and their futures. What you carry could bring safety for them all. It's time to go. Come on.'

⊤ ❈ ⚕ ⚖ ✦

Several hours later, and with muscles aching in places she hadn't known they could, their wildbeest waded out of the sea. Water streamed from Elissa's legs in hundreds of tiny waterfalls, and the split robe chafed her thighs. The warm, smooth hide of the beest stopped her from shivering, and her knuckles grew white from gripping tightly to the handle of the chest harness. Rossi rode his own and lead hers using a long rope.

'Hold tight. We need to cross this headland as quickly as possible since the surrounding coastline is much too steep to ride around. Being on land will expose you, so keep an eye out for xotryl. I'd love to think we're free of them, but the fact they even attempted the land bridge worries me.' Rossi looked at her with concern when she laughed.

'I'm holding so tight my hands have cramped. I couldn't let go if I wanted to.'

Rossi grinned and slapped his beest on the neck. 'K-k-k,' he called, and the wildbeest snorted, then started to run. Elissa's followed, and slowly the lumbering creatures worked up to a steady, rolling gait. Their clawed feet thundered across the ground, sending small creatures scattering to either side. The smooth hide of the beest made it hard to sit the gait without sliding, and Elissa bounced and rocked from side to side. She gripped on and focused on remaining mounted. Rossi sat calmly upright – as though he and the beest were a single creature – his legs barely moved. Flame the man, he made it look easy.

'How are you doing that?' she called as she was bounced again.

'Sit tall and relax your stomach a little. Let it move with the beest. Stop fighting it,' he shouted back.

Elissa's first attempt at relaxing ended up with her face in its neck, her second earned her a bruise as she fell and hit the ground.

'Rossi!'

He stopped the beest and sprung off.' Are you ok? We can walk for a bit if you need a break, but it will take us much longer.'

Elissa pushed herself up. Her aching muscles, combined with the pressure in her foot, caused her legs to wobble uncontrollably, and they gave way. *A gentle sit would be better than another bump.* She sank back down to the floor and shut her eyes for a moment, focused on breathing. In ... and out, breathing out the pain. Every muscle in her body wanted to sit and stay. Every part of her mind wanted to get going. It was only a matter of time before the awldrin flew across the narrow land bridge. They needed to move, to get to safety.

Elissa rolled into a crouch and repositioned her feet. She shifted her weight over her good foot and pushed up. Wobbly but upright, she leant against her beest, then grabbed a handful of the strap around its neck and hauled herself on. As her weight transferred to its back, the beest shifted and grunted in displeasure.

'Hoy! No!' she heard from Rossi. 'You! Stand.'

Elissa managed a thin smile. 'Let's go.'

His mouth twisted up at one corner, and he gave a small shake of the head. 'Hold on then. Try not to fall off again.'

'I *was* holding,' she muttered under her breath. 'There has to be a more comfortable way to sit on this moonstruck beest.' The loping stride of the animal interrupted her as it took off again. She gave up copying Rossi and just gripped as tightly as she could with her hands and thighs to stay on its back.

⊥ ✳ ⚹ ⚜ ✦

A soul-shredding screech rent the air. Elissa saw Rossi glance in its direction. They'd forced the xotryl across the land bridge; it must have left with the sun that morning. Elisa's heart sank. All the people on the northern side of the sea were in danger now, all because the awldrin wanted her.

'Hold tighter,' he shouted back. 'We need cover fast! The speed they fly, that xotryl will catch us before we get to the other side of the headland. There's marsh ahead – if the rains have filled it – but it's the in the wrong direction.'

The pounding thunder of their wildbeest hooves matched the pounding of her heart as they raced for the marsh. *Again*, Elissa thought, a grimace crossing her face at the thought of further bites and cuts. Why couldn't the other humans live somewhere nice and easy to get to? Without all the wetness. Or why not take another boat? If the human sericlaves were all on the water's edge, why didn't they just sail there in the first place? Surely, it would have been safer. Her life couldn't be worth all the people being enslaved by awldrin once they knew they were there.

'I think—' Breath was ripped from her mouth as she opened it to speak, and in its place, a bug entered. Trying to spit into the wind and hang on proved to be a step too far, so she bit the creature in two to stop it wiggling and swallowed it, gagging as she did.

The stone jar tied to her belt thumped against her hip, and although it shielded the big crystal, the one in her foot probably lit her up like a beacon. Another shriek raised hairs on her arms with involuntary fear, and she braved a look. The shape of the huge creature grew clearer by the moment. Before long, the xotryl's rider would be visible as well.

Reeds peeked from the ground, changing the texture of the land ahead, but the chance of them making it that far was slim. Between their beest and the marsh was an expanse of open ground. Rossi shouted and pointed to his right. 'That way. We're turning – hold on! I have an idea.'

The beest swung right and, for a heart-stopping moment, her body continued straight on. She slipped and slid, staying on by determination alone. As she struggled upright, she couldn't see anything ahead – no rocks, trees or any other cover. Why did Rossi turn away from the marsh? She peered around, searching for a reason. There appeared to be a more uneven texture to the ground, with some darker patches. They closed on the first within minutes, and Elissa realised they were patches of dark dragon glass protruding from the grass. The xotryl's wings were now distinct, and had it been a human rider on the xotryl, their small group would be visible. Could the faceted eyes of the awldrin see the wildbeest from that distance?

Her beest came to a sudden halt, and Elissa lurched forward.

'Get off and come here,' Rossi called. Elissa took a deep breath and slid off, wincing as she hit the ground. There was no part of her body that didn't hurt. She hobbled over to the large flat stone he stood near. 'I need you to lie down.'

'What? And make myself more of an easy target? No chance!' she snorted. 'I have not run from awldrin to lie down and accept my fate. I've spent my life hiding from them, and now I find out I have the ability to do something about that, and you want me to lie down and hide like an Untouched child! Either give me to them and run with the large shard, or let me fight.'

Rossi sighed. 'We don't have time for this. Lie down, tuck your foot under the ledge of that rock, push up against it, and allow me to protect us. Let the land hide you – let your crystal appear to vanish.'

Begrudgingly, Elissa did as he asked her, wiggling backward to get as much of her legs under the rock as she could. She doubted it would help and was convinced it would just trap her when the attack came. Elissa could move her legs freely, though; the space was bigger than she had expected. *Fine.* If they needed her, she'd do her best to be a stone.

Rossi nodded approvingly as she got into place. 'Elissa, I've been using these powers my whole life, and you can't even light a lamp! When you learn how to work your powers, by all means play the hero. We need you, not just your crystal. You. Every human on Tebein needs you – more than ever now the awldrin have crossed. Put your stone jar under there, too, just in case it's guiding them.' With that, he bent down and retrieved a small bag from under the ledge.

'What's in there?' she asked.

'We have emergency kits secreted around the main routes between each settlement. I don't know how long this one's been here, but I hope that it has ... Ah, yes.' He pulled a tiny bit of bone out of the bag, and two small balls, his hand shaking very slightly. Rossi then retrieved two hoods out of his own bag and covered both wildbeest's eyes.

'I'm going to set three wefts in sequence. I need you to hold this.' He passed her the shard. 'It's dragon bone. You won't be invisible, but it will make you hard to see. Their eyes will glide over, seeing only what's around you. The farther under that ledge you can get, the better.'

Elissa nodded mutely.

'The first weft will activate this, then I'll set off both a flash and flame globe. I could project it farther if I had time, but we don't, so I'll have to let them get really close. The one thing that's in our favour is that there's only one – they must be struggling to persuade the other xotryl to cross. Hopefully, the flash will scare the xotryl, and the flame will damage it enough that they have to retreat.'

Elissa watched in silence as Rossi set the first weft, a simple melody repeated twice, then placed the bone shard in her hand.

'When I'm done, I'll hide with you. If they don't fly away, I will take both beests and ride away to gain you extra time. Run for the marsh.'

A screech interrupted him. It was loud enough that the vibration cut through her teeth.

'If that happens,' Rossi continued quickly, 'Go to the marsh and follow the water down to the sea. Stay in the water and follow the coast to your right. Keep hold of the shard.'

He stood and ran toward the incoming xotryl, singing an ascending weft. The first ball launched at the creature as his song ended on a single clear note. The world went white.

Rossi began to sing again as Elissa blinked furiously to clear her vision. The notes were discordant and harsh. He ended with another rising scale, and as her vision cleared, a dark shape approached. Rossi launched the second ball. It burst into flames at the edge of the xotryl's snout, and it lashed out at him, but he ducked. The rider, presumably dislodged in the flash, was settling back into its seat as the second ball hit.

The strength of their bond was clear when the xotryl shrieked in pain and, immediately, the awldrin let out a guttural shout. They pulled up from their dive; the awldrin hung off the side to take a slash at Rossi in passing, but missed. It swung back into its seat where, mounted to the saddle, was a tall pole. Elissa watched in horror as the awldrin calmly pulled on it and something flew toward Rossi. A shaft of wood sprouted moments later from his arm.

Rossi dropped to the ground, dragging himself over to her and grabbing hold of the other end of the dragon bone. He was panting, pale, and shaking. 'We may have gained a few minutes. Our wildbeest give our location away, and there's only one of these bone shards. They can't pinpoint us exactly, so keep holding it until we remount. Control your own beest this time. If they return, I'll distract it again. The marshland is in sight. The elders in Shardeep are expecting you.'

Elissa understood his panic, but the dragon bone was strange and powerful; she could see his outline, but it was indistinct. They were hidden enough for the time being.

'Will it be poisoned?' she asked calmly, recalling the tales of her childhood.

'Probably not – it's been years since we skirmished with them. They probably forgot we existed.'

'Then why the kit?'

'There are other dangerous creatures out here too. Usually, we can scare them with a flash ball, but someone's already used one – hence, we only had one left.'

The screeching xotryl was still circling high above their heads, the rider clearly not wanting to lose their prey. It flew unevenly, shaking its great head from side to side. Fluid sprayed from the injury where the right side of its face was scorched and raw with one eye missing. If that was the power of the Souls of Dal, no wonder the awldrin were wary of them. Rossi said the elders were even more powerful? Why hadn't they just eliminated the awldrin years ago?

The xotryl flew low past them toward the marshes and then swung around. High on the xotryl's back, the awldrin readied its weapon again.

They came in low and fast, slashing one of the wildbeest with a claw. The wildbeest bellowed, and the second one took off, blind, away from the danger. The awldrin's weapon skimmed its thick hide, and it accelerated away from them. Their mounts gone, Elissa watched the xotryl fly off, flapping unevenly, back in the direction that it came from.

'Well, that's stuffed up the escape plan,' muttered Rossi.

'Maybe, but at least we're alive. Shall we head to the marsh on foot? It knows where it left us. We won't have long before it returns with re-enforcements.'

Rossi nodded. 'We need to move fast. It could be back at any minute if more of them crossed the land bridge.' He let go of the shard, sat up, and studied at his left arm appraisingly. 'Ever pulled an arrow out?'

'Arrow? Oh, that thing? No. Let's not forget that my success rate at pulling sharp objects out of people isn't exactly great,' Elissa said, gesturing at her own foot.

'Without the beest, we're going to take more than two days

to get to Shardeep round the coast. We'd be really exposed on a swim – it's indirect, and we'd need to rest in sea caves, if we could get to one before dark.' Rossi poked at the arrow as he talked.

The dragon glass was sharp, much like the shards she was used to, and Elissa scrabbled under the shelf, hoping that her hunch would be right.

'Try this,' she said, triumphantly passing him a jagged shard of the rock.

Rossi grimaced as he sawed at the arrow shaft. He managed to cut a groove cut in it. 'Can you bend it at this point?'

Elissa leant over him and grabbed either side of the groove. She bent the arrow upward, breaking the shaft off but leaving the head and a small bit of arrow protruding from his arm.

'Watcher's breath, that hurt,' Rossi hissed through clenched teeth.

Elissa scanned the landscape around them. 'If we don't stop tonight, could we reach the base of those mountains?'

Rossi looked at where she was pointing. 'Yes, if you think you can walk that far. We could use the caves and the old tunnels under the mountain. It's faster, but you'll be walking the whole way and there's a lot of dangerous creatures which call them home.'

'Can you swim with that arm?' Elissa asked.

He grimaced. 'I'm not sure, to be honest, but I can't fight either.'

'Can you make yourself better? You know, sing a weft or something?'

'Not without help.'

'Let me re-phrase that. Can you use me to help you get better?'

Rossi smiled. 'I wish I could, but you might make me worse if you get it wrong. Let's get going.'

Elissa stood and offered a hand to Rossi. He swayed slightly as she pulled him up. His eyes glazed for a moment, then he blinked a few times, reached for his bag, and swung it onto his good shoulder. Elissa reclaimed her stone jar and slung her small bag across her body. The two walked toward the marsh, limping and leaning on each other.

⋎ ※ ⚔ ⚖ ✦

Several hours later, wet through and with no sign yet of a returning xotryl, they reached a wide channel in the windweed.

'That way to the sea.' Rossi said, indicating down the channel to their left. 'That way' – he pointed across the channel to yet more marsh and the rising foothills behind it – 'to the mountains.'

'Maybe we should see if you can swim?' The large peaks ahead were a long way away. She felt confident she could make it, but it would be slow.

Rossi's one-armed floundering quickly solved their dilemma. Landward it would be. Elissa wasn't a strong swimmer, so towing him was out of the question.

They trudged on through the marsh. Light rain fell and persistent, pervasive drizzle soaked them thoroughly. At one point, they saw their masked wildbeest, but by the time they reached its location, the weeds had swallowed it again.

The sun was beginning to set, so xotryl would refuse to fly soon. The rider who'd pursued them would be back, or another would. Without shelter, tired, and soaked, Elissa decided she'd rather walk through the night than risk being attacked again the next day. Rossi needed help more than she needed rest, so they pressed on. Finally, as darkness closed in, they left the marsh, and Elissa fervently hoped it would be the last time she would ever have to be in one.

Blisters bloomed on both heels and inside her thighs where her wet clothes had rubbed. Muscles still not recovered from riding ached, but fear of the awldrin propelled her, shoving her forward like a gale at her back.

They stumbled along the raised pathway, winding between the wetlands for an hour or two, until they could no longer see their hands in front of their faces. Elissa reached forward to keep a hand on Rossi's back, and Rossi followed the path by feel as they walked.

'Stop,' he whispered. 'Did you hear that?'

Elissa listened, but could hear nothing. 'Hear what?'

A thin whistle cut the air, high and sharp.

'That!' Rossi said. He put his fingers to his mouth and whistled twice. An immediate response of three short whistles cut through the night.

'The elders sent someone out to meet us!' Relief infused Rossi's voice, and Elissa caught him as he sagged to the ground, his legs giving way.

Glowing light illuminated a short, stout-framed figure about Elissa's height, and a powerfully built man. The bobbing lights increased in speed as they collapsed on the path. Elissa held Rossi's head from the wet ground, watching the lights approach.

'What happened?' a soothing, musical voice called out.

'We were attacked by a xotryl-mounted awldrin. Rossi took an arrow to the arm. Part of it is still in there,' she replied.

'You must be Elissa.' The speaker was close enough that Elissa could see the lilac of her long hair in the dim lights. 'I'm Quin. Can you walk?'

'They will be back, especially now I'm out of the water. I will walk.'

'This is Bart. He'll carry Rossi to the old sericlave entrances where we can shelter, then I can heal him once we're safe and dry.'

Elissa took the extended hand gratefully and rose to her feet. She started walking and tried to ignore the sideways look afforded her by Quin as she limped.

'Can I help you? Are you also injured?'

'Thank you, but there's nothing we can do about this. Rossi and others have already tried. It hurts like dragon fire, but I can walk on it. Let's get away from here!'

With that, Elissa half strode, half limped off down the path, to shelter and – she hoped – sleep.

CHAPTER 25

DARIN

*The new landscape created by the Rending
created numerous problems for our ancestors.
The biggest of which was simply getting in and
out of the craters.*
History of Caldera, Post Rending

Darin's stomach lurched, and breakfast threatened to reappear with every pendulous swing of the basket. *Why did I have to look down?*

The crater wall curved away from him, hundreds of spans down to rock-strewn land below. The rickety, hand-pulled cage swayed perilously close to the cliff face at times. Darin's fear of heights immobilised him, and he gripped the edge of the basket as sweat beaded on his face and merged into a salty stream trickling past his nose.

The basket dropped abruptly as Chase fed the rope through the pulleys, and Darin's knees gave way. He found himself sat on the floor with his arms outstretched, gripping the rail. Star trembled alongside him, curling in close and whimpering in fear.

'Stand up and get control of yourself.' Chase's brusque voice cut through his internal fog. 'If you don't, Star will only get worse, and you will have a panicked hound who you won't be able to bring down here alone – and one day, you'll have to. So stop cowering on the floor and get up!'

Darin tried, but his unfaithful legs felt like jelly. It took several attempts to straighten them, and a few more to raise his eyes from their intent study of the basket's floor.

'Look up, not down,' Chase said. He shoved the rope into Darin's hands, then stood back, causing the basket to swing wildly. Darin's grip loosened as he felt himself get dizzy again.

They dropped.

Darin closed his hand, instinctively gripping the rope, which burned into his palm as it slipped through. He held on, and the basket stopped.

'Look up.'

Darin swallowed. He could do this. He could face a bar of drunken idiots, could speak to a hound in his mind. Watcher's breath, he could even do magic. So why wouldn't his legs straighten? Darin's hand was agony, but he had a feeling no help would come from Chase until they reached the ground. He narrowed his focus, looking up at the small pulley sets that the rope passed over. Then, he raised the hand holding the rope, gripping below it with the other, and repeated the action. Slowly, hand under hand, they dropped. The pulleys retreated into the clouds, and the cliff obscured his view of the sky. Maintaining a rhythm helped him stay calm and focused until the basket stopped with a bump, and the rope in his hands slackened. They were down.

Darin glanced to his side to see Chase grinning. Star's warm presence had stayed tightly pressed against his leg throughout the ordeal, but he no longer shook.

'I took at least three descents to do that!' Chase shook his head in disbelief. 'I wasn't sure you'd do it in five after that wobble up there. Next time, you'll have to glance down occasionally. One day there could be an ambush waiting or just a grazer below—'

'And I could be alone.' Darin finished for him. Since they'd left the tower and crossed the river that passed between the Talons, it had been Chase's most used phrase.

They unloaded the basket and re-filled the moonhound packs. Darin dug deep into his bag for the small set of poultices he'd brought. They had no wefts on them, but should stop the wound from getting worse. He bound one unevenly with his left hand and tied it off with the help of his teeth. Chase watched in silence.

'Which way?' Darin asked.

Chase pointed at the path which led away from the crater edge. *The only path in sight, of course.* It had seemed too obvious after the past few days.

They wound between huge boulders, many covered in smaller loose stones. The land was dotted with fallen debris, some old and moss-covered, while others had not been free of the cliffs long enough for their angry, angular edges to have softened. The farther from the cliff they walked, the fewer rocks blocked their route, and the path straightened, no longer having to meander around these remnants of a lost time.

The terrain also became noticeably more textured, plants were less spindly, and a wall of trees sprouted like guardians at the edge of the light. Animal trails crossed their path, and small paw prints ran along it. Away from the shadow of the cliffs, Dal crater sprang to life.

Darin searched the woods ahead for any sign of people.

Trees were cut back where they passed over the path, but no human footprints marked the wet surface. He dredged his memory for other signs to search for, determined not to ask Chase.

'What do *you* think?' was Chase's second favourite phrase, he was sure. Grasping for ideas, he decided to ask Star. *[People in the woods ahead]* Darin sent tentatively. He saw Star sniff the air and received *[A wood empty of people]*, quickly followed by *[A smoking fire]*.

'There's a fire up ahead,' he said, feeling a degree of pride that they'd worked it out.

'How did you know?'

'Star told me.'

Chase smiled widely. 'Good! About time too. You need to combine all your senses. We're near the edge of the village and our first stop. You'll find things in Dal a bit different from your travels with Hal.'

The village was tiny, a small cluster of houses, each with walls built from an assortment of rocks jammed between timber posts. Their overhanging roofs alive with plants and moss would be almost invisible from above. Some roofs even had small stones arranged on them. The central focus of the ring of houses was a large, lighting-shot tree, splintered at the core. Its charred remains stood proud, like a statue in a town square.

Chase walked directly up to the tree, rapped out a pattern on the hollow trunk, then stood quietly, waiting. Darin sidled next to him, attempting to mimic Chase's relaxed posture. Several minutes later, a door opened. A woman walked toward them, tall, proud, and confident. Long curls descended to her waist, glossy and black, with silver spirals mixed amongst them.

'Howler.' She paused. 'Howlers? I bid you welcome. I have both a request and a roof.'

'I bid you thanks. I accept your roof. What is your request?' Chase responded, bowing formally.

'Simple enough. I need a dream message carried,' she replied.

Chase nodded agreement, and she led them back to what Darin presumed must be her home. Chase was right – the woman knew about their magic and the Howlers. There was no hiding or big secret in Dal. How then had the Anchor forgotten about them?

The woman's home was sparse but comfortable. Thin branches sprouted from the floor and had been woven into a living seat, which dominated the room. The hearth was stacked with discs of wood fungus ready to light. Meat hung to cure over the fireplace, and a basket of vegetables sat abandoned on the table, a knife alongside them, waiting for someone to finish the task.

'I'd make you a hot drink, but ... well, you know how it is.' The woman shrugged.

'Later will be just fine,' Chase replied. 'So, who and where do you need this message sent to and why?'

'It's our report. I'd take it personally, but with increased sightings of the xotryl – even since you last passed through – it's getting risky for a powerless woman like me to make the walk.'

Chase's eyebrows shot up, and he gasped for air between snorts and laughter. Eventually, he managed to squeeze out, 'Powerless? You? Krista, you have more skill with a bow than any in Dal, and I've seen grown men lose an arm wrestle with you. Just because you can't weft does not make you powerless.'

'But you'll do it?' she asked.

'We're travelling to the Edgelands, rather than the northern edge, or I'd carry a message in person.'

Darin heard the continued negotiations, but was too tired to keep following it. Names and places filtered through his wandering attention. *Xotryl, huge scaly creatures, straight out of my books, and in this region. They only fly in the day because of their poor vision.* He rested his hand on Star, taking reassurance from their contact. Star was relaxed in her house, so he should be too.

'May I sit?' he asked.

'Of course. Put your bags in that room for the evening.' Krista pointed to a room at the back of the sitting area.

Darin followed her direction, and with Star in tow, left them to their negotiation. He should probably pay more attention, but the pain in his shoulders was calling for relief, and the blisters on his feet would thank him for loosening the ankle straps.

Once alone, he unwrapped his hand to check on the rope burn. Red welts rose across his palm. He rinsed it clean and applied a drosta leaf he'd picked from the side of the path. Its mild antiseptic properties would hopefully keep any infection away, and increased air movement would allow it to heal faster than under the poultice. He hoped so, anyway.

⊤ ✷ ✸ ✸ ✦

Krista lit the fire in the main room as night fell. Dancing flames fed his cold body with a little joy; the heady scent of burning fungus was musty and sweet. Darin watched with interest as Chase reclined on the seat, his arm resting on Sandy's head, and his eyes closed. His breathing was too fast for him to be truly asleep. Sandy sat at his side, alert and clearly unhappy, his ears pinned back against his head, and his tail tucked. He rested his head on Chase's lap and watched him intently.

Darin and Krista also sat in silence, neither daring to make a sound. Finally, Sandy's thumping tail broke the silence. His ears flicked forward again, and he nuzzled affectionately at his companion. Chase responded with a scratch of Sandy's ears and opened his eyes.

'All done. The Witness said to pass on that you were kindly regarded and welcome to move to the town should you, or the others living here, prefer to take refuge.'

'They always say that,' Krista replied. 'But someone has to be here for the lift. I'd prefer to take my chances out here than be trapped in a town as an easy meal for those creatures.'

'They don't hunt humans for food, though,' Darin offered. 'They hunt for sport.'

'And that is why he has a lot to learn.' Chase sighed. 'Darin, do you think being hunted for sport is better than food? Or maybe the better answer is not being hunted at all. Xotryl should not get this far. It is only as far from the Edgelands as Redpike is. The only thing stopping them is—'

'The river,' Darin interrupted again. 'I know. They prefer to eat the lumbering cattle that we call faat – because they are. I do read.'

'There has only been one xotryl in Dal for many cycles,' said Chase. 'But recently, another more aggressive one has joined Big Red. This one is smaller, battle scarred, and flies much farther into the crater, according to Krista. We need your hand healed urgently.'

'If they don't fly in the dark, surely we can just travel at night,' Darin suggested. It was so obvious.

'As we get closer to the Edgelands, we will. But in this area, the bigger danger is being trampled by rhinocorns and stunk out by graaken. Most Edgelands creatures can't get up this far, but we definitely don't want to stumble into either of those at night. There are big graaken encroachments here, and their scent makes Sandy unwell for hours. We need our hounds and can't afford them to be incapacitated. Now, talking of hounds, you need to use Star to get that hand healed.'

'Use Star? How?' His hound was playing with a piece of fungus, rolling it around and pouncing on it.

'Send a healed hand to him. Picture his nose against your hand, and see if he can help you. He might be able to, if you are bonded closely enough.'

Star could heal him? That was amazing! It must be some of the magic the Howlers had mentioned – things they could do with hounds that no others could. Darin sent *[Star's nose to his hand with no cuts or burns]*. He took his wrapping back off and offered it to his hound. As he did so, he felt a little of his power trickle away, like a small rivulet running toward Star. Star licked his palm, and the redness faded almost immediately.

'By the two moons, it worked.' Darin turned his hand over in surprise. There were no welts, and the scar tissue that had appeared was red and angry, but it was healthy and he could use it. Darin flexed his fingers and found everything working as it should be. He fussed over Star and threw his arms around him, trying to send thanks and love through their bond.

'Good. Two things you should be aware of, though, Darin. There's a limit to how much and how often you can do that. Your reserves are not infinite. The second is, never do that in the palace.'

'What about Krista?' Darin asked. She'd watched the whole thing.

'Dal is different. They live in the shadow of the Aulirean Gate and deal daily with the consequences of the past. While the rest of Caldera has forgotten us, in Dal, they've always relied on the Howlers. Our families were forged here, and few ever leave.'

'Do they not send people to the Redpike trials like everywhere else?'

'No. All warriors with skills are needed within the crater, and potential Anchors are carefully tested by the Witness family, who is, of course, from Dal. All the So'Dal families who were originally here moved to Redpike's safe community after the Rending. The Witness family has true So'Dal blood, and their family keeps Dal secrets close. Occasionally, new talent appears, who will choose the safety of Redpike over life here.'

'So there are some in Redpike who know about the Howlers?'

'Some, but they keep that information close. It protects their families, especially as local relationships with Howlers have, on occasion, resulted in new additions to the Howler pack.' Chase chuckled. 'The trouble is, we've all got too old to add any more human pups.'

Darin looked at Chase. 'Surely, you are not so old you couldn't ...' His face heated as he found the words unwilling to vacate his mouth.

'Not too old, no, but I'm not interested in women. I've been with Tian since we first met. And therein lies the issue with begetting my own issue! You know you should not really exist – a Howler coming from outside Dal.'

'It's Tian we are going to see?' Darin asked.

'It is. He'll be surprised to see me again so soon.' Chase's face lit up as he spoke.

I hope someone feels like that about me one day. 'My family travelled around Caldera for many years and generations, before they set up the inn. Maybe it's not as odd as it appears.' Darin replied. He had relatives in just about every other crater apparently, so why not Dal too?

Krista had remained quiet, observing the exchange from her seat by the fire. At that, she rose and swayed over to them, exhaustion writ clear across her features, and her eyes deeply hooded with sleepiness. 'If you need more Howlers, my bed is available. I promise to make it worthwhile,' she murmured in Darin's ear as she passed him. Flustered, he tried to gather a response, but she'd already gone into her room.

Chase stifled his laughter. 'It makes a good change not to be the one propositioned,' he eventually managed to spit out. 'Be ready. We leave at dawn.'

CHAPTER 26

SURIIN

*The creature's gleaming grey skin reflected the
sun's light as it sat astride the huge xotryl. Its
savage pointed teeth snarled, lipless, as it took
a single arrow and pierced the heart of the
weft leader. She fell. We know nothing of
their anatomy, and retaliatory shots fell
apart from any critical organs. It stayed
aboard and, making the horrible clicking
sound we think is laughter, turned the huge,
red beast in the air and flew away back to the
mines.*

<u>Battle Strategies of the Awldrin</u>

S uriin had followed old, forgotten passageways through the
mountain for three days since bonding the crystal, and it
still muddied her thoughts. On the second day, it had been so
distracting, she tried to leave it in her room. Five minutes later,
as she was about to enter the old passages, she'd felt dizzy and
only just held her breakfast down. As she staggered back to her

room, the nausea and dizziness had reduced, vanishing completely as she hung its pouch around her neck. For the hundredth time since she'd bonded it, she wondered why it was so important to use the stupid thing. She hadn't needed one when she'd helped to heal her father.

Suriin shook her head to clear her thoughts. She needed to get back to the present, or she'd get lost – again. She looked both ways and listened carefully for the whisper of footsteps. Confident that no one was around, she pulled out the small section of map she'd search through that day.

On the first day of her exploration, she discovered that some of the old passageways were bricked up. A fact that piqued her curiosity further. After all, if a perfectly serviceable area existed, why block up the entrance? They were all cramped into the castle as it was. She had so much to explore once her father was better.

None of the rooms she'd copied from the stewards' map were marked with names, just symbols – and the library had been decidedly unhelpful in deciphering them. Ancient symbols had probably changed usage over time, so Suriin hadn't been entirely surprised. After reclaiming her crystal, she'd worked through the passages toward a vaguely sword-shaped symbol the day before. Checking each route, room and tunnel as she passed, then marking down any changes, made for slow passage, but it did mean that she could finally push on to go much deeper into the mountain.

It took Suriin half the time to reach the point she'd finished last time, then she was into new territory. The next turn on her right was exactly where it should be, and the map suggested that it led toward the icon of a plant. The button operated and sank into the wall smoothly, the door slid open silently. It was so well cared for that Suriin tensed as it opened, half expecting to find someone on the other side.

A smooth opening mechanism was unusual. In her experience, most of them had been stiff, and mechanisms abandoned for centuries were hard to move. Many doorframes were filled with eroded rock debris, affecting their ability to open, and she had no choice but to give up. Their magic still worked, but the physical movement of those doors was stilted and grinding. The new one, however, was regularly used, and far more recently than any of the others.

 ⁂

Once Suriin realised the passage was dark, she felt safer. No one was in there, and if it was in use, then whatever was up there would be known about. Was it even worth investigating? By the dim light of her globe, she studied the pathway ahead. The clean, dust-free floor was also a stark change from other passages. Suriin wasn't prepared for a meeting with any So'Dal – she was too far away from the areas she should really be in. While there were no rules on where she could go, she had no reason to be here.

Suriin tried to prepare plausible reasons for being in the old tunnels as she walked, but her mind came up empty. Her heart pounded louder and louder as she continued down the passageway until she was certain that its beat would give her presence away long before the sound of her feet. She reached the next set of rooms without event and checked her map.

The corridor continued on ahead, dusky and dark. To either side, doorways stood. The one on the right was intricately carved with plants entwined all over it – much like a larger, more intricate version of her own room. The foliage was in raised relief, lifelike and delicate.

The one opposing it was simple, unusual in that it was wooden. It had a drop latch on the outside, like the ones she'd seen on the holroom. *To keep other creatures out ... or in?* The thought flitted unbidden through her mind. She reached for the handle, then at contact with it, drew her hand back; the wood was probably not straight anymore. If the bolts got stuck, she might not be able to close it. If the passageway was regularly used, a broken door might bring about questions.

Suriin held her lamp over the map. Should she go straight on to the sword symbol? Or through the plant carved door? Her map showed a vast chamber behind it and she was getting cold. Suriin hadn't copied the distances accurately, but she recalled that it was a particularly long stretch to reach the sword room.

Awldrin relics or possible seeds? The choice stretched before her. The presence and location of the ornate carving matched descriptions of the deep underground seed library that she'd read about. It was well away from the main mountain accommodation and secure – a good place to save their plants when the craters had first formed.

Each original plant was sent to Redpike in case they'd been unable to grow any longer. A protection against the possibility of the Gardeners running out of components for essential magic. Maybe there were further libraries with seeds, perhaps even sections from Mythos or Tebein. Maybe like the hot room, it would be lovely and warm!

With that idea growing in her head, Suriin checked around her one last time. *Ridiculous. I'd have seen a light,* she thought as she pushed on the button next to the door.

It slid smoothly into the wall slot. She walked through, anticipating a big, open space. Instead, she found herself in a short corridor. Suriin took a step forward and felt a gentle movement under her foot. Too late, she spun around as the door closed behind her.

She tried to quell rising panic. It moved swiftly, and her

desperate pushing didn't slow it. She pulled her hand back quickly before it became caught in the frame. Suriin was trapped.

If she'd thought her heart was loud, the small, confined space amplified each breath. Her palms grew clammy, and Suriin wondered if maybe she should have told someone where she was going. Breaths came fast and short as she realised that if she didn't get out, they'd miss her on her kitchen shift, but no one would know where to look.

She pulled the glow lamp out and, with a quavering voice, sung it brighter. The small chamber was only three steps long and an arm-span wide. The door she had entered by – which was firmly closed – was plain on her side. Heavy fabric coated it from roof to floor, and no matter where she looked, there was no obvious way to reopen it. She tried stepping on other stones, but there was no movement. More worryingly, she could not work out exactly which of the small tiles she had stood on to close it in the first place.

Fear and frustration started to build in equal measure. Her father would wonder where she was, surely? Or would he even notice? What would her mother say if they found her there? She'd be in even more trouble.

My father.

The thought of his immobile form forced Suriin back into action. She was there for him, and there was no point leaving until she'd got something of use, or ruled out the store as a useful source of help. She might be late anyway, so may as well make the telling-off worth it. Suriin drew a deep breath. *Onward then.*

Three paces from the first, was another door, much like that on the opposite side of the corridor. It was stone, but otherwise the heavy, metal drop latches looked similar. It wouldn't be easy to get through on her own.

Suriin pushed the lower lever up to rest on the edge of its keeper. She then grasped the top lever. As she lifted it, the bottom one dropped back into place. She stepped back and re-assessed the situation; memories of home and the Skaa-rak barn came to mind. The levers were metal, not wood, but the spacing was similar. If she put the lower lever on her shoulder ...

Suriin crouched against the door, cold stone leeching heat through her robe. She rested the protruding handle into her shoulder and raised her arms to reach for the second lever. As she extended her legs and pushed up with her arms, the cold metal knob pushed into her shoulder. It slowly moved, and as Suriin lifted the bars, she realised she had no idea which way it was going to open.

The levers both freed from their keepers, and her weight caused it to swing open abruptly. Suriin landed in a heap on the floor, sore, but triumphant.

The cold hit her as fast as she had hit the floor. The room was bone-freezingly cold. Her clothes were simply not thick enough to allow her to be in there for long, assuming she could get back out. Before Suriin moved from the doorway, she checked the other side of the door. Two hefty levers – like the ones she'd just lifted. *But I'll need to pull this time.* It would be impossible. The risk of being caught, rather than frozen alive, was worth wedging it open. She pulled her sketchbook out of her robes and tucked it under the lower edge. Satisfied that her jamb would hold, Suriin took in her surroundings.

Stretching into the darkness were shelves. On each shelf sat rows of stoppered glass balls, each labelled with tiny writing; every ball appeared to hold seeds and was numbered with a unique code. Suriin peered at the closest jar – CA EYE01Agr. As she moved along the shelf, she noticed that they were labelled similarly, the first five letters of the code being the same. She tried the next row of shelves and found, again, that they all started with CA ANC. Suriin checked along the rows – all the shelves started CA until she reached the far side of the room. There sat a smaller set of jars marked MY instead.

Suriin puzzled for a few minutes until she realised that CA must be Caldera and MY was Mythos. So, all she had to do was find Tebein. Excited, she ran around, searching. Maybe a cure would be there! She ran between aisles toward the far wall, until she found the initials VE and OU. Suriin stopped, puzzled. There were rows upon rows for both VE and OU.

She fumbled in her robe for her sketchbook to write them down, panicked for a moment when she couldn't find it, then recalled that she had used it to prop the door open.

The cold was already slowing her thoughts. Suriin decided to only allow herself a little longer, then return better prepared. She'd need far more clothes on to spend longer in there. As she walked back to the door, she read the labels aloud, still not seeing any with the tag TE. Frustrated and shivering so much that she could barely keep her teeth quiet, Suriin headed back to the exit in abject resignation.

She pulled the sketchbook out and let the door close behind her, guiding the bars back into their slots. They dropped into place, and a small stone popped out of the opposing wall of the small chamber. She had been so busy looking at the floor, she must have missed it. Suriin pushed it in and tucked her glow lamp inside her robes. The door slid back in its channel with a whine. She sidled back into the passage, checking for any sign of others. A puff of air ruffled her hair as the door moved silently back into place.

The comparative warmth outside the chamber was welcome, and for a moment, Suriin stood still in the darkness, soaking it up.

She spotted a distant glow – someone was coming. Suriin looked behind her into the darkness. That way would take her deeper, and she'd no idea how long she would have to wait or where they were going.

Suriin had two options, and in that moment, she chose the closest. Adrenaline fuelled her strength as she lifted the double bolts on the wooden door. It opened, and although she heard a quiet creak, she knew the noise-muffling of the tunnels meant that the newcomer wouldn't.

'Watcher, guide my steps,' she whispered as she entered the darkness. There were internal bolts too, so Suriin pushed them into place and slid down to sit with her back resting against the wood. She'd have to wait for the people to arrive – and leave – she supposed. Or they might continue past, and she'd have no idea when they would return. She was stuck.

⸬ ✳ ✸ ✵ ✦

Suriin pressed her ear to the door, listening for the sound of voices or hoping to hear the door opposite open. What if they'd heard her open this one?

Hoping the muffling of the corridors had saved her from trouble and difficult explanations, she kept her ear glued to the wood.

Several hundred heartbeats later, the squeal of the mechanism was just about audible. The returning click, she didn't hear. Suriin counted another 100 heartbeats, and, hoping that the visitors were fully into the frozen seed room, she dared to quietly turn her lamp on and look around.

The floor sloped gently down from the door. She pulled her map out to see what might be in there. It showed a short corridor and, on her copy, she had marked a dashed line across it, then a circle.

A small chamber should be to her right. Suriin looked

toward it. It was just outside her gentle circle of light. *I have time to investigate.*

There was a small area with a stone table carved out of the floor. Two carved chairs sat on either side of it. She reached out to touch the carving on the back, and the chair crumbled at her touch. Stone shelves cut into the walls lined the space, maybe – they'd once held books or glow lamps.

Nothing else caught her eye, so she passed the other chair, careful not to touch it, and continued down the slope. Nothing else on her map preceded the dotted line, but a glint caught her eyes. Suriin turned toward it to see a lock sparkling in the light; not magical, it appeared to need an actual key. Tentatively, she reached out. Might that door crumble like the chairs? She touched it feather-gently. Nothing happened, so she pushed it – still nothing. Had there been a key in the alcove?

She ran back, looked around the shelves, and felt to the back of the ones higher than her eye line. Nothing. It had been an optimistic thought.

Suriin was sure she had plenty of time before she could leave safely, so she temporarily gave up on that particular puzzle. *Just for the moment,* she told herself. Suriin turned back to the far end of the space and the circle on her map. There didn't look to be anything at the end. It was just a wall.

She ran her hands across the rough stonework in front of her. It felt solid enough. As she swept the glow lamp from side to side, Suriin looked for other clues. Maybe there would be displaced stonework, like in the seed storage. Nothing caught her eyes. No buttons, no aligned stones where an opening might exist.

Her map wouldn't make sense if she had to go through the locked door into a further space, but then, whatever was behind that wasn't on her map at all. Trailing her hand along the stones, she admired the veins of staramine glowing blood-red by her gentle light. One particularly large stone had an amazing red streak running across its face. She traced it with her fingers, following the curve as it wound across the stone.

Except that what she was seeing and what her hand was feeling didn't match. Again, she followed the staramine vein from the edge. Halfway across the rock, her finger was no longer on the cold smoothness of staramine, but the rougher texture of the black rocks. Her eyes were seeing differently. Carefully she felt around, closing her eyes to feel instead of see.

A few minutes later, she'd found the outline of an archway. The stones were above her head and wide enough for an entrance below it. She moved her hand down, following the pattern of bricks to find a mechanism that would open it.

If I couldn't see this, what else in these tunnels has been hidden in plain sight? Suriin wondered as she felt around. At waist height, she finally found a handle. She tried to turn it. Nothing happened.

Suriin opened her eyes and kept hold of the handle. Her hand appeared to be resting against the flat stone. She moved her hand again, and still it appeared as if was on a flat wall, even though she could feel herself holding the handle. It made her head hurt, working through the illusion with her eyes open.

So she closed them again, and bringing her other hand to the same area, she tried to hold the door and sing.

Only, she didn't know any wefts. Singing alone wouldn't work – nothing happened. Then Suriin remembered her crystal and its bonding. What emotion would open a door?

She tried feeling hopeful and singing. Nothing.

She tried feeling scared and singing. Nothing.

There were so many symbols on that table in Aslin's room to remember. Suriin tried to think through it logically. What would make you hide a door? And if you needed to both hide and lock it, what could be behind it? Something you were keeping incredibly safe?

What emotion would you feel if you were protecting something? Protecting – protectiveness?

Suriin tried to picture her brother up to one of his crazy schemes. How she felt when she was looking out for him. She struggled to push that through her crystal; it felt as though she pushed through syrup, but, it slowly began to turn. Her pulse raced, and with anticipation building, she kept pushing the emotion through her crystal.

The door swung open slowly. Suriin kept one hand on the handle as she watched her arm slide into the wall. She took a deep breath and then stuck her head through, as if she was putting her face underwater. She saw a cell with narrow bars across it. Water ran through one corner. At the back, standing taller than any human, with smooth green skin and their crystalline eyes pointed in her direction, sharpened teeth glinting black by the light of her lamp, stood an awldrin.

CHAPTER 27

ELISSA

The creatures native to Tebein are normally cold-blooded and furless. They tolerate a very wide range of conditions. Many of them go into a resting phase – or hibernation – over the cold wind season and re-emerge with the rains.
Animalis Non Localis

Elissa welcomed darkness' embrace as it beckoned her toward sleep and a chance to rest her weary muscles. Quin lit dusty globes on the walls, and the darkness receded, yet still awaited her.

'Only a little farther now. There's one of our scouting chambers ahead. It was empty on our way past, but it's worth checking before we shut ourselves in with something unpleasant. I'll go ahead.' Quin lengthened her stride, self-confidence oozing from every pore. Despite her being of a similar height to Elissa, Quin stood taller – the straightness of her carriage and her power worn openly gave her more presence than Elissa could imagine wearing.

Quin disappeared through a door to the left. A flash of light spilled into the corridor, and with it, several small creatures leaving at speed. Elissa only caught a glance of their strange, hair-covered bodies as they vanished into the darkness. She'd never seen anything like them.

'It's clear,' Quin called back. 'You can come in.'

The room was small, dry, and well-equipped. Several mattresses were packed into the space, along with a few cupboards. Bart carried the unconscious Rossi in, and laid him carefully onto a mattress,

'Can I help?' Elissa offered, sitting on the other side of Rossi.

'Not yet.' Bart gestured to Quin. 'She'll fix him up as well as we can out here.'

Quin was elbow-deep in a cupboard, pulling out packs of dried plants. She peered at them intently before selecting one and repacking the rest.

'I could remove this here, but it might still affect his arm in the long term,' she said as she sat next to Elissa. 'Can you hold this in place, please?'

Elissa held the pack against the arrowhead as Quin bound it gently in place.

'I'll try to ease his pain instead. They'll be able to deal with it more cleanly at Shardeep.' She placed her hands around the area and closed her eyes. A frown creased her forehead as she sat in silence.

'You aren't an elder, then?' Elissa asked once the woman opened her eyes.

Quin ran a hand over Rossi's forehead and smiled gently. 'He should sleep pain free now. No, Bart and I are a guard patrol. The elders received a message from Silverfish that xotryl had passed overhead and were worried for you. They thought you might need help – so we were redirected.' She rose from Rossi's bedside.

'They were right.' Elissa sighed. Rossi looked peaceful, and Bart was up and moving around the room. It was all very well to be in a safe place, but come the next day, they'd have to face xotryl again, and there might be more of them. She held back a shudder as she recalled the itchy feeling of being watched. 'How do we get to Shardeep from here?'

'Through these old tunnels.' Bart gestured back out of the room. 'This place is almost empty. Everyone's either in Shardeep or Hope. Only a small troupe of us live here to assist travellers and keep the tunnels mostly free from *unwanted* residents.'

Quin nodded. 'That sounds like the best plan, Bart – yes, that should work. Rest up, Elissa. You probably need it almost as much as Rossi. We'll not pass many safe places to rest tomorrow.'

Nowhere safe, but it was the safest route? Bart's bulk was sat in front of the doorway, a large hammer across his lap.

'Eat and sleep. I've got this,' he said gently.

Quin shared some dried fruits with her and a chewy, sweet bar. 'Sorry, we don't carry meat in the tunnels. It attracts the wrong attention.'

'It's still some of the best food I've ever tasted,' Elissa mumbled through teeth stuck together. It really was delicious. She laid on the nearest mattress. It smelt a little damp, but it was soft enough that she fell asleep easily.

⁂

Rossi was awake before her the next morning. His skin was pale compared to normal, but he flashed her a grin as he munched on another of those sticky treats. Bart wasn't there, and Quin packed blankets back into a cupboard.

'Are you ready?' she asked, offering Elissa a food bar too. 'Bart's just checking the way out is clear. He'll be back in a moment.'

'I can eat as we walk.'

The walls were green with moss where water dripped through porous rocks, and damp smells assaulted her nostrils. The lack of human habitation and total abandonment was clear. And yet, they passed a door with carvings on it, unidentifiable under a coating of slime moulds. On another wall, a light globe still worked, but needed a wipe from wet sleeves to make its light bright enough to see by. Despite the neglect, the similarities to the complex under Dragonsbreath were clear.

The tunnels were far from uninhabited. Unfamiliar noises drifted from side passages, shuffling, clicking, and a dragging swish of something big.

Quin lit each lamp they passed – the trail of lamps they left illuminated the empty space behind them and reassured Elissa they were alone, for the time being, at least.

Twice, Quin and Bart gestured urgently for them to freeze. Elissa obeyed without question. They stood still, barely breathing, to let creatures amble past. In confined spaces, the magic Rossi had used on the xotryl clearly wouldn't work – it would damage them all. Regaled by tales of all the creatures Bart had previously encountered and those they generally avoided, Elissa put the idea of heroics firmly in the back of her mind.

Quin told her about huge, six limbed, hard-shelled creatures called chitlins which walked on four limbs and used the front two as clawed arm-like appendages. Apparently, they were much smaller on Lieus, but the different environment on Tebein meant that they'd grown substantially.

'They hide in the caves during Rains, so we will definitely

come across one. As long as we stay still, they won't notice us,' Quin said as she finished her description.

'If they do, I'll bash them.' Bart laughed. 'Not that it'll hurt them, but it might make them change direction – or decide we are too difficult to eat. It usually works.'

Usually? Elissa swallowed the retort. Despite their kindness, they were still strangers – ones she was reliant on to help her own people. They didn't appear to bear any significant injuries, so they knew how to survive there. Relaxing wasn't an option, but if she was going to get through in one piece, giving them her trust was.

'What else lives in here?' she asked.

'Probably better not to know,' Rossi said quietly. 'Trust me – you'll sleep better that way.' The poultice around the arrowhead was still in place, and Elissa checked the knot on the sling as he walked ahead of her. He still looked pale, but the greenish light probably wasn't helping.

ⲧ ※ ⚔ ⚓ ✦

At one junction, an enormous creature with overlapping armour plates and many legs scuttled past. Its shining armour reminded Elissa of the shoulder guards awldrin wore. A swarm of small, furry creatures fled when they lit the globes in the next passage. Upon rounding the corner, they found the creatures had stopped.

'Whatever's in front is scarier than us.' Bart hefted his hammer and stepped forward. 'Flames, just what we needed. We have to get past one way or another. That's the main hall of the old sericlave, and that many eyes could well be a full pack of snalber. They're so toxic we can't risk coming into contact with them.'

Night-blinded by the globes, Elissa peered into the darkness. Several sets of eyes reflected back. She glanced at Quin and noticed a slight shrinking of her presence – just a fraction, but enough to worry her.

'Elissa, you'll have to help me.' Quin turned to face her. 'Do exactly what I tell you to do. It's the only way we'll reach the other side of the mountain. Firstly, gather your power and centre yourself. I want you to gather together all the fearful thoughts you have and any scary memories. Take how they make you feel, then push that feeling through to me, as if you are pouring them away. You can do this, Elissa. We need to scare these creatures away.'

It didn't make a whole lot of sense ... pouring emotions? But a few days earlier, singing a light into life would have sounded ridiculous. Elissa sank deep into her thoughts. She remembered the sweat on her palms when she saw the awldrin descend in the lift. The sensation of hopelessness when the xotryl was coming down to attack. She felt a hundred small things and incidents; mostly fear of discovery, fear of death. Elissa gathered all these things and held them, her mind floating on an ocean of fear. She could feel her hands clenching, her heart rate rising, and her breathing becoming shallow.

'Good.' Quin's quiet voice intruded into the sea of fear. 'Now push it away.'

Elissa tried, but her fear of the creatures ahead, and of failure, stopped her. She began to drown in her own fear. Her breathing got shallower, and panic set in. She couldn't control it; she needed to bury it again, deep down where she always hid it.

A warm hand rested on her shoulder. Rossi was standing with her. 'You can do this. You didn't want to be the one hiding from danger. This is your chance.'

He was right – it was what she was born to do. Elissa slowed her breathing and imagined the fear gathered up into a ball, then she mentally pushed it at Quin.

Quin staggered at the impact as Elissa felt herself empty. There was no fear left – she was calm.

She watched, entirely detached, as Quin braced herself against Bart and pushed her shaking hand out toward the glowing eyes of the creatures. They had moved closer; the small furry creatures ran through her legs at speed.

Quin dropped her arm. The eyes ahead widened, and the reflections grew, then narrowed for a moment. A collection of growls and yelps echoed through the chamber, and the standoff broke as the creatures turned tail and scuttled off into the darkness ahead. Elissa saw it all and felt nothing.

They walked into the big room, unopposed. Rossi lit a few of the closest globes, and Quin still leant on Bart heavily.

'Does it come back?' Elissa asked.

Quin sank to the floor. 'Yes, but it won't always be that strong. You will learn to collect emotions, treasure experiences, and bathe in the way they make you feel.'

'Does it always take the emotion? Leave you empty?'

'No. With control, you can use far less for the same effect. But it does always take – it depletes the emotion you use.'

'Couldn't you have frightened the xotryl away like that?' Elissa asked Rossi. 'Surely it would have been less risky?'

He shook his head as he walked back to join them. 'No, that skill comes with being a woman. Flames, I wish I could! You can sing the magic – you can do it all. But singing is always limited by needing something to act on.'

Elissa walked in silence into the centre of the domed chamber. It was smaller than the hall of records in Dragonsbreath, but there were similarities. She took in the familiar layout of small alcoves surrounding the room, while passageways opened on the far side.

'The Souls of Dal's rooms were down that tunnel when they lived here.' Bart pointed to an ornate archway. 'We need to go that way.' The tunnel he pointed at was simple and dark.

'How many lived here?' Elissa asked, the spark of an idea forming.

'About fifty, we think. It was small, but it supported most of the travelling Souls of Dal. Obviously, it's ruined and empty now. The rooms are still there, but there's nothing in them but mountain critters. Everything of use was moved to Silverfish, Shardeep village or, if it related to the Souls of Dal, to Hope,' Bart replied.

'Hope moved them personally. That's what the old manuscripts show. While Sorrow and Regret fought at Dragonsbreath, Hope moved people to safety and even carried precious books and artefacts to the island. They hoped to keep them safe from the awldrin.' Quin's voice was melodic, and she smiled as she spoke. 'Imagine meeting one of the dragons!'

Elissa tried not to. Xotryl were fearsome enough; dragons were a whole xotryl larger if the pictures she'd seen in the books were anything to go by.

Many steps and hours later, Elissa blinked in bright sunlight as they left the old sericlave. The open valley below her was a patchwork of fields. Flowers and crops grew in profusion; freshly seeded brown patches were interspersed with lush, verdant leaves. Reds and golds shone, and the funnelled breeze through the valley caused the edges of the fields to soften as plants swayed in response.

A stone path wound between the crops toward a walled sericlave which had spilt out of the opposite mountain. To her left, white crests danced on the waves of the Ameryth Dar Sea, decorated by small, triangular sails. A round stone building dominated the centre of the sericlave, surrounded by houses and huts, all brightly painted and welcoming.

ᚱ ⚔ ♅ ᛉ ✦

They scrambled down the plant-cracked path to join a well-maintained one in the valley. The people they passed wore smiles, and many waved a greeting; everywhere Elissa looked, children played freely in the open air. The relaxed atmosphere seeped into her and unknotted the tension she'd held like a lifeline since they left Dragonsbreath. She exhaled and let it drift away. Her shoulders released their tightness and, if walking wasn't so painful, then she might have had a spring in her step. The place felt happy. Laytha would love it! Makin would be so happy! There had to be a way to get them there.

ᚱ ⚔ ♅ ᛉ ✦

A group of old people were arrayed across the gates to the sericlave as they approached. The elders, Elissa supposed. Most stared directly at her with curiosity etched on their faces; she glanced down at herself and suppressed a laugh. She was filthy – again. Mud and dust coated her clothes while the stone bottle clanked against her hip. That would be a bruise to be proud of. The blisters she'd tried to ignore would not stay whole much longer, and then walking would be even more impossible. Could she push pain away like she had the fear? She should ask Quin.

Elissa glanced across at her companions. Rossi attempted to walk normally, but with his arm tied up, his balance was also out. Quin still leant on Bart – the only one of their small party to appear unaffected by the events of the past few days.

The laugh didn't quite stay down, and a snort escaped her. Rossi glanced at her, and she spotted his own lip twitch. The hysteria of tiredness and exhaustion combined to make the laugh unstoppable, and the pair of them both chuckled. Quin turned around in surprise, almost falling as she twisted. Normally, that would elicit concern, but Elissa was too far gone. Laughter erupted as relief and happiness flooded into her. It was what she could bring her sericlave to – to another life that humans had been living.

It was all too much. The laughter turned to tears, and she sank to the floor.

'Give her a moment,' she heard Rossi say, his own laughter ended. Voices filled with concern floated across the space between their groups, and she could sense the closeness of him, protectively hovering between her and the elders. Hushed voices whispered, but her sobs blurred the sound so she couldn't quite make them out.

'Would you like some help?' she heard Quin say, so quietly no one else would have heard it.

'Normally, I'd say no, but yes, please,' Elissa replied. She took the offered hand and felt a trickle of trust and joy flow into her. Just enough to help gather herself together. 'That's amazing,' she whispered. 'But ... have you just given me your happiness?'

'Remember – just a little. I saved plenty.' Quin winked at her. 'Come on. The elders can't stand there too long. They are old, after all.'

Elissa smiled, pulled herself back up, and walked to the gate. As they reached it, a small child flew between the legs of the elders.

'*Daddy*!' she cried, and flung herself at Rossi. He crouched down, small arms hanging around his neck, and showered her with kisses.

'Hello, sweetling. I'm back. Let me go see the elders and take Elissa there, then you can take me home and tell me all about your adventures while I have been away. Vinjii gave me a shell for you.' The girl held his hand tightly as they walked the last few steps.

A woman at the centre of the group stepped forward, flanked by two wizened and bent older men, her bright and lively eyes belying her age. She reached out with both hands, palms facing toward herself, and inclined her head.

'We welcome you to Shardeep, Elissa Shard-bonded. You will find both rest and refuge here. Guest quarters have been prepared, and you will find a meal in your room. We will meet properly with you tomorrow to discuss how we can help each other.' She then turned to the others. 'Quin and Bart, you have leave for two days. Your patrol has been covered. We hear rumours of xotryl flights over the marshes, so need you to return to your post after that. Rossi, go home and get your injury treated, then return to the tower for debriefing.'

⋎ ※ ⹋ ⹌ ✦

The lamp on her chamber wall lit easily – she copied the woman who'd brought her there, turning it on and off just to check she could. For the first time, she was aware of her magic's presence inside her, waiting to be used. She noticed the heat globe tucked against the wall absently; it felt warm enough to ignore for the moment – she had other concerns.

The spread of food in front of her was like an end of Rains feast. Fresh tangs burst from fruits, and her mouth watered with anticipation of each mouthful. Spices she'd never tasted before seasoned the meats, and the clear, clean water was delicious. Elissa ate until she could eat no more.

Sat in her comfortable suite of rooms, sated and relaxed – safe – she reflected on the quiet authority of the lead elder. She reminded her of Laytha, someone entirely confident in her own skin. *I wonder how Laytha and the others are getting on.*

Knowing how little her friends would be subsisting on added notes of guilt as an aftertaste to her meal.

Surrounded by the comforts of Shardeep, Elissa tried to examine how she felt, her fears. When she considered things that had scared her, there was not much emotion. It felt blank, almost hollow.

'Could be useful,' she said aloud. But it was fear which had preserved her for so many years. Not quaking and shaking immobility, but the healthy respect of what-if.

Elissa avoided excessive risk because of it. Fear had never stopped her – it just made her careful. What would happen to her if she emptied of emotion as she used it? Would she then be both powerless and empty, detached from those around her? Would she lose love for those she cared for if she used it in magical workings? She had a lot of questions for the elders.

Chapter 28

Darin

A true musician is a treasure. A true soul makes music that can bring tears and joy to all who hear it.
A musical instrument maker must, therefore, be a welder of true power. By their hand is the tone and quality of music raised to new heights.
There are few with the raw talent to make magic with their hands.
A Traveller's Guide to Caldera

Trilling birdsong and sparkling fire sprites softened the edge of the early morning chill. Darin walked quietly, trying to pick out new noises as he went. Dal was filled with unique birds and animals, and many were entirely unfamiliar to him. Thick woodland hid the owners of loud, guttural calls and small squeaks alike.

Star sent occasional pulses of worry through their bond,

but Darin couldn't see any reason to be concerned. Chase appeared relaxed, so Darin tried to follow his lead.

A loud crack came from his right; Star stopped in front of him. Sandy and Chase had also frozen. Sandy's nose was in the air, with his nostrils flared as he tried to pick up the scent.

Another crack, but from behind – then another, from the left.

Chase tapped his spear, and Darin checked that the tip of his own was tightly screwed in. He hefted the short spear into a guard position and readied himself for whatever came through the trees. Chase saw it first. Darin peered in the direction he indicated and saw movement as something big passed behind the trees.

Star held his tail tucked between his legs, and its tip flicked from side to side. Darin rested a hand briefly on his back to help calm him.

More twigs cracked and branches snapped. A heavy head preceded a large, solid body. Sturdy and covered in fine black hair, its legs resembled the trunks it trampled through. The creature's horned head was framed with a bony, flared ridge. A rhinocorn. They were even bigger than he'd expected, and the horn more menacing.

Darin lowered his spear point and broadened his stance. It felt like he held a toothpick facing such a creature. Burn it, but he missed his own staff. He'd have to try to get that back before he came to Dal again. Star growled, a rumble building in his chest, and Sandy joined in.

As the hounds crouched, ready to leap, Darin and Chase sprung toward the rhinocorn, one to either side. Adrenaline coursed through Darin's body as he prepared to strike. He focused on where he would attack it, searching for a weak spot. Just there, behind the ridge. He readied the spear to strike. The moonhounds filled the point of their triangular formation. Just as he began to move his spear, Darin's vision filled with *[A herd of rhinocorn off to Chase's side]*. Star could smell them. He held his throw.

'Did you get that too?' Chase called as he backed up, opening up an opportunity for the rhinocorn to run.

'Yes,' Darin said and sent *[Both of them charging at the rhinocorn]* to Star. Together, they ran toward the rear of the rhinocorn, Star and Sandy barking, and Darin with his spear lowered.

Thankfully, he reflected afterward, rhinocorns were herd animals. When threatened, it fled for safety. The aftermath of the altercation resulted in little more than battered trees where the rhinocorn had charged past Chase with hounds snapping at its heels. It was desperate to rejoin its herd, rather than engage in a battle with two pointy sticks and a pair of moonhounds.

The trail of broken branches and flattened shrubs in the stampeding herd's wake left a clear route through the densest part of the wood.

'Let's follow. We need to go in that direction.' Chase clambered over a fallen log and headed after the herd.

Sunrise cut through the trees with a pink glow, and it wasn't long before the air was lit. Red sun shone through clouds of dust left in the rhinocorns' wake. The spaces between branches glowed with the promise of fire, that all things would one day be returned to air and dust – yet that morning, the dust itself revelled in its own beauty, dancing between the boughs. They picked their way over branches and crushed vegetation for a few hours before the sun rose fully and the glow receded, leaving the harshness of daylight. The rhinocorn trail faded as they slowed, and the herd changed direction toward the north of the crater. Hopefully, that meant they wouldn't come across the beasts again in a hurry.

They left the woods and emerged onto a well-used path.

Darin followed Chase and Sandy along the right-hand fork; before long, houses came into view. A gust of wind blew past his feet, picking up leaves and floating them on air cushions as they skimmed the ground. Spiralling and twisting like small dancers, the group of leaves spun and danced until they came to rest on the threshold of a wide-fronted house. Its solid door writhed with carved animals. Farbrox cubs cavorted around the bottom, and birds decorated its upper section. Carved and intricately painted, they had been caught and frozen in pose, ready to bring to life at any moment.

'Welcome to my other home,' Chase said as he strode to the door and knocked twice. The door opened gently to reveal a small man, with gnarled hands at the end of gnarled arms and shoulders hunched from years of detailed close work.

'Chase! So soon?' he asked, his face brightening. Chase enveloped him in an embrace. Tian glanced at Darin and raised his eyebrows questioningly.

'Training expedition.' Chase grinned. 'Tian, this is Darin and Star. We have a little challenge for you.'

'Come on in. As ever, my roof bids all Howlers welcome!' The door swung open, as though the home really did welcome them. Wall-to-wall racks hung from the ceiling, loaded with implements and tools. The sturdy work bench dominating the space was grooved and scarred from years of service, and the warm glow in the room had a steady light. Glow globes around the edge gently illuminated everything.

Darin looked at the globes, his brow furrowed.

'I thought only So'Dal could use these?'

'He's an untrained one—' began Chase.

'Untrained by the Watcher's great claws!' interrupted Tian. 'I trained alright, but in wood craft and music, not that stuff you call training in the Black Palace. Not for me, all that wiffle and song. I can sing through the wood of my creations.' He took up a position behind the great workbench, his eyes twinkling as he studied Darin. 'So, tell me, young man, what am I making?'

Darin withdrew the slide whistle from his robe and offered it to the woodworker. Tian turned it over, then looked down its length, running his finger along the decorative edging.

'Nowt wrong with this one, considering I didn't make it.' He peered at the engraving at the base. 'Ah ha! I thought it was Wilf's work. He's done well, that boy has.' His eyes snapped back to Darin and to Chase. He raised it to his lips and played. Mournful notes floated through the air as the whistle sang out, and Darin understood why Tian chose music over magic – his talent was beyond anything he'd ever heard.

As the last note hung quivering in the air between them, Tian's gaze flicked from Darin to Chase and back.

'It's a beautiful noise. Nowt wrong with it.'

'It's not that it doesn't work ... it doesn't *work*,' Darin said reluctantly.

'Take a seat and explain this further. What more does it need to *do*?'

'This is your scheme, Darin.' Chase reached into his pack. 'Tian, shall I prepare some lunch?'

Tian frowned at the large, dead bird Chase waved around his workroom, and the feathers flying off it. He nodded in agreement. 'That sounds like a good plan. Get those feathers out of here!' Then he returned his steely gaze to Darin.

'This plan?'

⋎ ✳ ✙ ✦ ✸

Several hours later, Darin and Chase sat replete and in silence; Star's fur was soft and warm under Darin's hand. Tian stood at the table, mulling over ideas. He sketched drawing after drawing and turned the pages from side to side. Only the scratching of the pen and yet another sheet of paper being thrown into the corner punctuated the quiet. Tian was developing a design that would give them the full range of notes they needed, including the top end of the three separate whistles if he could.

The training globe sat in the middle of the work desk. They'd decided to leave it with Tian along with one set of whistles, rather than risk them in the Edgelands. Darin was relieved that he wouldn't have to worry about breaking it for the rest of the journey.

'We'll leave first thing.' Chase looked out the small window. 'Tian, the weather should hold for us to get to the Edgelands, right?'

'Aye, but the xotryl are another matter.'

'We heard Big Red was out on the rounds again – with a smaller one. I suppose we should count ourselves lucky that they reproduce so slowly.' Chase rested his chin on his hands, gazing into the fire. 'If I could only find the other one and stop them breeding altogether, it would be so much better.'

'Will there be more rhinocorns?' asked Darin.

'There's only the one herd in the crater. I've no idea how many are in the Edgelands, though.' Tian said, not glancing up from his scribbling. He held a page up in triumph. 'I think I may have it.'

Darin glanced at the page; it was covered in scribbles and numbers. Maths had never been his strongest skill, and the complexity of the calculations astounded him.

'You need to bring me about seven long tubes,' Tian said. 'They'll need to be at least a forearm in length, and consistent in width. I'll make you a ring you can check their width with to take with you.'

'Thank you,' said Darin, still trying to follow the workings, and eventually giving up. 'That sounds like a lot of wood. How big will these whistles be?'

'They'll be small enough, don't you worry.'

'Impressive, isn't it?' Chase asked, glancing back over his shoulder. 'This is why Tian is the best. Imagine what sort of So'Dal he might have made with skills like that!'

'A bored one!' Tian shouted back from the worktable. He'd moved away while Darin was reading the diagram and was measuring and cutting a section of wood. 'Your dark tunnels and crazy rules would have driven me senseless.'

'I can see where he's coming from. It is good to be out of the palace,' Darin mumbled to Chase. He was rewarded with a wry smile.

'You can understand why I'm so rarely there, except to check up on the others and catch up on news.'

'Can't I just apprentice to you and be done with it then?'

Chase sighed. 'Once upon a time, that's exactly what you'd have done. But we can't afford to do that anymore. Without new Howlers, we're the end of the line. You need to learn as much as possible to bring the threat back down. I'm sorry, Darin, but like me, you may spend many of your years working alone.'

'You are hardly alone. You have Tian. Living in this community, you must have friends here too.'

Chase smiled. 'Friendship? I suppose so. But it's always a friendship one step removed. We lead a strange life.'

With that thought ringing in his ears, Darin rested his hand on Star's head and imagined them older and greyer. Star must have felt his sadness, as a wave of reassuring love patted at him like a mental wag in his direction. His vision was replaced with *[Darin and Star sleeping]*.

'I'm going to rest up then,' he said, sending *[Them sleeping on the rug in his pack]* to Star at the same time. Sending was definitely getting easier. 'Is there anywhere in particular you'd like me to rest or avoid?'

Tian mumbled, pointing toward the back of the room where a curtain divided a section off. Darin walked through, pushing the tanned leather aside. Behind it was a small room with a bed. Star walked up to it, sniffed, and sent *[Tian and Chase lying on it]* back to Darin. As if he couldn't guess that already.

He rolled his rug out on the far side of the room. Weeks of lying almost on the floor next to Star before they had their own room had got him used to wooden floors. Star curled up alongside him, and Darin knew that he would, as ever, have dreamless sleep.

⊤ ※ ⚒ ⚒ ✦

He awoke many hours later to the sound of snoring. Tian had climbed into the bed at some time in the night, and the resonant nasal orchestra assaulting Darin's ears would be hard to sleep through. Quietly, he nudged Star and sent *[The workshop]*. A sleepy thud of a tail answered him, and Star padded alongside as Darin carried their blanket through. The curtain didn't block the sound by any means, but it certainly reduced it.

He looked around for Chase, but couldn't see him. The dark room was hard to navigate without bumping into furniture, so he let his hound lead him. Star guided them to a clear space, and the two of them laid back down. No sooner had Darin dropped back off than he heard the door gently click shut. He felt Star rise on silent feet and heard his gentle sniff at the air. Darin saw *[Chase and Sandy, stood by the door]* through Star.

'I know you're awake,' Chase called quietly.

'What were you doing outside?'

He heard the shiver in Chase's voice as he replied. 'Getting us a little help.' The room was illuminated with a flickering glow as Chase brought out a glow globe from under his cloak. It was filled with fire sprites. Tiny, angry creatures buzzed around inside it.

'Won't they need food?' He wasn't sure he liked the idea. It seemed cruel.

'Yes, but we can release them when they stop buzzing, and then we'll find more. It's best to use the least magic possible, and right now, we can't just make and light up a glow lamp.'

'I can.'

'If you get it wrong, we might set light to the whole workshop.'

⊤ ※ ☒ ☲ ✳

Morning dawned too fast. Tian gave them a bundle of dried food to save them foraging and refreshed their water skins. Darin tucked the bulging skin in his pack on top of the folded blanket, screwed his spear tip on, and double-checked its tightness.

'Carry the fern-wood in this.' Tian handed him a long leather roll. There were pockets in the bottom half to tuck each branch into, and when rolled up, it would stop each one making contact with the others. 'It will minimise the chance of breaks and scratches. You need to use this for the widths. If they're slightly wider, I can work with them, but no narrower.' He held out a short cylinder of wood. As Darin watched, he took opposing sides and slid his hands in opposite directions. The cylinder split into two halves, lengthwise.

'Oh, that's clever!' Darin nodded appreciatively. 'I'd wondered how I was going to get that around the tree in one go.'

Tian wrapped it carefully in a soft red cloth and handed it to Darin. 'Good luck to you both. I wish you speed and safety.'

He stepped closer to Chase and leant forward, whispering something into his ear before embracing him. Chase bent down and kissed him gently, then Tian retreated to the company of the carved animals on his doorway. Darin felt his eyes on their backs as they left. Given the injuries on Sandy, every goodbye could be the last.

A winding path led away from the small village past a flock of skaa-rak pecking at plants in a small paddock, and flickering lights illuminated small windows as the inhabitants started about their daily routines. Patches of dappled light scattered across the path between soft shadows. It looked inviting enough, given their destination. Just as long as they could avoid rhinocorns, graaken, and xotryl.

He was going to the Edgelands! A flutter of nervous excitement tickled his insides. Star lolloped ahead down the path, his tail wagging as Darin adjusted his pack one last time.

'Are you ready?' Chase asked.

'Let's go!' replied Darin and, with a spring in his step, excitement overriding the potential danger, they started down the path.

CHAPTER 29

SURIIN

The land rose up, the land fell down
The mines had disappeared
The dragon came and sent them home
The monsters that we feared
Children's rhyme, with actions

Suriin pulled her head back through the false wall, and her hand shook as she attempted to re-lock the door. She was panicking – couldn't access her power. Was the door far enough from the bars that it would remain closed if she ran? Could the awldrin reach it? What if she let it loose?

She ran her hands through her hair and grasped the crystal pouch at her neck. She could do this. Suriin tried once more. Nothing happened. The door remained stubbornly unlocked.

'Think!' Should she have spoken aloud? What if it heard her? Suriin tried to still her shaking and focus. What did she have plenty of right then?

Fear. She tried to gather her fear and use it to lock the door. Fumbling around with magic she had no real idea how to use, she wrapped the handle as though it was an apple in syrup. Would that lock it? Watcher knew she had plenty of fear to draw on. Suriin removed her hand from the door handle, then replaced it and tried to turn the knob. Nothing happened – it was holding.

She backed away from the false wall and sank to the floor. Relief washed over her in a wave, swiftly followed by crushing nausea and panic. By the Watcher's flames, what was an awldrin doing in the depths of Redpike? Suriin reached for her glow lamp, seeking the comfort of light, and her hand found sharp fragments of glass in its place. She must have dropped it.

There was no option. She'd have to leave and wait in the darkness beyond the seed library. Suriin would follow the others when they left – assuming they hadn't already – and could follow at a distance until they reached the lit sections.

What if they'd already left? It would be almost impossible to find her way back to the main tunnels in the pitch dark.

Suriin walked up the gentle incline until her outstretched hands felt the wood of the door. She pressed her ear against it and heard nothing. *It's the only way.* She opened the door, sliding back the bolt from the inside. Once out, Suriin dropped both heavy bars back into place and pushed the heavy lock across.

She walked quickly into the darkness, running her hand along the wall for guidance. The weapons sigil had been marked down there on her map, but with a vision of the awldrin seared into her mind, the only place she wanted to be was safe in her room.

It felt as though she'd shivered in darkness for an eternity by the time light finally spilt from the seed library. Suriin followed the pair of So'Dal walking companionably side by side, being careful to stay as far back as she could and relying on the polished black rock to absorb her gentle footfalls. *Farbrox tracking was finally paying off,* she thought wryly, placing each step with quiet care.

At the end of the long corridor, their light vanished, leaving her alone again. Suriin ran to catch up. Her stomach ached with fear, or possibly hunger, and she realised that by then, she would have definitely been missed.

She felt around the doorframe for the button, found a stone protruding, and pushed it in hope. Much to her relief, it slid open. Suriin stepped through and left it to close behind her – following the others had to be the priority. Far to her left, the light bobbed. She hurried after it, plunged into darkness each time they went through a passage or a curve. Suriin knew there were few areas in use so far from the main palace, so they had to be heading back to the main area ... she hoped.

More than once, she called on the Watcher for guidance, and ran, hoping that her memory wouldn't lead her false. As they drew closer to the main tunnels, glow globes welcomed her with their light embrace, and she held back to let the So'Dal get farther away. Suriin counted to one hundred, then darted back toward her room.

⚭ ※ ⚛ ⚜ ✦

She closed her door with shaking hands and tried to calm her panicked breathing. An awldrin, a Watcher-flamed *awldrin* was in Redpike. In her home – well, the deeper section of it.

Who should she tell? Did the Anchor already know? What would happen to her if she told the Anchor, and no one was supposed to find them? Suriin needed time to think. *I'll have to pretend I am sick.* That way, if anyone had knocked for her while she was exploring, she could claim to have been asleep.

Her usually cosy room was pitch black without the glow

lamp, so she decided her best plan was to climb into bed and wait to be found.

Enveloped in safe darkness, the smooth, green face etched itself further into her consciousness. Why would an awldrin be in a cell under Redpike? Who put it there? How had they got to Lieus, and how long had they been imprisoned? Round and round her mind worked, question after question. Like a spider spinning an ever-increasing web, each thought led to more possibilities.

The chair had disintegrated; no one had been in there for a long time. But those So'Dal knew their way to the store opposite. Why was the awldrin forgotten about? Or was it? If no one had been in there, how was the awldrin not dead from starvation? Her head ached.

She needed light to write the questions down. Maybe reading them would help her see some answers.

⟆ ✵ ⬡ ⬧ ✦

Finally, after what felt like hours, she heard a knock at the door.

'Come in,' she croaked, forcing a crack into her voice.

Fresna stood outlined in the doorway moments later.

'Where have you been? I tried to find you. I tried here, too, but you weren't answering, and your door was shut.'

'I was here. I just feel awful,' lied Suriin, hoping that years of avoiding chores at home were about to pay off.

'You poor thing. I'll run and let Chef know you were poorly. Next time, you really need to let someone know. It was almost impossible today without enough people in the kitchens.'

'Couldn't one of the new arrivals have helped?' Suriin asked, adding a big sniff for dramatic effect.

'They barely know the way to their rooms. I think they'd

have been in the way. Where's your glow lamp? You shouldn't sit in the dark.'

'I, um ... accidentally broke it. Too many books in my pile – some fell and knocked it off. I haven't felt well enough to get a new one yet.' Suriin wasn't convinced Fresna would accept the story, but a beaming smile grew across her friend's face.

'That's something I can help with! I'll leave you with mine for now. I can get a new one once I've let Chef know you're sick. Do you want to try eating something?'

Suriin tried to push herself up, but her still trembling hands made it hard. She certainly felt shaken – probably looked it too. She nodded feebly. 'Please. You are so kind!'

As Fresna gently closed the door behind her, guilt flooded Suriin. She was lying to her only friend there. Great.

She closed her eyes and sank back onto her pillow. The gentle light from Fresna's lamp bathed her room in a soft glow. Too tired to think straight, she dozed off, her mind wandering. At first, dreamless sleep claimed her, then slowly the events of the day invaded her subconscious. In her dream, she was facing the awldrin from the open doorway. But Suriin was braver than before and took a step closer. As she did, she heard a voice.

'I knowed you will come back.'

The voice was soft, yet with clicking noises in places that none should have been. The words, though, were clear.

'Come back where?' she replied, still only half aware she was dreaming.

'To me,' the voice replied, and Suriin realised with a shock it was the awldrin speaking.

'Let me be gone. None will know,' it said.

'No. I don't even know who you are or why you are here.'

'I will help you. What you want? I am strong.'

Suriin shook her head and tried to tell herself she was dreaming. She tried to create a safe place to step away from the awldrin when a loud knock at the door cut through the dream and woke her abruptly. She sat up, sweating.

'I'm back!' Fresna called, and without waiting for a response, she breezed into the room, a plate laden with food balanced on her arm. 'Watcher's fiery breath, Suriin, you're even paler than when I left you! Here, eat up. I was going to leave you while I went to get a new lamp, but I think I'll stay a bit longer. You look as though you might fall out of bed any second.'

Grateful for the interruption, Suriin tried to return the smile and dug into the small mountain of food that Fresna brought. Swirling around the back of her mind was a growing realisation that the awldrin was waiting; that any time she dreamt about that moment, the awldrin could make contact. Oh, flames! Whose dream had she woken from?

'You know about dream walking, right?' she asked Fresna, trying to keep it as casual as possible.

Fresna nodded as she swallowed the mouthful she was chewing. 'Yes, we study it more in the second part of our training. Did your parents teach you about it? After all, you grew up out in real Caldera.'

Suriin shook her head. 'I got taught how to dream shield if I was outdoors. Otherwise, I have always slept in stone, so it's never really been a problem.'

Fresna laughed. 'Oh, you can still dream walk from within stone. But only if you know where you are going. It's harder, and no one can find your dreams accidentally. You could meet at an arranged place, though.' She winked. 'It's useful for meeting a sweetheart.'

Her peals of laughter at Suriin's open-mouthed response helped Suriin to relax, and the rest of their meal was finished in companionable chatter about which So'Dal had yet to find their Soul Anchors. Fresna even suggested places where one might meet them, so no one else would find out accidentally.

It reminded Suriin of her father's dream walk, when he had shown her where he met her mother. Watcher, but she missed them both. What would her mother do if she met an awldrin? Suriin hoped she arrived soon. Would she have told her if she was here? Maybe.

⁂

Two facts resolved themselves in the quiet moments after Fresna left.

The awldrin could not get to her unless she went to it. So, she just had to not dream about it. There, one problem solved. The second was the realisation that she could have spoken to her mother all that time Or maybe even – through dreams – her father? It stood to reason that it should be possible if they'd been dream walking in a place she knew well. Suriin could have spoken to her father, helped him feel less alone. She could have told him she was trying to find a cure. A lump rose in her throat. Gulping it back down, she tried to be objective.

He'd probably just treat her like a baby again and tell her to leave it to those who knew what they were doing. Maybe she wouldn't say a word about a cure, just try to chat with him. Suriin wished she'd paid more attention to the marketplace he showed her. It was Redpike, he'd said. She should go out and explore, learn what it looked like. That way, she could meet them herself. There was also home, so maybe they met there?

Suriin resolved to visit their home regularly from then on, just in case. She lay back on the pillows and tried to visualise it. The steep sides of Golden, the cosy farmhouse and the rainbow rug, Gwynn and his discoveries.

The body has a way of dealing with trauma, and it wasn't too long before, once again – despite her best efforts – Suriin found herself in front of the awldrin. Was it actually smiling? Or was that a grimace?

Everything looked just as it had earlier in the day. She tried to step back and found the door had gone. She was trapped with the awldrin.

'Your skill is weak,' they said. 'I keep you here for long as I want, or until you not sleep.' Suriin tried desperately to open her eyes. The creature bared their fangs with a hiss, and its eyes refracted the light oddly. They faced her, but with no pupil, she was not sure if they were focused on her.

'You can run, but you never hides from me now. Let me be gone.' The clicking that punctuated every sentence made the voice as alien to her ears as the face was to her eyes. Whatever clothes they had once worn were long gone.

Before she could stop herself, Suriin blurted, 'How long have you been here?'

'How long is night under mountain? Tell me, how did my Hive lose?'

'Why do you say they did?' Suriin asked. The word *hive* had not been said. The awldrin had made a strange noise and created an image. Hive was the word that her own brain filled in to explain the image of warriors swarming out of a mountainside – dark clouds of them – like insects pouring from a hive.

'If they won, I not still be here. They need me.'

'No one won,' said Suriin. 'From what I've read, the stories say The Watcher intervened.'

'The stories ...' The awldrin paused. 'How long is that?'

'Watcher's fiery breath,' breathed Suriin as realisation struck her. 'You've been imprisoned here for over 500 cycles?' Her fear had almost faded with the calm posture of the awldrin, who'd remained sitting at the back of the cell throughout the exchange. She was locked in, but not under threat – yet. Suriin reminded herself to be vigilant.

The awldrin hissed again. Was that a laugh or a threat? Suriin's heart raced, and she tried to focus on her breathing. She was in a dream; she was safe. The creature couldn't actually touch her.

'What you want, young human? If you let me be gone, I kill someone for you? Choose your price. The door open now. I see you soon.'

The awldrin blinked out of her dream, and she was alone in the cell. Suriin turned around. The door was visible, so she opened it and walked through it to wakefulness.

CHAPTER 30

ELISSA

There is nothing as sweet to a person as Hope.
Graffiti on the dockyard wall at Shardeep

Cold bit into her feet, drew patterns in the air with every breath, and – despite ramming her frozen fingers into thick gloves – Elissa couldn't feel her fingertips. It was the kind of bone-aching cold that stayed with her for days. She'd never really appreciated the warmth the firestone furnace must add to Dragonsbreath sericlave until then; for a second, a very small moment, she recognised that awldrin must need the heat too. That the icy reflection of Dragonsbreath mountain must make the mountain top eternally chill. It still didn't give them the right to treat humans so badly. She shook the sympathy away like a crawling bug and wrapped the blanket from her bed around her more tightly.

The tunnels of Shardeep were abandoned in a different way. Unlike the ones she'd arrived through, the rooms were well appointed. Her room was full of luxuries and well laid out, as were others she passed on her way to it. Could they be guest accommodations for visiting elders? If she needed to sleep under rock, then surely the same applied to them.

Elissa wanted to explore, but the cold restrained her to the limits of her sight and the imaginings of her mind. It was no wonder the sericlave had relocated outside. Surely, magical powers could make the rooms inhabitable and as full of life as they must have been when the Souls of Dal lived there, but if those with talent were mostly on the island of Hope, she wouldn't want to stay in a cold, dark tunnel either.

Elissa flicked a frustrated glance at the stupid heat globe in the corner. They must have run it before she'd arrived to make the room so welcoming. Overnight, heat had leached into the walls, and she was suffering for not having rewarmed the room before sleep.

'Just use that for heat,' they'd said. *Just* was a pretty hefty overstatement. She knew what she'd done in the abandoned tunnels, and she'd watched Rossi teach Laytha to light a globe carefully enough that she'd managed to copy it, but a blast of irritation wasn't going to light a heater, was it? What would she be left with if it failed, if she drained herself dry? Would she feel even more empty with no fear or irritation? Maybe she'd feel calm, or some other emotion would rise to fill the void, but what was utterly certain was that she'd still be cold. Elissa knew she should head out into the warmth of Rains and see the elders, but failing such a little task as warming her room, turning up to meet them, shivering and cold – no, that didn't sit right with her. Laytha wouldn't let her give up, so she wouldn't allow herself to either.

Elissa Shard-bonded – a grand name for someone who couldn't even warm her room.

Anger. She tried pushing anger out. Nothing happened.

Love. The stupid heater resisted lighting.

She tried the same note that lit her room before, but that didn't work either, and she ended up in the dark. Sighing heavily, she re-lit her room. Next, she tried to sing a scale starting as low as she could sing and reaching as high as she could manage. Still nothing happened, aside from another brief plunge into darkness.

In frustration, Elissa picked the ball up. She'd been cold so long it was clearly not going to be hot or burn her, but she'd be grateful for either at the moment. Elissa studied it more closely. Under the base was a small lever. She flicked it to the opposing side and saw a spark.

Hope filled her. It hadn't been turned on? It seemed a silly idea, but anything was worth a try. She worked through everything again. Nothing happened. Burn it! There had to be a way to make it work.

She flicked the switch again, absently playing with it as she watched clouds of her breath spiralling upward and considered her options.

It sprung to life. The heat and light were so sudden, she almost dropped the globe. Elissa placed it gently back in the middle of her room and drunk in the heat greedily. She'd been using magic, and it was a simple flame stone after all – not everything needed magic, and not everything would have it. A few days earlier, she wouldn't have made that assumption. She needed to stop and use what she knew first.

Her fingers prickled with pain as they regained warmth and, as heat seeped into her, she stopped shivering. It was a lot to take in. She felt like a child again, in an unfamiliar place surrounded by new objects, learning new skills – but with no Laytha to guide her through the new society. It made Elissa aware that her whole life so far, all their lives at Dragonsbreath, had been mere survival.

No veins of lumina rock threaded across the cave roof, and

she had no way of knowing how long she'd been in the room, fighting with the cold. *Better than fighting awldrin,* the thought came unbidden.

She could just hide in the caves – then she'd be safe. But no one else would be.

With the return of sensation in her feet came the return of the sharp and persistent throbbing in her foot, a painful reminder that, for some reason, the Shardeep people believed Elissa could help them.

Maybe she could, but she wouldn't. Not for them. She would help them for Laytha, for Makin, and all those trapped at Dragonsbreath. If there was a way out, she'd find it. Elissa sat stewing her thoughts for a while longer, then experimentally nudged the heater over on the floor. She poked the switch, but the flame didn't go out.

'I needed the room heating anyway,' she muttered, and placed it safely back where it'd been. Elissa straightened her clothing, folded the blanket carefully on the bed, and left the room, heading for the exit.

The sun was so low in the sky that it must be afternoon. She'd slept – and frozen from stubbornness – through an entire day. Down in the valley, children played, and chimney smoke drifted out of cosy homes. Peeking out above the houses, awaiting her presence, was the squat brick tower of the elders. It was time to see what they wanted.

⁂

The door swung open with a gentle push to reveal an empty hallway. Muffled voices drifted through the crack of an open door at the furthest end. Smaller doors to each side were closed and unmarked. Elissa approached the open door quietly.

A hush descended when she knocked. She opened the door wider, and every person in the room turned to look at her.

'Come in. We've been waiting for you.' The elder who'd greeted her the previous day gestured to an empty seat at the round table. 'Would you like a drink?'

'You haven't been waiting all day?' Elissa asked in horror.

'We heard you were on your way. No need to be concerned. It sounds as though you needed the rest.'

Elissa sighed with relief and sat in the indicated spot. 'Calfa, please – if possible.'

The elder gestured to someone by the door, who slipped out and returned moments later with a steaming cup of calfa.

'We've had Rossi's report of your journey and have a few remaining questions we need to ask you, and you alone.' The wizened man's grey beard jumped like a tunnel creature with each word. He paused expectantly. With her mouth full of calfa, Elissa could do little but nod, hoping he took it as a sign to continue. He did.

'We need to know how you blood-bonded with the shard. How many other talented are in the Dragonsbreath sericlave, and whether you have more crystals hidden there.'

Elissa swallowed the last mouthful and placed the cup slowly, deliberately on the table as she composed her reply.

'I stood on the shard in a river whilst fishing, a small part of it remains in my foot. The larger part is safe and with me.' She reached for the cord around her neck, dropping her hand as she felt its absence. 'I didn't do anything to the shard. You are all telling me I bonded with it, but that idea has never come from my own understanding. There are thirteen other Untouched women – those you call talented – within the sericlave. Of them, Laytha is the most senior.'

She saw the woman nod. Clearly, she was agreeing with what Rossi had told them already.

'As for your last question. To my knowledge, there are no further crystals. If that was the reason the awldrin came for me – came stalking through our sericlave – I cannot imagine that they would let one remain unfound.' Elissa paused as her own words sank in.

'There have been several times in my life that they have behaved as they did this time, though ...'

The elders shared a glance.

'So, they *may* have found others after they were brought to your sericlave?' No-beard said quietly.

'Or there may be others that had been successfully hidden,' added Beard-face.

Elissa nodded. Silence hung in the air, thick and pregnant with possibilities. A knock at the door broke the moment. Elissa met the eyes of the woman, but they were calm, and her face remained still.

'Enter,' she called, sliding her gaze from Elissa and toward the door as a man dressed in oiled leathers entered the room.

'M'lady, the boat's ready. We can depart whenever you choose.' He bowed deeply and with a flourish.

'Then we travel at sundown. I trust you are sufficiently rested to travel tonight, Elissa Shard-bonded?'

That name again. Elissa felt her heart sink. She tried to keep a composed face; she'd wanted time to explore the sericlave. Perhaps send a message to Laytha via the woman. They had someone set up to receive messages, so surely someone there could send one – Rossi even. Maybe in the next couple of hours, she could arrange something.

'I have little to pack, so I can travel tonight, but why so soon? I thought you wanted my help?'

'That's exactly why we're leaving. Tonight, we travel to Hope. The sooner the Chosen can teach you what you need to learn, the better it is for all of us. Especially if—'

Elissa knew that the unspoken sentence said more than they wanted the sailor to know. *Especially if the xotryl are hunting you.* She willed the woman to say it, to voice concerns that she held close herself, but her face returned to pure calmness, unreadable and serene.

'Elissa, pack your belongings. I expect you at the dock as the sun rests on the horizon. We will talk more on our voyage.'

Was she supposed to leave? Elissa glanced around the table. The old men were in conversation with each other, low and murmured; some of the others were studiously avoiding her gaze. The elder nodded gently.

Elissa rose, trying to leave with as much composure as she could. They had waited all day just for that? She stepped out of the main building into the warmth of the sun. Rain loomed on the horizon, and dark cloud shadows crossed the valley. Which would be Rossi's house? How would she know?

'Hi, um, can you help me?' she called to a child. He seemed around the same age as Rossi's daughter. Maybe he could help.

'Yes, probably ... maybe. You're the Shard-bonded!' His eyes grew wide as he stared at her. 'I thought you'd be dressed all fancy like the elders, not in rags.'

She stifled a laugh. 'Sorry about that. I'm sure I'll get fancy clothes soon. Can you tell me where to find Rossi?'

He nodded like a flower in the breeze, enthusiasm and energy filling every movement. She couldn't help but compare him to the lethargic children she had accepted as normal until a few days earlier.

The boy led her to a beautifully maintained house on the edge of the sericlave. Bushes in the garden were bursting into leaf and readying for the growing season.

'Thank you.' She turned to find the child had already left, running back down the paved path. Elissa knocked on the door.

A woman she hadn't seen the day before opened it. 'Hello?'

Her hair was lilac, long, wavy, and shining. She had kind eyes, and despite her brief appraisal of Elissa's clothing, she felt safe, friendly even.

'Are you *her*?' she asked.

'I think so,' Elissa replied. 'Is Rossi okay? I have to leave tonight, and I wanted to say thank you and goodbye.'

'He's resting. The wound was starting to go bad. It's taken more healing than I'd have liked.'

'I imagine you'd rather you hadn't needed to heal him at all.' Elissa clapped her hand over her mouth. 'I'm so sorry.'

The woman smiled. 'That's true. I'll make sure he knows you said goodbye. Once you learn to dream walk, you can talk to him yourself.' She frowned and tilted her head as she looked at Elissa's clothes once more. 'I don't want to disturb him. I'm sorry. I suspect your arrival heralds significant trouble for all of us. He will need to be as well as possible, as soon as possible. Wait there a moment.'

She shut the door, leaving Elissa stood in the garden. Dream walking – that was what Rossi had called it when he spoke to her and the elders. Someone else she needed to reach. All those people she might never see again except in her sleep. Elissa shook her head. What a strange world she had woken into after one exhausted doze.

The door opened again, and the woman passed her a bundle of fabric. 'I'm taller than you, so it will have to be a skirt, but these are clean and dry. Take them.'

Elissa reached for the clothes. 'Thank you.'

'Safe voyage, and best of luck in Hope. May you be all we hope you are. I saw the *Cloudsailor* on the dock.'

'Thank you.' She'd already said that. 'I hope the troubles that follow me are minor and don't find you. I'll do my best – for everyone.'

The woman nodded and closed the door. Elissa clutched the bundle of clothes to her chest and left the garden to begin the climb to her room.

CHAPTER 31

DARIN

*Only two Craters are incomplete. Inviting golden
sands line the seaward side of South Crater.
With its view of the Talon sand banks, it
makes for a pleasant place to rest and relax.
In contrast, few travellers will ever see the
tumbling waterfall over the high cliff edge of
Dal, descending to an unknown pool in the
depths of the Edgelands.*
A Traveller's Guide to Caldera

He was tired. Not of walking; the growing strength in his legs reminded him of the man he had been, rather than the scholar he had become. No, Darin was tired of the dark. Part of the pull of their expedition had been an escape from the darkness of the Black Palace and Redpike Mountain. Yes, the xotryl might spot them in the day, but he'd risk being seen in exchange for some daylight – even though he knew it was a stupid thought, he yearned for some light.

They neared the edge of Dal and its open crater edge. If it

was light, they would soon see the sea, a sight entirely new to Darin. South Crater opened onto the ocean and Conor had excitedly discussed the pleasures one could have on a beach at the water's edge.

No waves caressed the shores of Dal, its crater floor was a hundred spans above sea level. The collapsed cliffs and sunken land below the plateau made up the Edgelands, a region filled with vegetation and creatures from the distant moons that had encroached through Lieus's Aulirean Gate.

'Where will we hide today?' he asked Chase.

'You'll see in a minute. It's not far now. We'll need to start our descent as the sun begins to set and before it is fully sunk.' Veiled tension threaded through his voice. 'It is a risk whenever we go, but this exposes us for the least time. The route is treacherous, and we need some light to see our way.'

⊤ ※ ⚄ ⚅ ✦

As the rising sun cast its rays across the ground, it revealed the cliff edge. The trees thinned ahead, and sunlight shimmered from sparkling waves on a distant sea. It was beautiful; a thin sliver of water beyond the lush green of the Edgelands. A tower perched precariously near the cliff edge, twin to the one they'd slept in on their first night, over a tide ago.

'Is that another of our watchtowers?' Darin asked. They'd be sleeping over a hundred span drop – just what he wanted to think about as he fell asleep.

'Yes. Once, we had both enough numbers to man it and enough risk to need to,' Chase said. 'It's been at least two hundred cycles since it was permanently occupied.'

'This one appears well looked after. It's in much better repair than the first one.'

Chase nodded. 'It's more important. Should we ever have a

major breakout from the Edgelands, this is the only staging post we can use,' he muttered quietly. 'A staging post for a pack of four.' He sighed.

'This is the watchtower that Aggi meant, isn't it?'

Chase nodded again. 'If there was a way to stop them coming up or to contain them by using magic without exposing others, it would make a huge difference. As it is, I cannot be in all places at once – let alone dealing with the one headed to the south.'

Darin thought on Chase's words as they walked. If Tian was talented, maybe there were other Howlers in Dal. Maybe, If the whistles worked, they could be used as an easy way to test for magic – to see if anyone had the potential to bond with a hound ... The roar of falling water swelled as they neared the tower, interrupting his thought. Darin couldn't see any rivers to feed a waterfall, and so, assuming it was hidden like the door in the mountain, he followed Chase carefully.

'What are you doing?' asked Chase several minutes later as he span around to see Darin placing his feet into his footprints.

Darin mumbled, 'I thought the river must be hidden, and didn't want to fall in.'

'Ask a simple question of me, or even Staramine.'

'I didn't think to ask him.'

'Start thinking. If you can't trust your own senses, check his. It needs to be second nature.'

It was a fair point. Chase was right – he should have done it. Darin sent *[River running over the edge of the cliff]* to Star and saw *[Water over the edge of the cliff, but none on the land in front]* in return. The image was confused – Star had a pool of water in the air, but none on the land. Clearly, he didn't quite understand what was ahead of them either. 'He doesn't see it up here, so it's safe to walk anywhere?'

'Yes, the waterfall comes out ten spans below the cliff edge, next to the tower. It flows underground to the edge, then falls down. We will climb down it this evening.'

'Climb down the waterfall?'

'Yes.'

Darin gulped. Watcher's wings, it had been bad enough going down in the basket. He'd hoped there was something like the ramps found on the other craters. Climbing down a slippery waterfall? He felt nauseous even imagining it.

ⵕ ※ ⵝ ⵣ ✦

Darin leant out over the high sill and looked down into the Edgelands. Chase had gone straight to sleep, but thinking about the descent had stopped Darin relaxing. He'd woken intermittently throughout the day, and eventually, the lure of the unknown pulled him to the window.

He deeply regretted it. Even safely inside the tower, it made his stomach churn. Darin's legs buckled under him.

His dad used to say that the more he did something, the less scared he would be. Getting in and out of the craters on the way to Redpike and into Dal had involved either a lift or a steep ramp. If his knees betrayed him, he'd just sit in the basket or slide a few spans. The cliff edge would be different. How in Watcher's name was he going to climb down a waterfall, let alone with a moonhound?

To distract himself from the impending doom of the evening, Darin looked farther from the pool at the base of the cliff and out over the rest of the Edgelands.

The glow of invasive Mythese plants didn't show in daylight. Instead, a hundred shades of green and red painted the land. Birds soared from tree to tree; the Edgelands was a true, wild area. No humans had set foot there – he revised that thought – Only the Howlers would have been there in the last five hundred cycles. He wondered how many animals and plants had found refuge there that were scarce on the Surface or extinct in the craters.

As the sun descended, the calls emanating from the forest intensified. Darin felt rather than heard Chase move up behind him.

'It's quite something, isn't it?' Chase said. 'If you look toward the coast,' – he pointed over Darin's shoulder – 'that's where the river meets the sea. We're headed over there.'

The area of trees he pointed at didn't appear particularly different to any other part of the forest from there. Maybe they were taller?

'Any minute,' murmured Chase. 'Keep watching.' The sun continued its slow descent, then a brilliant light shone out from the forest.

'What's that?' he asked.

'The Gates – or as much of them as remains, at least. Dragon magic is resistant to plant growth, it seems, so they stay ever-shining and golden. Shining, but very definitely broken. One day, I'll take you there.'

Darin stared out at them for a moment longer as Chase turned away. The Aulirean Gates – another thing he had relegated to legend until recently. He glanced up, searching for the moons the Gates once led to. It seemed impossible. Well, it would have a few tides ago. As the light moved on and the reflection dimmed, he turned from the window.

⋎ ✴ ✖ ✖ ✦

They repacked their bags as lightly as they could and left Star's pack in the tower to allow him more freedom of movement. Darin was desperate to ask how'd get down with no ropes, but

not wanting to raise the ire of Chase with too many questions –
and a little afraid of the answer – he resisted.

'Ready?' Chase asked, eventually.

'Yes.' His voice sounded confident, even if his knees
quivered.

'Follow me.' They returned to the ground floor, where
Chase rolled a heavy rug back to reveal a huge sliding door. He
lifted a whistle to his lips and blew. The door dropped, then slid
into the base of the tower, exposing a staircase.

'This takes us to the river bed.'

The steps were slippery from damp and lack of use. Darin's
relief that they wouldn't go over the cliff edge was soon lost
when he slipped on the first step. Star had no problem, despite
his gangly legs. *Maybe his oversized puppy feet are useful here.*
Darin grabbed at the rail as he almost slid into Chase for the
fourth time. How did the man make it look so easy? In the light
from Chase's lamp, Sandy leapt down steps with comparative
ease.

'Keep your weight down through your foot,' Chase called
back, almost as if he'd read Darin's thoughts. 'Stop being so be
tentative, or you'll fall again.'

'Sorry,' mumbled Darin.

'No sorry needed. One day, you will do this alone with no
one to catch you. Once we leave the cave, if you slip, you will
probably fall all the way down.'

What a cheerful thought. Darin focused on doing as Chase
had suggested, aiming to place his feet with confidence. It was a
slower process, but steadier. Why was everything always about
him being alone, though? Maybe there would be more Howlers
bonded by then; perhaps he needed to go hunt for them
himself. There had to be more than just him born in twenty
cycles, surely.

Flickering blue light danced on the wall at the base of the steps. Chase blew the whistle hard as he passed it, his own body illuminated for a moment. Far above them, the grinding of stone indicated the door closing. They were shut down there.

'Still a bit of daylight. That's good,' Chase said. 'We'll be behind the waterfall, but we're still visible in places. It's been dry over the last few days, so keep an eye and an ear open – there may not be a lot of water to hide us. There are bolt holes in the cliff wall if you need cover, but we don't really want to get stuck in one.'

'Cliff, wet stones, xotryl, bolt holes. I think I have it.' Darin grimaced.

With a nod, Chase strode out of the cave into mid-air. Darin couldn't hold back his horrified gasp. Chase stopped and floated next to the waterfall. He crouched down, put one hand on the floor under his suspended feet, and raised his whistle, then looked back at Darin with a twist of amusement on his lips.

'Come on – you've seen our illusions enough times now! Although, I have wanted to do that ever since Aggi did it to me many years ago.'

Stone appeared under Chase's feet as he blew the whistle. A hundred spans of wet, slippery steps, *with no railing*.

The light faded fast as they trod the zig-zag path behind the waterfall. The hounds found it easy, as did Chase. Although he sounded relaxed and chatty as they descended, Darin could see frustration writ across his face as Chase turned to encourage him over yet another particularly slippery bit.

'We really need to be at the bottom before full darkness. Fire sprites aren't known for hanging around waterfalls, and I need my hands for my own balance. Can you go any quicker?'

'I am going as fast as my knees will take me. If I go any faster, I swear they'll throw me over the edge,' Darin replied. His legs were so wobbly it took most of his concentration to keep moving.

In places, the stairs widened, and as they reached the end of each short stretch, they broadened toward the turn. On one corner, he clearly saw a darkened area beyond a smaller, cruder set of steps – presumably, one of the hideouts that Chase mentioned. Darin tried to focus on one step at a time, whilst trying to not look over the precipice. Star followed behind, his presence a comforting calmness against his Darin's fears. He was so intent on his footing that he didn't see the creature approaching over the Edgelands. He was nearing the next turn when Chase said, 'Get under the waterfall!'

Darin glanced up as shade fell over him. The low sun behind the creature cast a shadow that fell just to his side of the waterfall. Its hide glowed like fire in the setting sun, giving it an even more fearsome appearance. *Almost like a dragon, but its head is wrong.* Dragons were elegant, and if the records were to be believed, at least twice as big as the incoming creature. The elongated, pointed head with dagger-like teeth and strange eyes swung from side to side. *Just like the stories.*

His fear of the xotryl – Big Red, he guessed – turned out to be stronger than fear of falling, and he managed to get himself under the waterfall with Star trembling quietly alongside him. The xotryl may not be as big as a dragon, but compared to other living animals on Lieus, it was massive.

'A right pair of xotryl fighters we make, quivering under here,' Darin mumbled, stroking Star's head.

To continue down, he'd have to exit on the side of the

waterfall the xotryl was flying toward. He risked a peek down. Why was Chase not under too? Sandy barked loudly from that side of the waterfall – they must need help. Darin moved carefully closer to the noise. Surely it hadn't reached them already.

'Where are they, Star?' he muttered. He couldn't ask – there was no way he could manage double views while he was on the cliff. It felt better talking to him, though. Darin crouched down and peered over the edge. It was only about twenty spans down – not far until they reached the bottom. He wondered how deep the pool at the base was. A flash of light illuminated the water from Chase's side as a screech from the xotryl shredded his ears and left them ringing.

He was hit from behind. Darin's knees buckled; he lost his balance and reached for the edge of the step, but his body had other ideas. He slipped and slithered, the wet steps under the waterfall evading his grip. The weight of his pack pulled him further off balance, and he continued to stumble. His feet slid off the edge of the step, and Darin made a last desperate attempt to grasp hold of the rocks.

As Darin's fingers lost purchase, Chase's horrified face peered up from the stairs below.

'Hold on!' he called, running up the steps – back toward the xotryl. He kept glancing at Darin, and their eyes met as Darin's hand finally slid off the step and he fell backward. The weight of his bag tipped him head down. Darin heard Star's loud barking as the wind rushed past his head, blood-red light reflecting off it.

The water soaked his upturned face.

The water was falling faster than him.

His head jolted forward as he hit the pool, and the weight of his bag dragged him under.

Tumbling water threw him around, and the darkness of deep water started to close out his vision. Darin kept his mouth closed, hoping to be pushed out of the churning mess he was in. Then he felt his pack catch on something. Darin struggled to get himself free of the straps, but his limbs grew heavy, and he couldn't free either arm.

Then he felt nothing more.

CHAPTER 32

SURIIN

Suriin adjusted her blue scarf carefully. She smoothed down her flowing dress and tucked her crystal inside its high neck. Nausea overwhelmed her whenever it was too far away, and her head span when it hung openly. How long would it be before she could wear hers like her mother or the Anchor? Exposed and proudly. As it was, she dared not wear it free of its pouch. How many of the rest of her new class would do the same that morning?

She checked her sketchbook was tucked in her pocket and found the map scrumpled alongside it. Suriin couldn't think about that or the awldrin yet. She shoved the map under her mattress with the other nights' notes on the tunnels.

Aslin expected her soon. Suriin shut her door and ran a hand over the flower as she did every time she left – it had become her small ritual. The flower, she'd discovered, was an agrium. All her research had taught her a lot about plants; that was one positive to come out of everything. *And maybe another.* She tried to squash the thought as fast as it arrived. Her father would not want her to risk so much for him. But what damage could a single, lone awldrin do? Her thoughts carried her as fast as her feet to Aslin's room.

⟡ ⁎ ⁑ ⁂ ✦

Whilst she'd been exploring, others had arrived and bonded their crystals. Suriin noticed a small group of unfamiliar women growing more numerous by the day on the far side of the hall at mealtimes. One of the new women had arrived with an apprentice So'Dal, apparently; they could be bonded already. Suriin had tried to work out which of them it might be. The dark-haired one looked the least unsettled. Maybe it was her? The group was very diverse in appearance. Although lilac hair was a defining feature of magical ability, several of them had hair so pale it was almost silver.

⟡ ⁎ ⁑ ⁂ ✦

Outside Aslin's room were the same group of women. Most were very well dressed, but she didn't see any crystals on display; it made her feel a little less nervous. One other woman stood slightly to the side. She offered a tentative smile. Suriin grinned back – there was nothing to lose by being nice. She needed to get through the first lesson, and then work out what she was going to do next about the awldrin and her father. They wouldn't be in there all day, she was sure.

'Hi, are you from Redpike?' the woman asked. 'Only, I'm sure I saw you working in the kitchen, and you came from somewhere different from the rest of us?'

'Where are you all staying?' She'd assumed they were roomed somewhere near her.

'The guest tower.' The woman pointed out the window at the stone building adjacent to the wooden guest quarters. Suriin tried not to roll her eyes. As if she didn't know where it was.

She had to work and learn with those women, though, so she bit her tongue; Suriin had looked forward to starting lessons for years. Nothing would upset her that day, and she didn't plan to make trouble.

'Oh, is it nice there?' she asked, trying to steer the topic away from herself – not wanting to explain why she'd arrived before the rest of them.

The door opened silently, exposing Aslin sat at the centre of her table.

'Please come in,' she said. 'Take your seats.'

They looked at each other, trying to gauge who should enter first. Suriin hung back until one of the silver women walked forward and sat down. Suriin followed, continuing around the table until she found the symbol for remorse she had used to bond with. If it was her base emotion, then maybe it would be easier to use. She sat down, confident that the others would probably no more recognise her symbol than she would many of theirs.

Slowly, the other six took their seats. Most sat close to the door and around to Suriin's right. Was love over there? She tried to remember. Suriin was the only one on her side of the table. She hoped there was some randomness to the arrangement of the symbols, that the negative emotions were spread around.

Hello, my name is Suriin, and I bonded with remorse. Please

Watcher, let us not be introducing ourselves ... She took in the bright, excited smiles facing her. *That should have been me too.*

⊤ ❋ ⚭ ⚜ ✦

'Crystals out,' Aslin said. 'Now choose a symbol near to you. You all know at least one. I would like you to very gently focus your emotion onto that symbol through your crystal and make it glow. Remember how they glowed when you bonded.'

Suriin smiled – that was easy. After all, she'd already tried it. She inhaled slowly and felt for the power she knew was at her core, then pushed it out, steering it through her fingertips. As it had in the hidden room, it felt different. When she'd healed her father, the power had released in a torrent, but she only felt a trickle of power. Maybe she'd used too much remorse bonding her crystal so enthusiastically? The smile fell from her face as she concentrated. One student over the other side of the table had lit up her symbol. It must be the one with a bonded So'Dal, Suriin decided – if they were in love, an ever-filling well of emotion would be available to her.

'Focus on the emotion, not just the effect you want. Gather it and then push it out,' Aslin said, looking intently at Suriin.

She focused on an image of her father; on his disappointed face when they'd told her they would leave early. Suriin's emotion began to swell. She wished she hadn't done it, hadn't agreed to the adventure. Gathering her regret into a ball, she pushed it out through the crystal. The symbol flashed with a bright green glow, then went back out.

'Too much, too fast. Try again,' Aslin said as she watched the symbol flash. 'Concentrate more – it's almost there,' to one of the silver women. 'That's lovely, just hold the glow,' to a smiling woman opposite Suriin.

Several attempts later, each of them had held a steady glow for a few moments.

'Now I'd like you to try another emotion,' Aslin said. She drew a pack of cards from under the desk and dealt them one each. 'Find your new symbol and make it glow.'

Suriin's card was an unfamiliar double-wave symbol with JOY scrawled underneath it. They moved around the table, trying to find their new challenge, and Suriin found hers close to the door. They were far more spread out. No one appeared to be working on remorse. Good. That was a facet of herself she preferred to keep covered for a little while longer.

Suriin considered what made her happy. She pictured her father and mother, but the feeling changed almost immediately to sadness that she may never see them together again if her father couldn't battle through. She tried to picture her brother, but the same problem occurred.

No family-related thoughts. *Simplify it.* Favourite food ... yes, there was a little bit available. Friends – Fresna! That was better, although guilt crept around the edges of the joy. No, she needed to stay on simple things.

Suriin concentrated on food. She pictured brose sauce. The pleasure of drawing and creating beautiful pictures. Gently – slowly – the feeling built.

She tried to keep her focus, and for a very brief moment, a flicker of yellow light glowed on the symbol. She glanced up to see Aslin smile at her – she had noticed. Suriin's sense of achievement swelled, and a little more joy grew. Soon, the symbol glowed, gently but steadily.

'Remember this moment,' said Aslin. 'For most of you, this will be an opposing emotion to that which you originally chose. It will consequently have been harder to illuminate. But by the time you leave here to begin your role in our society, you must have mastered every one of these symbols. Your assignment for tomorrow is to have learnt the meaning of a further five. You will find the library a useful source of information.' She nodded and gestured toward the library area of the palace.

'Most of you have yet to be assigned a role here. Please consider the skills you can offer with most confidence and return with suggestions for how you will earn your keep in this afternoon's session. Once assigned, you will move out of the shared guest rooms and into your own private quarters.'

ⲧ ※ ⵝ ⵥ ✦

The door opened without Aslin appearing to have done anything. Suriin studied where Aslin stood, certain that – having seen the push-stones in the seed bank – there was a hidden button in the centre of the table somewhere.

'Thank you, Soul Anchor Aslin,' she said, as she followed the other students out of the room.

'Would you like to join us for lunch?' asked the silver-haired woman. 'I'm Xedra, and this is—'

'I'm sorry,' interrupted Suriin, 'I really am, but I have to work. I eat afterward and wouldn't want you to wait for me. I'll happily show you around the library later, though?'

Xedra huffed, 'Well, if you can spare the time from your chores, I'm sure we'd be grateful for your presence. Come on, ladies. Let's eat.' She turned on her heel and stalked off, with four of the others following behind.

'She thinks she's important because her parents are apparently influential and wealthy in Port Crater,' muttered one of the three remaining women. 'Xedra has been talking down her nose at us since we arrived.'

'Xedra doesn't understand how it works here. I can't wait

to see what jobs they will assign her,' said another. Suriin looked carefully at the women speaking.

'Are you ...'

'Twins? Yup. You must be Suriin. We are from the Witness family based in South Crater. It was our garant that flew you here.'

'Thank you!' Suriin relaxed and smiled widely at the women. Their eyes were as dark as their deep purple hair, and despite being a similar age to her, their tanned skin showed the hints of what would turn into laughter lines around the eyes. There was no tension in their faces. Suriin decided she liked the women.

'Did it get you here in time?' one of them asked.

'Sort of. He's still alive but unwell. Can we not talk about it right now, please? Did you fly up on her?' Suriin asked.

'No, she's been delivering messages and other things for the Anchor ever since. We aren't sure what's going on, but it's been really busy. Da decided we were better travelling by land. That's why we're so late. Would you show us the way to the main hall? We only arrived yesterday, so haven't really got our bearings yet.'

Suriin smiled and gestured for them to walk with her. 'Let's go then.'

'I'm Joy, and my sister is Merri.' Joy gestured to the woman who'd originally greeted Suriin, but had since remained silent, having watched their exchange from a slight distance. 'This is Skye.'

Skye waved shyly at Suriin.

'Merri and Joy?' Suriin asked, an eyebrow raised.

Merri rolled her eyes. 'Yes, we know.'

Suriin pointed out the routes to other important places on the way to the main hall, including the passage that led back out to the library. The corridor opened up a little more, and light streamed through the windows as they entered the hall.

'Shall I meet you after lunch to go to the library?' she asked as she prepared to head into the kitchen. They glanced at each other and nodded.

'Great! I'll see you shortly. I'll try to finish as soon as I can.' Suriin left them at an empty table and strode toward the kitchens. Once in, she draped her scarf over her peg by the door and grabbed her hair cap before setting to work on desserts.

It was mixed berry medley with a smooth herbal dressing, all cradled in curved sugar cakes. Fresna was pulling the sugar cakes out of the oven as she arrived in their shared work area.

'You look so much better than last night!' she said, hugging Suriin with sticky hands. 'How are your new classmates? Are they nice?'

'Some are, some are rude.'

Fresna laughed. 'I'll bet the rude ones are the first-generation lilacs. We had one last year. She turned her nose up at every job offered to her for ages until she finally worked out that the offers were getting more and more unpleasant.'

'What did she end up doing?'

'Stall cleaning. She thought working with the animals would be cute. We all learnt just how bad skaa-rak droppings smelt that first tide until she worked out a better system. It's a very small room to get stuck in with that sort of stench.' Fresna chuckled to herself. 'Anyway, the Collective came in early today. We had better get these done.' They worked well as a team and made short work of the berry dessert, working swiftly until it was time to eat themselves.

Suriin retied her hair at the end of the shift, promising to catch Fresna up on her day later that evening, and dashed back into the hall to lead the others to the library.

⋆ ✳ ✳ ✵ ✦

The library was silent. Merri and Joy stared in awe at the surrounding frescoes, while Skye rushed over to the bookshelves and muttered as she searched through them.

The Librarian's seat was empty, but the big listings file sat on her desk. Suriin searched between the book cases for her before giving up and opening it.

She flicked through the file – what would symbols be under? Magical languages, channelling power, or maybe emotional power. There was nothing under any of those headings.

'Over here,' Skye called. She wielded a small leather-bound book as she sat at a big table; they gathered around to see what she held. Each page had a beautifully drawn illustration of a symbol. Suriin pulled her sketchbook out almost without realising.

She sketched the outline of the first one; it was much like a wave. Underneath it said *serenity*. That wasn't one she could try any day soon! Not the way her mind whirled.

'Were there more copies of this book?' she asked.

'Several similar ones – I thought this appeared the simplest, though.' Skye pointed at the shelf. 'Over there.'

Suriin and Merri – *or was it Joy?* – crossed to the shelf and collected a few more, returning with them to the table. They spent the remainder of the afternoon copying symbols and trying to learn them, quietly testing each other as they went. Suriin decided to learn a range. But, with the awldrin firmly in her thoughts, she ensured vigilance and fear were two of them.

Vigilance was a series of straight lines, intersecting at angles – if she squinted, it could almost be a shield. Fear was an ever-narrowing and tightening spiral. It made her think of a deep hole and was deceptively hard to copy.

As the sun descended below the windowsill and shadows crept across the library floor, Suriin made her excuses and left. Her father's room should be empty of Gardeners by the evening, and she wanted some time with him. The courtyard was busy with guard training and some of the Collective sparring, so she skirted the edge, watching the sword play. Clanging steel covered up the sound of oncoming footsteps, and had it not been for her fast reaction, she'd have ended up in the arms of a freckled Soul Anchor. Behind her trailed a pack of young hounds out for their evening exercise. Mumbling an apology as her cheeks reddened, Suriin lowered her gaze. Once she was past, she risked a peek back. The woman had continued on her way, apparently unbothered by the encounter. Suriin hurried through the arch and down the passageways to her father's chamber.

He was alone, as she hoped. The sharp scent of unemptied bedpan filled the air. His once immaculate hair was knotted, and stubble on his chin was fast becoming a beard.

'Mother wouldn't recognise you,' murmured Suriin, kissing him on a thin cheek. The darkness had spread farther up his arm and started spidering across his face. 'I tried to meet you last night,' she said. 'I dreamt I was sat in our kitchen. Maybe you'd like to meet me there? That would be nice. I'm going to tidy your hair now – Mother will arrive soon, and you should look your best. I'll be very gentle.'

She pulled a comb from her pocket and began to gently work through the knots. An old nursery song came to mind, and she hummed the jolly tune as she worked. As she sang, the song changed tune slightly.

The click of the door closing was the first notice she had that anyone had entered.

'That's not a tune to sing, Suriin. You don't want people knowing you broke the rules before you started.' Ronin glowered at her from the doorway.

'I wasn't expecting anyone,' she replied, realising as she spoke that she'd been humming the healing weft. 'Anyway, I'm crystal-bonded now, so it's okay. I've been practicing using my power in class. Why are you here anyway?'

'It's my turn to lay the healing on him to sustain him a little longer. You should really leave before I do it.'

'Let me stay. I'll be quiet. Maybe you could use a boost?' Suriin stretched her mouth into what she hoped was a persuasive smile and tipped her head to the side.

He laughed, momentarily dropping his guarded pose. 'You can stay for a moment, but you need to go before the rest get here to check my work.'

'I'll just keep brushing his hair. Ignore me.'

Ronin opened Yorynn's shirt, placed his hands in the centre of the black marks, and sang softly.

Suriin studied him from the corner of her eye. He was good-looking, despite being bossy, arrogant, and self-absorbed. Yes, they worked well as a team, but he'd need a special kind of Soul Anchor to love his other faults. She snorted at the thought and tried to focus on the song. It was not the same as the weft they'd performed on the way. The tones and notes were complex, deeper. It was still repeating, and by the third repetition, Ronin was drooping.

Without really thinking, Suriin placed her hand on his and gently sang along with him. Startled, his eyes flicked upward.

'You can't do that here!'

Suriin recoiled, her hand breaking contact immediately, and awkwardly tried to finish her father's hair. Once she'd untangled as much as she could, she leant forward and whispered in his ear, 'The kitchen – remember.' Then, after kissing his cheek one last time, she turned away and left the room.

⊢ ✻ ⅏ ⅋ ✦

That night, Suriin took a moment to compose herself before she closed her eyes. Hope fluttered in her stomach like a butterfly as she tried to build an image of her kitchen at home, beginning with the spiral rug and crackling fire. She sat on the step and waited, trying to stay calm and controlled as she focused on building the details of the room. The fire tools in their holder. The heavy table pushed back from the hearth. Suriin sat for what seemed like hours. No sign of her mother or father. She was about to give up when a flicker of movement caught her eye; sitting in the armchair was a shadowy, veiled silhouette. Suriin rose and glided toward him. Through a mist shrouding his form, she could just about make out her father's features.

'Can you hear me? I told you I'd be waiting,' she said.

His eyes flicked in her general direction, but stared through her, unfocused. He looked up, and for a second, their eyes met. Then they slid past her again, and the butterfly of hope fell, swatted by despair. Her father didn't *really* see her.

He couldn't even be there properly. She was losing him, and it was all her fault.

⸱ ✤ ⸱

Suriin opened her eyes. She sat up, reached for the glass on her table, and gulped down water to ease the dryness of her throat. Closing her eyes one more time, she began a second dream walk.

Chapter 33

Elissa

Hope: A cloudy emotion, hard to define.
It is thought to be related to both joy and antic-
ipation.
Yet neither manages to put into feelings what the
first sight of Hope does to the heart.
We sailed that day, bearing hope to Hope.
Excerpt from The Captain's Log onboard
the Cloudsailor

It was quiet.

An incessant barrage of rain had pounded the cabin roof ever since they'd left Shardeep, creating a grey haze on all sides when Elissa had ventured briefly on deck the day before. For the first time, she could hear water lapping past the hull and the slap of the bow as it hit the waves. Loose sails flapped loudly, and on the deck above her cabin, the thuds of running feet cut through her rain-dulled consciousness. Elissa scrambled up the ladder to the deck, and brilliant sunshine warmed her immediately.

The curved prow of *Cloudsailor* had no painted figurehead, unlike the small fishing boats she'd seen on the Shardeep dock – they'd worn all manner of creatures proudly. Not *Cloudsailor*. The whole boat was unadorned and plain, with sails as grey and mottled as the sky and sea. From the shore, it was barely visible. Elissa could finally see how truly effective it was at sea; the colours matched perfectly. She rested her hands on the rail and gazed over the water, searching for a coastline.

A sailor approached Elissa and inclined her head slightly – in respect, maybe? It was a gesture she'd seen used in Shardeep toward the elder. Unused to the status she held with the Shardeep community, it made Elissa extremely uncomfortable.

The sailor pointed over the bow at a cloud bank and uttered a single word, 'Hope,' then continued with her work.

The boat's rolling motion – a familiar companion over the last few days – decreased, and the water calmed to mirror flatness as a circle of clear sky hung above them. Elissa hobbled to the prow and stared at the cloud bank. It didn't fill the horizon. Rather, it appeared to be a mountain of cloud emerging from the water. With no true concept of their speed, other than how fast they had departed Shardeep, she judged that they might be there by nightfall. As the day wore on, she glanced often at the strange clouds, and soon realised that despite sailing in their direction for hours, the cloudy peak remained distant, seemingly unchanging.

Something nudged at the back of her mind, a gentle prod for attention. Elissa looked around for the elder, thinking that maybe she could talk in her mind while awake, but she didn't see her on deck. As Elissa swung her head to search in the other direction, movement in the water drew her attention back to the sea.

The eyes were back – the huge green eyes. She could make

out a small section of scales around them. The water broke up the image as though it was a reflection.

Was it above her? Instinctively, Elissa ducked and looked up, but the sky was clear. She turned back to the water; it was gone.

'What was that?' she murmured.

'Watcher.' A crew member stood next to her, his knuckles white as he gripped the rail. He turned with wide eyes.

'My da saw one of them once,' he said eventually. 'Said it had black eyes and black scales. He was sailing a group of Chosen back to Hope. Never thought I'd see one.'

'What is it?' she asked.

'Da didn't know, and everyone laughed at him when he asked – well, all but one Chosen.' He shook his head as if to clear it. 'Da used to claim it was the Watcher itself, but now I know that ain't true. He must have been lied to because Watcher is black. Everyone knows that. Black in every painting, every book. That, what we just saw – that was green!'

'Do you know which Chosen?' Elissa asked. Maybe she could arrange a chat herself.

'Aye, he said it was the one with the grey streak in her hair.'

Elissa resisted rolling her eyes with frustration. The crew member still stared into the water, shifting his weight from side to side and muttering, clearly unsettled and unhappy. If his father had seen it, then a grey-haired woman could be one among many. Still, it was a start. Maybe she should ask the greyest. The Watcher – a name from history. The dragon who ended it all.

⊤ ✳ ✗ ✤

Finally, they entered the cloud bank. Cool, damp cloud saturated her clothes, and the world closed in to the ship's rail.

The air grew thick, and she found it hard to draw breath. At first, she fought the rising panic, then, realising that it was from fear, allowed herself to accept it – to feel it but not act on it. She would treasure emotions and save them all for later, just like Quin had suggested.

Cloudsailor turned, and then immediately again, the crew unhurried but deliberate. At the prow of the boat stood the Captain, statue-still in his oiled leathers and staring intently at a device in his hand, calling out orders that the crew followed immediately. Elissa squashed herself against the railing, trying to keep out of their way.

She lost count of how many times they changed direction in the greyness of the cloud. The wind shifted constantly, and she was utterly convinced they'd sailed in circles. They continued their twisting route through the fog for hours until, finally, the fog cleared.

Under the grey shadows of a still-clouded sky, Elissa saw Hope for the first time. Sandy coastlines ran under towering cliffs, themselves topped with unfamiliar plants that stretched their leaves toward the sky. At the base of the cliffs, a small cove with a harbour came into view. To her surprise, they didn't head for it, but turned around the coast. The Captain continued to stare at the object in his hand, ignoring the land ahead, while the crew continued to follow his orders. They slipped past other coves with numerous landing places and more cliffs. Hope was so much bigger than she had been led to believe; the island stretched across the horizon.

The elder approached her. 'I always enjoy this bit. Nothing on Hope is quite as it seems. Hold tight and trust the Captain.'

Elissa hadn't seen her since they boarded. Maybe sailing didn't agree with her – she certainly was a little pale. Elissa was about to comment on it when the Captain raised his arm.

'Turn about ... Now!'

Cloudsailor swung to face the cliffs. Elissa held tight, fighting the urge to leap overboard as they drew ever closer. They would hit it at any second. She felt a reassuring hand on her own, but still she grabbed the rail, braced for collision. Her eyes squeezed closed, and she waited for the splintering of wood and a shuddering impact.

Instead, a tingle ran over her skin, a spark passing through her body from front to back. She was left cold to the core, but unharmed. Slowly, she opened her eyes.

They were on open water. Elissa snapped her head around to look behind them – there was no trace of the cliffs. She could see the grey wall of cloud in the distance, but nothing else.

'What in the Watcher's flaming name just happened?'

The elder smiled at her. 'The first time is always the best. I couldn't spoil it for you!' She gestured for Elissa to look ahead.

There was another island, much smaller than the illusion they'd just sailed through. No soaring cliffs scraped the skyline; instead, a gentle slope rose to a slender golden tower. It protruded from a dome and reached into the sky. A ring of smaller buildings encircled it, and a brightly coloured town squatted around a beach of black sand.

Several of the crew leapt from *Cloudsailor* into shallow walkways either side. The sails flapped merrily in the breeze, while men in the water steered them through a landing channel that fitted *Cloudsailor* like it was dug specifically for it. She glanced behind as the captain clapped the helmsman on the back in congratulations. He closed his device and stowed it in a pocket.

A group of women arrived on the beach as the crew tied the boat to posts. They wore simple, clean white and gold robes. Every one of them with hair in shades and tones of purple; they must be the Chosen. Elissa searched for one with grey hair and found several older women. Later, she might ask about eyes in the water.

⋎ ⸎ ⚝ ⚜ ✦

'M'lady,' a voice cut through her thoughts. 'You'll have to get wet, I'm afraid.'

Elissa laughed at both the term of address and the idea that water would bother her in Rains. She took off her wraps and stepped over the rail onto the small steps carved in the hull. Her dressing would need changing again, but no matter. She was sure they'd have something to help.

The woman at the front of the greeting party held out her hands with the same self-facing gesture Elissa witnessed at the Shardeep sericlave.

'Elissa Shard-bonded, welcome. Be yourself among us. May we assist with your belongings?' She reached for the small bag Elissa clutched to her chest and gestured to it. One of the other Chosen stepped forward, but Elissa held it tight.

'Thank you, but there's no need. I'll manage just fine.' She had no intention of handing her shard over to them just yet. The woman stepped back and offered a friendly smile. 'This way.'

Elissa followed them up a winding cobbled path, through a hotchpotch of buildings with rooflines at improbable angles and painted a riot of colours. As they strolled alongside each other, the Chosen gestured expansively around her.

'Welcome to Gallimaufry, the only village on the island. Thanks to the boldness and bravery of the Captain, everything you need can be bought here.'

'About that,' interrupted Elissa. 'The fog, and the other island?'

She nodded. 'Ah yes, the only protection that the great golden dragon, Hope, left us. What an illusion! It's produced by the tower and has kept us hidden since the Gates closed.'

'How many of you live here?' Elissa asked.

'One hundred and twenty registered residents. However, of those, at least twenty are out on patrol around Shardeep or assisting our people at any one time. I understand you met Quin and the Shardeep elder. She doesn't sail well – most unfortunate for one who has to visit her area regularly.'

Elissa glanced behind. The Shardeep elder trailed at the back of the group, but looked considerably better than she had on *Cloudsailor*.

The path from the village was well cared for, and furry animals, like the ones near Shardeep but bigger, bounced around the hillside with their rear ends pointed upward into a fluffy point. Crops flourished there, despite it so recently being the end of Winds.

'What are these creatures?' she asked, as one bounded up to her.

'Farbrox. They're lovely, aren't they? They eat the pests for us.' The Chosen leant down and stroked the head of a passing farbrox; it raised its tail and wiggled it around. Elissa wasn't sure she liked the odd thing.

⋎ ※ ※ ※ ✦

The ring of buildings was broken by the protruding dome at the base of the tower. Each round house was arranged so that its entrance faced inward. A little like a selection of cave rooms opening into a central area, but the mountain had been melted from above them.

'Would you like to see your room first? You can take a rest, and we'll meet with you properly after the evening meal?'

Elissa looked around at the Chosen who had spoken. Whilst her voice had been calm, Elissa noticed signs of impatience; her foot tapped gently, and she fiddled with the ring on her finger. Behind her, others were exchanging glances, and one shrugged at her closest companion. They were polite, but clearly wanted to talk to her right away. It wouldn't be a good idea. Speaking to them straight after the experience of entering Hope's waters would not give her time to process what she had learnt, or what she needed from them. They may hold the control and be able to use their power, but she held what they needed. She would risk it.

'I would like that, thank you,' she replied. Pursed lips and frowns adorned the Chosen's faces. Yes, that was the right decision. She might be untrained – uncultured too, in their eyes – but she was no child to be pushed about.

They led Elissa to one of the buildings. She thanked the Chosen and entered, closing the door behind her. Just the one entrance and no window. If things went wrong for some reason, she wasn't getting out easily. A small bed rested against the wall, and a jug of water sat on a table, along with a small selection of food.

Elissa tapped her finger on one brown object – it was sticky. She raised it to her nose, and her mouth began to water at its scent, so she popped it into her mouth whole. The coating was sweet, and fresh, juicy fruits burst as she bit down. She sank to the floor by the table and chose another. All the food she'd been given since leaving Dragonsbreath had been incredible – there was no need to starve after all.

Hungrily, she ate a couple more, then saved the rest for later. Old habits are hard to break, so she hid them in case they were cleared away.

Inside the safety of the stone room, Elissa lifted the large chunk of crystal from the stone jar and hung it around her neck, tucking it under her clothes. If the elders were safe there from awldrin eyes, then hopefully, she would be too. Despite that, she'd feel safer knowing exactly where the crystal shard was at all times.

Next, she lifted her foot across her lap to check the sole again. The wound had healed over completely, and the scab appeared ready to fall off. She poked it gently, hopeful that when it did, the shard would come out with it. Elissa wasn't ready to accept that it might be permanent – she refused to be lame and unable to work.

After a drink of water and some time off her feet, the walls of the house grew oppressive. When had that happened? Small dark spaces had always been her place of safety. She was fed, rested and as ready as she'd ever be, so Elissa pushed open the door. Someone sat in her direct line of sight. *My own personal watcher.*

By the time Elissa reached the entrance to the tower and dome, the waiting Chosen had reached her side.

'Shall I show you around?'

It was a little irritating to be under escort, but Elissa decided to hide it. After all, it was the best chance to get her friends out of Dragonsbreath. She gestured ahead, offering the Chosen the chance to lead the way.

The path ended at a narrow pond. Elissa stroked the smooth rails as she passed over silver fish and flowering plants. The surface was decorated with splash rings where insects dared to land. Fish greeted them with hungry mouths. The pond stretched around both sides of the tower as far as she could see.

Elissa was surprised how easily the pair of heavy-looking doors swung open. Much like the one in Shardeep, it was fingertip-light to push. Steps to her right spiralled upward, but it was the large stone doors across the hall that drew her toward them. A restraining hand rested on her arm.

'Not yet, Shard-bonded. First, you need to meet with the rest of the Chosen.' The woman gestured up the stairs. Elissa stole another glance at the doors. Black, like the mountains of Shardeep and Dragonsbreath, with an ornate golden symbol engraved across both doors.

The stairs were a challenge she hadn't expected. Unable to adjust her weight as she did on the flat, it took her a while to climb to the room on the first floor where a semi-circle of women sat waiting. What was it with elders and Chosen waiting for her? Surely, they had other things to do. She sighed inwardly.

At the mid-point of the circle was an old Chosen. Her back stooped with age, and her lilac hair was broken by a white streak running down one side of her face. She looked up at Elissa and smiled brightly.

'Welcome, Elissa Shard-bonded. Do take a seat. Would you like anything to eat or drink?' she asked.

Elissa shook her head, sat on the lone empty chair facing the Chosen, and folded her hands calmly on her lap, waiting for them to begin. There was much looking at each other, and she caught whispers circling the room.

'Does she even have it?'

'Have you seen the state of her.'

'How are they surviving at Dragonsbreath?'

'She is so ... rough!'

Elissa held back a smile. Laytha would be pleased with her patience, but patience was something she was very good at. After a few moments, the leading Chosen quietened the women, and Elissa felt certain that she was supposed to have heard them. Rising with more steadiness and poise than her curved spine would suggest possible, the woman walked directly toward Elissa.

'Before you enter the dome, before we share our secrets with you, you must be tested.'

'You brought me across land and sea because you need me, and only now do you think to test me?' asked Elissa. She forced a smile on her face and remained seated and still. Over thirty-five cycles of hiding from awldrin made an old woman, no matter how powerful, seem pretty tame.

'It is true you may be the key to a lock we have been trying to open. But if you're merely an accident and your powers weak, then nothing will be gained by admitting you.'

'So test me.' Elissa rose to her feet, trying to stay as steady as she could. Her foot pulsed with pain, but she stood firm. They would see no weakness from her.

'Can you push emotion at me?' the older woman asked.

'I'll try.'

Elissa held her arm out as she had seen Quin do in the caves and heard a small snigger from her right. Her first instinct was to use fear, as she knew she could. Would that help? Probably not – she needed the women to work *with* her. Elissa decided that she would try to surprise them. She gathered thoughts and feelings together; Laytha, Rossi, her brother. The people who had helped protect her in Dragonsbreath. Then she pulled the strength of that feeling together into one ball.

Raising her head, she met the eyes of the old Chosen and pushed it toward her. The woman's eyes widened, and she let out a peal of laughter that belonged to a woman half her age.

'Elissa Shard-bonded, you are as clever as you are strong. You send me trust. If I was to send that away or fight it, I would lose yours. The power you just showed for someone so untrained is impressive. Will you accept my tuition?'

'If you tell me about the eyes that watch from the ocean,' Elissa said.

'A strange request, but one easily met. It's always been thought that the eyes were those of the Watcher. They were commonly seen in the same area, maybe where some of the echoglass crystals were dropped or have collected with the currents. But no one has seen the eyes for many, many years.'

'I have – twice now. Today, one of the sailors was stood with me, and he saw them too.'

The Chosen stepped closer to Elissa. 'I am Andra, and given this news, I must also ask – do you have the shards with you?'

'I do, Andra, although one is buried within my foot.'

'May I see? I might be able to help it out?'

Elissa sat back down and unwrapped her foot, grateful that she'd changed the dressing on it before entering the tower. Andra knelt – to a gasp from the others – and raised the foot up to inspect it.

'There is no wound there? Just a scar. Even with distraction or other magics, I can't pull it out. How big was it?'

Elissa shrugged. 'I didn't see it before I stood on it. It feels big enough to cause damage, but as long as I don't stand directly on it, I will be fine. The other piece is much bigger. How will it help? How do I use it?'

'Come with me,' Andra said, and slowly she crossed the room to the spiral stairs.

One of the others called out, 'Is it her magic, elder one? Has she clouded your thinking? Should you take her in so soon?'

'It certainly isn't. We have little choice right now, and elder Shardeep has confirmed that her story checks out.'

They proceeded down the stairs and across the hall. Andra laid her palms flat against the black doors, each resting on part of the huge symbol made from two curved waves facing outward, away from three intersecting lines which had further joins between them. It came to life, glowing as the doors parted, and swung open to reveal a soaring space. The ceiling and wall to her right were entirely covered in paintings depicting the island of Hope and the tower they stood in; they portrayed an enormous golden dragon, with eyes as black and dark as the mountains. Elissa crossed to it and ran her hand over the tip of the tail that coiled down the wall. The artist had engraved each individual scale. It was the most beautiful thing she had ever seen.

'Is this Hope?' she asked.

'Yes. Hope gave us survival, this island, and her protection.' Andra stood in the centre of the space, leaning on the only object in the entire dome. 'Hope also left us this.'

It was a tiny gate, waist high and as golden as the dragon. The metalwork formed plant-like tendrils, coiling around a central oval where something must have fitted once.

'It is a section of the Aulirean Gates! I saw a picture in Dragonsbreath. I thought they had been blasted to glass?'

'They were, except for this piece. Hope saved it and tried to re-grow it here. But she was young and didn't have The Watcher's power. For hundreds of cycles, every shard of echoglass found has been brought here in case it fits. This time, we're certain yours will be the missing one. We finally have a chance to get humans off this moon.'

Andra reached inside her white robe. Pulling out a pouch similar to the one that Rossi had given Elissa, she opened it and poured out a chunk of echoglass. Andra held it against the gate – it sat perfectly in one half of the oval space. A hint of blood red marked its broken edge. Elissa pulled hers out and matched them together. The missing shard was a thin sliver, less than half the width of the crystal, surrounded on both crystals by a blood red line.

'I knew it.' Andra smiled.

Elissa frowned at the gap. 'Will it work without the shard in me?'

'I don't know, but including that shard, we may have the key to open this gate. We are a step closer to going home.'

CHAPTER 34

DARIN

Among the many innate behaviours of moon-hounds, one in particular bears close consideration. They are known to form strong bonds with both human and hound members of what they consider to be their pack. They also seem able to assist with healing those close to them. The exact mechanism of this energy transfer remains elusive, but there is no doubt that it requires both a degree of altruism and sacrifice on behalf of the hound, as well as an exceptionally close bond.
Moonhound History and Care

He couldn't feel his toes, and his feet were cold and wet. Darin tried to lift a leg, and cold water poured from his boot, down the back of his calf. Watcher, it hurt. Aches and pains radiated through his body. He tried to stretch, stopping abruptly as something in his back hurt so badly that it drew tears from his eyes and a moan escaped his cracked lips. He laid still. His side was warm – something licked his face.

Darin cracked open his eyes. There was no sign of the waterfall, no sound either, for that matter. A quiet whimper called for his attention, drawing him from the deep haze of exhaustion; he turned his face toward the source of warmth and the wet tongue. Shallow panting and another whimper dragged him to the surface of consciousness.

'Star?' he whispered. The licking of his ear slowed, and Star flooded his vision. The images were faint, but Darin could make them out. *[Sandy barrelling into Darin. Darin falling. Star running down the steps, leaping after him into the waterfall. Him swimming down and grabbing the bag in his teeth.]* He saw himself through Star's eyes. *[Darin struggled to free himself, and Star fought to raise him to the surface.]*

'You did it,' he said. He tried to send a question *[Chase and Sandy by the pool?].*

Star either had no answer, or wasn't strong enough to send it.

Sharp pebbles dug into him as he shifted his weight and levered himself upright. He held the shivering hound close. 'You saved me. Thank you, Star.'

The river ran over his partially submerged feet, an occasional wavelet reaching past his ankles. Wet feet, check. His back was painful, but being dragged out of the water by a hound or bounced along a river bed would do that. How far had they been swept? Chase would surely catch up with them soon enough. After all, they could only have travelled in one direction from the waterfall. That's if the xotryl left.

To his other side was his bag. Thank the Watcher he hadn't managed to remove it after all.

The sun peeked over the trees, gently bathing his pain with

a caress of warmth. He must have been there all night. Chase should have found him by then. Star needed him, he needed food, and they both needed warmth. Darin pulled his feet from the water. Before the xotryl spotted them, or any of the other creatures that lived here, he needed cover from the forest canopy while they dried out.

Darin carefully studied the surrounding plants. That one was poisonous, that one would help with fever ... was he hot? No, but he needed to avoid that bush. Slowly and painfully, he checked the other side of them. Ah, a massive tree trunk. That would do – for the moment.

He leant forward and brought his legs under him one at a time. They were heavy, but nothing bar aches appeared to be wrong; he'd probably be as mottled with bruises as the pebble beach soon, though. Darin pushed himself upright, stood unsteadily, grabbed his bag, and dragged it to the tree.

He expected Star to follow, but the young hound remained still, lying on the foreshore, the white tip of his tail dragged by the current to point downstream.

Star looked up at Darin with sad eyes. He tried to get his legs under himself, but failed, flopping back down with a thud onto the riverbank.

Darin's heart sank, his gut gripped in a knot of worry for Star. He had to hide it, to push strength and confidence. 'No giving up, boy.' Darin sent *[Star sleeping under the tree]*. Star tried again and failed.

An image *[Darin carrying Star]* filled his view.

He could barely carry himself! Darin mustered as much energy as he could and struggled over to his moonhound. It took a couple of failed attempts, but eventually, he gathered Star's legs together in his arms, bracing his elbows against his waist whilst Star leant against his chest, his head resting on

Darin's shoulder. Darin's legs shook with the strain as they moved over to the tree, one slow step at a time.

Once they reached the safety of the roots, his legs buckled and they sank to the ground. Star struggled free and flopped next to him. They collapsed against the broad roots, utterly exhausted.

Darin rested his hand on Star's back. 'Sleep, boy. It's my turn to keep watch.'

Star licked his hand and closed his eyes. Something sharp dug into the back of Darin's neck as he leant against the trunk; he reached for it, and his hand closed around the shard of dragon bone. It might help, might hide them. He pulled his whistles from his jacket, but they were too wet to work. Until they dried out, the tree was all the shelter and protection they had. He pulled other items out to dry, arranging them alongside him.

Hours passed, and Star barely moved. His sides rose and fell with shallow but steady breathing. As Star slept, Darin took the time to check his own injuries. He pulled his tattered sleeve up; a fresh, red scar snaked down his forearm. Surely, they'd not been on the river bank long enough for a cut that enormous to heal. He ran his fingers over it. It was raised, tender and sore. Star whimpered, and Darin turned his attention back to stroking his hound.

Several times during the morning, a shadow passed overhead. Each time, his heartbeat quickened, and he readied himself to grab Star to move farther into the forest. The sun was in front of him, so he worked out that the xotryl, if that's what it was, would have to be on the other side of the river for its shadow to fall over the water. He hoped it stayed there.

Narrowing his eyes against the sunlight, Darin peered across to the other bank. Would he see Chase or Sandy if they were over there? Would they see him? It was dark under the canopy and, part-blinded by the sun, it might be almost impossible.

The red fabric which the measuring tool was drying on caught his eye. Maybe if he put that out in the light, it would help attract their attention. He eased his leg out from under Star's head and took the red fabric to the lowest hanging branch over the water. It had smaller side branches, so he tied the corner of the fabric around one of them, allowing it to flap in the breeze.

The scar caught his eye again in the bright light. It reminded him of the one on his palm. Oh Watcher, no. Star was still asleep. Could he have done it? What had Chase said? Healing used his own powers, but the moonhounds could use them within the bond in a different way.

Darin felt for his reserve. It was very faint, almost nothing left. That explained why he felt empty. What had that much healing done to Star? Darin found the energy to run back to his bag. He dumped the remaining contents on the floor and frantically rummaged through his belongings, searching for the healing drafts. He found the small pouch and opened it with relief flooding through him. It was still there. Shards of glass fell into his palm as he tipped the small vials out. They'd all smashed.

He rummaged through the herbs and plants he'd brought and collected, then sat back to survey the result. Darin still had everything needed to make the healing draft. Some leaves were a bit battered, and he wasn't quite sure how much to use of the dried leaves instead of fresh, but they were all still useable. Unless he could sing the right weft, though, it wouldn't help a lot, and there was only enough for one attempt. If he was making a glow lamp, there would be plants there in the Edgelands, but the most potent of the ingredients he needed for the healing draft was from the far south of Caldera.

Darin didn't have enough of his own reserves to help Star, either – not that he knew how. His beautiful hound had both saved and healed him. Somehow, Darin would find a way, even if he had to carry Star back to Redpike alone. He stroked the soft black ears and tried to squash down the sadness and fear that threatened to overwhelm him. Star needed positivity.

A few hours later and, having eaten some slightly soggy food from his bag, Darin was ready to move. Star had finally woken, but his legs still couldn't hold him up. Darin tried to offer him a drosta leaf, but Star rejected it flatly. He had at least shared some not-very-dried meat, and Darin felt hopeful that, given time, his hound would recover. Time was not something he had much of out there. They were somewhere in the Edge-lands, alone.

'I'll just have to get out of trouble myself. Chase said I had to be able to go it alone. I just wasn't expecting it to be this soon.' Darin packed his belongings away as he talked to Star. He needed fern-tree wood. If he could find some, get back up the waterfall, and back to Tian, then he could make the potion.

'You might be young, but you're still heavy!' he said, and sent Star an image of how he planned to carry him.

Darin folded the blanket in two, passing it widely under Star's stomach. His legs would hang loose out at either end once lifted. Star stood, wobbling unsteadily, over the blanket, as Darin tied the corners together on each side. He crouched and put an arm through each loop, then carefully stood up. Star hung across his front, with his legs dangling; he turned his head toward Darin's shoulder and gave him a lick. Darin felt a gentle waft of affection through their bond, as though Star was a very long way away.

'This should let me take your weight more easily,' he muttered, hoping the sound of his voice would help keep the hound still. He sent the request, too, just in case.

They couldn't move fast, but any progress was better than staying there indefinitely. Especially if Chase was gone. He hadn't really let himself think that the xotryl might have got them until then, but he needed to accept the possibility. To survive alone.

He sent *[Fern-tree wood]* to Star. Darin had only seen pictures, but the distinctive fronds and circular branches protruding from the base should make it easy to find. He wasn't sure how Star could help, but talking to him helped keep a lid on his own anxieties.

Darin chose a fairly straight path from the river into the woods, resting frequently and marking his position each time. He scuffed his feet as he walked – easy to do with the extra weight he was carrying. If nothing covered his tracks up, he could follow his own trail back to the river.

Several stops later, Darin noticed a small fern on the ground. He put his hand around the stem and squeezed. It didn't flatten like a true fern would. It was way too small to be any use to them, but there was surely a parent tree around somewhere. He needed the wood, needed to get back. If the xotryl had caught Chase, he was alone. The other Howlers and himself were an entirely inadequate barrier between creatures of the Edgelands and the population of Caldera. Their pack neither large, nor powerful enough to forestall the need for the So'Dal to be seen as their true magic-using selves by the population of Caldera. Surely in Dal, it would be okay? He could just try to find out who was from Dal, and they could fight?

Darin wobbled unsteadily onward, searching for trees until his legs gave up. He should search in Dal anyway. He'd speak to Chase when he got back – if Chase was okay. The thought of those scars, the damage on Sandy, and the size of the xotryl that they'd seen caused his stomach to churn.

He put Star down with his bag against a trunk and told him

to stay there, then searched outward in each direction, using the small fern as a starting point. But try as he might, he did not see a parent tree. If it was any other type of plant, then the seed might have been carried by a bird. Fern-trees had spores; not small, light ones, either. He had seen a tree spore once in Tralkion's workroom. They were the size of his thumbnail.

He returned to Star and leant against the rough tree trunk alongside him. Maybe he should climb a tree to help him see the canopy.

Darin shuddered at the thought, but Star's gentle presence strengthened him. He'd do anything for his hound.

He looked up to see which tree would support his weight the best. The canopy was thinner there, and light filtered down, lending a tiny bit of warmth to the area. Enough light that a shadow passing overhead blanked out all the sunspots.

Darin noticed two things simultaneously. The sky was clouding over, and the canopy directly above him was made of fern leaves.

He was sat against the base of a gigantic fern-tree. It didn't look at all like the drawings. A true trunk rose for a few metres before it branched, but once the canopy sprawled out, it was unmistakable.

It must be incredibly old. The base of the trunk had been smoothed – by passing animals, he presumed, as he studied it more closely, noticing claw marks on it. Darin sighed in relief. He only had to climb one tree, then he could get the wood and head back to the river. If it was that old and had been in the Edgelands for so long, then maybe its wood was really magical.

Thudding footfalls broke the quiet of the forest. Something moved toward him fast. Darin pushed himself upright and stood in front of Star protectively. He wished he still had his spear. He snapped off a nearby branch and held it ready to fend off the intruder.

An enormous, grey hound barrelled into the clearing, sliding to a halt at Darin's feet.

'Sandy?' Darin said, reaching forward to stroke him. 'Where's Chase?'

'Watcher's charred scales, you're safe! The red flag was good thinking. It saved us time trying to track you.' Chase's voice carried ahead of him as he ran into the clearing.

He pointed at the tree behind Darin. 'That's a big one. Not the easiest to climb, but you found one. Well done.' He held out Darin's spear. 'I found this on the river bank just after the waterfall. Thought you might want it back.'

Chase stopped talking abruptly as he saw Star. He crouched down and put a hand on the moonhound's chest. 'He's not looking good. What happened to him?'

'I think he healed me,' Darin said, showing Chase the scar. 'So, now you're here, I need to climb this tree and get the wood. We need the whistle urgently. I can make a general healing draft – if I have a whistle. Chase, he can't stand alone.' His voice cracked, and his shoulders slumped. At least with Chase there, the pressure was slightly reduced.

'With an injury that big, he saved you – he didn't just heal you. How did you get him this far from the river?'

Darin showed him the blanket and was rewarded with an approving nod.

'That's pretty clever. If he did what you think, we need to get him home and soon. If nothing else works, dragon bone will.'

'Can we give him the bits we are wearing?' Darin asked with hope.

Chase shook his head. 'We can't grind it, and in this form, it would cut his insides. We need fine powder.'

So be it. He had a tree to climb and a hound to heal, then a pack to heal in a different way. Darin eyed up the tree, deciding that he'd rather fight a full bar of drunks than climb it. There were some rough sections on the lower trunk that he might be able to get purchase on.

'Keep an eye on my pack. Can you pass me a knife? I'm going up.' He tucked the measuring tube into his waistband and the knife into his boot, then started to climb. *I'm doing this for Star. Just keep looking up.*

Darin reached the first branch, but none of the fronds were narrow enough. Three branches above, he spotted a thick branch with numerous side branches. The main one appeared wide enough to take his weight. *I can do this.* He reached upward, his battered body hurting with every motion, his feet grappling for purchase on the trunk.

The branch was scaly and wet. Parts of it came off on his hands as he shuffled along, with feet hanging either side. The side branches were almost perfect, and he breathed a sigh of relief. There would surely be enough sections the right size.

Darin reached for his knife. As he did, his gaze slid downward; the forest floor was a long way away. His palms grew clammy, and he froze. Darin felt himself go cold, and the edges of his vision closed in. Then, instead of the ground, he suddenly saw straw – just a big pile of bedding straw.

Confusion overwrote terror for just long enough to realise Star was trying to help. He looked up quickly, the image of the straw fading fast.

Darin shuffled along, keeping his eyes firmly fixed on the branches and his task. He cut and dropped all the suitable ones, hoping Chase caught them before they broke from the fall. He cut and dropped, cut and dropped, entirely focused on finding branches that fitted the guide.

'Darin, stop – we have enough. Work backward and take care getting down. Feel with your foot. Keep your eyes up,' Chase called.

He pushed himself backward along the branch. It was harder to move in that direction as the old frond growth pointed outward and caught against his legs. Slowly and carefully, Darin worked back to the main trunk. He swung his legs around it and sought out a stable ledge. The upward-pointing, broken frond growth that remained at that height made easy shelves to descend on.

He reached the smoother section near the base, and couldn't find any footing.

'Let me know when I'm low enough to drop,' he called down.

'Keep on coming. Move your right foot to the right,' Chase said. 'Now your left down a bit more.' Step-by-step, Chase guided him most of the way down.

'No more foot holds now. How do you feel?'

'Honestly? Exhausted, shaky, and desperate to get to the floor.' Darin laughed nervously. 'Can I drop yet?'

'Well, you could, but you're still way over my head.'

'I can't hold on forever. I'll just have to try slowing my fall.' *This is going to hurt.* Darin gripped with his thighs and slid his hands around the trunk, then moved them down toward his waist. He then tried to shuffle his legs down, gripping as hard as he could with his arms. He slipped as he did so, but his encircling arms caught the ledge his feet had been on a moment earlier. The jolt hurt his back. Darin re-wrapped his legs as far around as he could and, deciding that he really needed to know how much farther he had to go, glanced down.

'Fancy catching me?' he joked.

'I'll stand close and try to help you land, but catch you? No thanks. You're bigger than me!'

Darin loosened his legs and arms, sliding down the trunk. He reached the floor with a crunch, his ankle twisting as he landed, but it took his weight. He was down. Darin sank to the floor next to Star, and Chase joined him.

'Well done. Let's get these branches sorted, then you should eat.'

They measured and cut the sections of fern-tree wood, wrapped them in the leather case, then Chase tucked them in his pack while Darin ate a less soggy bit of dried meat and a sweet bar of grains that Chase offered him.

'Should we take some of the rest too?' Darin asked. There were a lot of branches still scattered around.

'We can take a few, but if Star can't walk, we already have more than enough to carry.'

They decanted light items from Darin's bag into Sandy's packs, then Chase rose to his feet. 'The blanket wrapped around him was a great idea. You'll make a full Howler yet.' He bent to stroke Star. 'Can I carry you for a bit, boy? Let's give Darin a rest, eh?'

'Shall I ask him?'

'No need – Sandy already did. He's happy to let me,' Chase said as he crouched down to take the weight of the makeshift sling. 'Oof, you're heavy,' he mumbled as he stood, bracing his legs. 'You'd better not get any ideas,' he said to Sandy.

Darin shouldered his pack and picked up a few extra sticks for Tian. His ankle was painful, but they'd make it, and he could use his spear to lean on.

Chase started to walk. 'Come on, then. It's at least a day's walk before the waterfall. It's easier going along the river's edge, and if we're lucky, we'll have moonlight to help. We won't stop for sleep until we reach one of the waterfall refuges.'

⚊ ✷ ✷ ✷ ✦

Darin led the way back along his trail toward the water; Sandy followed, and Chase brought up the rear. The sounds of the Edgelands forest filled the air. Finally having time to listen, Darin heard the shrieks of an animal from the direction of the coast, and the clicking insects in the leaves increased in volume as the afternoon heat cooled. Once he spotted water through the trees, he turned upriver – every saved step would count.

CHAPTER 35

SURIIN

*The crystal bond is one of the three bonds every
Soul Anchor will make, and the least understood. Even the meaning of the draconic
words used to bond to the crystal has been lost
with time.*
The Bond of Three

The bars of the cell formed in her mind. Suriin focused on
picturing the small space behind them with its trickle of
water.

'I knowed you be back. Have you choosed a price?' the
clicking voice whispered from a shadowed corner of the cell.

Suriin tried to imagine her own clothing; she dressed herself
in expensive clothes with her blue scarf wrapped how her
mother wore them. She created a calm image of herself –
appearing more composed helped her bargaining position.
Suriin needed to look as though she could achieve things, could
make things happen – not project the image of a scared child.

'Not yet, but I do have a question.'

The awldrin stepped forward, illuminating the cell. Their own attire was detailed and intricate; no helpless prisoner faced her. Suriin held back a gasp at the sight of the warrior. The awldrin's black and red scaled armour rippled with each long stride. Their hands were covered by shining black spiked gloves. A huge sword at the awldrin's hip swung freely as they walked, and multifaceted crystal eyes glinted with a rainbow intensity. Standing upright, the awldrin was almost double her own height.

'I listening,' they said.

'How do you survive a xotryl wound?' Suriin asked.

The awldrin tipped its head to one side, and pointed teeth parted. 'We don't. Need old magic.'

'Can you teach me?' Suriin asked.

'Can you make me be gone?' the awldrin clicked back.

'If I free you, you could kill me, and I gain nothing,'

'I help you, you get cure. I get no free.' The awldrin rested a hand on the hilt.

They stared at each other in stalemate. The awldrin appeared calm, Suriin thought; like a creature unused to failure. How on Lieus had they ended up in there?

She tried a different approach. 'My name is Suriin.'

The awldrin responded with a strange sound, and Suriin tried to copy it. 'Na-at-Ker?'

'For human, that almost good. Nat-ke,'

Suriin tried again, making the *k* at the back of her throat and cutting short the *e*. 'Natke'

The awldrin nodded. 'You not afraid? Sad that my name lost its fear. So, Sooreen, now us reach agree. You need cure. Is not for you. I hold life in hands already.' To illustrate the point, the awldrin held out a clawed glove and mimed squeezing it closed. 'But you hold key to me free. I not wish 500 cycles more. My hive need me.'

Suriin was about to say that the gates were closed, Natke's people banished, and freedom would do little good, when she realised that would lower her bargaining position. She stood taller.

'Can you teach me?'

'When I know you get me free. Let me think.' The awldrin sketched a bow and blinked out of her dream.

Suriin woke, feeling much calmer than she'd anticipated. There was a lot to think on, but for the first time, there was also hope. Could she get a cure and back out? Not free the creature? She reflected on the way Natke had dressed and grabbed her notebook. Suriin sketched as many details as she could remember. The sword with the thick handle was familiar, but she couldn't recall why.

She ripped the page out and hid it under her mattress. She could return the original map to Ronin. Her new solution would not need his – or anyone else's – help.

Υ ※ ✲ ✦

Sleep tried to claim her, but Natke's surprise at not being recognised dug at her subconscious, and she couldn't settle. She relit her glow lamp and reached for her pile of books. *Battle Strategies of the Awldrin* was still there. Suriin flicked through the pages, uncertain what she was searching for. There were many pictures of xotryl-mounted awldrin, their black armour a little like Natke's. None had red scales interwoven in the design; one warrior had the spiked gloves.

Suriin checked for a caption, but nothing was written under them that would help her. Then, on the centre spread of the book, she saw a familiar picture. It was a frieze from the far end of the library. A Soul Anchor was fighting a xotryl-mounted warrior. The awldrin warrior was drawing a mounted bow, and the purple hair of the Anchor was shown haloed around her head, her hands exuding a stream of almost unimaginable power.

Suriin studied the warrior. That armour didn't have red on it either, but there was a sword at the rider's hip – a long, black sword with a red stone pommel. If it wasn't the same one, it was its twin. She squinted at the tiny writing, a picture of the plaque below the painting, but couldn't read it. That would be a job for the next library session. She closed the book, lay back on the pillow, and put her guard up. Suriin drifted off to the sleep of the exhausted.

⋎ ※ ※ ※ ✦

She woke up startled, then heard a loud bang on her door. Suriin padded across the room and opened it as she rubbed sleep from her eyes.

'Hurry up or you'll be late – again,' Fresna shouted.

When she finally had neighbours, they'd get so annoyed with that. She couldn't find her favourite dress in her wardrobe. Where had she left it? Suriin sighed as she glanced down. Watcher's flames, she must be losing the plot – she'd slept in it. As she sniffed her armpit, Suriin wrinkled her nose in disgust. It was sweaty and grim; there was no way she could wear it. She bundled it into her laundry bag, along with the last few nights worth of sweaty clothes, and quickly pulled another dress off the shelf.

'Can we stop to drop this off?' she asked as she closed the door.

Fresna looked at the bag and nodded. 'Come on, then!'

With her laundry deposited, they rushed to the kitchens. Chef stood at the door, waiting for them.

'One more time, Suriin, and I will speak to Aslin. Punctuality is a key attribute of a Soul Anchor. Fresna, you should know better!'

'Yes, Chef!' they chorused, and rushed in. Both women kept their heads down and worked as fast as they could on breakfasts. Only once they were eating their own did they have another chance to chat.

'How did yesterday go? I loved my first sessions on the table!' Fresna said once they had gulped down their food.

'It was good. Harder than I expected, though. I think I may need a lot more practise than I first thought.'

Fresna grinned. 'Yeah, it might be a few cycles ago now, but I remember that sensation. It caught me out too.' She leant forward, whispering, 'I used my powers once before I was bonded – accidentally, of course – and I swear it was easier without the crystal. But with one, it is more focused and precise, with less chance of accidents, I suppose.'

The revelation almost made Suriin explain that she felt the same. Only her promise to Ronin held her back. She may not need him anymore, but she couldn't risk upsetting him while he was taking care of her father.

'Talking of Aslin, I had better get moving!' she said instead, and hugged her friend.

'Go. I'll take them.' Fresna gestured to the plates. 'My session starts late today. The Anchor has a meeting this morning.'

Suriin didn't need to be told twice, and hastened to Aslin's room. Merri, Joy, and Skye greeted her. Smiles of excitement beamed from the twins, whilst Skye gave her a more reserved wave from behind them.

'Good morning,' said Merri. 'We spent loads of time last night testing each other. Are you ready for this?'

'I suppose we'll see in a minute,' Suriin responded.

Aslin opened the door and peered out. On seeing just the

four of them, she scanned the corridor to either side. Her eyebrows raised momentarily, but then the smooth veneer of Soul Anchor calm returned.

'Come in, ladies. Please sit by one symbol you learned yesterday.'

Suriin hunted around the table for the symbols. She could spot three of the four. The other one must be there somewhere, and she'd just overlooked it. Wanting to start the day well, she reached inside herself to determine whether she could feel any of her four more strongly. Fear was definitely there. It wasn't the most sensible one to show off to her new classmates, but she needed it to unlock that door again. She didn't want to use blind fear – she needed to be in control.

To her surprise, Skye sat alongside her. Suriin felt the itch of eyes on her and looked up to see that Aslin stared at them both from the door. She checked the corridor one more time, then appeared to make a decision. Aslin closed the door, turned, and flickered, reappearing in the centre of the table.

'Watcher's breath, how did you do that?' Suriin asked before clapping her hand over her mouth. 'Sorry, Soul Anchor Aslin.'

She saw a sparkle and a small smile as Aslin pointed to a symbol on the table. 'When you combine this with this one, you can produce interesting effects. When you can tell me what they are called and show me you have control, I will teach you a few tricks.'

Suriin and the others leaned forward, straining to see the symbols she was pointing at. They weren't ones they'd researched the previous day, but she was sure they'd all study them that afternoon.

'Skye, please start.'

Skye reached out toward the centre of the table and placed her hand on a swirling symbol – similar to fear. She closed her eyes, and Suriin watched closely as she held her other hand around the stone on her neck. Within moments, the symbol glowed a steady dark red.

'A core emotion is a good choice, although terror is an unusual starting point.' Aslin had sympathy etched in her face. 'Being able to *drain* terror, however, is a very useful thing. Terror stops rational thought. Fear is much safer to use, although less powerful.' She moved her gaze to Suriin. 'Please illuminate your first symbol.'

Suriin reached for her fear and recalled the moment she'd first seen the awldrin as she directed it through her crystal. A glimmer of light appeared. She added in her father, slumping forward on the garant, and the light grew.

'Good,' Aslin said and moved on.

Merri was the last to go, and as she placed her hand on love, there was a knock at the door. Aslin ignored it and nodded for Merri to continue. She tried again, and another knock sounded. Suriin could see the wrinkling of frustration across Merri's forehead. Her twin placed a reassuring hand over hers. Merri had another attempt at the symbol, and it lit with a soft white glow.

'Well done. Working under distraction is always harder. Please locate your next symbol.' Aslin flickered to the door again and opened it. Outside, red-faced and scowling, were the others from their class.

Aslin swished out and closed the door behind her.

'Will she be all right?' whispered Skye. 'They look awfully cross.'

'She is a full-blown Soul Anchor. I'm sure there's no problem,' Suriin said. 'Come on – let's find our next ones. What are you looking for?'

'This one,' Skye replied, touching a symbol next to the wave of serenity.

Suriin laughed. 'Serenity is mine – although I think it will be my hardest to achieve! I cannot remember when I last felt calm.'

'With the condition of your father, I'm not surprised,' Skye replied. Suriin looked at her in astonishment.

'People talk, and I grew up here - I know everyone.' Skye shrugged. 'They will find a way, Suriin,' she said, giving her a gentle squeeze on her arm.

'Wait, if you grew up here, how do you have anything to be so afraid of?'

'I was born in Dal.' Skye shrugged again. 'That close to the Edgelands, terror is a normal occurrence. I have few strong memories of early childhood, but all your animals being eaten by a massive, red xotryl – that's pretty terrifying.'

Aslin returned without the other students, and they spent the remainder of the session working through their other symbols with varied success. They ended the session with instructions to learn two further symbols, then Suriin was dismissed, while Aslin kept the other three back to discuss their new roles. Suriin waited outside the door for them, then they strolled across to the library together.

'If we get this work done now, could you show us around afterward, Suriin?' Merri asked.

'I'm sure Skye could too,' Suriin replied.

Skye shyly nodded. 'The gardens are my favourite part. Although, wait until a full moon market, and you see the stalls and the town. It's so beautiful!'

'Skye, why are you sleeping in guest quarters if you already live here?' asked Joy.

'I didn't want to stand out. I thought it would be easier to make friends,' she said.

'It worked.' Merri laughed and hugged her. Skye went stiff at the hug, but given no choice, finally hugged back.

The library was quiet again, so they collected the same set of books and sat down.

'Why aren't the others doing preparation work?' Suriin asked as they started searching through them.

'I know that Xedra turned up with a load of books that her parents had paid for.' Merri rolled her eyes. 'She's going to find life so different once she realises that money means nothing as a Soul Anchor.'

'She'll have to start being nice.' Skye grinned. 'Won't be long before she finds that out.'

Suriin nodded. Xedra really wasn't nice on their first encounter. She tried to follow the conversation the others were having as they attempted to find the symbols involved in the 'flicker,' but the frieze showing the awldrin was just visible from behind a far shelf.

'I'm a little stiff. That bench in Aslin's room is hard. I think I'm just going to stretch my legs for a moment,' she said, and, shooting a smile at them, she uncurled from the low seats and pretended to stretch.

As Suriin strolled down the library, she could hear Merri and Joy laughing quietly. She rounded the corner of the bookshelf. The plaque was there. Suriin leant forward to read it, but the writing was too faint. The ink had faded to pale brown at some point in the past. She sighed in disappointment.

'My ma always talked about this picture when I was small.' Skye was standing right behind her, and Suriin jumped at the sudden voice.

'Firstly, how are you so quiet? Secondly, why this picture?'

'I told you – grew up in Dal until I was about six,' she said, it as if it explained everything. 'Secondly, Ma used to say this picture showed that real power has always been held by women.'

'Because it's a female human defeating the awldrin leader?'

'Not quite. Because it shows the two most powerful creatures in history were female. That awldrin was their last queen.' Suriin caught her breath as Skye continued. 'When she was finally brought down, they stripped her of all her possessions and killed her, I think. See that red-pommelled sword? It hangs in the reception rooms of the Star Tower to remind all visitors of what we can do.'

Suriin's knuckles grew white as she gripped the back of a chair. 'Do you remember her name?' she managed to squeeze out, attempting to hide the tremor in her voice.

'No, but I believe it was something like Nastik or something,' Skye said. 'How are your legs feeling now?' She frowned. 'Are you okay? I'll help you back. Maybe you're better off sat down after all!'

'Maybe,' Suriin mumbled, letting herself be helped back to the others, her mind racing.

⊢ ※ 🗲 ⅏ ✦

After lunch, Suriin and Skye took the twins to the steam lift. 'I know you've a steam lift in South Crater, so you're used to them, but it amazed me the first time. Hold tight.' She grinned at the hooded So'Dal as he pulled the lever. Merri and Joy whooped with delight as the lift shot up, and Suriin decided their parents had truly named them well.

They wandered around the garden for a while, admiring all the herbs and flowers as Skye showed them around the Dal section.

'I don't remember the names of most of these,' she said.

'But I know they are from home. It makes me feel more connected.'

'Where's South Crater? Oh, there!' Joy said, pointing at a stand of tall plants at the far edge of the crater with long spiky leaves.

'You'd need to come back up later in the evening to appreciate the Edgelands ones that line the rim of Golden,' Suriin said. 'These are a whole lot safer to sit around.' While she was desperate to get to the awldrin and ask more questions, the chance for a slice of normality amongst friends was just too pleasant to rush.

⋎ ⚹ ⚝ ⚌ ✳

'We must stop meeting like this.' His voice carried across the sandy area in front of them. 'Please introduce me, Suriin.' Ronin's eyes were locked with Merri, though he broke the gaze to glance her way briefly as he approached.

'This is Ronin, my father's apprentice,' she said. 'Ronin, this is Merri. She's in my class.'

'Not for much longer. I will take my final assessment soon,' Ronin said, still looking intently at Merri. 'I've met you somewhere before. I know I have.'

'Yes, at my – ouch, Joy! Our Father's home in South Crater,' Merri replied, equally engrossed in Ronin.

Suriin and Skye looked at each other, rolled their eyes, and laughed at the synchronicity. Joy sidled up close to Suriin and Skye and whispered, 'Shall we leave them for a moment?'

Suriin and Skye both nodded, and the three of them quietly slipped away. They strolled to the central pagoda and sat on the bench, facing the northern side of the crater. Suriin gazed up into the evening sky at the green moon and the shadow that was Tebein beyond it. The adventure she had dreamed of hadn't happened the way she expected. But she would find a way to save her father, to set her life back on course. For the moment – in fact, for the first time ever – Suriin enjoyed the chance to relax with a group of friends. She dropped her gaze to the two women to her right and felt a smile begin to grow.

Welcome to Hope.

Choosing this home shows strength of heart.

I found Joy in the solitude and its peace can
never be under appreciated.
There are some important things you need to know
about your new home.

1. There is an old spring at the back of the garden.

2. Don't use magic in it. The house hates it. It tolerates
this refilling basket only because it is outside.

3. You will share this home with wildlife that also
lives on Hope.

4. Keep the green chair. It holds its own treasures.

Watcher Guide You.

Nakia

CHAPTER 36

———————

ELISSA

My Dearest Nephew,
There are many sailors on the Ameryth Dar, but
there is only ever one Captain.
The time has come for you to take the helm.
All my love, Aunt Andra.

'You can learn how to control your dreams quickly if you want,' said Andra. 'Your guarding needs a lot more work, though. It's intermittent and you're far too easy to find.'

Elissa chewed on the thought as they walked through the village. She wanted to speak to Laytha, and maybe her brother, so whatever it took, she'd do.

Every now and again, Andra would point out an unoccupied house for Elissa to consider, but they were too crowded for her liking. Still, she didn't feel comfortable sleeping in the round houses near the tower, and that meant finding a place to call home, even if only for a short time.

They were passing out of Gallimaufry and returning to the tower when a small house caught her eye. Set back and alone, its crooked wooden timbers defied any reasonable logic to remain standing. Yet, its weather-aged wood belied that idea – it was old. Small windows faced the beach, though she doubted anyone inside could see the water; an overgrown tangle of plants scrambled for light around the building.

'I like that one.' As soon as she saw it, Elissa knew it was the right house. The constant companion of unease departed, and she was drawn toward the door.

Andra arched an eyebrow. 'Really? That old place?'

'Yes, it feels right.'

'I'll send someone to clean it up for you, then.'

'No! Please, I mean – thank you for offering. But I think I want to do it myself.'

They pushed through vegetation to the door. It was slightly ajar. Elissa pushed gently, so as not to loosen it if it wasn't well hung; it creaked a welcome. Inside, the scent of green and brown filled the house. Warm sunlight filtered through dust-covered windows, and old furniture was arrayed in haphazard positions that made no sense to her.

A faded green chair, straw stuffing protruding like straggly hair from the seat, caught her eye. It was positioned in what should be the warmest part of the room, next to an empty fire grate. Struggling rays of evening light just reached it. The sunken cushion looked welcoming, despite its dilapidated state. She crossed the room, dodging around the small table to sit in it.

As she reached for the arm of the old chair, she saw eggs nestled amongst the pulled-out reed straws. They were tiny; delicate, speckled jewels, luminous with colour, the promise of future life almost overshadowed by their current beauty. She'd never seen anything like them.

Elissa scanned the room for their parents. Small footprints in the dust ran between the chair and a crack in the wall.

'Then I shall leave you undisturbed,' Elissa murmured.

'What have you found?' Andra peered over the back of the seat and gasped. 'Charver eggs – how beautiful! I'm betting you've never seen one before. They're creatures from Mythos. This island is the only place in the whole of Tebein where they survived.'

Andra opened a nearby cupboard and, finding a frayed scrap of fabric, tried to clean the window. More light crept through the smears, and dust soon clogged her cloth. She stepped outside to shake it off.

Elissa looked around with happiness swelling in her heart. It would be dark before long, and she had no firestone or any light sources yet, but it didn't matter. She joined Andra.

'I think I'll stay here tonight,' she said.

'It does have a special sort of charm,' Andra replied. 'Join us up at the tower for food first, though. You don't have a way to cook yet.'

'I will, thank you.'

Andra passed her the cloth. 'I think you might need this.'

'Thank you.'

'I'll see you shortly,' Andra called as she headed back up to the tower.

Elissa turned to re-enter her new home, and an object tucked behind twisted vines caught her eye. Hidden on her new doorstep was a covered basket. She crouched down, brushed dead leaves off the cloth cover, and reached inside carefully. Her hand grasped a rough textured object, a small log of wood. Feeling around a second time, Elissa pulled out some candles, a couple more small logs, a jug, and a hand-written note.

She unfolded the tattered fragment of paper and frowned at the spidery scrawl across it. Elissa could make out a few words, thanks to Rossi's help back in Dragonsbreath, but they were all short ones that didn't help her understand what it said. She recognised other letters, but could not decipher it.

Near the bottom, she recognised the word *Wa-t-ch-er,* and she assumed that the word at the very bottom was the writer's name: *N-a-ki-a.* Other than that, few words stood out. She hoped it wasn't anything important. They'd soon learn not to leave a note for someone who could barely read. She chuckled at the thought of the things she could pretend to miss out on. Still, once she had settled in, maybe she'd find someone who could help her read it. The fact it appeared to have a list on it was interesting. She tucked the paper into her pocket and took out the wood.

Wood was useful, and having candles instead of a glow lamp made her feel a lot more relaxed. Elissa tried to pick up the basket. It resisted her efforts and stayed stubbornly fixed to the step. Elissa tried a second time. She would have found it easier to lift a wildbeest than move the stubborn basket.

Huffing in frustration, Elissa stomped back indoors and found a pot in the small kitchen. She returned to the basket and emptied its contents into the pot, then frowned at the basket grumpily one last time before closing her door.

� ⁂ ⚕ ⚜ ✦

Gentle candlelight flickered around the room, unfamiliar shadows forming around her as she tidied her new home.

The only other door in the house led to a small sleeping chamber along with the expected layer of dust and debris. Threadbare and dust-clogged sheets covered the bed, but it appeared soft and inviting under them. Elissa folded the outer sheets into themselves carefully, trying to move gently and minimise the dust she raised as she cleared the room. She trapped the dirt into the folds and placed it gently by the wall.

The bed was useable, though all the sheets would need a good wash. She'd have to ask where to get water.

Elissa gently closed the door to the bedroom, then leant down to inspect the tiny footprints. The freshest had no dust on them at all; hopefully, the parents wouldn't be too scared by her presence. She put logs on the fire grate ready for the evening and opened a window to let the sea breeze freshen the musty air before leaving her new home for a meal in the tower.

As she hobbled up the hill, Elissa wondered if the distance might be a bad thing. A glance back at her little house reassured her as she passed through the ring of soulless round buildings on the hilltop.

Her stomach rumbled in appreciation as the scent of spiced meat wafted down the stairs and out of the open tower door. The chamber they had met in earlier was transformed, and small tables were loaded with food. Chosen sat in groups, and relaxed chat filled the atmosphere.

The only remaining spaces were on Andra's table. Elissa hesitated, but Andra patted the seat next to her, and in that moment, Elissa was again reminded strongly of Laytha. Maybe she could talk to her that evening, as she was safely on Hope.

Everything was delicious, and Elissa found herself comparing the luxury these women lived in to their equivalents in her sericlave.

'Have you heard any news from Dragonsbreath?' she asked.

'None, but we didn't know you were there until our shard turned red and we began the hunt for you. We'd assumed that all talented descendants there had been wiped out. As far as we knew, only those we saved survived the awldrin's purge hundreds of years ago,' replied Andra.

'Rossi was going to keep in touch?'

'He tried, but as he only knows the entrance and a few locations inside, he's had little success. No one has been able to make contact since you left.'

'Most of the population live in the main cave. The Untouched like me live in tunnels behind our homes. I will try.'

Andra sighed, 'I'm sorry, Elissa, you can't. When you dream walked, you lit up like a glowing beacon because of that shard. You're safe when you shield, but you cannot go. If *They* catch you, all our efforts to retrieve you could be undone, and you'll endanger those you try to protect.'

Elissa could feel her nails digging into her palms under the table as she responded. 'These are my friends – my family – I came to you to help them. Not to save you, who already have lives filled with privilege and power.'

She stood as she spoke, and every face in the room turned her way. Blushing furiously, but standing her ground, Elissa said, 'I will make contact with Dragonsbreath tonight.' She pushed back her chair and moved to leave the room.

'Elissa, you have so little control that you just almost drowned us in a wave of your anger,' came the quiet voice of Andra. 'Anywhere outside this room, you would have created hostility both toward yourself, and others as a result.'

Elissa stopped. Distrust was writ plain on most surrounding faces.

'I am sorry,' she said 'I ...' She sank to her seat again.

'I can shield her. I had to do it on the journey here. Besides, we all need to know what's happening. Now, did I miss my invite to dinner again?' The Captain filled the doorway; without his oilskin, he was still imposing. Concern lined his weatherworn face. 'My boats have been spotting xotryl around the edges of the sea. They won't cross at the moment, but it is only a matter of time until they try.'

'Fine, you shield her. But we'll do it here – in the tower – with others on hand to wake her the second we have any concerns,' Andra said.

'Agreed. You had best lay out some comfy beds then.' The Captain laughed. 'It's been a while since I had so many women in my bedchamber.'

Elissa winced, but it was an opportunity she wasn't willing to miss. 'I agree to be shielded. Thank you, Captain.'

⊤ ⁂ ⚭ ⚇ ✦

Two mattresses had been hauled out and blankets acquired from somewhere. The Captain laughed at all the comfort. 'I can sleep anywhere. This is far more than I need.'

Elissa wasn't comfortable lying down to sleep in a room filled with awake people – the Chosen had insisted on two of them being on hand throughout the night as Elissa was uncertain at what point she would be able to dream walk. Not for the first time, Elissa wished she could just dip in and out of dream walking like Rossi could. But she'd only ever done it asleep.

'Start here,' The Captain said. 'If you start here, I can come with you. I'll wait in this room.'

The pillow was soft and the covers warm. Despite the audience, Elissa felt safe. She tried to remember everything Rossi had taught her and put her barriers up when she laid down. *I'll drop them when I see him,* she thought sleepily.

⊤ ⁂ ⚭ ⚇ ✦

'You took your time,' the Captain's voice cut through her observation of the tower staircase. 'Your shields are down again.'

'Oh Watcher's fire, sorry.'

'Don't you worry. I've got you safe. If Dragonsbreath is in trouble, then likely Silverfish will be, too, and I have family there. Hold my hand and bring me into your dream properly. Now imagine walking into the place we are trying to be.'

Elissa reached out and took the offered hand. 'Ready?' she asked.

'Yes, ma'am.'

Elissa stepped from the tower to the back entrance of Dragonsbreath. No one was there. 'We agreed someone would be here,' she said. 'Can we go in?'

'Yes, but probably not through any doors.' They walked into the passage and saw no one. The Captain pointed down at the floor. 'There are tracks.'

There was a trail of footprints, wet and larger than any human footprint she had ever seen.

'They found them,' she cried. She started to run, but was stopped by the grip of the Captain restraining her.

'Where would they hide?'

Elissa gritted her teeth. 'That's just it. They'd hide in here.'

'We're going no farther. Let's try somewhere else.'

Where would they be? Maybe it was just a coincidence. The awldrin had found someone because they were dreaming; the rest would be okay. 'Hold tight,' she said, and stepped again.

The walls of Makin's house appeared the same from the inside. But without him, something didn't feel right. On impulse, she tried to lift his pillow.

'I can't move it.'

'Let me – I'm a lot more practised,' the Captain said. Underneath the pillow was a full fish skull.

Elissa stared at the skull. She turned to the door and tried to peer through the gap at the side of the door curtain. The glow of the crystal illuminated the sericlave chamber.

'Can you open this?' she asked. The Captain moved the

edge of the curtain slightly and Elissa looked across to where her hut should be. It was flattened. All the false houses were gone. 'They found all of us,' she whispered.

'That doesn't mean they are all gone,' said the Captain, squeezing her hand reassuringly. 'What's the fish head about?'

Elissa had tried to ignore the strangeness of him holding her hand, but the squeeze made her try to pull her hand free.

'Elissa, you need me. I meant nothing by it. Think – the fish's head?' he said.

'I am trying to think.'

She caught fish from the river and left him the fish bone so he knew she was okay.

'The river! Upriver from here is a lake. On the way, are some caves. It's all I can think of, although I'm just grabbing at clouds.'

'Do you know it well enough?' he asked.

'I don't know. It's been a while.'

'Then try. As long as we don't end up on the peak, we'll be fine. I am tiring, so we don't have much longer.'

Elissa tried to picture the caves in her mind, but couldn't quite do it. 'I'll get us as close as I can.' She stepped onto the riverbank, much farther up river than the day she had stood on the shard, and scanned upstream. 'We'll have to walk.'

'Just take us as far ahead as you can see each time,' the Captain said. 'We need to be quick.'

Several steps later, they arrived at the area that Elissa desperately hoped to find.

'I see caves,' she said with relief. 'Is that—'

'A foot!' The Captain pointed at a cave near them.

Together, they ran to the entrance. A woman sat in it, looking down the valley. 'You found us!' she called.

'Hut one?' Elissa asked.

'One, three, and five made it out. They found hut two at the entrance, but they let us know before the awldrin found us.'

'Who else is here?'

'Everyone we identified as being able to light a glow globe, plus a few Laytha hadn't tested yet. We've been taking it in turns to watch for you. Makin thought you'd work it out, eventually. They destroyed our homes and made everyone sleep in the sheds. Everyone is soaked, cold, and hungry. The awldrin have killed one person each day to shock the sericlave into revealing where we've hidden. We need help.'

'Why haven't they exposed you? They might live.'

'Because we haven't told them where we hide. Although, it won't be long before someone gives us up.'

'Is Makin here?'

'No, nor Laytha's brother. They both felt too well known to the awldrin to vanish. They're risking being found to ensure we're not betrayed. They've told everyone that you will take them to safety, and you are a way to freedom from the awldrin forever. That's what's keeping them going. Rossi told them that his people believe you might be able to take us to Lieus. Is it true?'

Elissa's heart sank. She stood in silence for a moment, trying to compose herself. 'If it's possible, then I will do it. I'll get you all out of here somehow.'

'We need to go. I can't keep your shield much longer,' the Captain said gently.

Elissa crouched down. 'Tell Laytha I found them, and we'll bring you help.' She turned to the Captain. 'Ready? One last time?'

He nodded, and she stepped back to the tower.

⛬ ✳ ✳ ✳ ✦

She took a while to wake up fully, and when she finally sat up, Andra was in conversation with the Captain on the other bed.

He met her eyes, his own hooded with exhaustion, and gave her a smile. 'You did it.'

Andra followed his gaze and crossed the room to Elissa. 'You certainly did. The Captain has filled us in. We'll check in on the other villages now, and tomorrow we'll work out a plan. Do you want to return to your house? One of us can escort you?'

Elissa thought about her cosy cottage, but exhaustion claimed her, pulling her back onto the mattress. 'I'll just sleep here, I think,' she heard herself mumble before falling asleep.

CHAPTER 37

DARIN

The wheels of the cart,
Drive through the dust,
The song of the heart,
Leads where it must.
Excerpt from The Traveller's Song.
Unknown origin

The fire sprites flickered their last as Darin shook them into the bushes. They'd survive to glow another day. In the night-silent forest, the waterfall drummed its distant rhythm into the pool. It wasn't too far away by then, but the risk of stumbling over another root or uneven surface in the dark was still too high to travel with no light.

'Unless the clouds clear, and we get some moonlight, we need to stop,' Chase said as if reading Darin's thoughts. Chase had Star at the moment – they took turns carrying him throughout the evening and overnight, each stint shorter than the last as their muscles fatigued faster. It might not be a bad idea to take a short rest before they attempted the climb. Switching Star halfway up the waterfall would be a challenge, and slow their progress.

Darin rolled his shoulders. The muscles between his shoulder blades and up the length of his back burnt with the ache of carrying Star, almost as much as his heart ached for the sacrifice his hound had made to heal him. Darin turned around, and with hands outstretched, walked toward Chase. He could have asked Star for help, but the exhausted hound needed to conserve everything he could.

Chase laughed. He was clearly using Sandy to help him see. 'Catch hold of Sandy and come this way.' A wet nose pushed against Darin's hand, and he rested a hand on Sandy's back, grateful for the guidance.

⁊ ※ ⚇ ⚌ ✦

They sat for an hour or more; Darin lost track of time, and just as he dozed off, he felt Star's head on his lap, sending love and pain intermingled.

Darin shook himself awake and checked Star over, as he had each time they rested. Star winced as he ran hands under his ribs – the sling must be digging in. He tried to stand, but his legs were still not strong enough for more than a few steps; Darin showed him that they'd have to go up the waterfall, and that he could rest at the top. A single dull thud of his tail hitting the ground was all the reply Star could muster.

Finally, a pale glow lit the sky, and they could make out roots interweaving across the path.

'I'll take him.' Darin gently stroked Star's head. 'Once we're in the tower, is there anything we can use to build him a bed to pull, instead of carrying him? Something to help us travel faster.'

'There may be some chairs or a table we can break up,' Chase said. 'Let's get there before we worry about that.'

Darin nodded and adjusted Star into a comfortable position. The sling was as wide as he could spread it, and he checked that no folded bits rubbed underneath.

The stretch toward the plunge pool was easier walking, but it was more noticeably uphill. His calves ached, and shooting pains from his ankle reminded Darin of his own injuries with every step, but he pushed on. It was one thing having heard about xotryl, even meeting one, but realising the scale of the danger was quite another. Survival against the creatures wasn't enough. No spear or arrow was going to damage a creature that size.

More than once as he trudged, he thought maybe it would be better for the So'Dal to come out of hiding to fight them, to secure the continent. But would it be? He'd assumed they were administrators, healers – helpers. Would things be different if he'd realised they could use magic? Would he have been afraid? Maybe not, but more wary, less trusting definitely. Yes, it worked in Dal, and change wasn't a bad thing, but it *was* destabilising. A sudden reveal of the magic hidden throughout Caldera wasn't the way to go about it, unless lives were in danger. And they were.

The whistles would help to buy the Howlers, and by extension, the So'Dal, time. They needed to deal with the immediate threat first, and then he could broach the subject again. It was apparent that despite their extra magic – which, until then, they had refused to use – the Howlers were no longer enough to keep the Edgelands at bay, and unless the whistles worked as a temporary fix, there would be no choice but to expose at least one group of So'Dal.

Spray in the air heralded their imminent arrival at the plunge pool. Darin took out his whistle and blew once. The steps became visible, and without hesitation, he began the climb.

The steps from both sides of the waterfall met behind it, wet and slippery. Then, the oscillating climb began in earnest. From one side to the other, ever ascending, they kept moving until his calves were burning.

'I need to stop,' he called back.

'Take the next bolthole. We can rest for a short while. Remember, keep stretching your legs out, or you'll hurt too much when we restart.'

Darin laughed to himself. They were almost back to safety, and Chase turned straight back into his normal self. He looked up the cliff – they must be at least half-way.

Beyond the waterfall, the sky darkened. A train of black clouds heavy with rain drifted toward Dal. If they dropped their burden in the crater before Darin and Chase reached the top, it would become a much more difficult climb. He pointed upward.

Chase grunted. 'You've spotted them, then. I've been watching those come over from the sea. We can still stop if you really need to, or, we can stop just to swap and then continue up. I promise I will take as much care as if he was Sandy.'

Star licked Darin's hand and showed him that he wanted to be in the tower, sleeping.

'Let's do that. He needs this blanket off as soon as possible.'

They scrambled into one of the boltholes to swap Star across in the dry. True to his word, Chase went first and took extra care, re-testing some steps more than once for stability. They eventually reached the top and the tunnel beneath the tower when the flow of water increased.

'Hurry!' Chase called. 'It must be raining up top.'

They moved along the narrow ledge as Sandy ran ahead to the steps. He stood on the lowest one above water, barking and pacing in agitation as the water rose and flowed over his paws and he was forced up a step. Chase was next to reach them, and Darin watched with relief as he climbed onto the first one to settle Sandy.

The surge reached his feet, churning mucky and brown. The first wave reached his knees, pushed him off balance and he stumbled. He was thrown backward as his feet were swept from beneath him. Darin flung an arm up for the handrail. Hand over hand, he fought against the flood water, dragging himself upright, then turned sideways to present less surface to the flow and made better progress. He stumbled again and clung to the wall, totally spent.

From the steps ahead, he heard Star bark. A small wave of panic washed over him. Spurred into motion, Darin pushed himself onward. His eyes locked with Star's as the hound watched him creep ever closer. The bottom two steps were flooded, and upon reaching the third, he sank to his knees to catch his breath.

'No time to rest.' Chase reached down a hand. 'Come on.' He pulled Darin to his feet, and they struggled on up to the trapdoor. Chase opened it, and they climbed into the room, then he gently lowered the blanket over his arms and placed Star on the floor.

'A short sleep, and no more. We'll sleep, make a towing sled, and get going. The faster we get to Tian, the faster we can – hopefully – get this whistle made and decide whether we're heading straight back for dragon bone, or waiting for him to make the rest.' Chase patted Darin on the shoulder. 'You did well down there.'

⥀ ✳ ⚶ ⚶ ✦

The sun was near its midpoint as they prepared to leave.

'We'll have to risk it.' Chase scanned the horizon. 'I can't see any sign of the xotryl right now. In fact, the forest is eerily quiet. We need to get off this open plateau and into the woods as quickly as we can. Are you ready?'

Darin nodded. 'Let's go.'

He picked up the sled they'd created from the table and padded with torn blankets, stepped out of the door, and placed it flat, showing Star how he wanted him to lie. They tied him carefully, then took one side of the sled each, wrapped the straps across their bodies, and towed it away from the edge.

'This is still going to take days.' Darin sighed as they entered the tree-line.

'It is, but I've asked for help. There will be skaa-rak meeting us on the way, I hope,' replied Chase.

'Who did you ask?'

'Tian, before we climbed the waterfall,' Chase said. 'He said he would try to send someone. Watcher only knows who, or what story he spun them about how he knew we'd need help.'

'I thought he wasn't trained?'

'He's not – not really. But I taught him enough for our convenience. It's nice to see each other when we're apart for tides at a time.'

Darin pushed forward into his strap. 'Then let's get to these skaa-rak. They've had most of a day's travel toward us by now. Dependent on their speed – and xotryl – we should meet them tomorrow, shouldn't we?'

Chase nodded. 'They'll have to travel by daylight, which is obviously risky. But I imagine the riders will be armed, so the sooner we meet up with them, the better.'

'We have our spears.'

'And one very unwell moonhound. We don't want to be fighting, and I only have one flash-ball left.'

They pushed against the straps, leaning into them as they

kept the sled moving. It was heavy to start, but once underway, its momentum kept it going as long as they kept up a consistent pace. When it caught on roots, it took a lot of effort to re-start afterward, so they took the path of least resistance, both for Star's comfort and their own. Sandy had taken up position at the rear of their group. He loped along behind, watching over Star. At one point, he crashed off into the bushes at the side. Darin heard twigs breaking, thudding footfalls, then silence.

Sandy reappeared a few minutes later in front of them, proudly carrying a small animal in his jaws. He sat on the path blocking their way, so that they had to stop.

'You can try,' Chase said. Sandy trotted back to Star and ripped off a chuck of fresh meat to offer him. Hope swelled in Darin's chest as Star took it.

They passed an abandoned hut where they had slept a night on the way out. Fire sprites danced around it, so they refilled their jar and continued on after nightfall. Finally able to relax about the reduced threat from above, Darin stepped forward in a regular beat. Every step took them closer to Tian, and he found himself singing an old song in his head to the rhythm of his feet. If he had enough breath, he'd have sung it aloud. At least he knew Chase wouldn't criticise him for his lack of ability to hold a tune.

They walked for most of the night, taking short breaks, but finding it easier to continue slowly than restart, they were infrequent. Eventually, exhaustion claimed them both, and they settled down alongside the path.

⊢ ✳ ✸ ✦ ✴

Bitten by night bugs and cold to the bone, Darin woke up as the light hit his face through the branches. He was relieved to see that the blanket he'd pulled over them still covered Star, even though he'd thrown it off himself in the night.

Chase was nowhere in sight, and a pungent aroma was coming from where he'd been sitting. Darin leant closer and immediately regretted it. He drew back from the foul-smelling liquid on the bushes to quickly check his pack; all was good there.

'Chase?' he called.

'Over here,' Chase replied from behind a tree on the other side of the path. 'A graaken got Sandy. He growled at it, so it sprayed him. We now have one unwell hound and one who can't smell anything aside from the stench he's covered in. I thought I'd move away to save your nose when you woke up.'

'You mean you smell worse than that?' Darin gagged. 'This is going to be a fun day! I don't remember passing any streams or pools on the way to wash it off.'

'We didn't. When the skaa-rak arrive, take Star to Tian – no bird will let us near it smelling like this. Sandy and I won't be too far behind. Without the sled, we can probably keep up a pace that will get us there half a day after you, and we can travel at night for safety. Shall we get walking?'

Darin eased the sled back around to the path and prepared to leave. Chase was only mildly pungent, but the stench of Sandy made Darin's eyes water, and he retched.

'How on Lieus have you sat next to that?'

'I must have got used to it.' Chase shrugged. To the dismay of Darin's stomach, Sandy insisted on slinking along, tail tucked in, next to Chase.

'He feels lost without a sense of smell,' Chase explained.

'So do I.' Darin had never hoped for rain clouds so fervently as he did that morning.

Shrieking calls heralded the arrival of a rider. Broad and scarred, he rode a single skaa-rak with three more in tow.

'Now that's impressive,' Darin said.

'Whoa!' the rider said to his beast as he pulled up. 'Did you see them? Did you find out why they're heading inland so often?'

Chase winked. 'I told you he'd have told someone something.' He looked back at the rider. 'Indeed, we saw them. They are definitely restless, but we could not find the cause. Can you get our injured party member back?'

'I wish the Watcher-flamed xotryl would just die out,' the rider replied vehemently. 'One was bad enough, but the smaller one's really causing panic. As for getting you back to Tian, of course I can. It worried him that you'd been longer than he expected. He thought one of you might have taken an injury.'

Darin stepped aside. 'Yes, he has.' He gestured to Star. 'Can we get him on a bird?'

'Will he lie still?'

Darin had no idea how Star would take to being carried on a skaa-rak. But he sent an image and Star seemed to agree to it. 'I am sure he will, if he is in front of my saddle.'

'You ride much?'

'I used to. It's been a while though. I've been ... busy.'

'Right, well, they say you don't forget. Your brain might not, but I can assure you that your muscles will have. I'm sorry, one of you smells awful!' the rider said, covering his mouth and nose.

'That's us.' Chase waved cheerily. 'We'll follow on foot and save your noses.'

'Good, I think the birds would struggle otherwise.' He leapt off his mount and held the head of the stockiest bird. Its feather crest was shorter than the others, but its back was wide. 'This old boy is very smooth gaited. He'll get us underway.

We'll have to change to the other two skaa-rak in a while to rest these up.'

The big bird folded its legs under to allow Darin to mount, and the rider hefted Star high in the air, gently placing him across the front of the saddle. The skaa-rak pecked at him gently, then seemingly happy to accept Star as a passenger, it straightened itself up. Darin gripped both the saddle and Star as they were jolted upward.

The rider swapped the saddle from his own mount to one of the others, wrapping the chest harness carefully under the wings. Darin shuffled Star across his lap to even out their weight as the rider leapt onto his own mount.

Darin waved at Chase. 'Wash before you get home,' he called, and taking the loop in one hand, the other supporting Star, they set off.

⋎ ✳ 🜨 ⚜ ✦

By the time their exhausted skaa-rak struggled into the small hamlet, they'd switched mounts for the third time, leaving the other birds to find their own way back to the flock once they had rested.

Darin's muscles ached, and his ears rang. The squawking of both birds had intensified once they heard their home flock in the distance; the noise a part of riding he'd gladly forgotten until then.

They stumbled to a halt in front of Tian's door, where his mount collapsed to allow them to dismount.

'Thank you,' he said, and scratched the bird's neck.

Tian's door flung open, and he rushed out. He took Star in his arms, his strength belying his size entirely as he slid the moonhound off the skaa-rak and ran back into the house. Darin climbed down, stretching out immobility from his legs.

'Go through. Get him comfortable, and talk to me in a moment.' Tian reappeared and headed toward the rider – why hadn't he thought to ask the man's name? He heard the two men chatting and caught the phrase 'graaken spray,' accompanied by chuckling laughter before Tian followed him into the house.

'He's a good man. I'm glad he found you both. I take it Chase will detour via some sort of water on the way home?'

Darin smiled. 'Yes, he stank, but poor Sandy was the one really suffering.' Even remembering the stench made his stomach clench. He pointed at the case of fern-tree wood on the workbench. 'How fast can you make one?'

'Don't you worry lad,' Tian said. 'I took apart a whistle as soon as Chase explained the situation. I need a few hours to shape the wood, then we can check it works as you hope it will.'

'I only have one shot at the healing potion, or I need to get Star straight back to Redpike.' Darin tried to quell the rising panic before Star picked up on it. Tian was calm and relaxed, so Darin tried to take comfort in his presence.

'I know. If it's doable, I can do it. You look exhausted. Go. Sleep while I work, then I'll call you when it's ready to test. Be assured, I understand the need for these whistles, and the love for your hound. If these will keep Chase safer, I'll use every skill at my disposal – I fixed his old whistle, so I know I can do this. For the first time, there's a way my skills can really help him.'

Darin opened his bag and withdrew the other branches. 'We also brought you these spare bits in case they're useful for anything else.'

Tian glanced at the spare sections of wood. 'Thank you.' He reached for the roll and unfurled it. 'These are great – well done. Now rest, both of you.'

The plants needed to be freshly ground to make the healing draft, so Tian's suggestion of sleep was sensible, if he could sleep. Darin checked on Star again. His breathing was shallow, faster, and his eyes were glazed. On impulse, Darin sent the image that Star had sent him the very first time *[The two of them walked through mountain passageways under Redpike, staramine veins running through the rock around them].*

He hoped that he didn't imagine the small feeling of affection running back through their bond – it felt as though Star sent it from a world away. Pushing down rising concern, he tried to stay calm. *What I feel, he mirrors.* Breathe, focus on calm, slow breaths. Taking Tian's advice, he curled up next to Star and tried to rest. Redpike was still a long way off, and the skaa-rak might not be available for it.

He awoke to a gentle shaking from Tian. 'It's done. I think it might work, but without your training, I cannot be entirely sure.'

Darin hauled himself up off the floor. 'The training globe?'

'It's on the table.'

It was a simple whistle with no fancy engraving or ornate detail like Wilf's, but it had a sliding component and the ring of white bone. Darin picked it up. The wood was smooth and retained heat from having been recently worked. It was very light, and he could see the delicate inlays of bone and crystal.

He reached inside himself. A small store of magic was available. He carefully sang the glow lamp note, and the training globe illuminated – it was the only note he could guarantee to hit. Darin lifted the whistle to his lips and played it with no weft. He slid the slider up and down until he felt he was close to the right point, then added his magic through the note. A gentle flicker appeared. His heart soared with hope.

Darin tried again, moving the slider until it played the same note, and the training globe glowed with the right colour.

'Can we make a notch or a mark so I can tell when it is

exactly at this point?' he asked, trying to keep his excitement under control.

'I was going to suggest that. Keep it still a moment.' Tian reached forward, marking the slider.

Darin had a starting point, so it was easier to work out the rest of the notes. Together, they worked through the globe, right up to the white-violets that came from the notes of the Howler whistles.

'How long will it take to finish?' Darin asked, trying not to sound impatient as Tian cut small grooves in the slider.

'A few minutes.'

'Thank you! Do you have a bowl and a grinding stone?'

'I have one for spices.'

'That should work.' Darin searched the kitchen shelves until he found them, then carefully prepared and ground the leaves. Fresh leaves had a different potency to dried, so he hoped his quantities were right. Darin took each step steadily, adding the leaves in the same order as he had with Tralkion. He boiled the mixture in water and then carried the steaming bowl back to the work area.

'What have you put in that?' Tian asked.

'It's heavily loaded with healing leaves and a few others found in the Edgelands,' Darin replied. 'If there's any left, I am sure we can leave you some. To be honest, I'm hoping that Star will drink most of it.'

Darin practised moving the whistle from note to note through the sequence without adding any power. The five-note combination had eluded him with his own voice. He repeated the process a few times, using the training globe as a focus. The lights skipped when he missed a note, so he tensed up, causing the next note to squeak too.

Tian rested a gentle hand on his arm. 'Relax. Remember, both music and magic come from the heart, not just the voice.

That's why it works. That's *how* it works.' He picked up the original whistle Darin had brought and accompanied Darin as he played the notes over and over.

Darin felt himself relax and tried to add the weft again. He repeated the sequence on the globe to check, then carefully adjusted his focus to the bowl in front of him.

He let his hand repeat the pattern once more, then finally added the weft into the melody. After two repetitions, a gentle flash of gold travelled through the bowl, and the liquid turned vibrant green. He lowered the whistle and couldn't suppress the tear that snaked down his cheek.

'Tian, you did it.'

'*We* did it. Now, get that into your hound. I'll make a start on the rest of the whistles. You'll still want to get back to Redpike for him to finish recovering.' Despite playing his role down, Tian's upright posture showed his pride, and the twitch of a grin was desperate for release.

Darin transferred the draft to a cool bowl, carried it to Star, and sent *[Star drinking it]*. He received clear disgust in reply, but Star drank the whole bowl with more urging. It wasn't a cure – Tian was right. Star would still need rest and possibly stronger intervention like dragon bone once they got back. But he hoped it would at least let Star walk back to Redpike and stabilise him.

⋎ ✳ ✖ ✵ ✦

By the time Chase arrived the next day, smelling considerably cleaner, Tian had completed three further whistles. There were just two more to make before they could leave. Chase watched them working with close interest, eventually trying one for himself. On discovering that he could make the training globe work, his face lit up.

'This changes *everything*! We can finally make our own potions and use the battle-magic in the texts. If we combine that with our ability to fight with hounds, we have a stronger force and can discharge our duty once again. We just need enough extra men to take these xotryl down before they harm more people.' His excitement was palpable.

'Just.' Darin smiled.

'I know. Big Red has been living well off the increased food by hunting in Dal. We really can't afford the Anchor sending teams down to Dal, untested in battle and unprepared for what they face.' He grimaced as he continued. 'We simply don't have enough dragon bone left to heal every So'Dal who gets overly brave.'

'So we do it ourselves,' Darin replied. 'I need more practise at balancing hound and spear before we face one in a fight to the death, though. We really do need to find more new Howlers too.'

'I'll train you up – we'll use the weaponry. It has a big enough space for practise, and now you and Star are starting to work together, I have a lot to teach you.'

Sandy woofed and wagged excitedly. He ran past Darin to the back room and returned with a much happier Star, who walked steadily and wagged slowly. Darin's heart soared. *[Crunching on juicy meat]* filled his vision, the strongest image since he'd woken on the river bank. Star was going to be okay.

'A few more hours, and we should be able to get him home without carrying him. You did a good job, Darin. Well done,' Chase said, reaching down to stroke Star.

When the last whistles were ready, they prepared to leave, and Darin braced himself for the question he knew he should have asked first.

'Many thanks for the whistles. What can I do in return?'

Tian laughed, long and deep, as musical as his instruments. 'You already gave me what I have always sought. A true place in history, even if not recognised.'

Darin shook his head. 'That's not enough.'

'The next time you pass, bring me a bottle of that wonder potion you brewed up. I know the sequence now, but I don't know what you put in it, and I doubt I can find all the ingredients here.'

'You're right. I can leave you a list, but you might struggle to get the ingredients. I'll make you a big bottle! Although, it doesn't seem much for what you did for us, and for Star.'

'You did the hard work – you got the wood and worked out the idea. I only made it. If this helps you Howlers get Dal back to normal, it's worth it. If it keeps this man safer, then it is more than worth it.' He stood by Chase and squeezed his hand. Chase looked down at Tian and smiled.

'I am not sure I could ever consider Dal normal,' – he chuckled – 'but I'll ensure Darin makes you one of those potions and teaches me how too.' He enveloped Tian in a hug and whispered something in his ear.

With all farewells said, Chase and Darin departed for the lift and Redpike.

CHAPTER 38

SURIIN

Born of Dal, always of Dal.
Proverb

Her father's dim form flickered in the chair in the corner. She still couldn't get through to him. She'd tried for hours with no response.

When she'd returned the map to Ronin, Suriin had been non-committal about its usefulness. It was better he knew as little as possible – there would be less interference in her plans that way. In return, he told her he'd tried to dream walk to her father, but none of the Gardeners had found him yet. She considered telling them where he was, that she could take them and maybe they could help him there, but seeing her father in his poor state once again reminded her how little help the Gardeners had been so far.

It was her battle to fight. Suriin held tight to the remorse that kept her pushing forward to find a cure. She glanced down. Good, her clothes were still in place, despite her loss of focus. She kissed her dream father's misty cheek, stood tall, and stepped from her parents' kitchen straight into Natke's cell.

Natke looked down at her as Suriin tried to take in more detail of the awldrin's armour to help steady her nerves. She could add it to her sketchbook when she awoke. Natke wore the sword again. Suriin exhaled gently, feeling centred and ready. She slid her gaze from the sword up to the crystalline eyes.

'Is beautiful, is not?' Natke drew the long, black sword from its scabbard. Gentle light flickered from the blade. It looked like black glass with intricate carvings decorating its length, the symbol for vigilance amongst them.

'What is it made from?' she asked, building up the courage to return to the conversation they both knew was hanging over their heads. The balanced line of tension they walked was as fine as a gossamer thread of spider silk.

'Dragon glass,' Natke said, turning and admiring it. 'I miss it. It is part of me once. Now is save me again and be tool of my freeing.'

Suriin felt nerves flutter in her gut. She could never steal a sword without anyone noticing.

'You know it, do you not?' Natke clicked. 'Your face are so easy to read.'

Suriin nodded. 'It is painted on the wall of a library.'

Natke hissed. 'Then you know who am I?'

Suriin took a step back. Despite it being her dream – and knowing she could step away at any time – her fear was building. She tried to give herself a wall to touch, a solid object to ground her fears against.

'I have offer,' Natke hissed and clicked more forcefully.

Suriin struggled to compose her voice as she replied. 'What

can you offer me if you will not teach me how you survive?' *I am in control. I can walk away. She has no true power over me – keep breathing,* she told herself, over and over as she waited what felt like an age for a reply.

'Find sword, remove red stone. Twist in way sun rotates. Inside hollow. Is store for powder to heal. Enough will be to give human more healing. But not fully cure. Put in the mouth. When it works, return. We talk about how you get more and get me free.'

Natke had barely finished speaking when Suriin stepped out of the cell. She stepped back into her parents' house, confident that it would be safe. Suriin thought she spotted a movement past the kitchen door and ran toward it, hoping for her mother, but no one was there.

Leaning close to the flickering silhouette of her father, she whispered, 'I'm coming, and I will fix this. I love you.'

After taking one last look around the kitchen, Suriin returned to her room in Redpike and allowed herself to drift into a normal sleep.

⋏ ※ ⚛ ⚜ ✦

The next few days passed in what had become a regular routine. They had lessons every morning and spent afternoons in the library. Xedra hadn't been late since the second lesson. Whatever Aslin had threatened them with appeared to be enough. She'd still made snide remarks about kitchen maids when they headed for lunch, though.

'What is your job?' Joy had asked.

'I don't need one. My parents will pay for me to stay in the guest tower as long as I need to,' she'd sneered, and Suriin had covered her mouth to hold back the giggle that tried to escape.

As they headed down to the hall, she'd told her friends

about the woman in the year above them, and lunch had been greatly enhanced by trying to imagine what job Xedra would finally have to accept, were she to stay.

⋆ ※ ※ ※ ✦

What spare time Suriin could find between her evening chores, visiting her father, and her studies, was spent watching the comings and goings of people into the Star Tower. She tried to mask her spying by sketching the people and creatures around the Black Palace as she waited.

On the third day, Suriin felt she was getting a handle on regular timings, and she wasn't entirely sure that she'd have long enough to get into the reception area unnoticed, let alone to get to the sword.

A loud crack of someone bashing at the gate made her jump. It swung open to admit another of the red-robed skaa-rak riders like the one she'd seen with Fresna a few days earlier.

The rider flung their harness strap at the nearest guard and ran for the Star Tower. Moments later, three of the Collective rushed out. Whilst not quite running, they moved at a considerably faster walk than normal.

One went under the archway and toward the kitchens, while the others headed for the passageways that led to the gardens and the rest of the network under the mountain.

⋆ ※ ※ ※ ✦

The sun had dropped behind the palace wall when they returned. Suriin sat quietly in the shadows as the first of the Collective returned with Aslin. The others were accompanied a few moments later by two older So'Dal. One was a Gardener – she could see the green trim on his robe even in this dim light –

and the other man, Suriin recognised. She'd seen younger So'Dal bowing before him at mealtimes. He must also be important.

They all entered the Star tower, making it clear that she wouldn't get in there that evening. Whatever information the messenger had brought must be serious. She sighed and rose from her seat, stretching the stillness out of her legs. With her sketchbook tucked back into her pocket, Suriin headed toward her rooms.

Evening sun was warm on her back as she walked out of the wall's shadow. The whistling song of the small, golden enna birds perched around the top of the wall brought with them warm memories of Golden in the evening, riding around the fields with her brother. One alighted on a bale of hay next to her. Its blue eyes sparkled as it tipped its head to one side and regarded her with curiosity, before whistling and fluttering off again.

She changed her plan. A quick visit to her father, then she would head up to the crater garden to just enjoy the plants and birds by starlight. The black moon was full, and it would be beautiful up there. Maybe she would draw a new plant. Sometimes it was small things in life that brought enough joy to keep her going, while she battled against the big problems. A smile played on her lips as she headed to her father's rooms.

Seeing his prone form brought her crashing back down again. What were the small things, after all, when he lay like that? How could everything just carry on while he was so unwell? She felt foolish – as if she was betraying him by even thinking about being happy.

Suriin sat by his bed, holding his thin hand. Tendrils of blackness crept through the skin across his knuckles. Hot tears flowed freely down her face, and she lay carefully on the edge of the bed, hugging him gently.

She was still in that position, dry-eyed but holding her father close, when the door opened. She rubbed her puffy eyes as she tried to take in the short silhouette in the doorway.

'Suriin, I need you to come with me,' said Aslin.

'Can't you find someone else?' Suriin sniffed as she spoke, her head pounding from crying.

'No, I am afraid the Anchor needs to speak to you now.'

Suriin kissed her father on the cheek and tried to remain as calm as she could. Had someone seen her after all? Had someone checked the awldrin and it told them about her?

'What about, Soul Anchor Aslin?' she asked, as she straightened out her robe. She tucked her hands into the pockets to hide their shaking and trudged reluctantly to the door.

'It's not my place to have that conversation with you, as much as I would like to warn you in advance.' Aslin's lips were tight, and she wouldn't meet her eyes.

Suriin raised her hands and tried to massage her temples to relieve the headache, then sighed. 'Let's go then.' She turned back to her father. 'I'll see you later. Rest well.'

The weight of silence as they walked to the tower was as suffocating as a heavy blanket on a midsummer day. Each step was harder and her feet grew heavy. She'd been so close to helping her father. They climbed the tower and, as they passed into the waiting room outside the meeting chamber, Suriin saw the awldrin's sword. It was mounted exactly as Skye had said, above the fire. They didn't stop there, though. Aslin walked straight through, and the doors swung open at her touch.

Suriin expected all the other people who had arrived earlier to be in the room, but only the senior So'Dal and the Anchor were there, sat in two heavily embroidered chairs.

'Anchor, Master, I have brought Suriin as requested.' Aslin bowed as she spoke, and Suriin heard a tremor in her voice.

'Suriin, please sit.' The Anchor gestured to an armchair. 'Aslin, would you wait outside? I will speak with you again shortly.'

Aslin left the room, pulling the doors gently closed behind her.

The Master leant forward in his chair. His eyes were sad and his hands clasped in his lap.

'I am afraid we have had some worrying news, Suriin.' His voice was musical, each word almost sung, every syllable crystal clear. Suriin tried to sit tall; defiantly, she looked him straight in the eyes. Even sitting, her height meant she was looking down at him.

The Anchor walked around and put a hand on Suriin's shoulder gently. Suriin felt herself tense. She was getting thrown out.

'When you and Yorynn arrived here, we sent support to your mother to allow her to come here. The new Witness and Soul Anchor, who were to take care of Golden, were sent immediately. Your mother and brother left Golden upon their arrival.' The Master rose and walked to the tower window, gazing out as he continued. 'Whilst you have been here, they have been travelling toward Redpike. However, several days ago, we received a messenger bearing worrying news.'

That wasn't what she expected – it was worse. A lump rose in her throat. Why had they needed her there to tell her? Why had it needed a messenger?

He turned around and looked at the Anchor. Suriin saw the Anchor close her eyes and nod in some unspoken agreement. She then turned to Suriin.

'Your mother has gone missing. We've been hunting for her ever since we heard. We had no way to get in contact with Gwynn as he is not thought to be talented – and he is too young for it to have manifested yet, even if he was. We've searched everywhere. Aslin has been dream walking every night. As your mother's oldest friend here, we had hoped she might find her, but we have found no trace.'

Suriin crumpled. The silence stretched out as she tried to take in the news.

'Your mother has always done things her own way,' the Master said, breaking the silence. 'She was always a little unpredictable. She may be alive and well, but we cannot find her.'

'Why not? Surely she has my brother and Fluffy with her? They can't all have vanished. Did they not see anything? Can they not help you find out what happened?' The questions poured out of Suriin.

The Anchor returned to her own seat and leant forward, resting her clasped hands on her knees. 'Do you think we have not already tried that line of searching? We found your brother a few days ago, in Scarton crater.'

Suriin interrupted. 'Then send the garant! Please.'

Calmly the Anchor continued. 'We can't – he is not alone. He is with Fluffy.'

Her mother was missing, and had been for days and days. No one could find her. Her little brother was travelling alone with her mother's moonhound. Moonhounds didn't leave the people they bonded to. Her mother was gone.

The room felt claustrophobic. She needed some space; she was going to burst. 'May I step outside? I need a moment to myself,' she asked politely. The Master looked at the Anchor and nodded.

'You can take a few minutes for yourself in the waiting room. Please send Aslin in. We need to speak to her, and that will give you a few moments to gather yourself. Remember, you are to be a Soul Anchor. You must be able to handle difficult news. I will need to ask you some questions, in case we've missed anything in our search. Come back in when you're ready.'

Suriin stood and rushed toward the door, grief beginning to blur her view with rising tears. She made it through the door before letting them fall. Aslin rose to enter the room as she left.

As she passed, she leant toward Suriin and whispered, 'Do not give up hope. Only the Anchor has more power than your mother, and there's something else you probably don't know about her. She was born in Dal.'

Suriin didn't understand the relevance her mother's birthplace had on the situation. But the first part lit the tiniest flicker of hope. She mustered a weak smile.

'Thank you,' she said, and watched as Aslin closed the door behind her.

Suriin sank into the soft chair Aslin had sat in, and for the second time that evening, tears fell freely. Finally, when she was dried out and hollow, the tears stopped falling. Suriin raised her head from her hand, took the end of her scarf, and used it to dry her eyes. In the dim light, a glowing red caught her eye.

Suriin stood. She unwound some scarf, and using the edge of the blade on the wall, she cut the wet section off.

'I may only have one parent left – We may only have one, by tomorrow, maybe none,' she whispered to herself. 'What's left to lose if they catch me?'

The sword was mounted length-wise over the fire, so she stood on the closest chair and steadied herself against the wall to study the pommel stone. *The way the sun rotates.* She gripped the stone and twisted it. To her surprise, it worked – the stone came off, revealing a small, hollow chamber in the pommel. Quickly, Suriin stuffed the wet scrap of scarf inside and twisted it around so it brushed against all the sides, then pulled it out and gasped – there was white powder on it, just as Natke had told her there would be. She refolded the scrap of scarf so that the powder was on the inside of the fabric scrap and replaced the pommel stone.

Suriin retrieved the sketchbook from her pocket, tucked the carefully folded scrap between two pages, and bound it tightly shut. With seeds of hope planted in both her heart and pocket, Suriin knocked at the door, ready to face whatever questions they would ask. Her mother wasn't the only strong woman in her family. She would show them.

ⲧ ※ ※ ⛭ ✦

It was dark when Suriin finally left the Star tower. She couldn't offer much new information to the Anchor. Her mother had no visitors that she could remember; she'd never had a conversation with Fluffy herself. Yes, her brother had always loved Fluffy and had a way with animals. No, she had never met any of her mother's family. So many questions, so many unrelated facts.

When they asked about family, Aslin had been standing behind the Anchor and Master, staring out the window. At the question, she turned around, and meeting Suriin's eyes, gave a tiny shake of her head. In the moment, Suriin decided that trusting Aslin seemed right, so she pleaded the same ignorance of her mother's family or their location that she genuinely had throughout her entire life.

They told her that a messenger had come bearing Gwynn's version of the story. The Anchor's bonded So'Dal, Hal, had taken two skaa-rak to speed their journey to Redpike, but Fluffy had refused to co-operate. As Gwynn refused to leave her, they were travelling at Fluffy's pace and had sent the other rider ahead.

He was due to arrive in about a tide. Apparently, Hal had left a few days earlier to guide Gwynn to Redpike and ensure his safety.

Apparently Gwynn and their mother had slept beneath the stars one night and he'd awoken to find her gone and Fluffy sleeping next to him. Suriin thought the story sounded ridiculous, even for her brother! He woke at a feather landing next to his pillow, and she had no doubt that he was hiding something. Once he got there, she could ask him, could try to talk with Fluffy. The Anchor and the Master were fairly sure something, or someone, had taken her. Everything they said was vague, couched in uncertainty.

Then they'd had to agree on what would happen when he did arrive. Suriin was old enough to not need a guardian until their father woke up or their mother made a miraculous return. Gwynn, being younger, would need a guardian when he arrived. Aslin offered, and Suriin couldn't think of a reason to say no, so she agreed on his behalf.

Aslin left the tower afterward with Suriin. They walked together across the moonlit courtyard, the green light of Mythos illuminating it brightly.

'If you look up tonight, you might just about see the sun reflecting off Tebein,' Aslin said. 'On days like this, where xotryl and other creatures' names are thrown around so freely, the dark moon feels a lot closer than it really is. Did you know when the Gates were closed, it trapped some So'Dal on the other side, along with farmers and other humans who'd been working on Tebein?'

Suriin shook her head, searching the sky for the shining glimmer of light that would indicate Tebein's presence. Much smaller in the sky than Mythos, its dark surface was hard to see in full darkness.

'I wonder if any humans still live there now?' Suriin said.

After all, there's at least one awldrin here. 'I'm not sure I can sleep, Aslin. Do you think it would be alright to sit with my father a while? I know it's late, but sometimes reading to him makes me feel calmer. Maybe he can hear me, and it helps him in some way.'

Aslin smiled up at her. 'After this evening, I think that sounds like a good idea. I'll see you in our lesson as normal tomorrow morning. You are strong, like her, but I feel that you are less impulsive – it might let you go far, once you have a full grasp of your emotions.' She waved and headed off in the other direction.

Less impulsive? Suriin resisted the urge to run to her father's rooms. But Aslin was right. Every decision she made was thought through. She weighed the risks, just like she had that afternoon, for what she was about to do. Calmly and coolly, she wound her way through the palace. The Gardeners would have visited him while she was in the Star tower, so no one should be due until morning.

She pushed open the door gently, peering inside. It was dark, and her father's breathing was calmer than it had been when she left. Suriin lit the glow lamp and checked his hand again. The Gardener's weft had pushed the black veins back maybe a finger's length up his arm, but the poison was winning.

Suriin pulled her book out, then hesitated. How was she going to get the powder into his mouth? She could hardly stuff the fabric in there. A jug they used to wash him down with sat on the table. She sniffed it – the water still seemed fresh.

She poured a small amount into the tiny cup that she normally helped him drink from. If his head was upright, his instinct to swallow still worked. Suriin lifted the book over the cup carefully, unfolded the fabric between the pages and, keeping the bottom of the spine over the top of the cup, she tipped it. A small amount of powder slid into the cup. Suriin let it settle; it sat like sand in the base. That was frustrating – she'd have to swirl it to stay suspended in the water. She inverted the fabric and washed the remaining powder into the cup. *Watcher, please let this work.*

Suriin sat next to her father's pillow and lifted the frail, light form of her father into a more upright position. Supporting the back of his head against her chest, she used one hand to open his mouth. He felt even hotter than usual. The fever was raging.

'I don't know if you can hear me, but if you can, I need you to try to drink this,' she whispered. The first attempt failed, and the small amount she poured in came back out without being swallowed, dribbling down his chin.

He spluttered a little.

Suriin mopped the drips up and tried again, swirling the cup to get as much powder in each mouthful as she could. Gently, slowly, Suriin poured a small amount in, and she felt her father swallow.

'Good, let's get the rest in now,' she murmured, and eventually, she'd got most of the powder in his mouth.

Suriin laid him back down carefully once she was certain he'd swallowed the last of the liquid. She wiped the rest of the powder out of the cup and replaced it on the table. Full of optimism, she checked his arm and neck. The black veins were still visible – nothing had happened. Perhaps it was slow working, or it needed to travel there. After all, he had only just swallowed it. Maybe her hopes were too high, or the dose too low to do him any good. Time would tell.

Watcher guard your sleep, she thought, looking back at him as she closed the door softly.

CHAPTER 39

ELISSA

When humans settled on Tebein, they spread across its habitable zone, as humans are wont to do. The most isolated community became known as Ice-holt. Not because it was cold, but due to the sheer amount of lumina crystals in the rocks there that reminded the settlers of ice.
The Black Planet

Elissa awoke to the sound of footsteps pounding down the stairs. She stretched as she sleepily took in the frantic activity; people ran in and out of the main door. Why were they all running? The Captain's bed was gone, and only hers remained in the room.

The flattened huts in Dragonsbreath flashed to the front of her thoughts. How much more of the sericlave had been destroyed? The awldrin must have found the library too. More runners passed her, none sparing her a glance.

Maybe the Chosen were already working out how to help

her friends. Her stomach ached with hunger or concern, probably both. Hunger, she could deal with.

'Shard-bonded, you're awake. Please, come on up,' a passing Chosen said. 'Andra wants to see you.'

Andra was still awake? Or was it morning? Elissa ran her hands through her hair – hunger would have to wait. 'You wouldn't be able to find me a cup of calfa, would you?' she asked.

'Of course. I'll bring it up.'

⌶ ※ ⚇ ⚇ ✦

The meeting room was full. Charts and maps lay spread across tables with people gathered around them, gesturing at marked areas. In the far corner, voices rose in heated discussion. Elissa tried to listen in, but the general talking in the room was too loud to make out the discussion clearly.

The Captain stood at the table closest to her with a map of the Ameryth Dar sea in front of him. He was deep in discussion with several crew members and two Chosen. When he noticed Elissa, a broad smile broke across his face, and he pointed upward, mouthing, 'Andra.'

She replied with a silent, 'Thank you,' and continued up the stairs.

⌶ ※ ⚇ ⚇ ✦

Andra sat on a comfortable chair in the middle of the room. Either side of her were Chosen, apparently sleeping. One was dressed in deep purple, and the other appeared to be wearing her nightclothes.

Andra was more hunched than the day before. She sat with

her head rested in her hands, watched Elissa cross the room toward her and sighed deeply.

'Come and sit with me,' she said, patting the cushion next to her. 'As we readied ourselves to work through our contacts,' – she gestured to the woman in formal attire – 'news came in from Silverfish. A group of awldrin arrived at midday, having crossed the land bridge. The remains of the village is smoking, and the boats cannot get near the shore to attempt to rescue any survivors.'

'Burn this shard! If I hadn't found it, then none of this would be happening,' Elissa said through gritted teeth, trying to clear the image of a burned young girl from her mind. Maybe the child had survived. 'What about Shardeep?'

Andra's shoulders dropped. 'Some xotryl carried on past. It's only a matter of time before they find Shardeep sericlave. We're trying to evacuate as quickly as we can. The Chosen there are refusing to leave, and the talented men are just as stubborn.'

'Rossi?'

'He will not leave his post.'

'His daughter?'

'She's on the first boat leaving tonight. They'll sail in darkness to reduce the chance of being followed. The Captain will meet them outside our defences and guide the boats that reach them through. Those who remain will either have to take refuge in the mountain or fight. I suspect they will choose to fight.'

⵲ ⚹ ⚹ ⵲ ✦

'No! Watcher, save us!' the night-clothed Chosen sat up. 'Iceholt is also empty. All the buildings are burning.'

'Also?' Elissa asked.

Andra nodded. 'That's the second village where there

appears to be nothing left standing. It doesn't mean no one survived, but it's too far for us to reach.'

'I'll try Silverfish again,' the woman said. 'I'll try the inn. It shouldn't burn.' She lay back down and immediately closed her eyes.

'What can I do to help?' Elissa asked. There had to be something. She'd brought the awldrin down on them – people died because of her.

'Tell us as much as you can about the awldrin in Dragonsbreath – anything you think might help.'

'Calfa?' interrupted The Captain, bringing a steaming cup to Elissa. 'I don't know how you can drink this stuff. Andra, we're leaving. I'll guide each ship through, then search the coastline for survivors.' He looked over at Elissa, tiredness still etched on his face. 'I can't get close to Dragonsbreath now. I am sorry.'

'I know.' Elissa sipped at the calfa. 'Without food, their chances are slim, but they're resourceful. If there's a way, Laytha will find it. It all depends on how long the rest of the sericlave holds out.'

The Captain put a gentle hand on her shoulder. 'I'll check in on them and let these dreamers know,' he said, gesturing to the two Chosen in the room. 'Don't go alone yourself.'

Elissa laughed and shrugged his hand off. 'Just because you held my dream hand doesn't mean you can hold me when I'm awake.' In truth, it hadn't felt as odd as she expected, but all physical contact still felt odd to her. He winked at Elissa, bowed to Andra, and left the room.

Andra took a pencil into her gnarled hand.

'That's part one of the rescue underway. We need to develop the rest of our strategy. Where do they live?'

'They live at the top of Dragonsbreath. Throughout

Winds, we power the furnace that keeps their part of the mountain warm.'

'Of course, they're cold-blooded. We have the advantage at night. Go on.'

'My brother was a lookman there. He said that every eclipse, they gather on the melted side. He never got close enough to see what they were doing, but he did say that there had been a few less awldrin there over the last few years.'

Andra raised an eyebrow as the pencil scratched across the page. 'Less? That is unexpected. They are almost immortal, exceptionally long-lived. Some of the same individuals are discussed in the histories over centuries.'

'I don't know a lot more. But ...' Elissa paused. 'Maybe this ties in to what you just said. They don't look like the paintings or the pictures in books. Their skin is dry, almost scaly and wrinkled.'

'Have you ever seen a smooth one?' Andra asked.

'No, and Makin hasn't seen a young one either.'

Both women sat in silence. Elissa had never really thought about that before. Where were the awldrin keeping their young?

The Chosen interrupted the silence again. 'Andra, the whole town is aflame. From the window of the inn, I can see flattened buildings. Flaming arrows hiss in the roofs, and there appears to be a bonfire of sorts under a gibbet.'

Elissa sat forward, horrified, as the woman continued.

'There's one other thing. A boat is heading out of the harbour. I couldn't see who or what was in it, but its sails are all wrong.'

'Children? Non-sailors?' Elissa asked.

'Awldrin have never been seen on water before, so hopefully it's survivors,' said Andra. 'Take a break, Clara. Send the next one up when you get downstairs.'

'Where's she trying to reach?' Elissa asked, pointing at the other woman.

'She's not. She is sat here, waiting for others to contact us. There has always been someone here, so that the villages can contact us. She will not wake until her replacement is in place.'

'That is normal procedure, m'lady, but I am sorry – you need to hear this now.' The woman still lay down, her eyes closed as she spoke. 'I'll be quick. The talent from Silverfish fleet says that there's a boat headed toward them loaded way beyond the safe waterline. He hopes that it contains survivors. It's being followed by a second boat sailing erratically. He has seen flame stone arrows being shot at the first boat and will attack in retaliation to slow or disable the pursuit. Once they have the occupants of the first boat in the fleet, they will attempt to meet up with The Captain. They are unable to return to shore.'

'Shardeep has also been in touch. Xotryl were sighted, heading toward the mountains by patrols. They anticipate an attack before nightfall. Shardeep is sending all boats as soon as they are loaded. I will await further messages.'

The brief, matter-of-fact delivery of the news left Elissa numb.

'Five hundred cycles we have co-existed. Not happily, but nothing like this has happened since the Gates were closed.' Andra's voice held a barely controlled quiver. 'What's happened? Why are they suddenly attacking us? This can't all be because of your shard.'

Elissa couldn't help but think about the kindness of her welcome in Silverfish. Those generous people, all probably dead ... the children playing on the beach. Were they there when the xotryl came? Was Vinjii on the overloaded boat? The innkeeper? Watcher's flames, what could she do? At Shardeep, Rossi would face the xotryl again. She doubted he was fully healed from their last brush with one. His wife was a healer – did that mean she would stay too?

'I'll take Rossi's daughter into my home,' she said.

'Thank you. Assuming they get here safely, I'll direct her to be brought to you. But I am not sure any guilt on your part is needed. This feels bigger than a lost shard. When other shards have been found, they have pursued, then given up. After all, they have no gate as far as we know, and there are many other shards out there to be found.'

Andra pushed herself out of the chair and paced the room as she spoke. 'If it *is* all about you, then they know something is different. Maybe they seek to use you.'

'But I don't even know where Ice-holt is. We didn't pass through it, so tracking me would not have led there,' Elissa said.

'Discovering that there is at least one fully powered human left when they thought us extinct could have been a trigger. They thought that they'd removed all those who could hurt them. Would that be enough, I wonder?' Andra looked out the tower window as she spoke. 'The awldrin are a warrior race. Without xotryl, they cannot track crystals, and they have few individuals who can dream walk. But no evidence has ever shown them to have other magic of their own.'

'So we should beat them easily at Shardeep?' Elissa sipped her calfa, inhaling the fumes as she tried to think clearly, to shake the last clouds of sleep from her mind.

'History has ever shown that we are matched. It's why the dragons intervened. To prevent full annihilation of one or both of our species.'

'Except they haven't been back. Over five hundred cycles alone, and now we are fighting again.'

Andra nodded. 'In truth, Elissa, I thought the Watcher had abandoned us.'

'He hasn't. I am sure of it.' She was very sure – she'd seen his eyes. If she could just reach him ... 'Do you have your crystal?'

'I do, but—'

'No time for but. Give it to me, please.'

Andra shook her head. 'I know what you're thinking. It won't work.'

'Let me try. I have to do something. What if this is my fault?'

'You have no idea what might happen.'

Elissa stood, still holding her hand out for the echoglass crystal. 'No, I don't. But I'm willing to try,' she said.

Andra took her crystal from around her neck, and held it in her hand, hesitant to hand it over.

Elissa spotted the thong hanging from her fist and prepared herself.

'Maybe if we work together,' Andra said. 'I'll call for help. If we practise pushing your emotions ...'

Elissa snatched the pouch out of her hand and ran. Her foot hurt, but it didn't matter, not anymore. People were dead, and it was her fault. The spiral was hard to run down, and she stumbled several times, determination alone kept her moving. From above, she heard Andra shout.

'Do not try this alone! Elissa, stop!'

Elissa ignored her. The large doors were in front of her. She took quick breaths, panting with exertion. The symbol! The Chosen were keen on their ideology, so she put her hand on the door and hoped it would open, pushing that thought at the door. Hope, need, anything else she could think of. The door moved, and she pushed harder until there was just enough space to fit through.

She ran to the small gate and pulled out both halves of the crystal. She slotted them into the space in the gilded spirals formed of twining stems and pushed at it. Nothing happened.

The small gate was barely up to her waist, but maybe if she focused, she could create enough space to get through to wherever it led and find help. Elissa put her hands to the crystal once more and pushed with every emotion she could muster. The crystal flickered briefly, but the gate did not budge.

Hands hooked under her arms from behind and someone caught her head as she passed out on the floor, completely drained.

CHAPTER 40

SURIIN

Suriin ran to her father's room straight after breakfast. Loud voices drifted down the hall as she approached, and she caught the odd word, including cure.

As she rounded the corner, three Gardeners turned her way, and silence fell like a cloak of snow between them.

Had she been tricked? Had she killed him instead? Suriin spared no thoughts for the Gardeners and sprinted toward his room. She burst in, expecting the worst. He tilted his face toward her and opened his eyes. Suriin collapsed to her knees, grasped his hand in both of hers, and sobbed hot tears of relief.

'Suriin,' he croaked, his voice rusty and grinding with lack of use.

'Are you cured?' she asked hopefully.

'I don't think so. But I do feel a lot better.'

'May I check?' Suriin asked, gesturing to his shoulder.

He nodded. Suriin unbuttoned his shirt to see his shoulder. Two of the Gardeners who'd been outside peered over too. She almost snapped, but decided to ignore them instead. From neck to wrist, his skin tone was mostly normal and the black spider had receded from his neck fully. His arm had only a small patch left. It looked like a black agrium flower with petals of poison spreading from the dark heart of the original puncture.

'It's almost gone!' She gasped. 'You're going to be okay!' Throwing her arms around her father, she hugged him.

'Um.' A Gardener cleared his throat behind her. 'It doesn't appear to be quite that simple. It shrunk overnight, but now it's growing again. To confuse things further, we're not sure what caused the improvement in the first place.'

Suriin sat up and met her father's eyes.

He returned the gaze steadily. 'It's true. I am sorry, and it appears to be spreading faster than the first time. You can almost see it growing in front of your eyes.' He smiled weakly. 'At least I get to say goodbye.'

Suriin's gut knotted, and nausea filled her. Natke had led her false after all. False hope followed by her father's swift death? There was no way she'd let that happen. If there was some of the white powder in the Black Palace, there must be more. She'd find some, would drag it out of Natke. Could she get any more from the sword? She swallowed hard, trying to avoid throwing up.

'No, you don't,' Suriin said, holding his hand in both of

hers. 'There won't be any goodbye. You can beat this. We can beat this.'

He looked at her with pride and sadness. 'I love you, child. Maybe when your mother arrives, she can help me. Until then, I need you to be strong. If she's too late, at least I got to tell you all I love you. You will pass that on, won't you?'

Suriin nodded through stinging curtains of tears. 'I'll be back very soon. Rest. I'll see you later.'

'Can you bring me paper and a pencil when you come back?' he asked her.

'Of course.' She bent forward and gave him a kiss on the cheek. 'I promise I'll see you later. I love you too.'

Suriin walked out of the room as calmly as she could manage. Once she was out of his sight and around the corridor, she ran, all attempts at decorum gone.

She barrelled into someone, almost sending them flying as she rounded the corner.

'Sorry, I'm late for class,' she shouted back as she continued, belatedly realising she had just run into the Anchor. Hoping that the current situation would afford her some leniency, she carried on running. She was due at class, it was true, but she wanted to go the other way, to run toward the possibility of her father surviving. Even if the sickness was moving faster, it would not be quicker than her class. He probably had a few days for her to work out a plan.

⋆ ✸ ✹ ✷ ✦

Suriin reached the door just as Aslin began to close it. Panting and out of breath, she leant against the frame. 'Sorry I'm late, Soul Anchor Aslin.'

Aslin loudly replied, 'Do not be late again.' Then, more

quietly, 'I heard about your father's recovery. Good news at last.'

Aslin paid her no more attention in class than any of the others. She offered advice on controlling her emotional flow and suggested symbols for each of them to practise. The only nod to the events of the previous night was her choices for Suriin of sadness followed by optimism. Was there a message there? Suriin tried to catch Aslin's attention subtly, but she was detached and polite, as she usually was in their lessons.

Suriin found sadness hard to control that day, but optimism was easier. The potential repercussions for what she was about to do were massive. She'd have to act soon, though – that much was clear. As her mind wandered, Suriin's light flickered, and the symbol went out. Aslin noticed and raised an eyebrow questioningly.

'Maybe you should try serenity again, Suriin. You appear to be having a little trouble controlling your emotions today,' she said. Suriin swallowed and rose to move to the serenity symbol. It might actually be a good idea. She needed to preserve some for later, so Suriin used the slightest, smallest trickle and created a very gentle glow.

Joy sat next to her. 'Oh, well done! That's really tricky. Can I have a go? Maybe with a calm emotion, I can get a glow instead of an uneven pulse.'

Suriin shuffled over and they took it in turns, trying to gently illuminate the serenity symbol. Aslin came past periodically, suggesting a different image in their minds, or trying to elicit a memory of a calm situation to help them. Then she asked them to try holding two emotions at once. Suriin tried optimism and serenity. She placed one hand on each and began to draw them through, using her memories of Golden; farbrox cubs tumbling about and trilling evening birdsong. As she practised, she felt her shoulders begin to drop, and although she was using up some serenity, Suriin found that she could generate more by holding the right thoughts. Gently, she fed the power through her crystal. She just had to master the rest of the table with the same level of control.

The class ended, and they were dismissed. To Suriin's surprise, Aslin gave them no preparation work. With the events of the last day, she had forgotten they had the afternoon off to attend the market in Redpike.

⟡ ✦ ※ ⚜ ✦

Suriin mumbled an excuse to Merri and Joy about needing to go to the kitchens. She wasn't due until much later that night, but it would be enough to put them off waiting for her. Most of the palace would be out that afternoon.

Ready or not, it was her best chance. Suriin walked past the kitchens, collected some snacks, and mumbled loudly about a headache. Hopefully, that would buy her some extra time if she was late back. Then she continued on down the passageway to her own room. She lifted her mattress to get the map and sketchbook and stuffed them in her bag, along with her glow lamp and the food. On impulse, she pulled a green dress off the shelf, throwing that in too.

Suriin closed the door behind her and hurried down the passageways, breaking into a run once she was sure no one was around.

'Watcher, guide my steps,' she muttered under her breath. Because of the market, everywhere was quiet. People were preparing to embrace their freedom and socialise; it was the perfect time. She tried to rehearse what she'd say, but could form no sensible, coherent thoughts. Emotion drove her forward, fuelled by the image of her father's face as he said goodbye.

Suriin had to double back a few times to avoid detection and was exhausted by the time she reached the far section of the tunnels. Her crystal bashed against her chest as she ran, so she moved it to the outside of her dress to reduce the impact.

Upon reaching the entrance to the corridor she needed, Suriin heard voices, so she extinguished her light and continued on past. From a distance, she watched the light get brighter as they approached. The So'Dal stopped and looked around, then paused, peering in her direction. She shrunk back tighter against the wall; she was outside their circle of light and her dress was dark. Suriin held her breath as she waited for them to carry on past, her heat hammering loudly in her chest, every beat like a thunderclap to her nervous ears. Eventually, they turned back toward the main palace.

She waited until the light had receded, then, sticking close to the wall, she returned to the door. Her hand guided her along the wall until her fingertips felt the frame.

Only once she was safely through, did she light her lamp. Every moment waiting was time wasted. She hurried to the seed store. Suriin traced the patterns with her hands, focusing on the beautiful designs of the plants for a few minutes to calm her breathing and focus her serenity.

Holding that serenity tight, she kept calm images in her mind and opened the barred wooden door opposite, closed it behind her and put her bag down in the alcove. Suriin pulled out the long green dress and food, then took a hesitant step toward the wall. An image of her father in his chair at home flitted through her mind, and she quickly pushed it down. She needed focus and detachment.

Suriin placed her hand on the wall, and after closing her eyes, found the handle easily. She combined serenity and added vigilance. It didn't turn.

When she left, she had been afraid. She needed fear, but

could not let it take over, so Suriin held serenity tightly and added a little controlled fear. It worked, and the handle turned. She took a deep breath and entered the room containing the cell.

Natke was stood near the bars. Suriin swallowed hard. She was even taller in reality than in her dream walk. The awldrin was, however, still naked.

Suriin decided nakedness was a good place to start.

'I brought you this,' she said, and stuffed the dress through the bars.

'It worked,' Natke stated. She picked up the dress, holding it up and turning it in front of her face. 'What is this?'

'A token of my thanks,' Suriin managed to get out, serenity slipping from her grasp. She stepped back to what she hoped was outside arm's length and shut her eyes. A moment longer than a normal blink. Thank the Watcher for Aslin's lesson that morning. She could handle it.

'I also thought you might appreciate some food.' Suriin held up the cakes. 'I know it's not much.'

'Silly human, you think I still be alive if needed food like you?' Natke's hissing, clicking laugh rang around the cell. 'I eat this.' She gestured around her. Suriin couldn't work out what she was pointing at to start with, then she saw the thin scrapes on the walls.

'Rocks?'

'Rocks. And there is enough small creatures float past in this stream to feed me. There is, too, staramine. The only thing for long life. You see, little one?' The clicks became louder as she approached Suriin, and the words harder to make out. 'You trap me with a very good diet.'

Suriin stared at the creature. Although she had felt a simi-larity with it – her – she felt the chasm between their species keenly.

'Then I hope I did not cause offence by offering it to you,' she said. 'Yes, the powder worked – partially. The person is healing, but the fever returns. How do I get more? Can you show me?'

Natke's teeth parted, and the narrow-pointed tongue was revealed.

'I have more, little one. It is with my things.'

'Where is that?'

'I tell you that? You will no free me. Where my sword?'

Suriin decided to keep its location a bargaining chip. 'I have hidden it,' she bluffed.

'My shield in this world,' Natke said, offering out a long-fingered hand. 'It will call me once I am out. Come with – I will help you heal person.'

'What is the recipe for the white powder? Please,' Suriin asked.

'It not of your world. I sorry,' Natke said. She bent down to pick up the green dress. 'Dress like you wearing be longer?' she asked, and Suriin felt as though her eyes stopped, lingering on the pouch around her neck for a moment.

'I only have one.'

'Help me to this one. We go find my shield, cure your person. Then I go home to hive.'

Natke was so calm, so open, that Suriin relaxed. She let go of serenity and talked Natke through how the dress tied. Natke stared at the scrap of fabric and eventually dropped it over her head. It fitted awkwardly. It caught on the protrusions on her back and barely reached her legs, but she was at least clothed – partly.

'Where do you think your shield might be?' she asked.

'Toward the sun-up from the mountain.'

'How will we travel without you being seen?'

'Not worry about that.' Natke showed her teeth again.

'That my problem.'

Having let go of serenity, Suriin's subconscious pushed through again. Fear and worry for her father surfaced, stronger than any other emotion, casting aside reason. She looked into the smooth green face.

'Should I trust you?'

'Who do you lose if you not? All I want is go home. I told you. My hive need me.'

Suriin studied the lock in front of her. It was an engraved disk that would need to rotate to open; she peered closely and recognised all the symbols.

She started with refilling her serenity. It wasn't on the disk, but she needed to focus. For a moment, reason started to resurface – should she even be considering it? Suriin pushed thoughts aside and focused on each emotion in turn, working them gently into a thread of power. Vigilance again, and anger, as well as several others. Calmly she added more, Natke's, relaxed posture helping her. Natke had taken a sitting position back from the entrance, watching her silently.

Suriin kept feeding power gently into the disk, then testing it. Eventually, all the symbols glowed gently. She could do it! Taking another deep breath, Suriin gave one more burst of power and turned the disk.

The door opened. Natke sprung from her position toward Suriin and punched her in the gut. Suriin doubled over in pain as Natke kicked her forward into the water. Prone on the floor, she looked up at the towering awldrin. Winded and hurting, she gathered her fear and tried to push it at Natke, who hit her again, breaking her concentration. Suriin made a grab for the gate to close it, but Natke stood on her arm, hissing with laughter.

'Puny humans. You've always been so easy to manipulate. "I need be free." As if I haven't spent so long waiting, talking to other Anchors, learning your words ... You are so weak and foolish, so gullible. All except *Her.*' She grabbed at the pouch containing Suriin's crystal, pinning Suriin's other arm down as she reached for it. 'I don't know why you have echoglass in this bag, but I'm taking it back. The Gate needs it.'

Natke kicked her again, and Suriin heard something in her chest crack. As she lay gasping for breath, the awldrin walked calmly out of the cell.

'The trouble with magical locks is that they re-lock when shut,' she clicked as she walked out.

The gate of the cell closed before Suriin could reach it. Natke paused briefly at the next doorway, then smashed it open with her fists.

'Enjoy the next few weeks – if you live that long. I have my people to avenge,' she called back as she strode through the doorway.

The farther away Natke got, the sicker Suriin felt. She felt every motion of running that wasn't her own. Natke had gone toward the weapon store. Suriin tried to focus on the lock, but every time she tried to push power toward it, she felt worse.

Natke had her crystal – that was why she couldn't focus. Retching into the stream, she watched as her stomach contents floated away, clogging up the tiny exit hole from the cell. She raised herself up again and crawled across to the gate. Her head was spinning, and the nausea was overwhelming. Suriin collapsed, holding onto the bars. Maybe if she could sleep, she could dream walk to someone, maybe her father. She had to hope that they would notice she was gone. Someone would call for her, would find her missing ...

The headache intensified further as the crystal moved away until Suriin could barely open her eyes. She sat on the floor of the cell, rocking and crying in pain and shame. What in the Watcher's name had she just unleashed on the world?

CHAPTER 41

DARIN

Star trotted by Darin's side, his tail swinging happily with each step. The trail of broken branches strewn across the forest from the rhinocorn had been partially cleared, a path free of debris running straight through the centre. They followed it, and Darin calculated that they should be at Krista's hamlet before nightfall. Maybe they could enjoy another home-cooked meal. Darin pushed on, the anticipation putting a small spring in his exhausted steps.

They reached the perimeter of the hamlet and froze. The lightning-split trunk had been toppled and the surrounding bushes flattened. The hut opposite Krista's was half demolished. Its door swung unsteadily on the top hinge, with a huge hole torn from the roof. Darin started to creep toward it until Chase reached a hand to still him.

'If someone is still there, we'll hear them. If whatever did this is in there, you'll be trapped with it. Wait a moment.' He strode to the fallen tree and kicked a rhythm on the old trunk. 'It's Chase. I'm here to help,' he called. They stood still, listening for any motion, any clue to life. But no one came out.

Darin couldn't wait any longer. He dumped his bag and fitted his spear point.

'I'm going in.' Time to use everything he had. *[Inside the hut?]* Star sent back a wave of fear and *[Blood-covered xotryl]*.

'He can smell xotryl.' Darin strode toward the hut, his spear extended in front of him. Star growled as he walked closer, head level with Darin's knee and his hackles fully raised.

'I know.' Chase ran toward Krista's hut.

Darin stopped outside the door, his hand ready to pull it open. It was silent. *[Xotryl in hut?]* he questioned. It felt too quiet for anything to be in there, but it did no harm to check.

[Empty hut, covered in blood]. Darin pushed the hanging door open. It screamed in protest. He stepped across the threshold to the bitter tang of metal invading his nose – the scent of blood mingled with urine and fear. The floor was sticky and the walls splattered with dark red spray. An arm lay to the right of the doorway, jagged bone protruding where it should have been connected to a body.

Darin found himself staring for a moment. He'd seen the results of many brawls at home – after all, it had been his job to break them up. He'd seen men stab each other and dealt with blood-spattered walls and broken limbs. Flames, he'd watched a man die once. But what he faced was ... a massacre. His stomach heaved, but he held it down. He needed to search for survivors. Darin struggled through congealing blood as it sucked at his shoes. A smashed child's crib was in the centre of the room, but no sign of the child.

'Watcher, guide you all,' he muttered. Star remained outside and barked as Chase appeared at the doorway.

'She's not there.' He stopped. 'Fire and scales, I hope she went to the Witnesses before this happened. Are there any survivors?'

'I don't think so.' Darin kept searching. Chase joined him in checking under blankets and the back section of the hut.

'Burn it,' Chase exclaimed from a corner.

'What is it?'

'It got them all,' he replied as he stood from examining something.

Darin crossed toward him, but Chase put a hand up.

'We don't both need this seared into our minds. Please, trust me. It got the child too. We need to get out of here before it comes back.'

'Shouldn't we bury them first or something?'

'There's not much to bury.' Chase sighed. 'Flames, Darin, if this thing has a taste for humans, we're in a whole crater of trouble. We need to get home as soon as we can. The Howlers need to know.'

They left the devastated hut behind them, walking into a forest as silent as Darin's mind was busy.

Their path remained clear; nothing moved on either side. It was even more unnerving when Darin realised he couldn't hear birdsong either. He sent to Star *[Birds in trees?]*.

Star replied with an image of *[Birds huddled together in silence]* and filled it with fear.

'The birds are scared,' he said to Chase.

'They are,' he replied. 'Sandy can't smell any other creatures close either. We need to get through this area and out of the crater as quickly as we can.' He started to jog.

Darin increased his pace to match Chase. Star kept up without panting excessively. So long as that stayed the same, he was in full agreement with the idea of getting away from Dal.

⊤ ✸ ✸ ✸ ✦

They were halfway up the lift when they finally saw it. From the far side of Dal crater, a small, dark green xotryl flew in with something dangling from its claws. Something human-sized. A streak of red stained the earth as it landed on the open area below them and waddled into the forest, along the path they had just left. It was only about the size of two faat, but its scars were visible even from there. It was no youngster, yet it was nowhere near as big as the red one.

'I've never seen Big Red so bold or so far from the Edgelands,' murmured Chase. 'I knew one had passed Golden, and a green one was sighted to the South in Nameless Crater. I wonder, has it moved north?' He paused, staring at the xotryl. 'If it hasn't, and there are three or more active, even these whistles may not help us enough. We still have to learn the magic we need.'

Darin took the rope from Chase and carefully continued the ascent. They couldn't hang in the air indefinitely – they were too easy a target if it came back out, and his fear of the xotryl was greater than that of heights, but Chase was right. It grew more urgent by the hour. The xotryl down there was actively hunting ... something.

The xotryl didn't come back out of the trees, and they reached the top with no further sightings. Darin stepped out of the basket and sat down, allowing his nerves free rein for a moment.

Chase sat next to him. 'You know, you've come a long way, Darin. You and Star make a strong team. Thanks to you, we have a sliver of hope against that creature and a real chance of resurrecting the Howlers. It's been a lonely few years, and you aren't bad company. Now all we need is to find more recruits to rebuild properly – once we deal with that xotryl.'

Star licked his face repeatedly until Darin had to choose between walking or being drowned in dog slobber. Darin tried to feel some of Chase's optimism; he didn't feel like he made much difference yet, so it was good Chase saw the same need as he did and wasn't assuming they could do it alone.

'Where will we find them?' Darin asked as he stood.

'Maybe back in there.' Chase indicated Dal.

Darin looked back into the crater and suppressed a small smile. 'It's worth a try. After all, if Tian is there, who else might be? We have a tool to find them now as well.' He patted his pocket. 'If they can't sing, they can use this.'

'See, you really are thinking ahead.' Chase squeezed Darin's shoulder and inclined his head up the path. 'Let's get home. I want to get resupplied, rested, and back here to deal with this as soon as we can – and with backup. There's no way the Anchor isn't going to hear of this soon, unless Krista ...'

'Come on. You can try to contact the Dal Witness as soon as we're safe,' Darin said. 'You said Krista was strong. I'm sure she got away.'

⫟ ✳ ✷ ✸ ✦

A few days later, they emerged from the Howler tower, still having established no contact with Dal. Their nerves strained with lack of knowledge, and their legs were exhausted from the pace they'd maintained. Star was still tired, but stubbornly loped alongside.

'I have a challenge for you both,' Chase said. 'Can you find the way back in?'

Darin thought for a moment. 'Yes, I think we can.' Clouds hung low over the peak of the Black Mountain. Somewhere on its side had to be a hidden entrance.

'Go ahead, then. I'll follow you.'

Darin asked Star if he could smell Sandy's trail and sent a specific image of *[Sandy entering a tunnel]*.

Star immediately scented around, and Darin was pleased to see that he appeared to be following the route they'd taken on the way out. He let Star lead, and for most of the morning, they followed the return track. Then Star stopped. He sniffed in one direction for a short distance, came back, and sniffed off in a different direction along a small trail. Darin's vision was flooded moments later with images of Sandy *[One version of Sandy was headed straight back up to the pass, the others all headed down the new path]*.

He confirmed they wanted the path with multiple Sandy trails, and they continued. The trail on the ground was so faint it was hard to make out a final destination. He couldn't see any caves in the mountainside, but that didn't surprise him; whatever entrance there was would be well hidden. Darin was scanning the cliff when Chase flattened him from behind.

'Get down! Stay still. Use your dragon bone, now!'

Darin rolled to the side and pulled his whistle out, setting the dragon bone. He worried that it hadn't worked, but he could only just make out Chase next to him. He told Star to lie down, and the hound dropped immediately into the grass.

Darin lay staring up at the sky, his view filled with the low flight of the green xotryl coming from the west. It must have flown a long way around the river source to get there.

He froze. The creature's blood-stained head swung from side to side as if trying to find something. It circled between them and the mountainside with its wings spread, quietly gliding. Darin was amazed by the effortless flight for a creature so big.

'I still think it looks like a dragon,' he whispered. 'Why's it here? It can't have tracked us – not coming from that way?'

'I agree. I don't think it's here for us. Stay still. It's not as clever as a dragon by a long way, nor as big. Can't reason with a xotryl. Well, *we* can't. The awldrin supposedly had a way to communicate with them.' Chase flattened himself and held Sandy close; Sandy's outline blurred slightly. Darin moved his shard toward Star, but he was still visible. The xotryl continued to circle overhead and Darin desperately sent *[Star as still as a rock]*, his heart hammering in panic.

A high-pitched clicking reached their ears as the xotryl turned mid circle and dropped to the ground, its body hidden by dense bushes.

Moments later, it sprung back into the sky, no longer alone. A tall figure sat astride it with green fabric flapping above exceptionally long legs and a hairless head. The creature's skin was as green as the fabric it wore and the xotryl it rode.

'It cannot be,' Chase whispered.

'Is that?' Darin couldn't bring himself to say it. 'Where's it going?'

'By the Watcher's flames, where's it come from?'

The xotryl flew back to the west, growing smaller in the distance.

⊤ ※ ✹ ✦

Once they were confident it wasn't coming back, they sprang to their feet and ran for the mountainside.

'Sandy, track it!' Chase called.

Darin whistled as they neared, and the tunnel entrance

appeared. He started to run toward it, but Chase restrained him.

'We don't know what we'll find in there. Empty your pack of everything that isn't a medicine or a weapon. We can come back for them later.'

They approached slowly, tucked their belongings into a small hole in the passageway wall, and released their moon-hounds to follow the scent. The hounds moved fast, and Darin struggled to keep up with them in the long entrance passage. Once they reached branches in the tunnel, they slowed down. They ran down several dead ends, only to turn back around again. The trail must have had got muddled. It appeared that the awldrin had not known which way was out.

'It didn't recognise the false wall,' Chase panted as they reached one dead end.

'Is that ours?' Darin asked, catching his breath as they saw the shining stone wall blocking the end of the passage.

'Yes, that's our normal way home.'

'Not now, though! We need to find where it's been, or come from – and if it was alone.' They turned their backs on the wall, and Darin gave Star a pat on the shoulders. 'Are you okay, boy? You can stay in there and rest if you need to.' He sent *[Star on the rug in their Howler room]*. Star licked his hand and ran after Sandy and Chase. 'Let's stick with our pack then, boy,' Darin said, and chased after them. Star was flagging and his legs were tired – every once in a while, he stumbled a little. Darin followed as closely as he could, worried constantly that Star would collapse.

They travelled deeper under the mountain and into the heart of the old tunnels. Dusty scents and crumbled door frames were all around them. Darin held his spear at the ready as he checked each side passageway they passed; eventually, they came to an open door leading to a wide passageway. The moon-hounds turned down it.

'The seed store and armoury,' Chase pointed into the darkness.

'Our armoury?'

'Yes, it's hidden. Hopefully, it hasn't been in there. We still have some awldrin artefacts collected and preserved.' They ran down the corridor, almost falling over the hounds who had stopped at a pair of doors. Both pawed at a large wooden door with big drop bolts.

'You know, I guess I knew this door was here, but I've never really noticed it,' Chase said. 'What on Caldera is in here that's important enough for a door which causes the eye to slip over it? Do you have your glow lamp still?'

Darin shook his head. 'Could the door have dragon bone embedded in it?'

Chase shrugged. 'I suppose so. It would explain why it is both invisible and not. You only see it if you know exactly where it is, but hounds aren't often fooled by it. We'd better check what's in there.'

They pushed up the levers to open the door as running footsteps drew closer. A teenage boy ran up to them, following an elderly moonhound. He slid to a halt in front of them as the new moonhound joined Star and Sandy in pawing at the door.

'What have you done with my sister?' the boy shouted, his fists curled, ready to fight.

'What sister?' Darin stood between the boy and the door. 'Look, I know nothing about your sister, whoever she is, but something just came out of that room, and it could be dangerous to go rushing in.'

The boy let out a cry and charged at Darin. He was much smaller, and Darin easily restrained him. 'What sister?' he asked again, but the boy kicked out, and the three hounds pushed into the room. 'Burn it.' Darin released the boy so he could rush after Star. Inside, there were a few stones strewn on the floor and an alcove to one side.

'Where is she?' the young man said as he ran around the room. 'This is her bag!' He picked up a bag from the alcove.

'I don't know who you're talking about. We only just got here ourselves.' Darin replied. He studied the room carefully, searching for any sign of other awldrin or a human. First, they see a xotryl-riding awldrin and then a hysterical boy – it couldn't be a co-incidence. What had happened to the sister?

They walked farther in and came across a pristine wall with more stones strewn around it. Those bricks came from some-where. If the door held dragon bone, there was a good chance the wall wasn't real. He blew his whistle, and the wall illusion vanished.

A smashed, open doorway stood in place of the illusion. Through it, they could see a young woman on her knees, trapped in a cell.

The teenager ran forward, reaching through the bars to her. 'Suriin, I'm here. I've found you. It's going to be okay.'

She looked up, her eyes red and face blotchy. 'Gwynn, How did you get here so fast? She tricked me. I tried to save Father, but it went wrong. Now, I can't open the door because she stole my crystal. I'm sorry.'

'What are you talking about?' Gwynn asked as he stroked her hand through the bars.

Chase glanced at Darin and shook his head. He crouched close to the bars to talk to Suriin. 'That was your doing? You released that awldrin from in here?'

Suriin nodded forlornly and threw up in the stinking water. 'Not just any awldrin. She's a queen who thinks the Gates are whole and wants to get home.'

Darin knelt by the cell door. 'We'll get you out of here first, then we can deal with the awldrin.' The girl's eyes lost focus, and she collapsed in the corner of the cell.

Chase sighed. 'I don't think you'll be returning to lessons anytime soon, Darin. Our pack is needed even more urgently, and sooner than we expected.'

'It is, but we're more capable and powerful than we were a tide ago. We'll free Suriin first, then we have work to do.' Darin looked at the teenager and his old hound. Maybe their pack was already growing.

CHAPTER 42

ELISSA

The murals around the dome were painted many hundreds of cycles ago. Two artists are permanently tasked with repairing damage to the paintwork. They have never had to repaint a single scale on the golden dragon Hope.
The Black Moon

Elissa faced the gate once more, but with a room full of Chosen. They'd poured in after Andra had caught her.

'If you are going to do this, you need control first,' Andra had said gently when Elissa woke.

Elissa nodded accession. 'Will you let me try again?'

'It's worth an attempt.'

They'd spent several hours together; Andra showed her how to control a basic emotional push, making Elissa repeat and repeat it until she was happy that there was a focused flow produced.

'I'm ready to try again,' Elissa said. Her friends were scared and in hiding. If she could help, she must. Everyone else had faith in her – it was time to believe in herself. Andra retreated, leaving Elissa facing the gate alone. *I am part of the crystal... The crystal is part of me.*

Elissa pushed against the fragment of Gate with all the power within her. She laid her hands on the crystal, trying to look through it, past the blood-red streak which darkened when she touched it.

Deep within the crystal, she could make out an eye looking at her. The eye receded, and a crystal-featured shadow appeared to nod. She swallowed hard. He saw her. She was certain it wasn't her imagination.

Elissa gave the gate one more push. It didn't move. Exhausted, she sat down, defeated.

'I'm not powerful enough. Maybe I just don't have the skill. I'm sorry.'

The room remained silent for a moment, then she heard Andra.

'Instead of seeing Elissa as the entire answer, maybe she is merely a key. We can all contribute to the force needed to unlock it.'

The elder from Shardeep had asked to check on her seri-clave and lay on a recliner brought into the dome. She sat up, and her eyes snapped open. The knuckles on her hands protruded, white and bloodless, as they gripped the edge of her seat. She looked not at Andra, but directly at Elissa as she spoke.

'Rossi says the awldrin have arrived – Shardeep is under attack. The ships with the children have left. At least one talented or Chosen is on each boat to protect them. All non-talented adults who are unable to fight are fleeing into the mountain tunnels for refuge. The elders and remaining guards are positioned to make a stand. He said the farmers have tried to protect what stores they can. Some guards have even headed into the old sericlave tunnels in search of the paralytic snalber poison. But they are yet to return.'

Elissa struggled to her feet once more. 'Then we will try this again and again until it works!' She stared defiantly around the room, expecting dissent, but all she saw was determination. A number of women nodded at each other.

'I lend you my power, Elissa Shard-bonded' one said and walked across the room to place her hand on Elissa's shoulder. A murmur of assent filled the room and the Chosen of Hope arranged themselves in a wedge shape; three women touching Elissa, and three behind each of those, widening out toward the back wall.

'What emotion do you need?' a voice from the back of the wedge called.

Elissa thought of her friends hiding in the caves upstream from Dragonsbreath, and her brother risking his life for them. She thought of the kind faces in Silverfish who made her feel human for the first time, of all the people she'd met on the way to Hope. She thought of Rossi's tiny daughter and her friend.

'I want hope. Please, Watcher, give us all hope.'

She touched the crystal again, and tears formed in her eyes, blurring her vision. Elissa quickly wiped them away, then returned her hands to the crystal. Where her teardrops touched the crystal, they ran into the gap left by the shard in her foot and gathered there, gently glowing. Elissa glanced around, but no one else had seen it. She reached forward with her other hand, and covering the red light, steadied herself.

'I'm ready,' she said, loudly enough for all to hear.

The power of the combined women of Hope washed over her like a wave, all three lines converging on her at once. The hopes of a room full of women trying to save their friends and families filled her, overwhelmed her until she worried she would overflow.

Every fibre of her body sung with optimism and positivity. As she pushed her power forward, the gate moved slightly. She moved one hand to the edge and pushed physically as well as with the combined force of all the magic funnelled through her. It shifted a little farther. There was room for a foot to squeeze through.

She could see a dark crack while cool air poured through the gate and over her legs. The Chosen behind her cried out in amazement.

'We can do it. More!' she shouted. In response, the surge increased. Elissa pushed toward the gate with a tidal wave of power, her sense of self afloat on a sea of hope. The gate opened a little more.

Elissa dropped to her knees and studied at the gap. She tried to stem the flow so that she could look at it objectively.

'I can get through.'

Without waiting for a response from Andra, she crouched forward, twisting her body into the narrow space. As she crawled into the darkness, tingles crossed her skin and passed through her entire body; it reminded her of passing through the defences of the island.

Still brimming with hope, she brought her legs through. It was cool on the other side, and there was no air movement. As her eyes adjusted, she made out a large silhouette.

Staring at her, with twin tendrils of smoke rising from its nostrils like entwining vines, was an enormous green dragon.

'It's you!' Elissa gasped. 'We need help. Where's the Watcher?'

The dragon turned its head to the side. A curled-up

skeleton laid nearby, its bones bleached and white. 'The Watcher has been gone for many, many cycles,' it said.

'Then hope is lost.' Elissa's shoulders sagged. Their plan was over.

The dragon's scaly eyebrows raised. 'The last time I saw Hope was only a cycle ago. Hope is definitely not lost.'

Elissa was confused. Then she looked up at the green dragon again. It looked back at her.

'You've been watching me?'

It nodded.

'What is your name?'

'I am Regret, and I watch in the Hall of the Watcher until we appoint a new Watcher.'

'Regret.' Elissa bowed deeply. 'Do you live your name in truth?' One of the dragons who had created the glass of Dragonsbreath, who had melted the gates, trapped them.

The dragon nodded, its face otherwise unreadable.

'Then help us now. The awldrin are attacking the last of the humans on Tebein. They're killing everyone, children and adults.'

Regret's head tilted to one side. 'How big is the space that gate is in?'

Elissa tried to imagine Regret fitting in the hall. 'The room is big enough for you, but the entrances are not.'

'Will there be room for two of us?' Regret asked.

Elissa's breath caught – two dragons! They may be saved after all. 'We will knock a wall down!' she replied.

'Then return. We will be with you soon.'

Elissa crawled back through the gate, her heart soaring. She'd seen and spoken to a real dragon. It was not the Watcher, but for them, in this moment, maybe it was better. She reentered a silent chamber. All the women were exhausted, resting in groups and leaning on each other for support. Their eyes fixed on her as she emerged.

'Help is coming, but we need to knock down a wall for them to leave this room,' she said.

The oldest elder gasped. 'The Watcher comes?'

'No, the Watcher remains at his post, but two dragons come instead.' It did not seem the right time to tell them the news of his death.

The occupants of the hall couldn't use magic to move a single stone, they were so spent, but word spread fast. Seeing an opportunity to help, people poured up the hill. Stone by stone, pieces of the dome wall were removed to allow dragons to leave the chamber. Whispers of disbelief mingled with words of hope passed around like flickering flames. Dragons were coming!

As the sun sunk into the sea, and the waves wore a rosy tint, the population of Hope Island gathered around the dome. Elissa sat with her back against the painted mural, facing the small, open gate, and waited for a sign.

A tendril of smoke curled around the golden vines.

'Get back,' she called, and everyone retreated to the edge of the room.

An emerald green, scaled snout flickered into view, and the gate appeared to grow. The air around it shimmered, and the rest of Regret's enormous body followed his snout. Regret swung his head until his gaze rested on Elissa, then bowed his head slightly.

Regret moved away from the gate, stretching his wings and shaking himself.

A golden snout entered the room. As the dark eyes looked into her, Elissa cried with relief. Around the room and on the hill outside, the same emotion was reflected on every face as the golden dragon emerged from her own gate.

Hope had come to save them.

A single flash of green reflected off the emerald scales as Regret flew across the Ameryth Dar and into the cloud-bank protecting the island of Hope. Somewhere in the same magical fog, The Captain and the crew of the *Cloudsailor* were following their erratic route through the magical barrier to guide the survivors of Silverfish and Shardeep to safety.

Elissa watched for a few more moments, then, breathing her hopes of safety and rescue for her friends into the wind, she turned back toward the tower.

The steeply winding ascent caused her pain. The shard within her foot showed no inclination to come out, and her awkward, rolling step, though tiring, was becoming second nature. Elissa had tried to walk more normally, but the pressure that put on the arch of her foot was excruciating.

Tendrils of smoke rose from Hope's snout as Elissa hobbled toward the tower. Her eyes bored into Elissa until the compulsion to speak to her overrode the need to meet Andra as she had arranged.

Elissa found herself a few paces from the great golden dragon. She bowed her head deeply in respect. 'What can I do for you?'

Hope tilted her head to bring her eyes level with Elissa. 'Regret tells me you are the one who called us here.' She touched her nose to Elissa for a moment.

'I see now. You have our magic within you. How can that be?'

'Your magic?' Elissa furrowed her brow in confusion. 'I have the same magic as the other Chosen, and I'm not very good at using it.'

'No, you have something extra – different. It is familiar to me.'

'I stood on the echoglass and have a bit stuck in my foot. Is that what you mean?'

Hope reached down with her snout and touched it to Elissa's foot. Heat enfolded her as Hope breathed out. 'It is there.'

Elissa studied the great dragon. She'd raised her snout and was facing across the sea. 'I can feel dragon magic scattered across this moon. It pulls me from all the places my brothers scattered it when we were last here. Only the bit in you pulses with life. It was not the other sections you put in the gate that opened it. They needed to be there, but without your extra power, from the blood bonded crystal that slowly becomes one with your body, it would never have opened. It was the power of the dragon who lives through you.'

'It's just a rock, though, isn't it?' Elissa asked.

'It is dragon bone. Only the eldest remember how it is made. The Watcher was one of those.' Hope's scaled face showed no emotion as she spoke of the Watcher. 'Do not share what I have told you. I need to think on this.' She paused, then narrowed her eyes. 'Does it hurt?'

'Yes.'

'All over you?'

'No, just when I stand on it.'

Hope stood, her bulk towering over Elissa, and she curled her neck around herself. A crack split the air. When Hope snaked her head back to Elissa, a section of broken scale glinted in her jaws.

'Use this under your foot. It will not flex or be pierced. You can walk with more speed then. I have a feeling that in the coming days and tides, you will need to. In time, I suspect the pain will fade as the shard becomes fully part of you.'

Elissa took the scale and sat at Hope's feet. She unwrapped her foot and inserted the scale inside the bandage. It was slightly smaller than her foot, but long enough to reach from heel to the ball. She retied the wrap and stood. True to Hope's word, the scale took the weight, and although she could no longer flex her foot, Elissa could stand straight for the first time in tides.

'Thank you.'

'No, thank you. My brother has long wanted to right the wrongs we did on this moon. Your summons gives him that chance. Now, go. I will speak with you soon.'

⊤ ⚹ ⚰ ⚎ ✦

Elissa considered walking into the tower through the gaping hole in the Gate chamber, then turned away. She'd use the front doors. Andra would be up in the top chamber with the Chosen on communications still. The villages needed to know that help was coming.

Although she had needed every one of them, she wished some of the Chosen had left with The Captain to help defend the people unable to protect themselves. By the time he returned, she planned to have enough control to leave with him. *If Rossi's family survives to protect the girl.* The thought flashed unbidden through her mind, causing her to dig her nails into her palm. Rossi would survive, so would the girl's mother – she had to hope. Until then, Elissa would take care of her.

She reached Andra's room in so much less discomfort that it must have shown in her step.

'Did it come out? You're walking better.'

'Hope helped with the pain,' Elissa said. 'What are we starting my studies with?'

She sat where Andra gestured and clasped her hands on her lap, leaning toward the elder in her eagerness to learn.

'Restraint,' Andra said, a twitch at the corner of her mouth giving away wry amusement. 'You need to be able to use only a little of your power at once, or you will have no reserves to draw on. You will always feel a surge of power try to push out. There will be times when you feel that you cannot stem that tide – or must not. But there are also too many times when you push it out subconsciously.'

'Like anger in that first meeting we had?' Or Laytha pushing belief and confidence.

Andra nodded. 'Yes, just like that.'

Elissa sat back. She stared at her hands, eyes unfocussed. *I can control this.*

'Hold your hands out, cupped like a bowl.'

'Like this?'

'Yes, make sure there are no holes.'

Elissa frowned and moved her fingers subtly to make the bowl complete.

'Good. Now instead of pushing emotions through your hands – like you have done until now – I want you to let trust trickle into the bowl from your palms. Visualise it filing up.'

'How will I know when it's full?' Elissa asked.

Andra smiled and held a finger suspended over the bowl Elissa had created.

'You will have to trust me to tell you.'

Elissa concentrated hard, trying to dribble trust through her fingers. She couldn't feel anything happen, and the more she tried, the more frustrated she got.

'Breathe,' Andra murmured, 'before you start to shoot out things you don't intend to.'

'Nothing's happening.'

'Did you find it inside you first? And then try to pour it out? There is not much of a store of trust in your fingers.'

I can do this. Trust. I need to think of Laytha, of my brother. There. I can feel something. 'I can feel something. It's in my chest. A bundle of feelings.'

'Good – isolate trust. Try to direct it in a stream to your hands.'

Elissa tried again, but found it too slippery to direct. She grabbed it with her mind and pulled a strand of trust out. It hung in the air before her; she could feel its presence. On impulse, she gently blew it. The intensity diffused away, and Andra sat back, surprised.

'I felt that. But there's none in the bowl.'

'I ... I plucked it.' Elissa paused. 'I couldn't pour it – it was too tangled. Not a pool. More like a ball of fibres all bundled together. So I just pulled one out.' She frowned. 'I think I can do it again.'

Andra tilted her head to one side. *Like an old, delicate bird.* 'Try again,' she said. 'I'll try to find it. Choose a different emotion this time.'

'Do I keep the bowl?' Elissa's arms were aching a little.

Andra shrugged. 'I don't know. I have only taught this to young students before. Maybe your age makes emotions more tangled. You never learned to separate them, so it's all a bit messy in there. Let's just see if you can do it again. Then we'll worry about how to work with it.'

Elissa shook her arms out, then recreated the bowl. It helped her to have somewhere to focus while she felt around inside herself for sorrow. It was there. Her parents, and being separated from them as a child, stood out starkly amongst the ball of emotions. She looked for a stream to direct, but as before, it swirled around like a small tangled cloud – undirectable in any small quantity. Elissa felt certain that she could almost push the whole ball out, like she had done with fear when in Shardeep caves, but a small bit was much harder to isolate.

Taking a deep breath, she reached again and plucked at it,

pulling a thread of sadness out. It snapped free, and in her surprise, she flung it forward. It hung nearby like the first one.

She nodded, and Andra moved her hands through the air in the bowl, shaking her head.

'Nothing in there.'

'No, because it's here. May I?' she gestured to Andra's hand.

'Go ahead.'

Elisa took Andra's thin, gnarled hand in her own and raised it to where she felt the sadness was. She watched as a single tear rolled down Andra's face.

'Watcher's breath, this is like nothing I've ever come across. Can you do anything with it?'

'I can spread it out – like blowing powder.'

'Could you choose where you put it?' Andra sat down as she spoke, withdrawing her hand from the fine thread of sorrow.

Elissa pondered the question. 'Maybe, with practise.'

Andra wiped the last tear away, and a thin smile formed.

'Then, Elissa, we need you to practise. If you can consciously place a small thread of emotion on an item, maybe you can work out how you are doing it and teach us all. Imagine if you could place a thread of hope or joy on a bandage for a wounded child. Normally, we pour emotion onto or into something, and then it disperses. We can direct the flow. But a fixed piece?' She shook her head, opening her palms and shrugging. 'I have never seen it stay whole like this.'

Elissa nodded. 'That would be wonderful.' *But if I could place a harmful thread on a weapon, it would be far more useful to us. She must surely be considering it.*

'Let me call for some more drinks. We'll practise for as long as you can this evening. The luxury of time is not ours, after all.'

Elissa found a comfortable position while Andra called out for drinks. She was clearly going to be there for a while.

With dragons and the possibility of creating weapons to destabilise the awldrin, maybe there was a way out for them all – and a way home, to a new life through the gate.

Acknowledgments

This book is where it all began. Before Black Hind's Wake –
before the selkies.

Elissa, Darin and Suriin have been living my my head for
many years, and it was finally time to share them. I hope you
enjoy visiting their worlds as much as I enjoy escaping into the
Aulirean system. This is the book my editor asked me to never
give up on. Diana, thank you for your consistent belief in Gates.

I cannot begin to count the number of versions of this book
there have been, but I fully appreciate all the friends it has
brought in my direction, including everyone from Bristol Con.

Timy and Julia, for being the first and last of my beta readers, thank you. I sincerely hope that Gates is no longer the book
you once read, Timy! Justin, thank you for the feedback, your
patience, and your friendship. No one should ever read a
chapter one that many times unless they are the author!

There are name checks hidden within the book to other
friends, who have helped along the way, in particular, Vinjii –
I'll try not to kill her in book 2. Natalie she's finally here!

Thavie, whose beautiful art graces the cover, thank you for
drawing Darin and Star so well!

My family have once again been awesome. There was much
agonising over this book, and they have supported me all
the way.

Lastly, thank you to all my readers. I look forward to
returning with you to the Aulirean Gates later in 2023 with
Gates of Regret.

Also by J E Hannaford

Black Hind's Wake

The Skin, Black Hind's Wake 1

The Pact, Black Hind's Wake 2

Black Hind Short story, SirenCall

sign up at www.jehannaford.com

Anthologies

So Alone. An Aulirean Gates short story in Through Shadows.

Dark Whale, Skybreaker Anthology